W9-CFK-497

▶ ▶❙ ◀)) 6:17 / 29:20

FGTeeV FAMILY BIOGRAPHY

8,857,752 VIEWS • 1 WEEK AGO 👍 283K 👎 8.5K ➜ SHARE ➕ SAVE •••

 FGTeeV
20.5M SUBSCRIBERS

Duddy, Moomy, Lexi, Mike, Chase, and Shawn are the stars of FGTeeV, one of the most popular family gaming YouTube channels in the world, with more than 20 million subscribers and 20 billion views. This family of six loves gaming, traveling, and spontaneous dance parties. To learn more, visit them on YouTube @FGTeeV.

4,120 COMMENTS

 Add a comment...

HARPERALLEY IS AN IMPRINT OF HARPERCOLLINS PUBLISHERS.

FGTEEV SAVES THE WORLD! COPYRIGHT © 2021 BY LAFFTER INC. ALL RIGHTS RESERVED. MANUFACTURED IN ITALY. NO PART OF THIS BOOK MAY BE USED OR REPRODUCED IN ANY MANNER WHATSOEVER WITHOUT WRITTEN PERMISSION EXCEPT IN THE CASE OF BRIEF QUOTATIONS EMBODIED IN CRITICAL ARTICLES AND REVIEWS. FOR INFORMATION ADDRESS HARPERCOLLINS CHILDREN'S BOOKS, A DIVISION OF HARPERCOLLINS PUBLISHERS, 195 BROADWAY, NEW YORK, NY 10007. WWW.HARPERALLEY.COM

LIBRARY OF CONGRESS CONTROL NUMBER: 2021934350

ISBN 978-0-06-304262-9

TYPOGRAPHY BY ERICA DE CHAVEZ. 21 22 23 24 25   RTLO   10 9 8 7 6 5 4 3 2 1   ❖   FIRST PAPERBACK EDITION, 2022

SAVES THE WORLD!

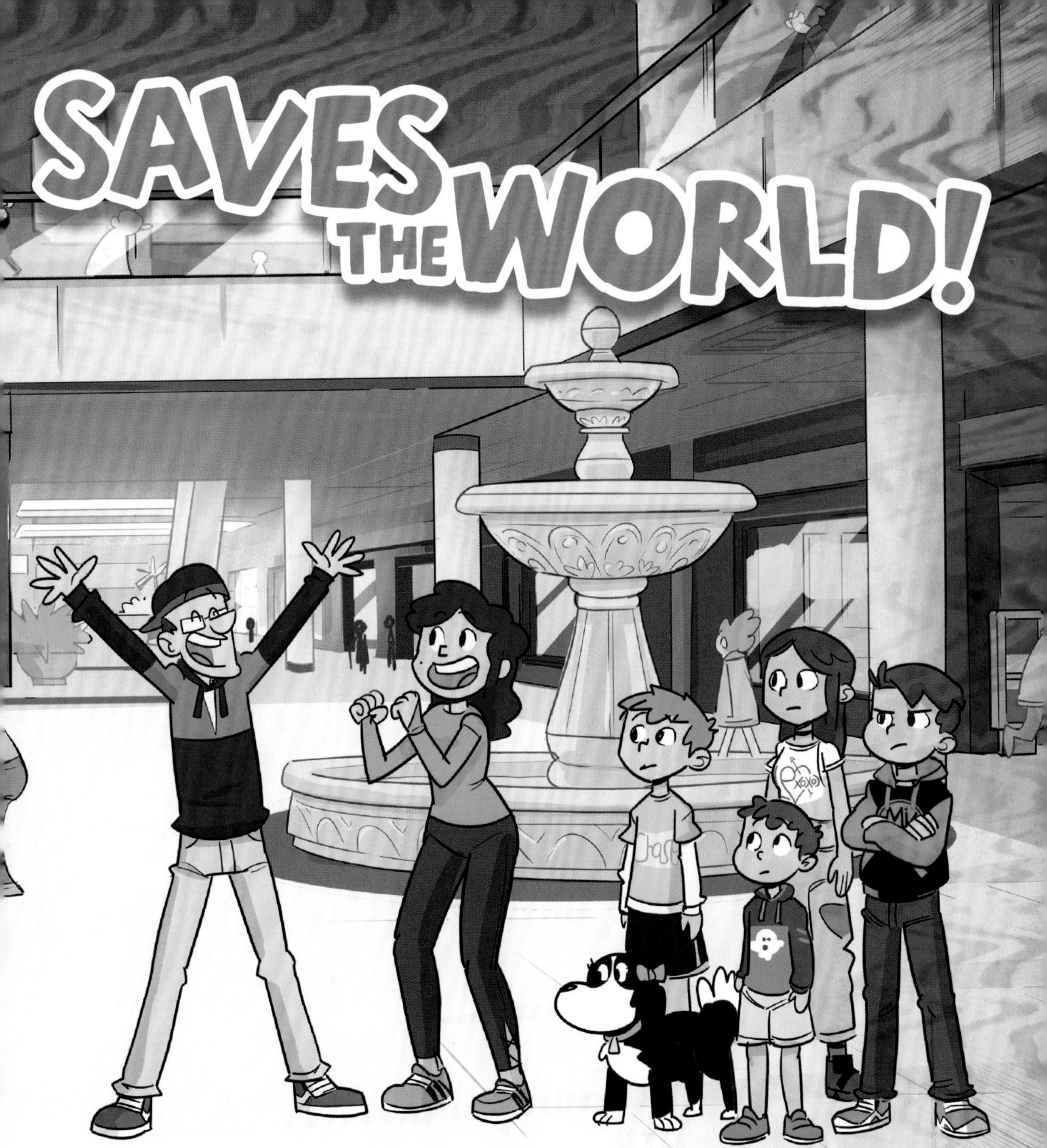

By FGTeeV

Illustrated by Miguel Díaz Rivas

HARPER alley

An Imprint of HarperCollinsPublishers

CHARACTERS

DUDDY/ DUDSTER

This fun-loving dad has more achievements and power-ups than the best gamers in the world. But will all that be lost to history—and his greatest hero?

MOOMY

Moomy keeps the fun train from going off the rails, but she's also sweet, as you can see by her chocolate-chip freckle!

LEXI/LEXO

The boss of the children; the master strategist who takes control with the confidence of her gaming know-how.

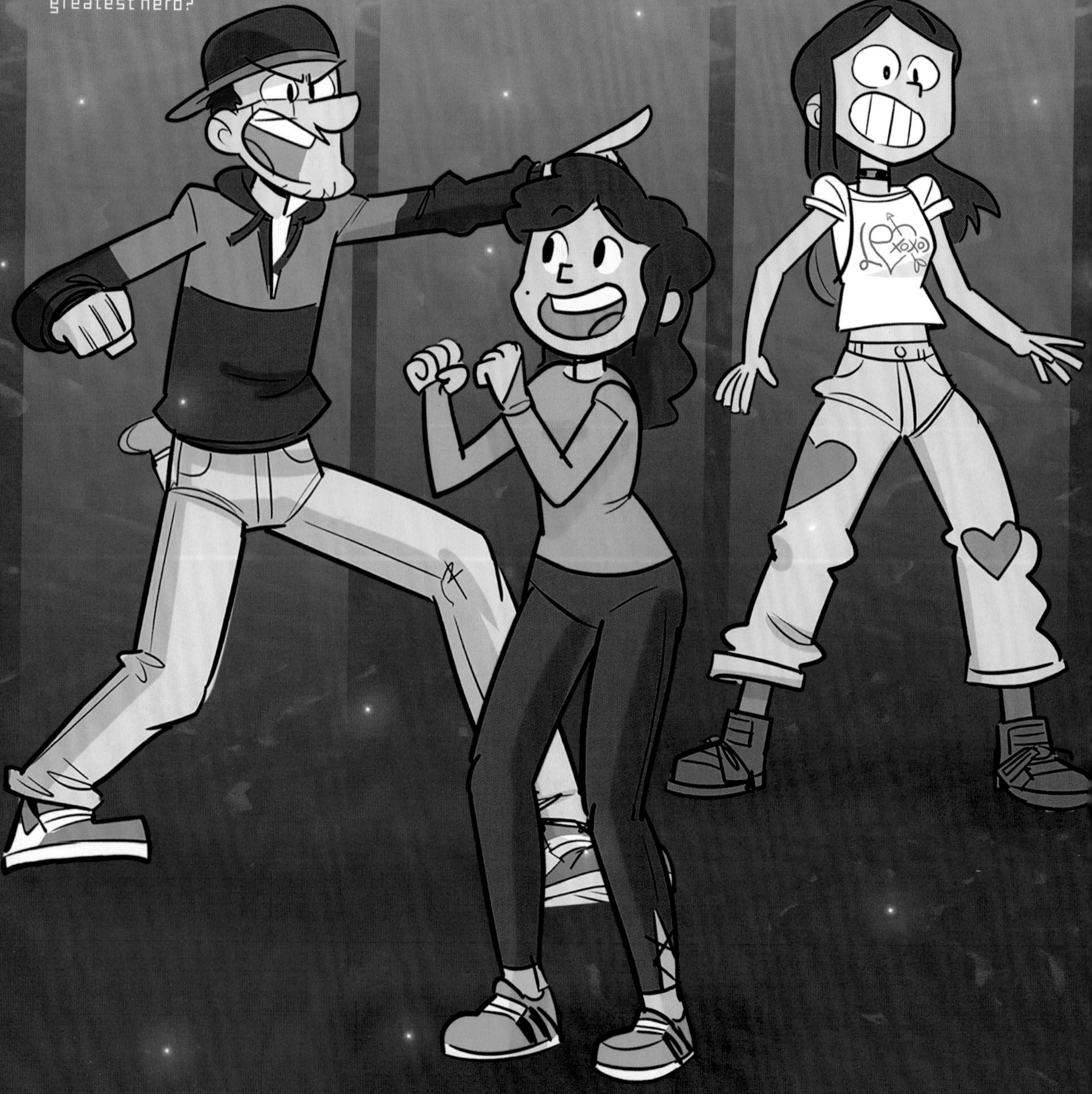

MIKE/ MICKSTER

The second-in-command. Mike respects Lexi's rules . . . but that doesn't mean he always follows them.

CHASE/ DRIZZY

He's the fearless sharp-shooter of the family—even when he's drinking a slushie.

SHAWN/GHOST PUNCHER

Shawn is curious about everything, which sure keeps the family on its toes! He also thinks everything, no matter how dire, is hilarious!

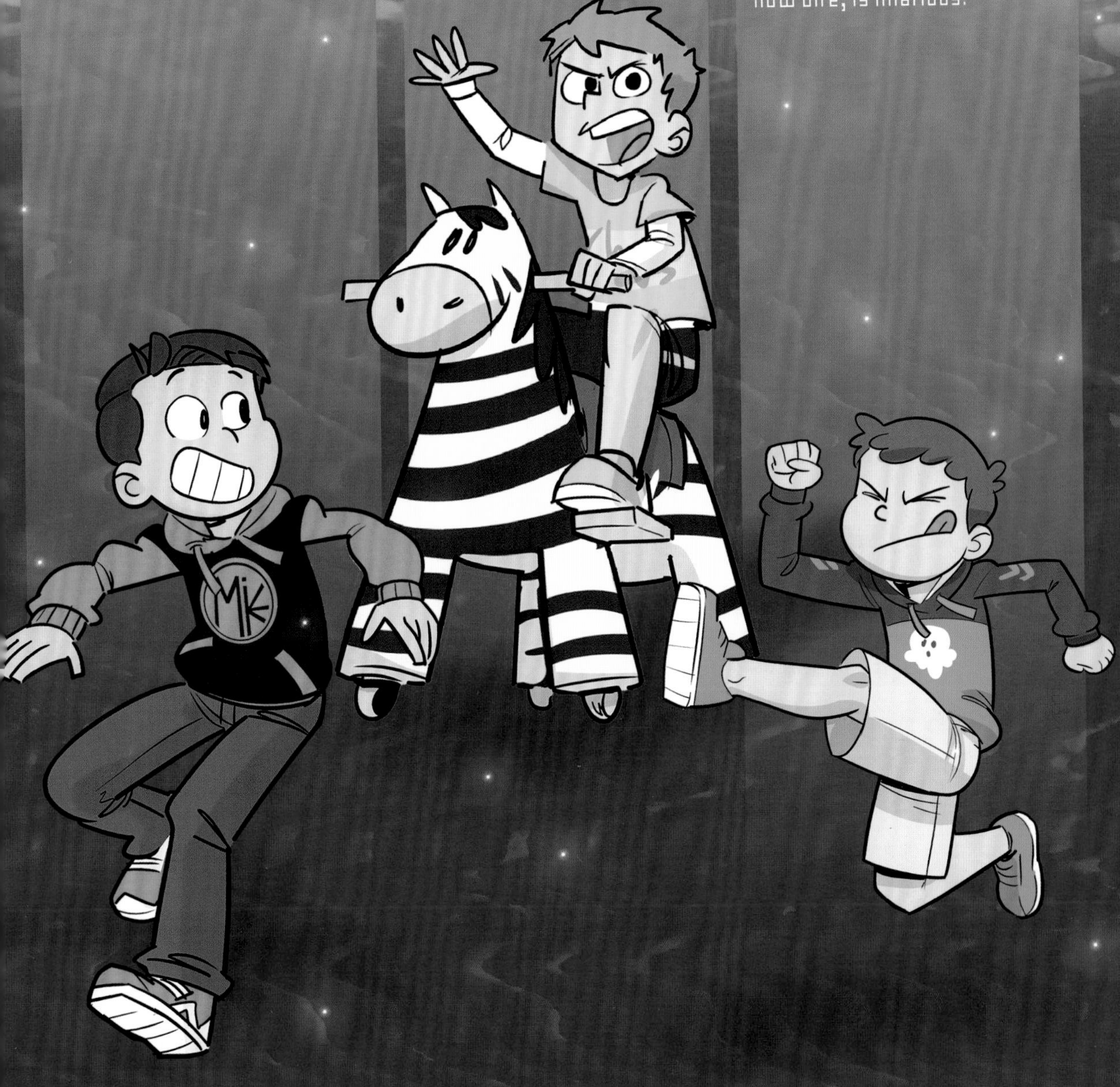

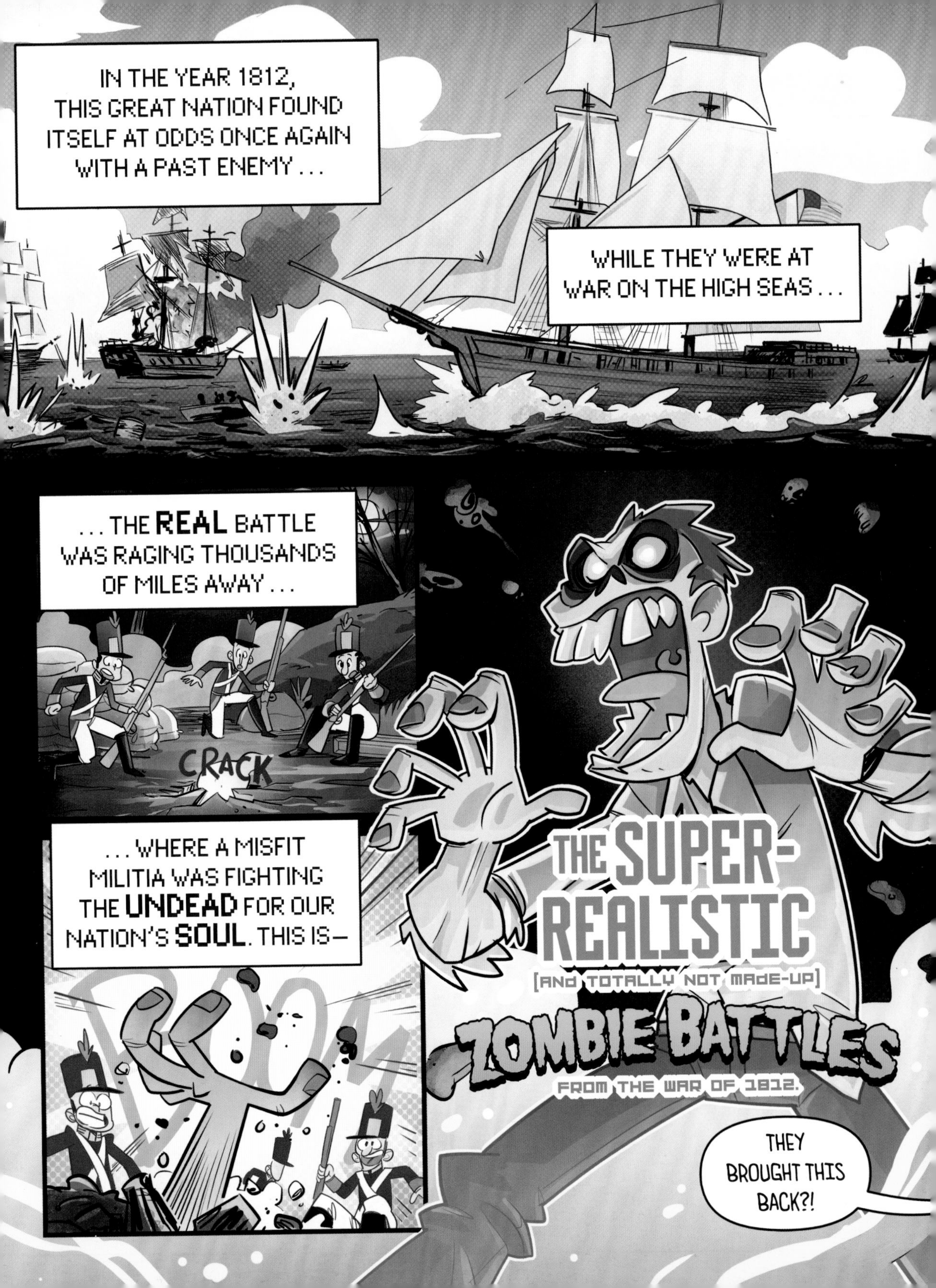

IN THE YEAR 1812, THIS GREAT NATION FOUND ITSELF AT ODDS ONCE AGAIN WITH A PAST ENEMY . . .
WHILE THEY WERE AT WAR ON THE HIGH SEAS . . .
. . . THE **REAL** BATTLE WAS RAGING THOUSANDS OF MILES AWAY . . .
CRACK
. . . WHERE A MISFIT MILITIA WAS FIGHTING THE **UNDEAD** FOR OUR NATION'S **SOUL**. THIS IS—
BOOM
THE SUPER-REALISTIC
[AND TOTALLY NOT MADE-UP]
ZOMBIE BATTLES
FROM THE WAR OF 1812.
THEY BROUGHT THIS BACK?!

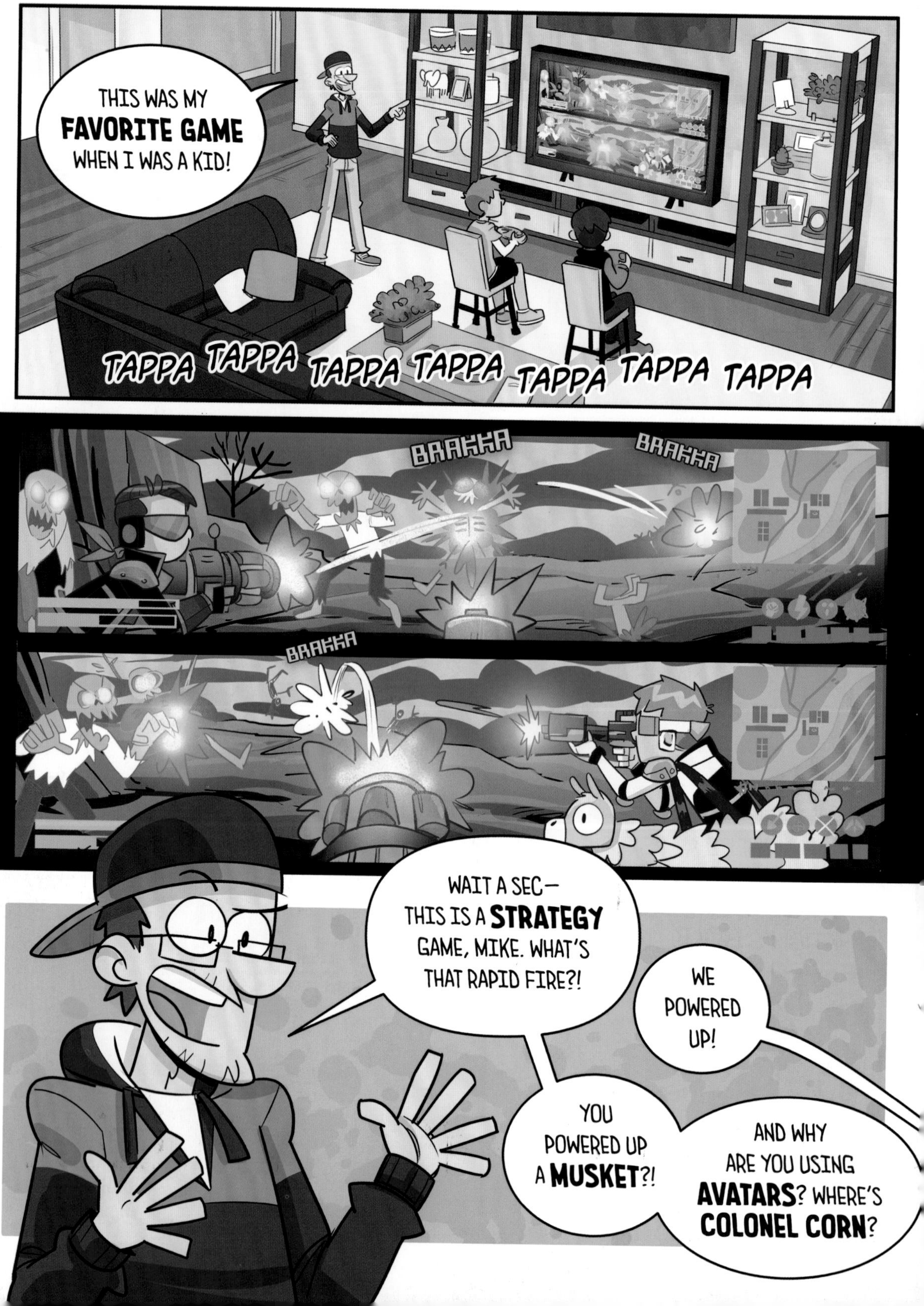
THIS WAS MY **FAVORITE GAME** WHEN I WAS A KID!
TAPPA TAPPA TAPPA TAPPA TAPPA TAPPA TAPPA
BRAKKA
BRAKKA
BRAKKA
WAIT A SEC— THIS IS A **STRATEGY** GAME, MIKE. WHAT'S THAT RAPID FIRE?!
WE POWERED UP!
YOU POWERED UP A **MUSKET**?!
AND WHY ARE YOU USING **AVATARS**? WHERE'S **COLONEL CORN**?

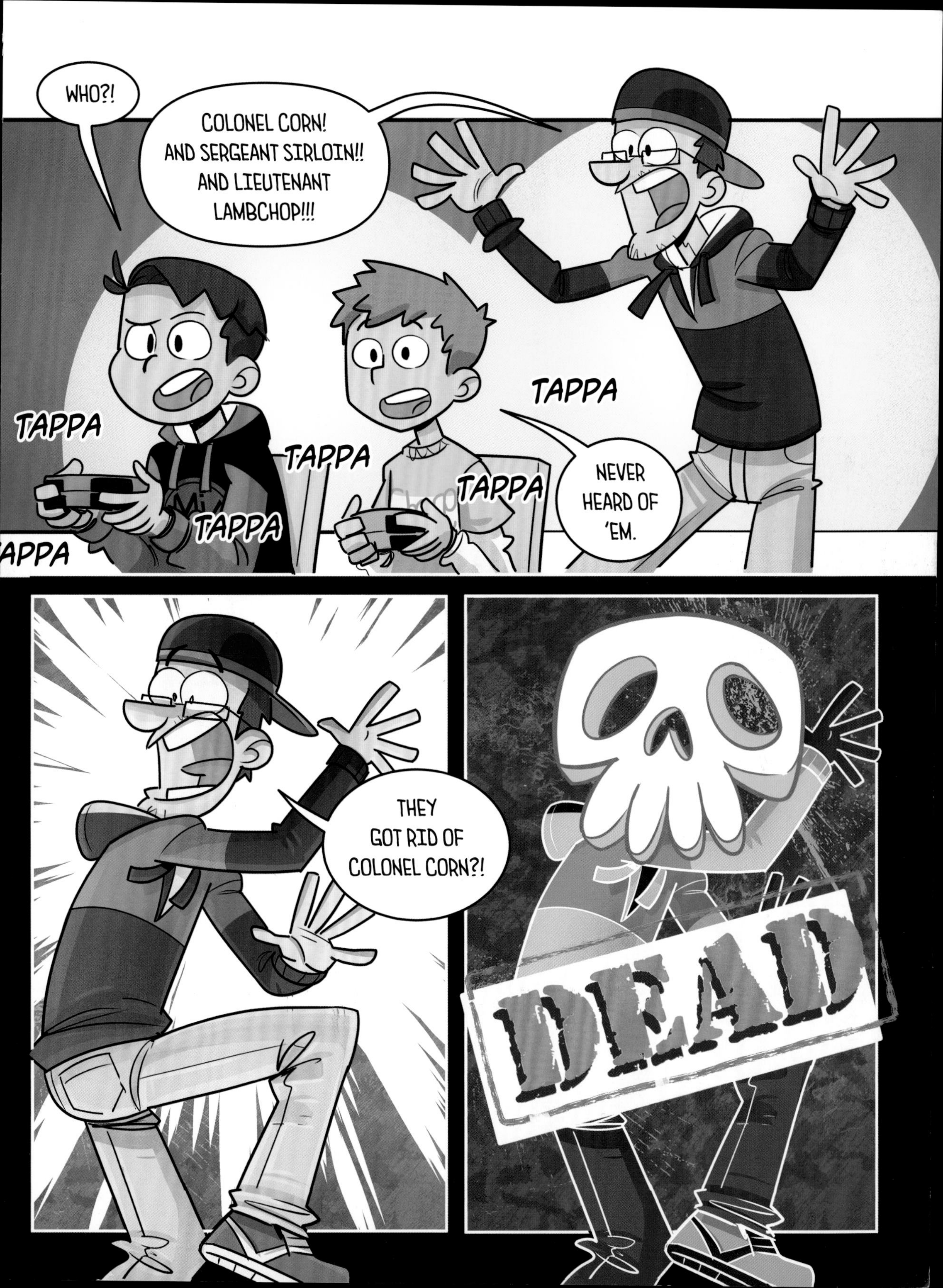
WHO?!
COLONEL CORN! AND SERGEANT SIRLOIN!! AND LIEUTENANT LAMBCHOP!!!
TAPPA
TAPPA
TAPPA
TAPPA
TAPPA
TAPPA
NEVER HEARD OF 'EM.
THEY GOT RID OF COLONEL CORN?!
DEAD

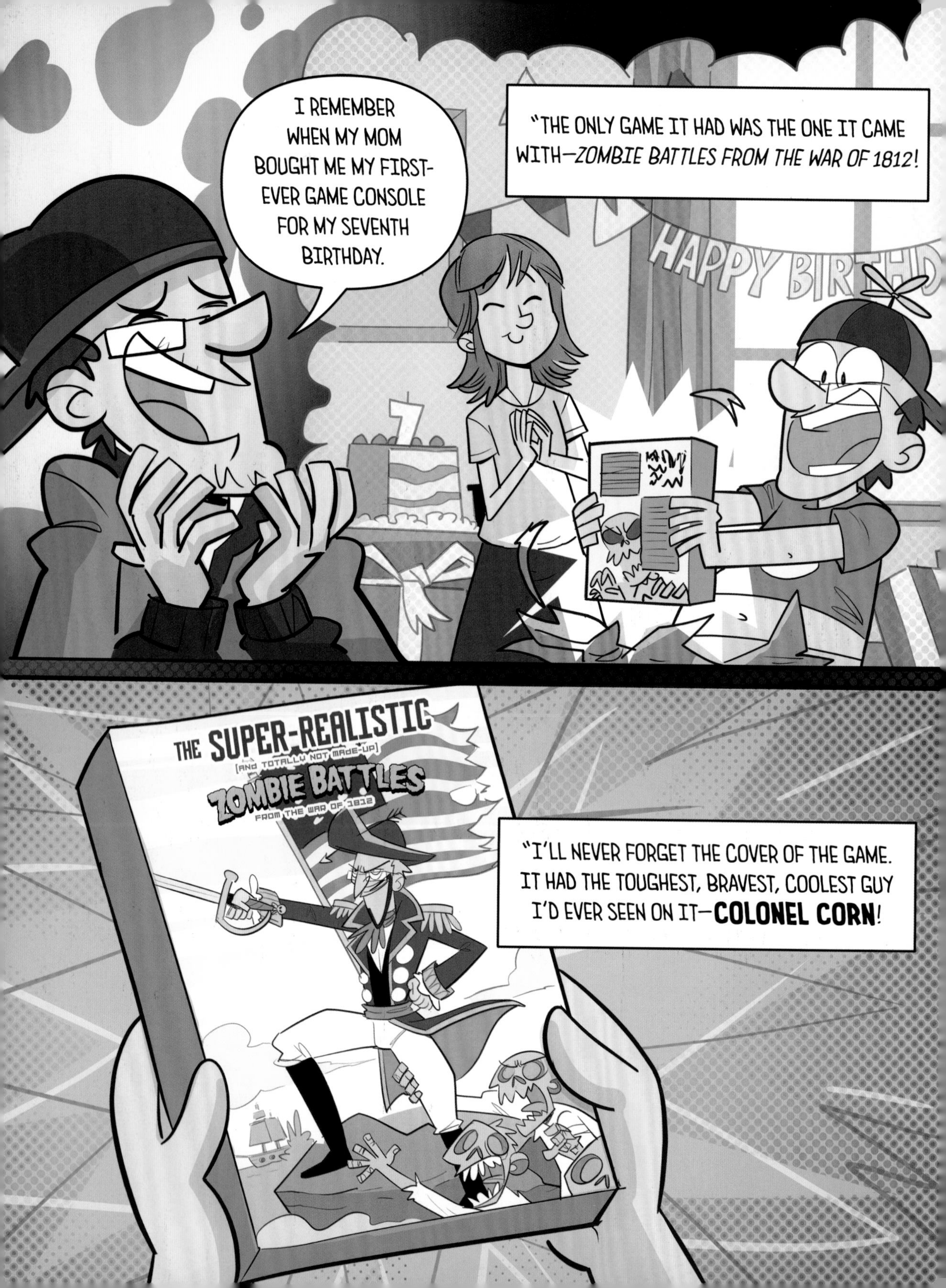
I REMEMBER WHEN MY MOM BOUGHT ME MY FIRST-EVER GAME CONSOLE FOR MY SEVENTH BIRTHDAY.
"THE ONLY GAME IT HAD WAS THE ONE IT CAME WITH—*ZOMBIE BATTLES FROM THE WAR OF 1812*!
THE SUPER-REALISTIC
(AND TOTALLY NOT MADE-UP)
ZOMBIE BATTLES
FROM THE WAR OF 1812
"I'LL NEVER FORGET THE COVER OF THE GAME. IT HAD THE TOUGHEST, BRAVEST, COOLEST GUY I'D EVER SEEN ON IT—**COLONEL CORN**!

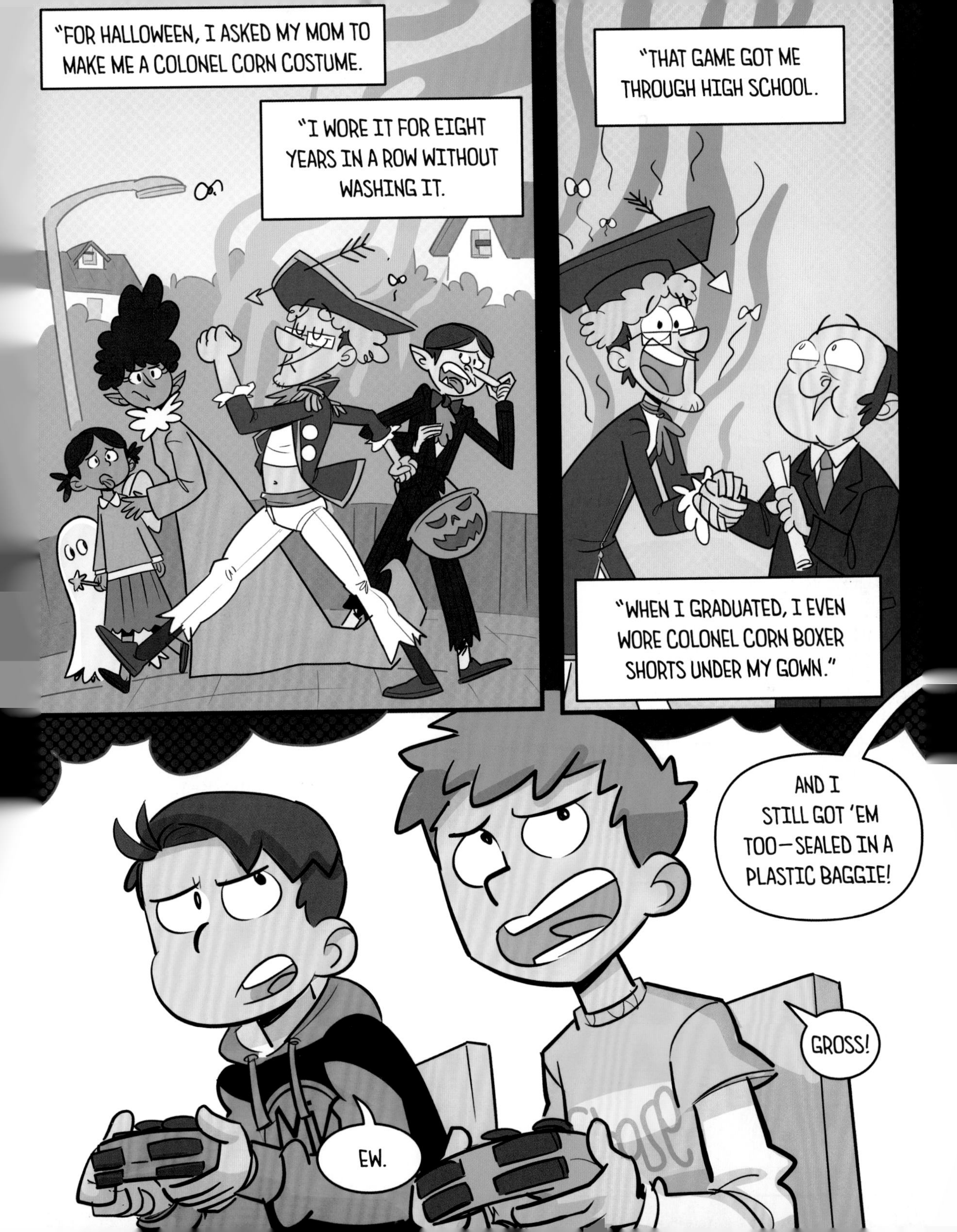
"FOR HALLOWEEN, I ASKED MY MOM TO MAKE ME A COLONEL CORN COSTUME.
"I WORE IT FOR EIGHT YEARS IN A ROW WITHOUT WASHING IT.
"THAT GAME GOT ME THROUGH HIGH SCHOOL.
"WHEN I GRADUATED, I EVEN WORE COLONEL CORN BOXER SHORTS UNDER MY GOWN."
AND I STILL GOT 'EM TOO—SEALED IN A PLASTIC BAGGIE!
GROSS!
EW.

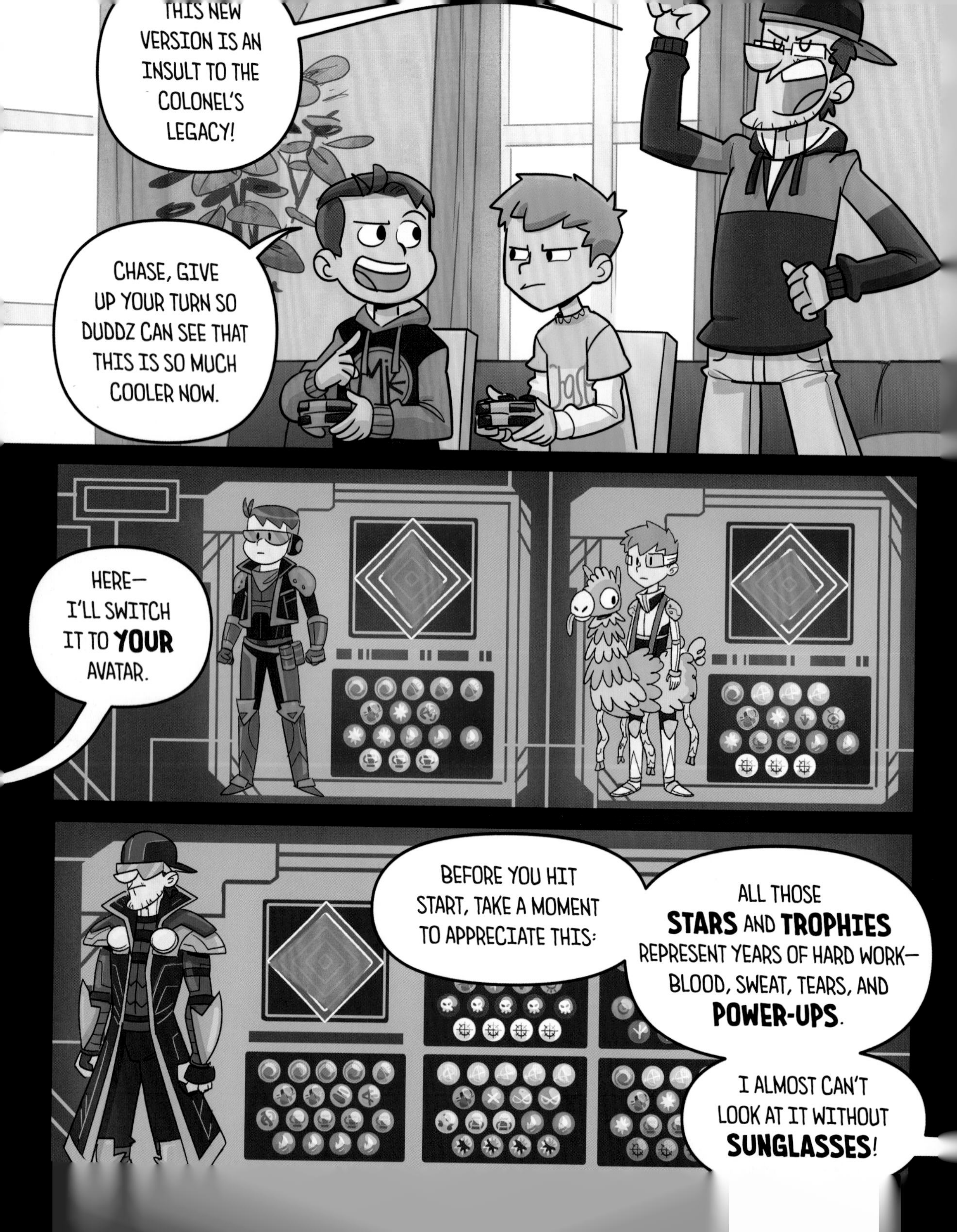
THIS NEW VERSION IS AN INSULT TO THE COLONEL'S LEGACY!
CHASE, GIVE UP YOUR TURN SO DUDDZ CAN SEE THAT THIS IS SO MUCH COOLER NOW.
HERE— I'LL SWITCH IT TO YOUR AVATAR.
BEFORE YOU HIT START, TAKE A MOMENT TO APPRECIATE THIS:
ALL THOSE STARS AND TROPHIES REPRESENT YEARS OF HARD WORK— BLOOD, SWEAT, TEARS, AND POWER-UPS.
I ALMOST CAN'T LOOK AT IT WITHOUT SUNGLASSES!

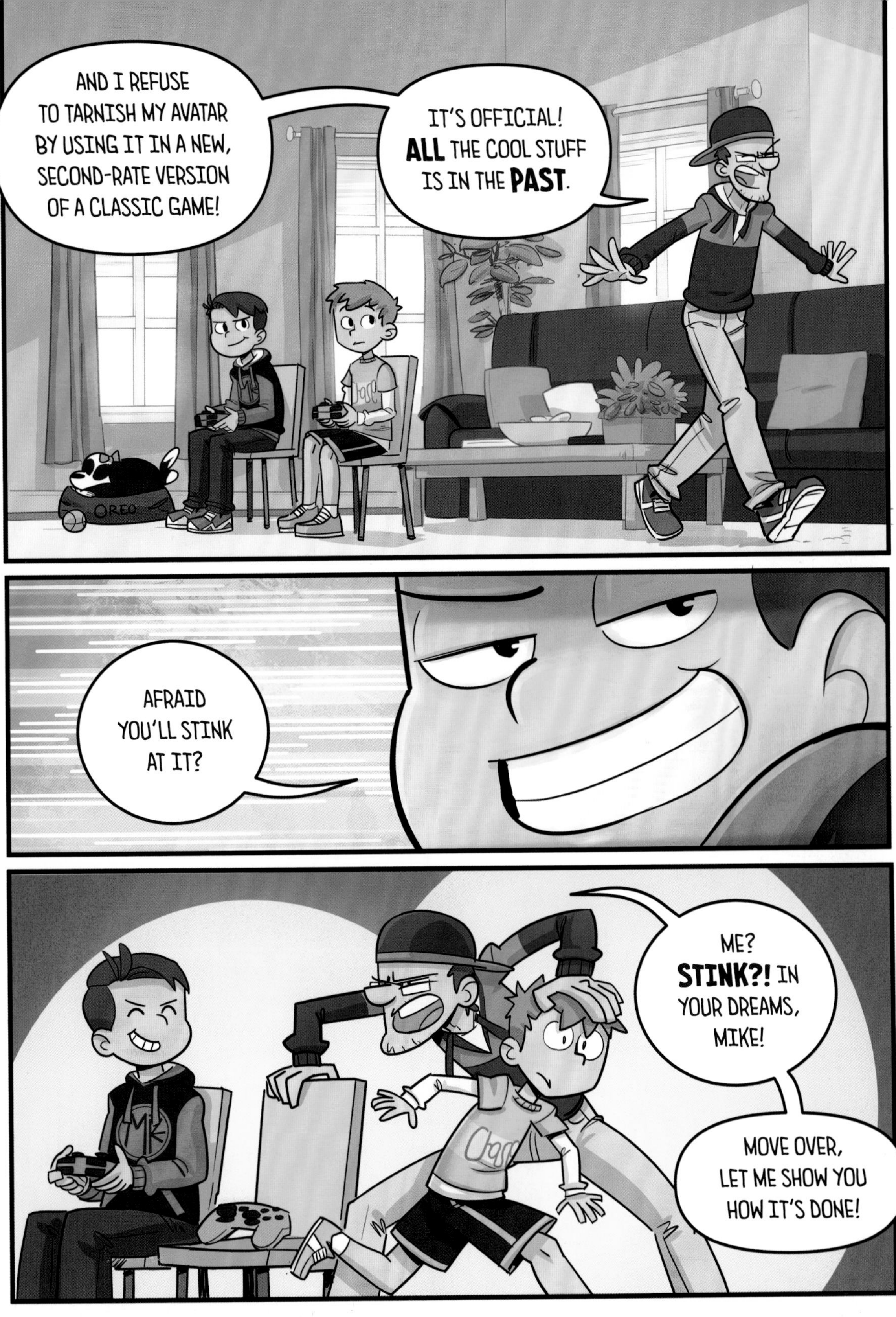

AND I REFUSE TO TARNISH MY AVATAR BY USING IT IN A NEW, SECOND-RATE VERSION OF A CLASSIC GAME!
IT'S OFFICIAL! **ALL** THE COOL STUFF IS IN THE **PAST**.
OREO
AFRAID YOU'LL STINK AT IT?
ME? **STINK?!** IN YOUR DREAMS, MIKE!
MOVE OVER, LET ME SHOW YOU HOW IT'S DONE!

SNIFF
SNIFF

OREO

TAP TAP TAP

TAP TAP TAP TAP

WHO WANTS FRESH-BAKED COOKIES?

MOM!! WHAT DID YOU DO?!

WEREN'T THOSE THE NEW **PANTS** YOU WANTED? THEY LOOK **CUTE!**

YEAH—WHEN I WAS **SIX**. EVERYONE AT SCHOOL'S GONNA CALL ME A **BABY!**

NO, THEY WON'T!

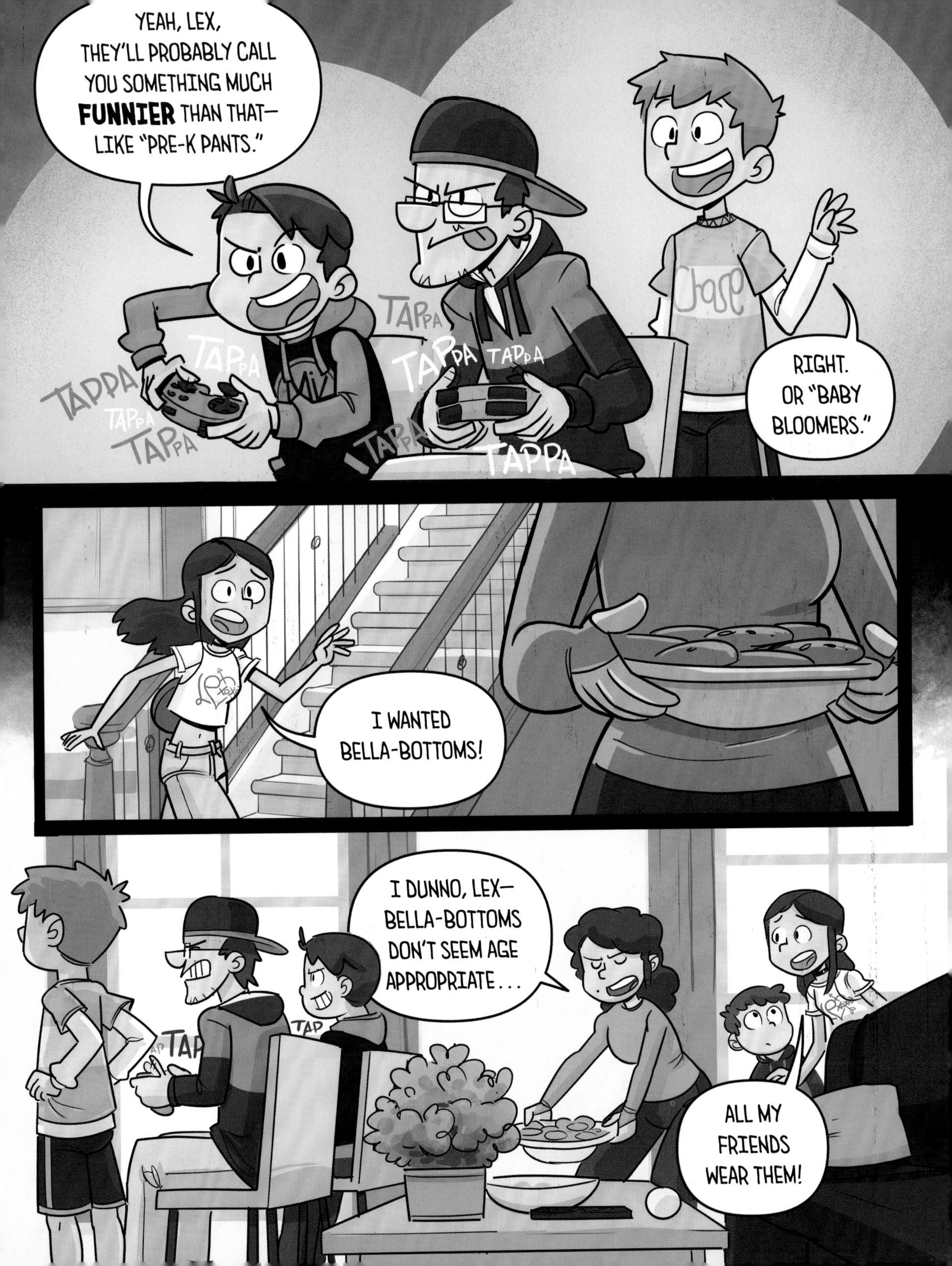

YEAH, LEX, THEY'LL PROBABLY CALL YOU SOMETHING MUCH **FUNNIER** THAN THAT— LIKE "PRE-K PANTS."
TAPPA TAPPA TAPPA TAPPA TAPPA TAPPA TAPPA TAPPA TAPPA
Chase
RIGHT. OR "BABY BLOOMERS."
I WANTED BELLA-BOTTOMS!
I DUNNO, LEX— BELLA-BOTTOMS DON'T SEEM AGE APPROPRIATE . . .
TAP TAP
ALL MY FRIENDS WEAR THEM!

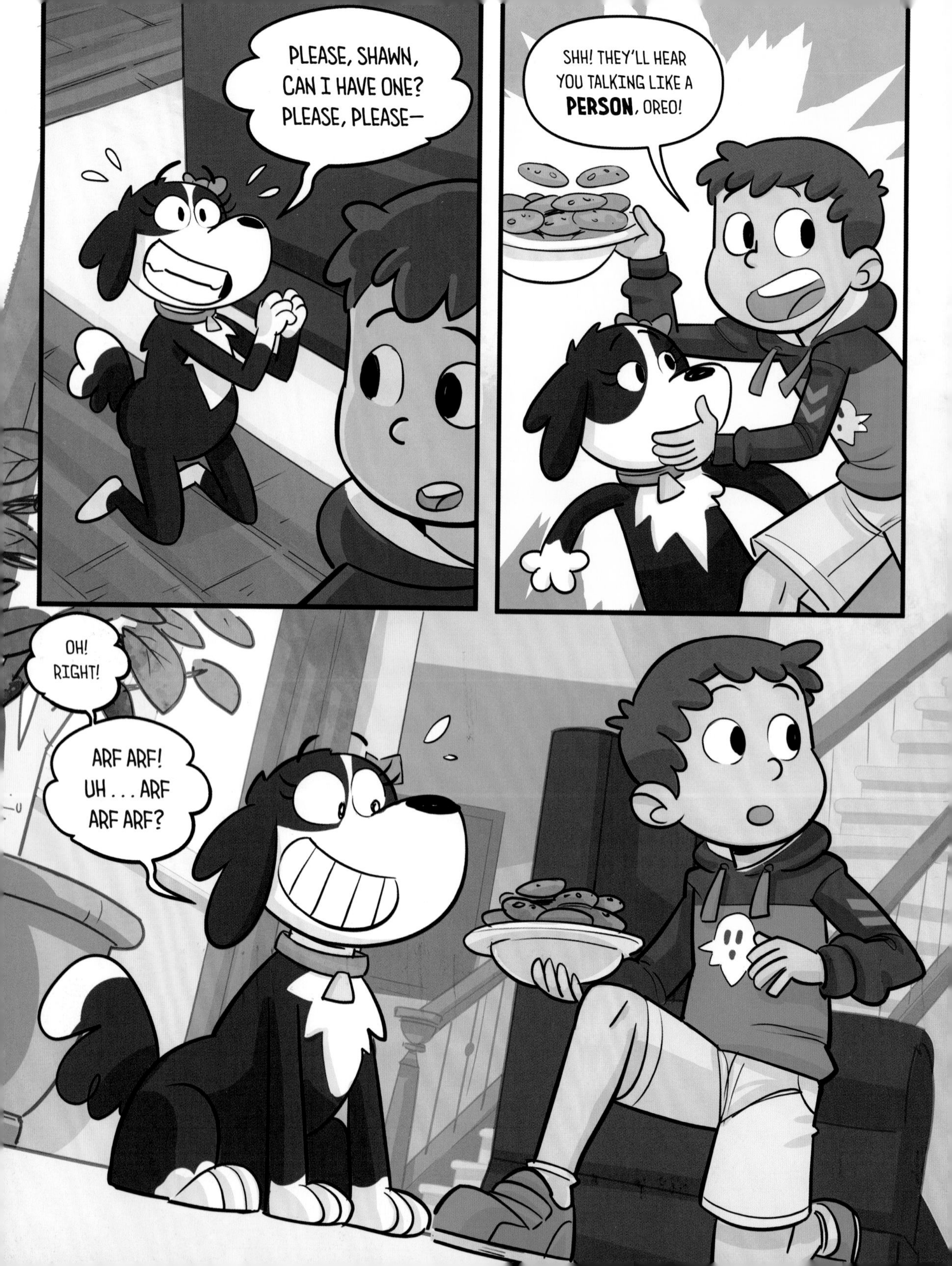
PLEASE, SHAWN, CAN I HAVE ONE? PLEASE, PLEASE—
SHH! THEY'LL HEAR YOU TALKING LIKE A **PERSON**, OREO!
OH! RIGHT!
ARF ARF! UH . . . ARF ARF ARF?

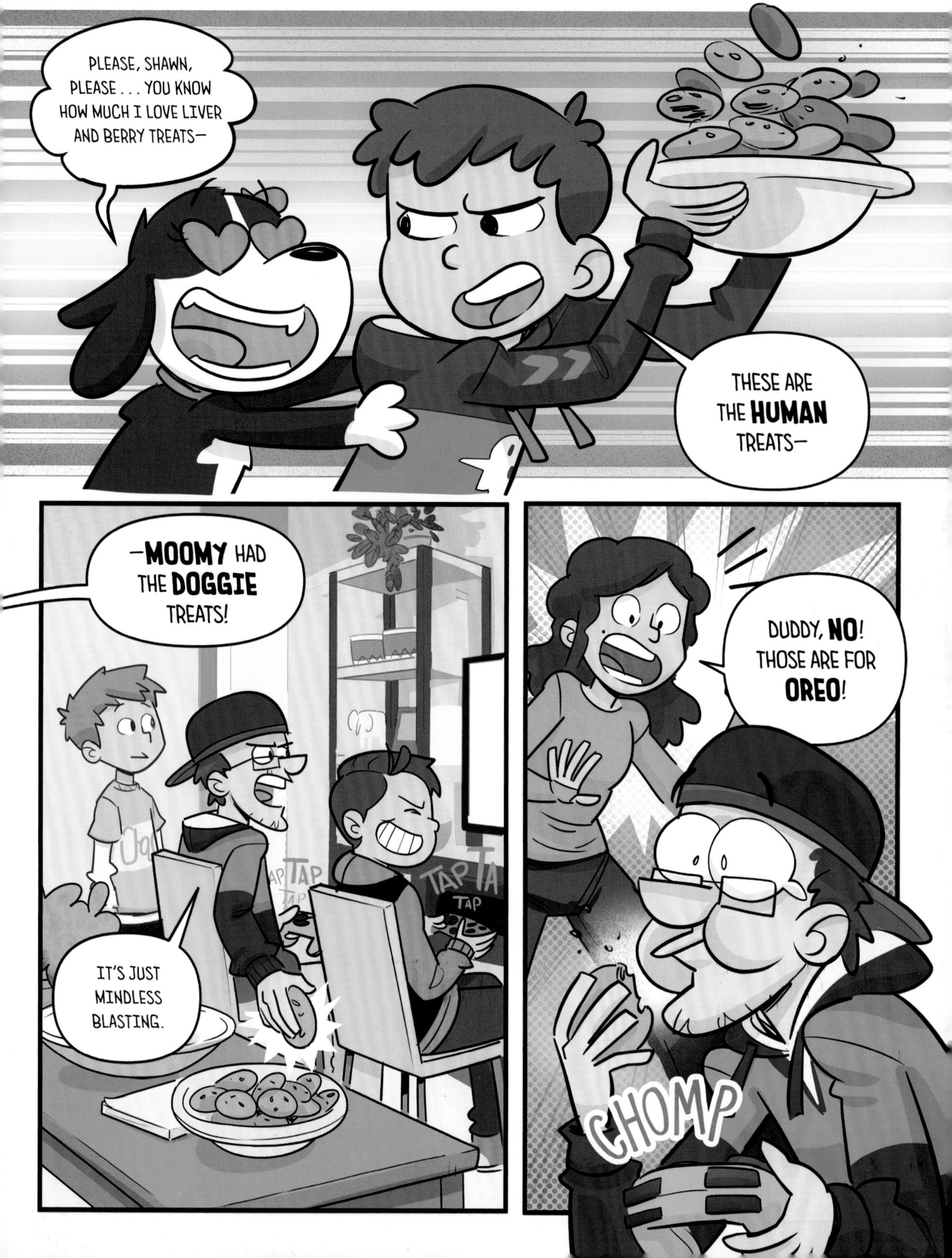
PLEASE, SHAWN, PLEASE . . . YOU KNOW HOW MUCH I LOVE LIVER AND BERRY TREATS—
THESE ARE THE **HUMAN** TREATS—
—**MOOMY** HAD THE **DOGGIE** TREATS!
TAP TAP TAP
TAP TA TAP
IT'S JUST MINDLESS BLASTING.
DUDDY, **NO**! THOSE ARE FOR **OREO**!
CHOMP

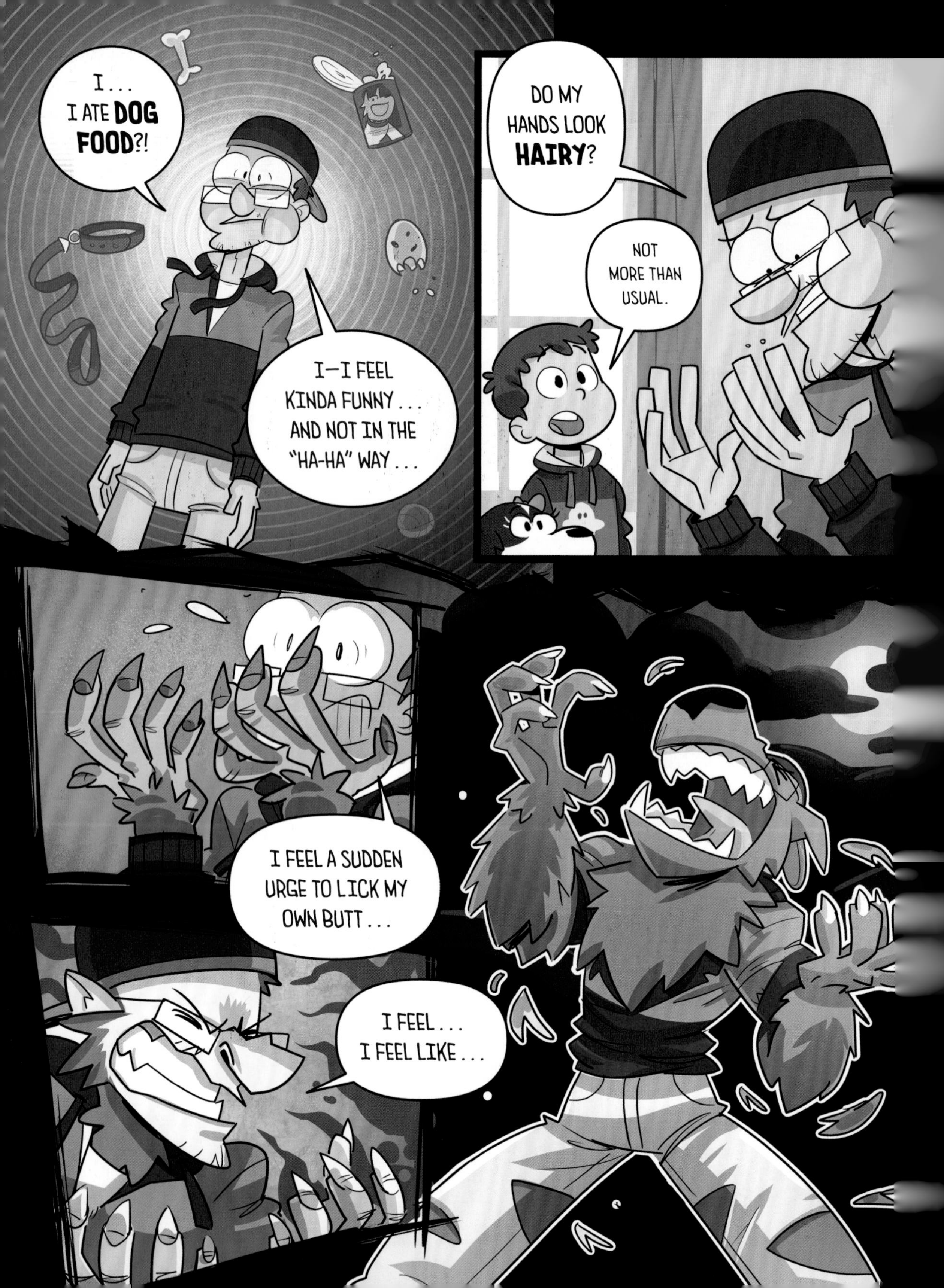
I...
I ATE DOG FOOD?!
I—I FEEL KINDA FUNNY... AND NOT IN THE "HA-HA" WAY...
DO MY HANDS LOOK HAIRY?
NOT MORE THAN USUAL.
I FEEL A SUDDEN URGE TO LICK MY OWN BUTT...
I FEEL...
I FEEL LIKE...

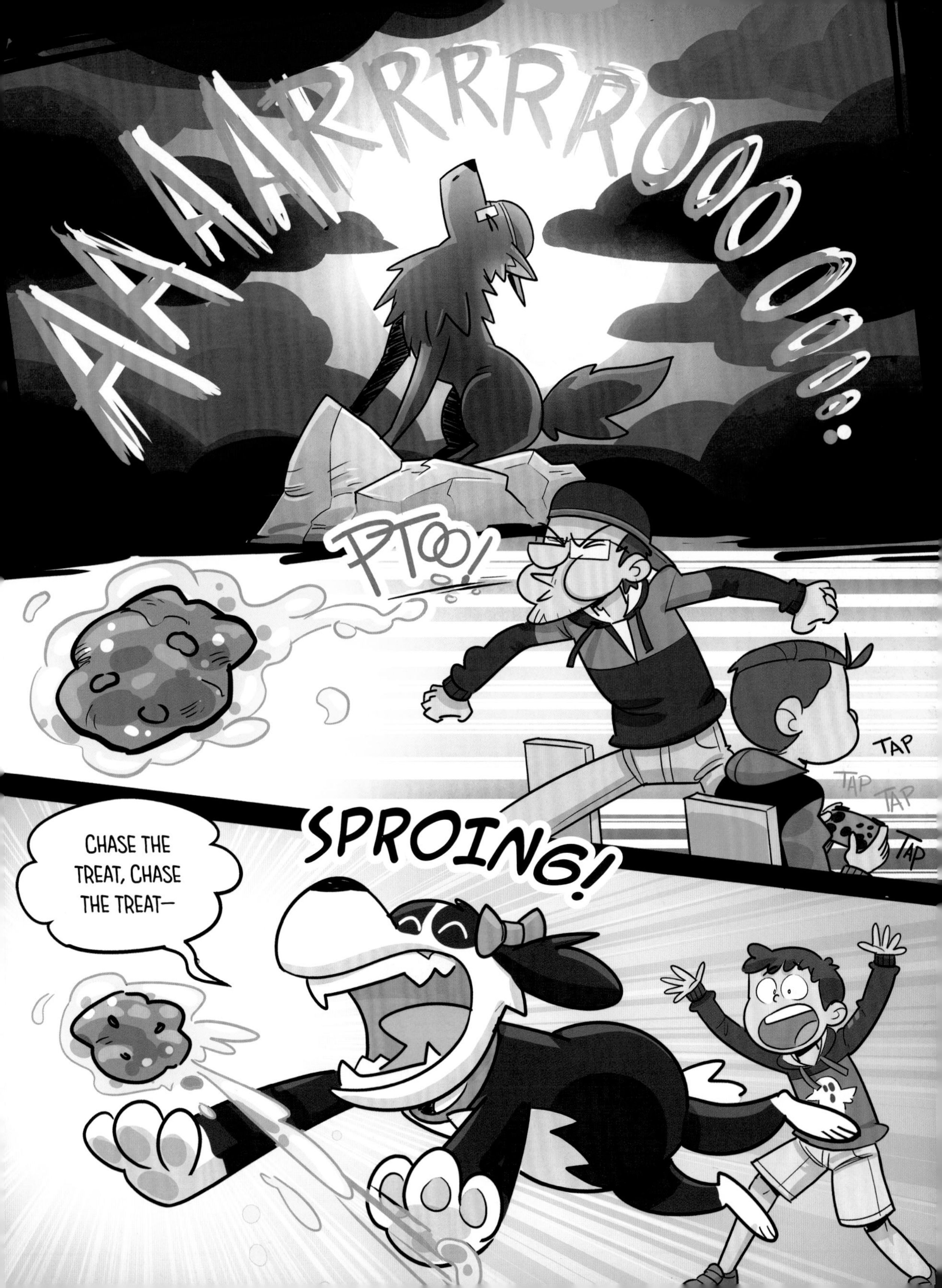
AAARRRRROOOOOOO...
PTOO!
TAP
TAP TAP
TAP
SPROING!
CHASE THE TREAT, CHASE THE TREAT—

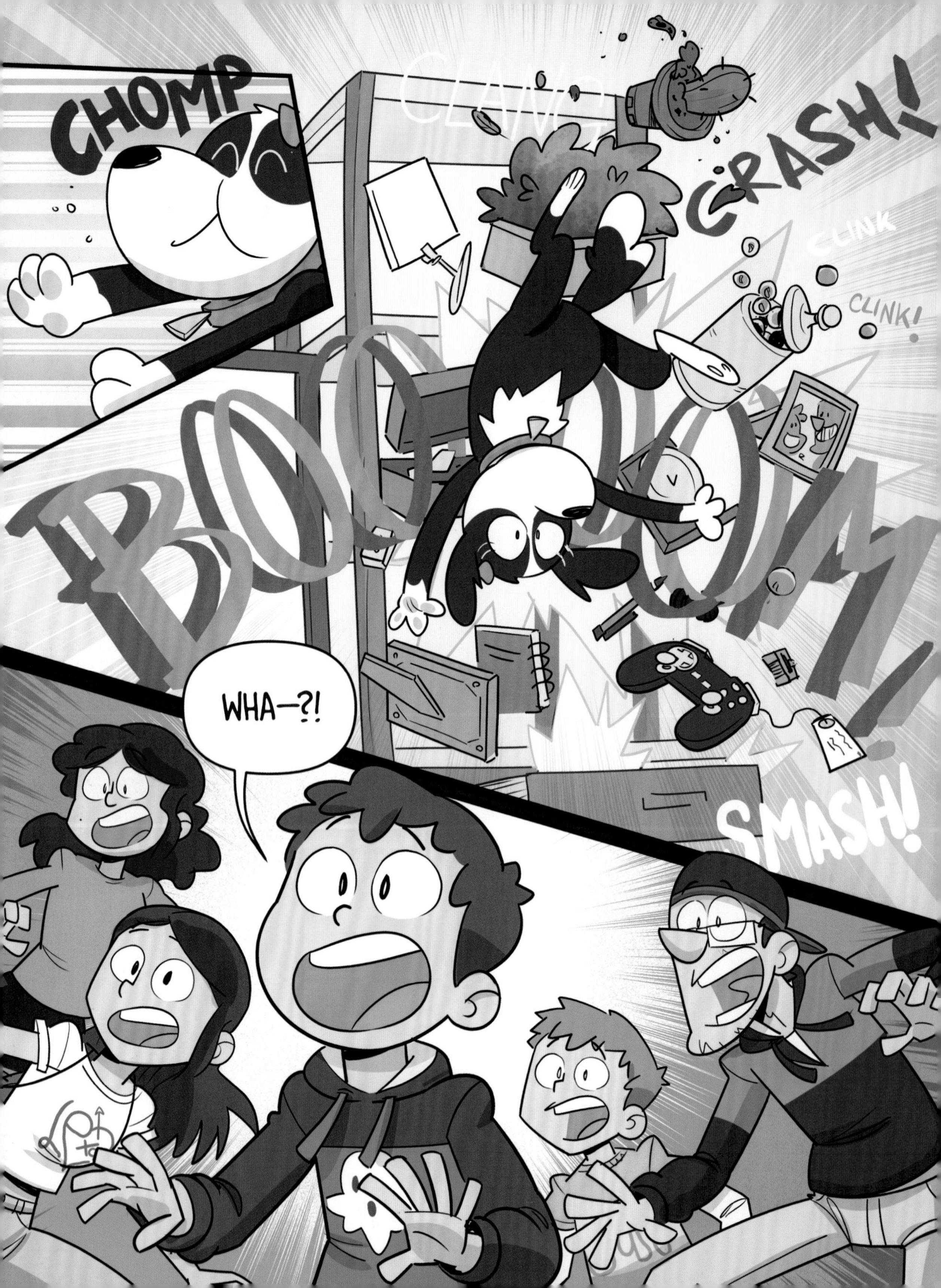
CHOMP
CLANG!
CRASH!
CLINK
CLINK!
BOOOOM!
WHA—?!
SMASH!

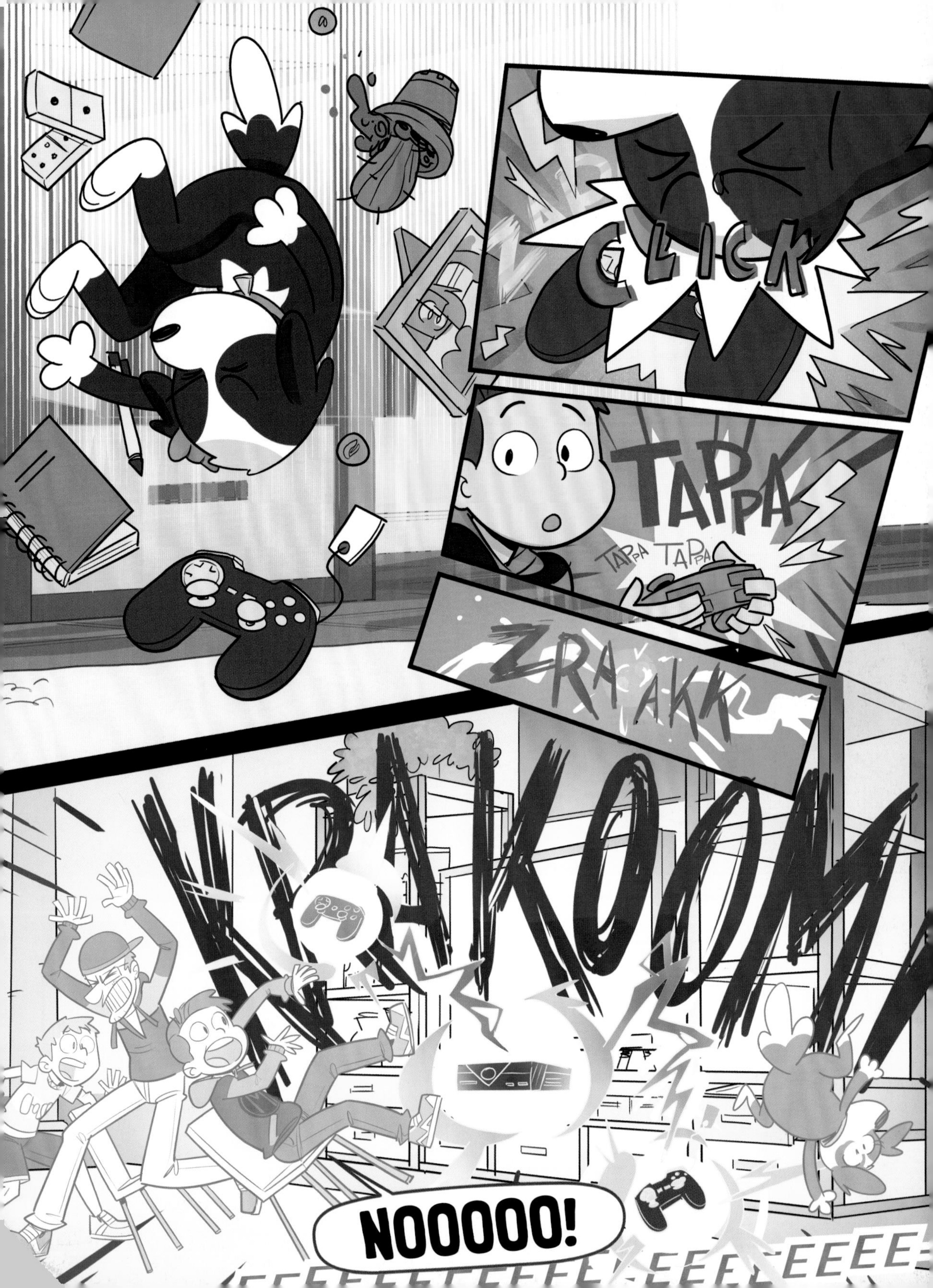
CLICK
TAPPA
TAPPA TAPPA
ZRAAKK
KRAKOOM
NOOOOO!
EEEEEEEEEEEEEEEEEEE

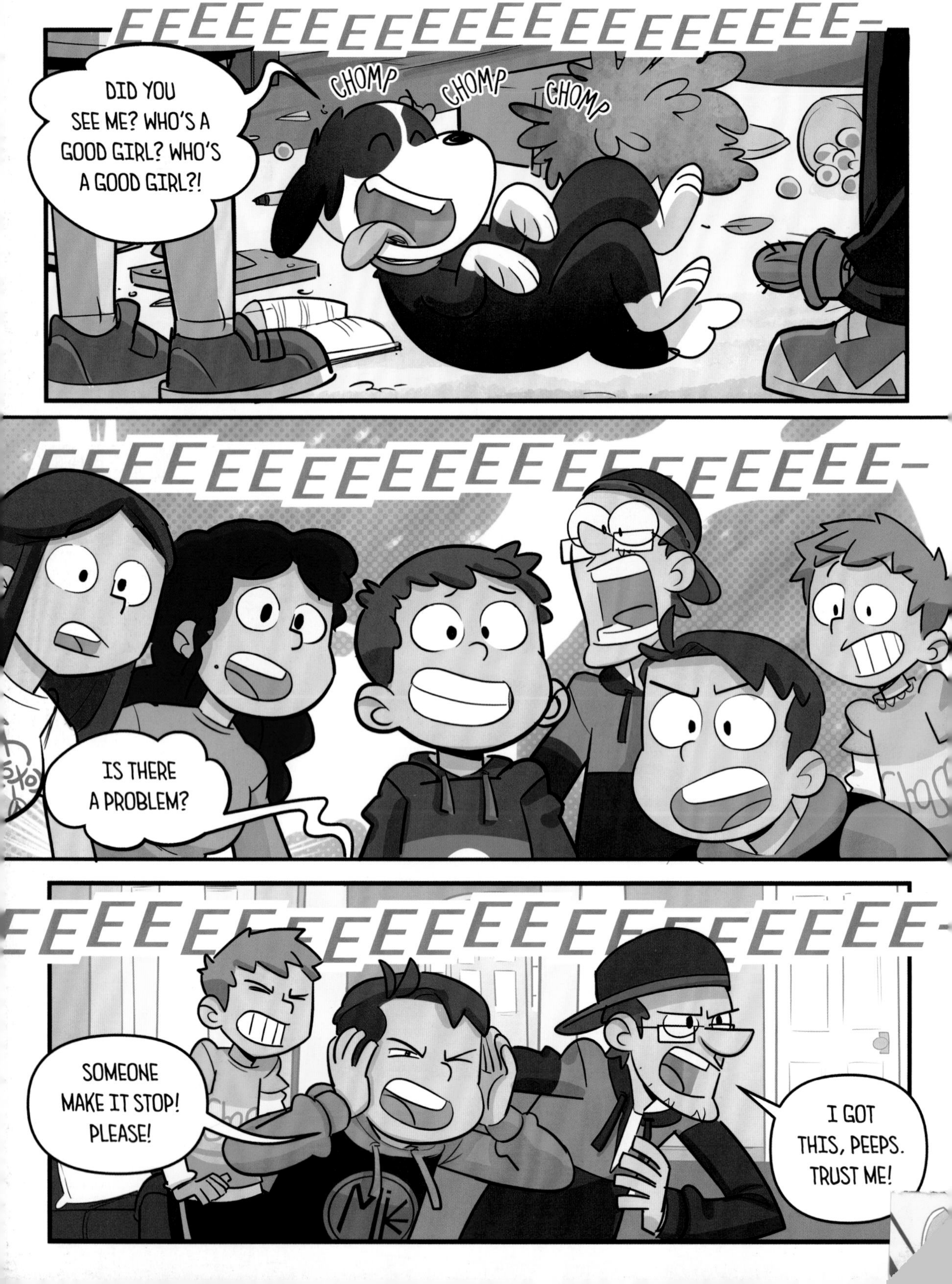
EEEEEEEEEEEEEEEEEEEE-
DID YOU SEE ME? WHO'S A GOOD GIRL? WHO'S A GOOD GIRL?!
CHOMP
CHOMP
CHOMP
EEEEEEEEEEEEEEEEEEEEE-
IS THERE A PROBLEM?
EEEEEEEEEEEEEEEEEEEEEEE-
SOMEONE MAKE IT STOP! PLEASE!
I GOT THIS, PEEPS. TRUST ME!

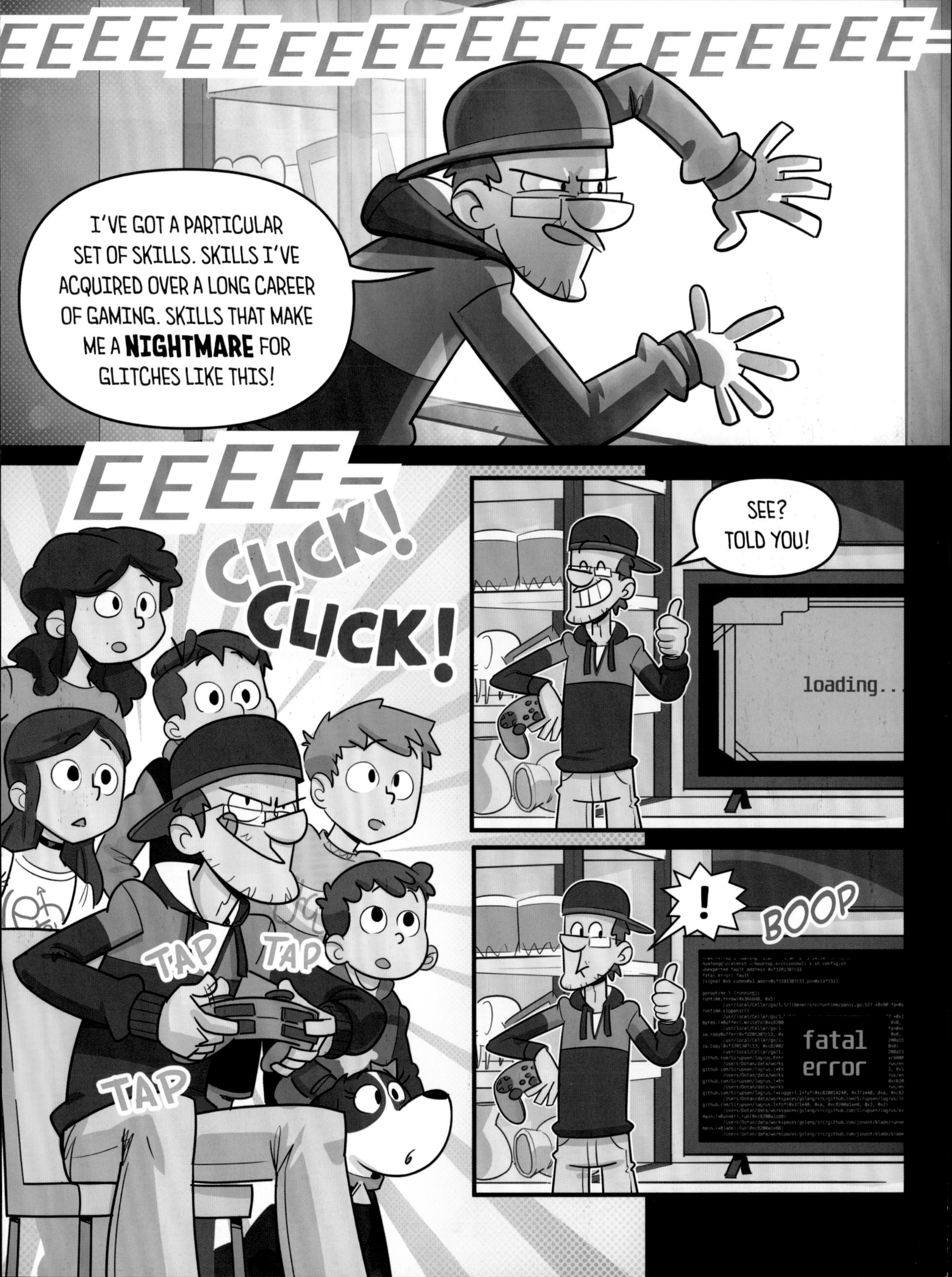
EEEEEEEEEEEEEEEEEEEEEEEE—
I'VE GOT A PARTICULAR SET OF SKILLS. SKILLS I'VE ACQUIRED OVER A LONG CAREER OF GAMING. SKILLS THAT MAKE ME A **NIGHTMARE** FOR GLITCHES LIKE THIS!
EEEE—
CLICK! CLICK!
TAP TAP
TAP
SEE? TOLD YOU!
loading...
!
BOOP
fatal error

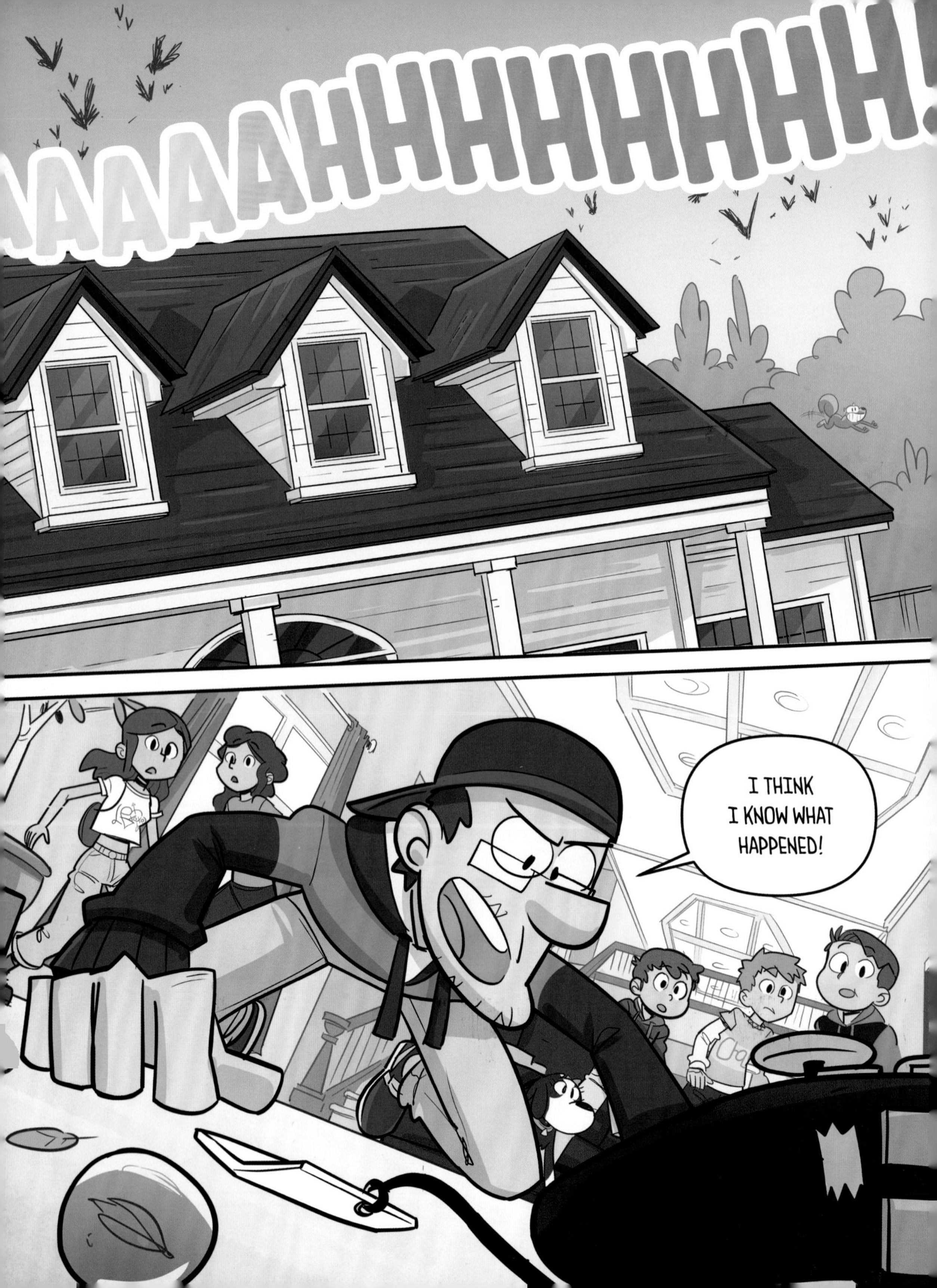
AAAAAHHHHHHHHHH!
I THINK I KNOW WHAT HAPPENED!

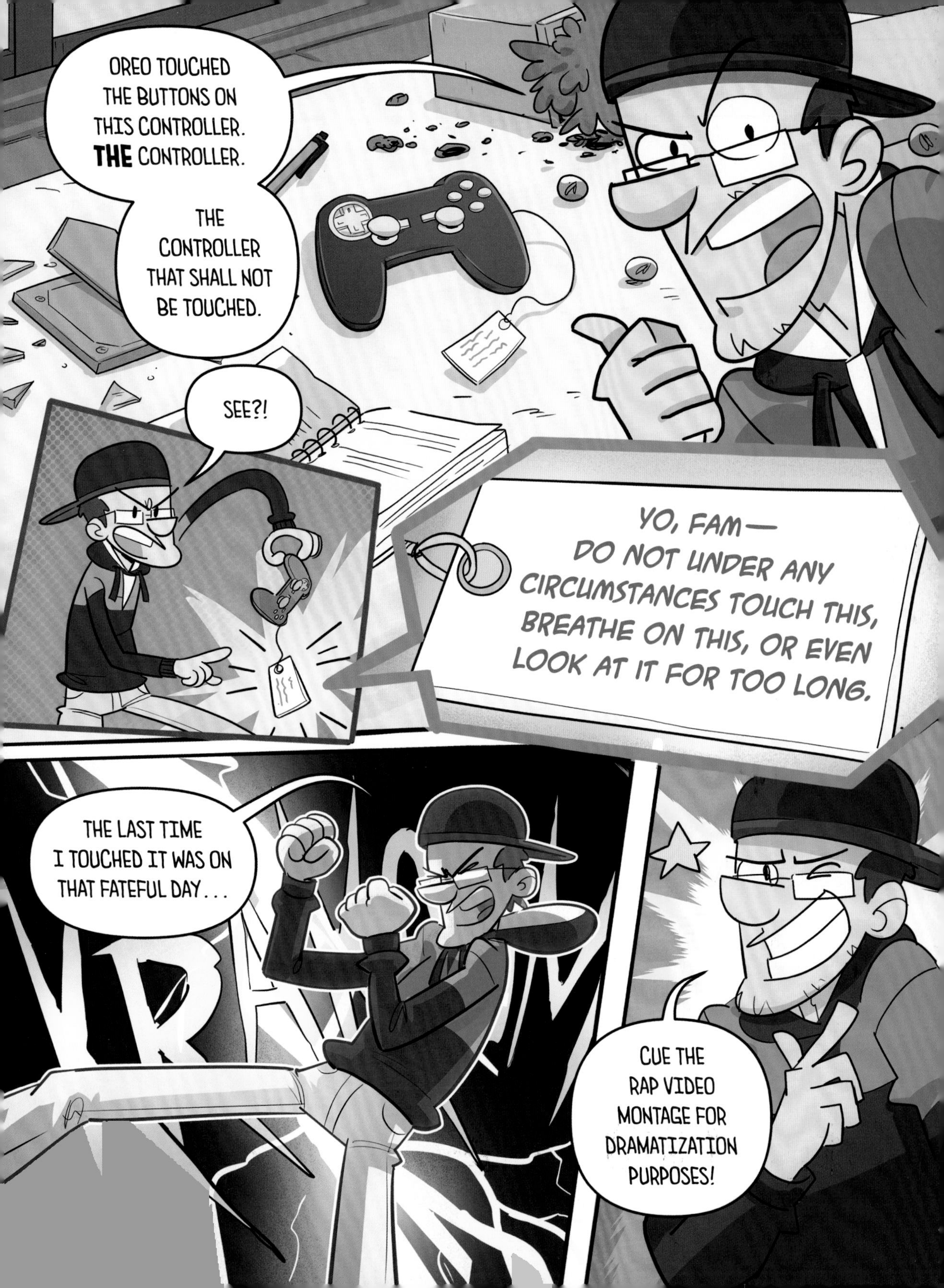
OREO TOUCHED THE BUTTONS ON THIS CONTROLLER. **THE** CONTROLLER.
THE CONTROLLER THAT SHALL NOT BE TOUCHED.
SEE?!
YO, FAM— DO NOT UNDER ANY CIRCUMSTANCES TOUCH THIS, BREATHE ON THIS, OR EVEN LOOK AT IT FOR TOO LONG.
THE LAST TIME I TOUCHED IT WAS ON THAT FATEFUL DAY . . .
CUE THE RAP VIDEO MONTAGE FOR DRAMATIZATION PURPOSES!

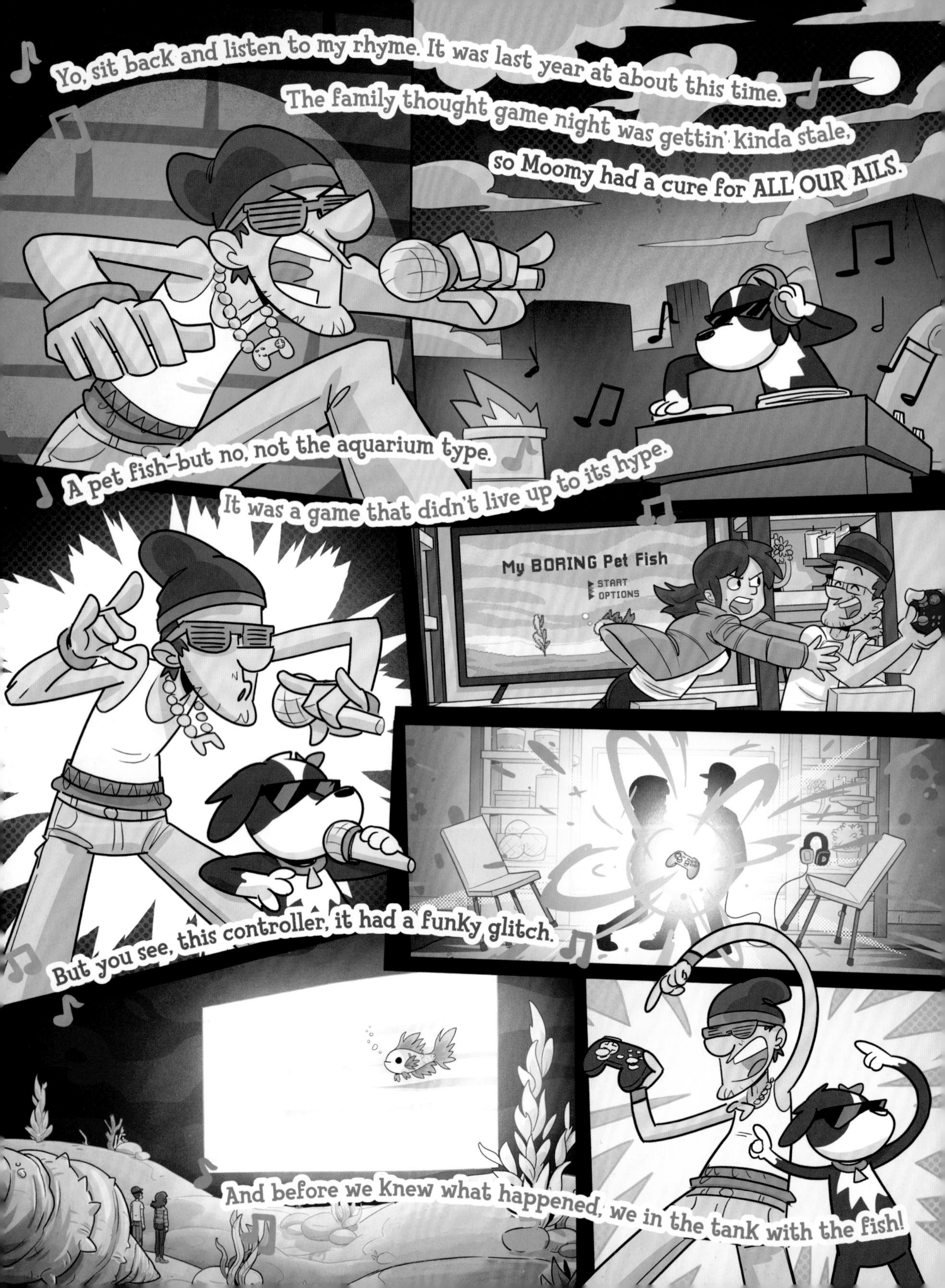

Yo, sit back and listen to my rhyme. It was last year at about this time.
The family thought game night was gettin' kinda stale,
so Moomy had a cure for ALL OUR AILS.
A pet fish—but no, not the aquarium type.
It was a game that didn't live up to its hype.
My BORING Pet Fish
START
OPTIONS
But you see, this controller, it had a funky glitch.
And before we knew what happened, we in the tank with the fish!

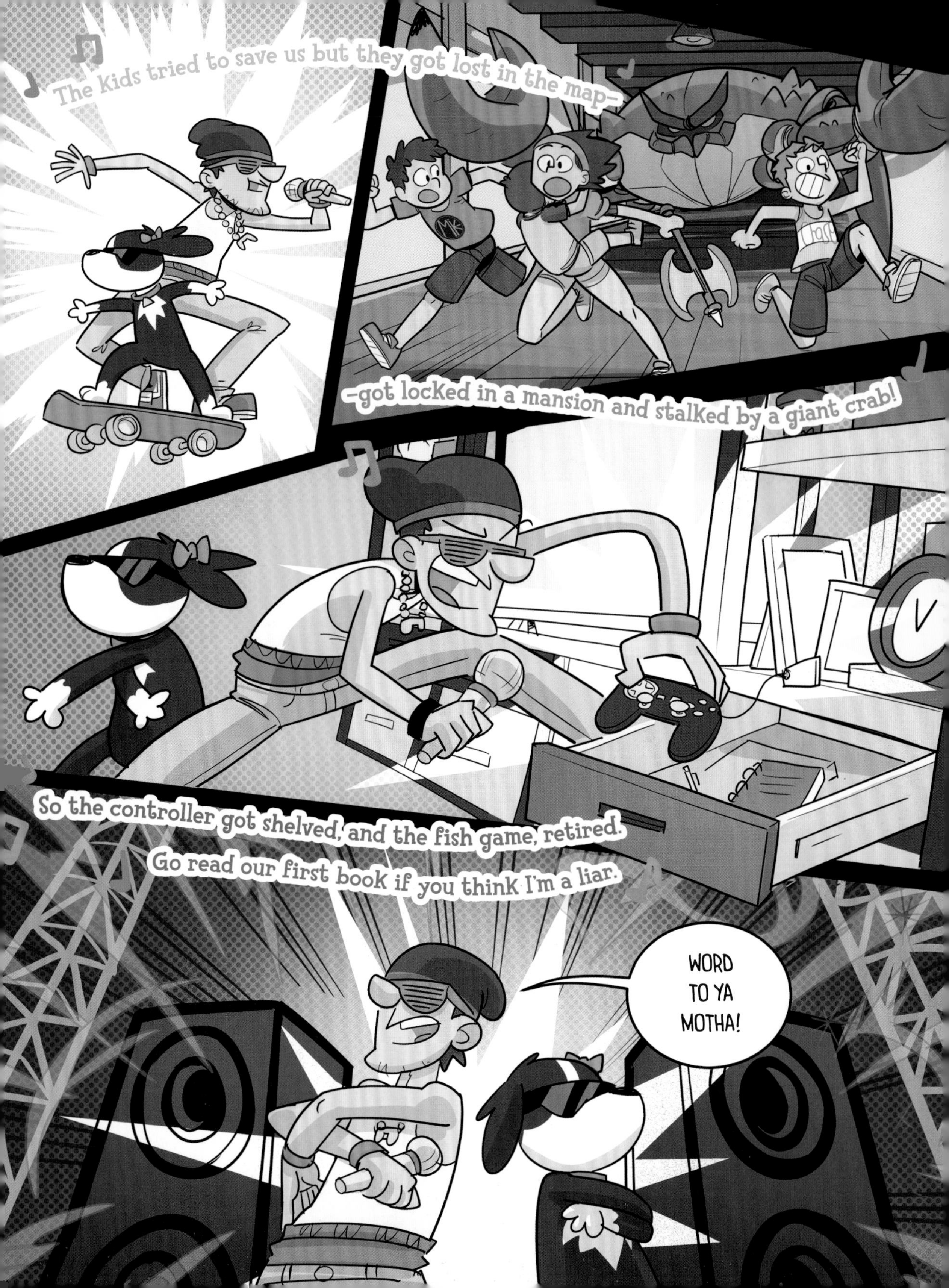
The kids tried to save us but they got lost in the map—
—got locked in a mansion and stalked by a giant crab!
So the controller got shelved, and the fish game, retired.
Go read our first book if you think I'm a liar.
WORD TO YA MOTHA!

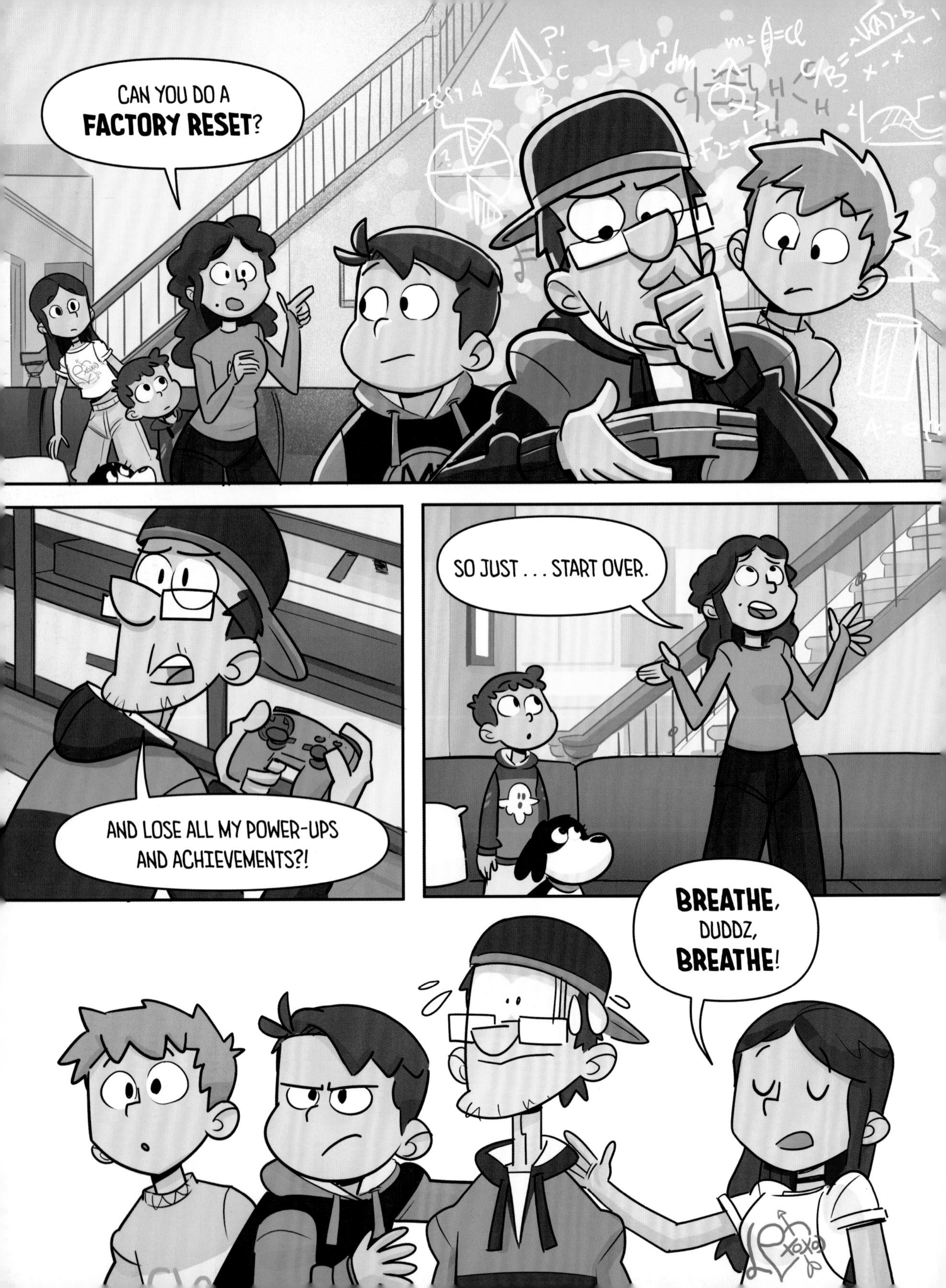
CAN YOU DO A FACTORY RESET?
AND LOSE ALL MY POWER-UPS AND ACHIEVEMENTS?!
SO JUST . . . START OVER.
BREATHE, DUDDZ, BREATHE!

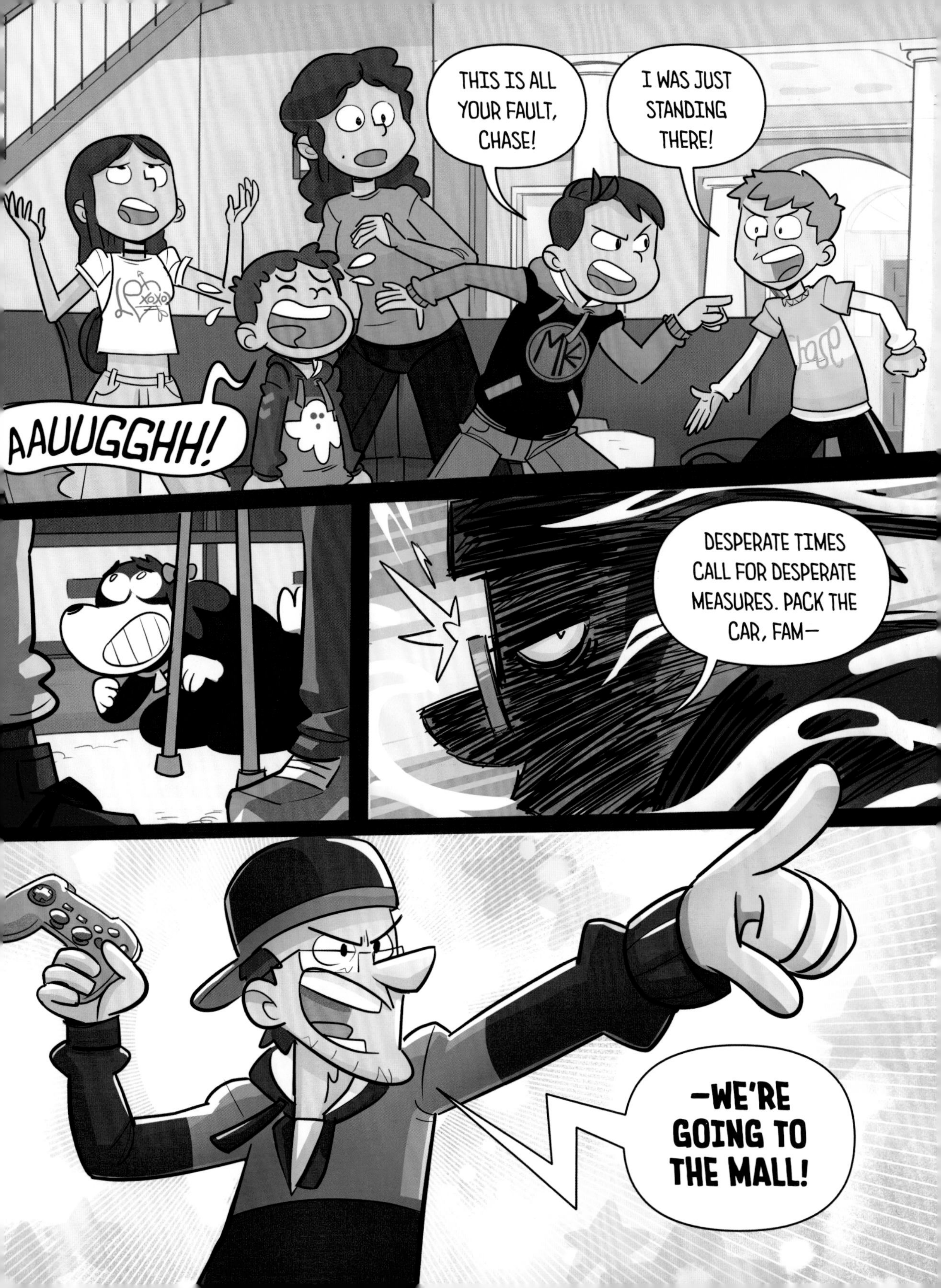
THIS IS ALL YOUR FAULT, CHASE!
I WAS JUST STANDING THERE!
AAUUGGHH!
DESPERATE TIMES CALL FOR DESPERATE MEASURES. PACK THE CAR, FAM—
—WE'RE GOING TO THE MALL!

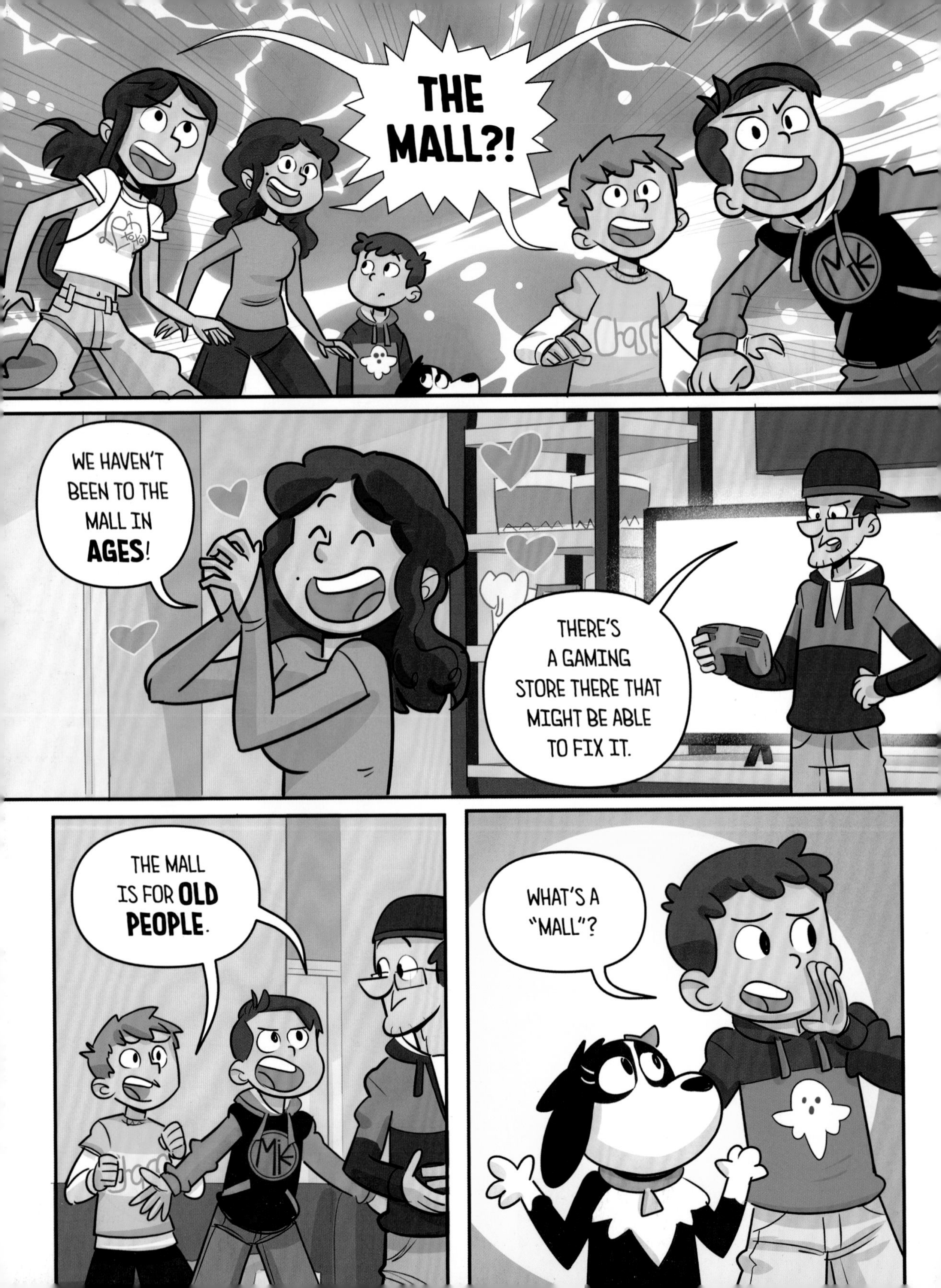
THE MALL?!
WE HAVEN'T BEEN TO THE MALL IN **AGES**!
THERE'S A GAMING STORE THERE THAT MIGHT BE ABLE TO FIX IT.
THE MALL IS FOR **OLD PEOPLE**.
WHAT'S A "MALL"?

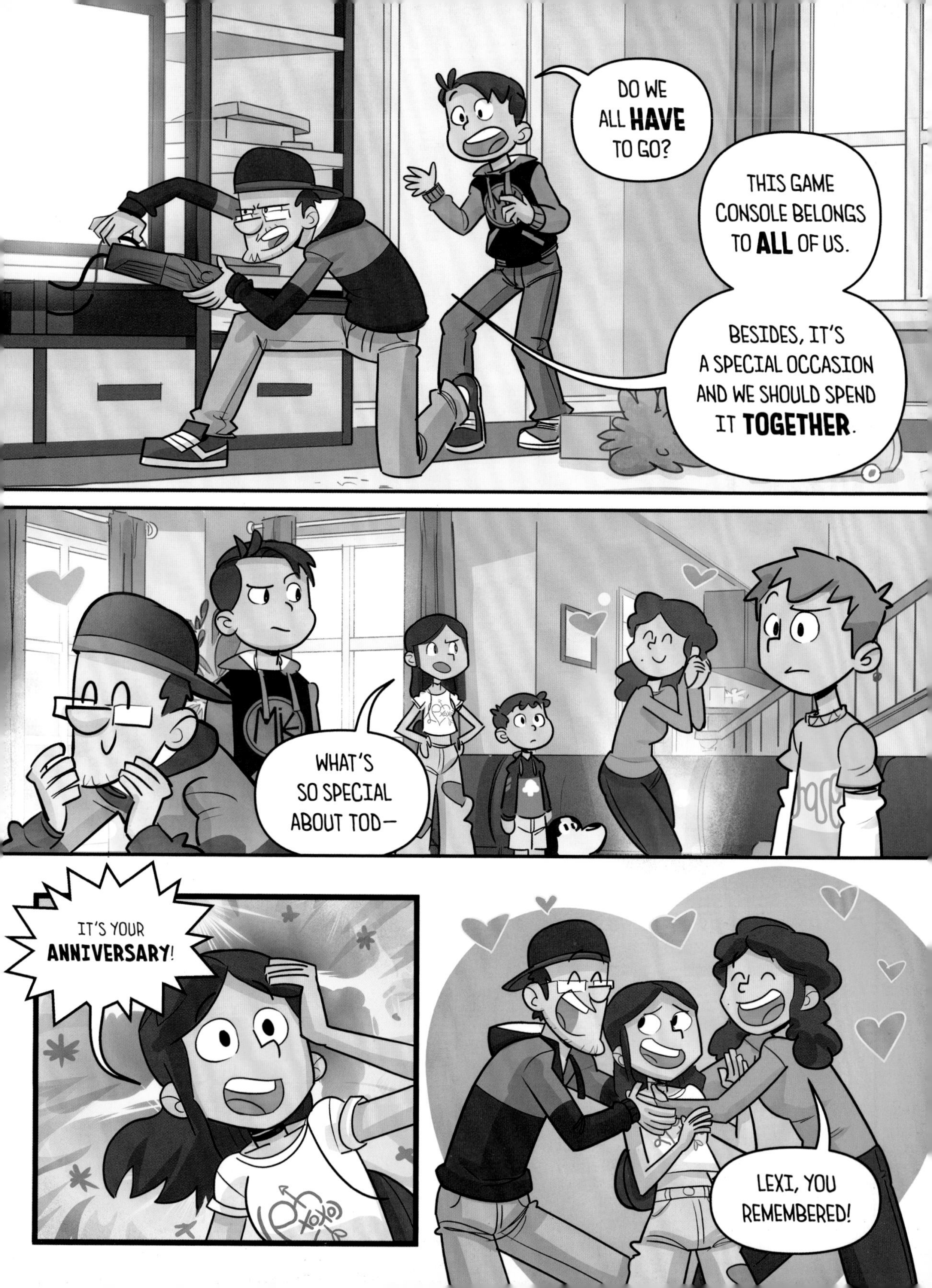
DO WE ALL **HAVE** TO GO?
THIS GAME CONSOLE BELONGS TO **ALL** OF US.
BESIDES, IT'S A SPECIAL OCCASION AND WE SHOULD SPEND IT **TOGETHER**.
WHAT'S SO SPECIAL ABOUT TOD—
IT'S YOUR **ANNIVERSARY**!
LEXI, YOU REMEMBERED!

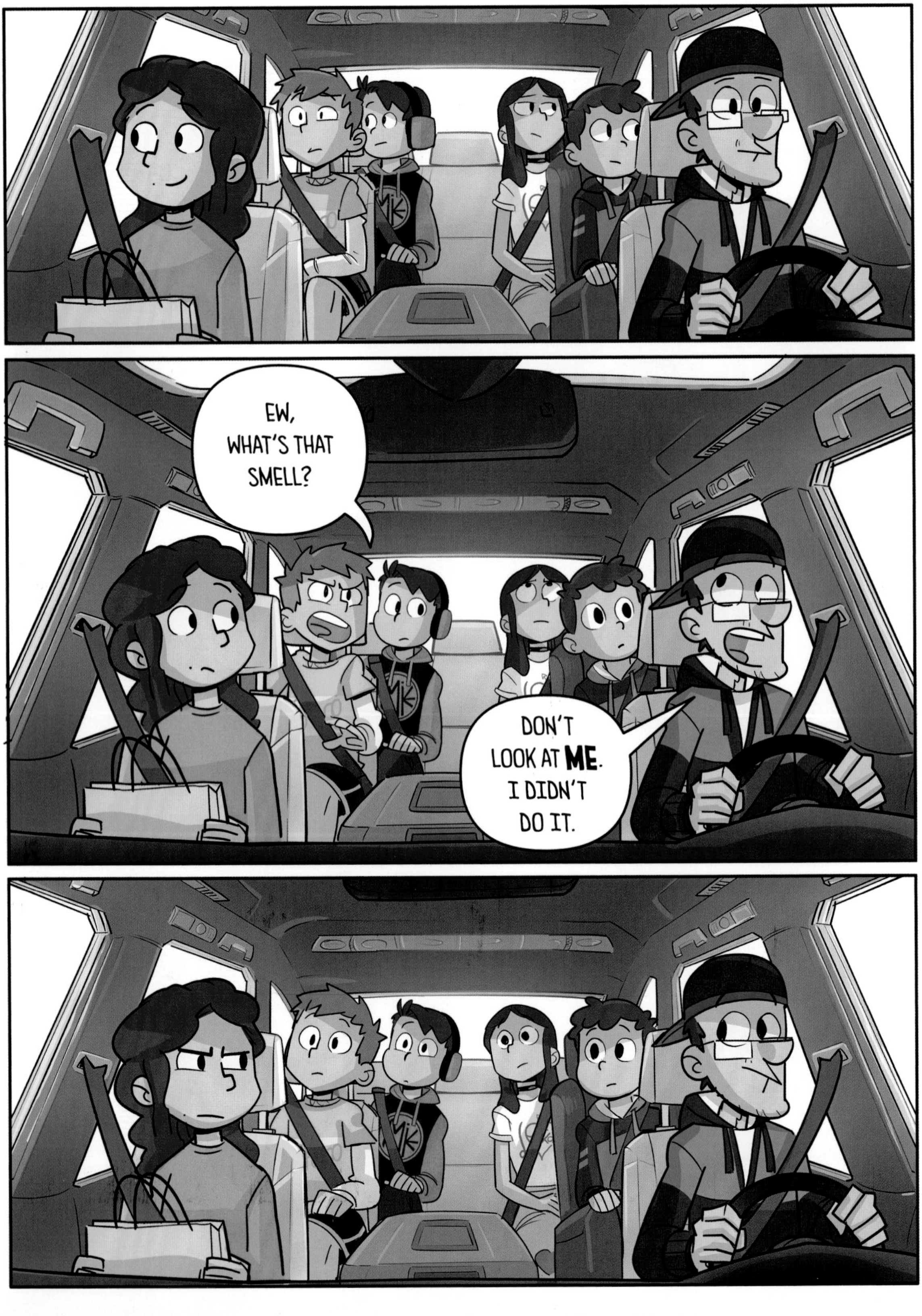
EW, WHAT'S THAT SMELL?
DON'T LOOK AT **ME**. I DIDN'T DO IT.

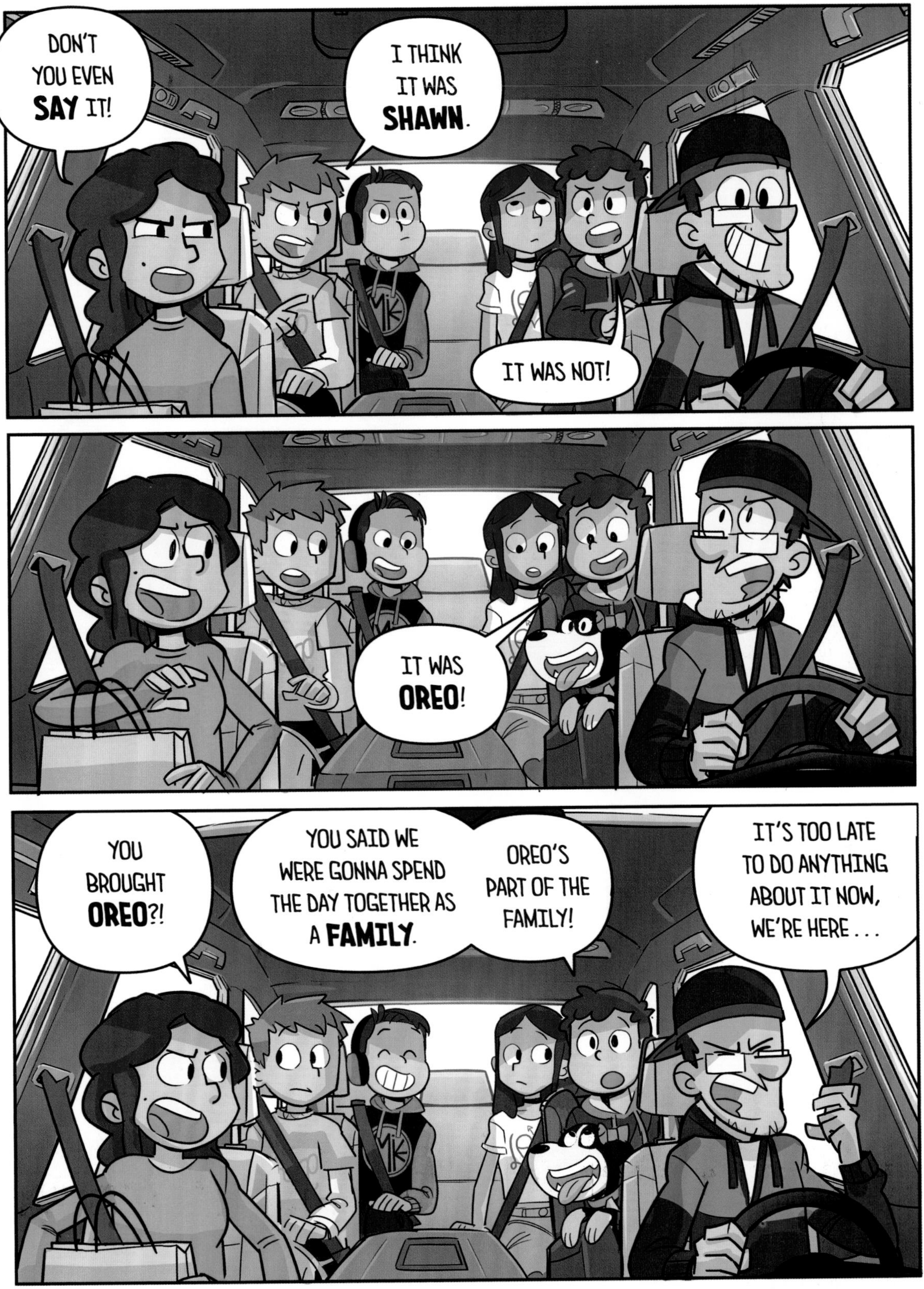

DON'T YOU EVEN **SAY** IT!
I THINK IT WAS **SHAWN**.
IT WAS NOT!
IT WAS **OREO**!
YOU BROUGHT **OREO**?!
YOU SAID WE WERE GONNA SPEND THE DAY TOGETHER AS A **FAMILY**.
OREO'S PART OF THE FAMILY!
IT'S TOO LATE TO DO ANYTHING ABOUT IT NOW, WE'RE HERE . . .

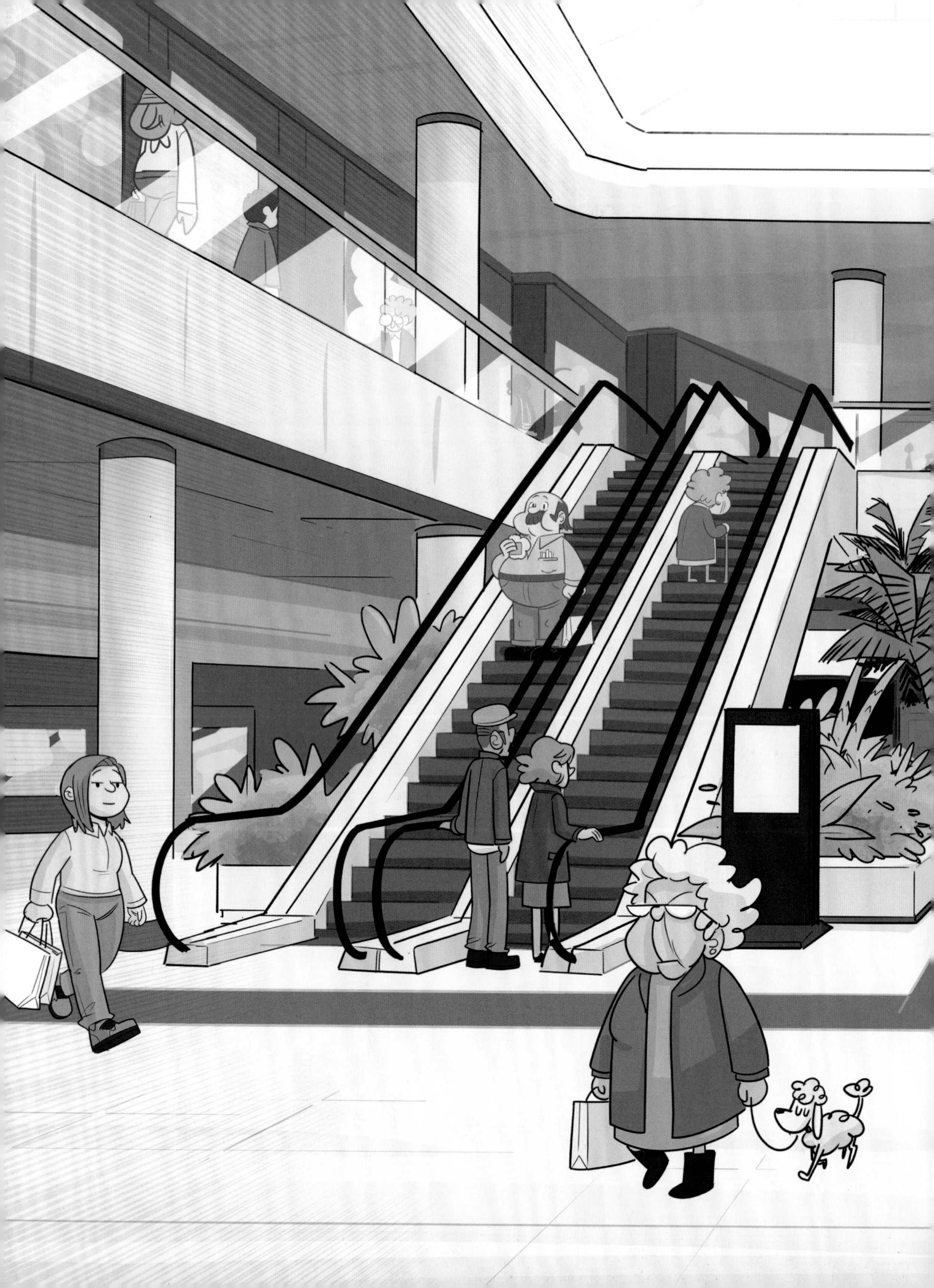

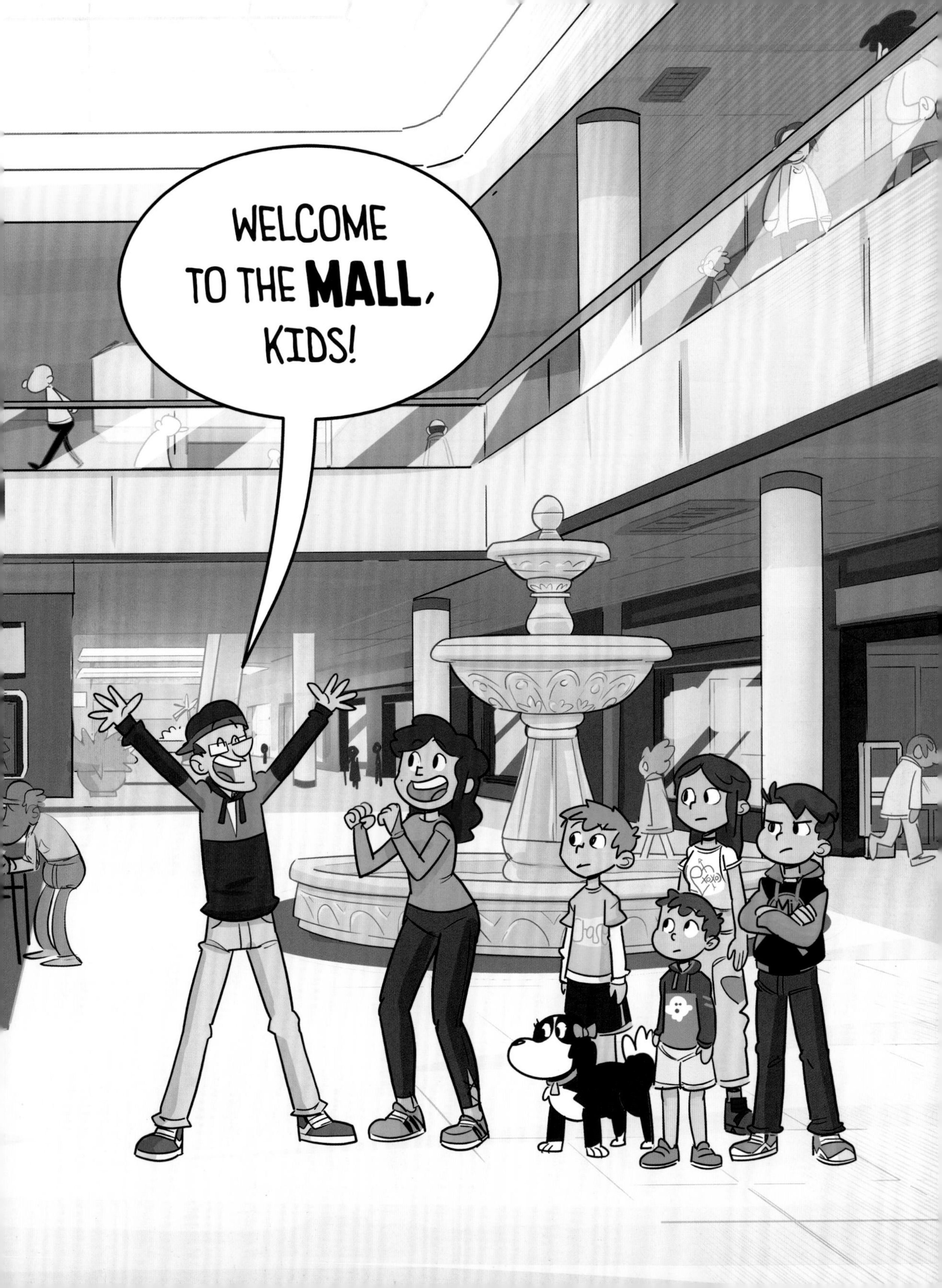
WELCOME TO THE MALL, KIDS!

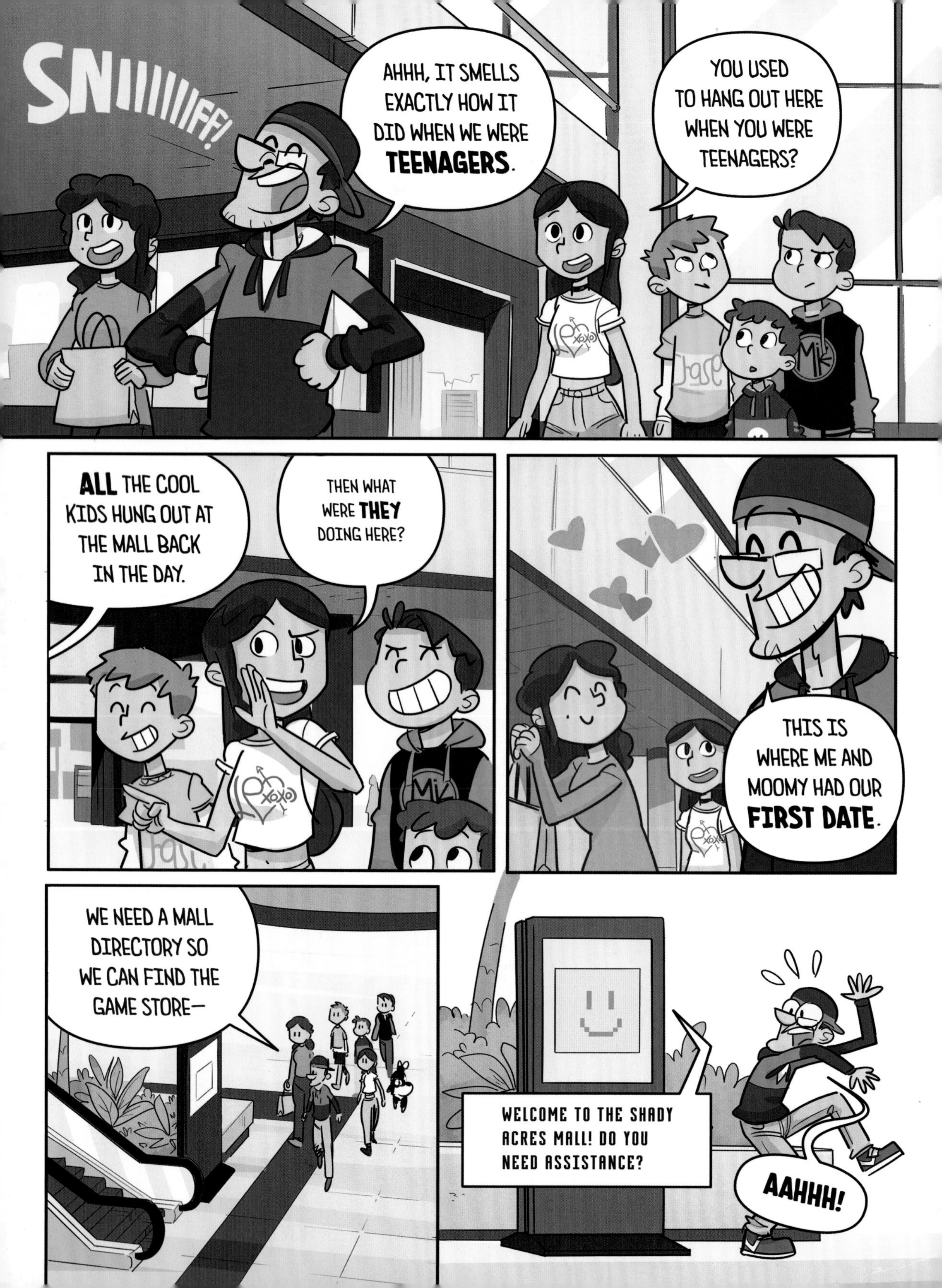

SNIIIIIIFF!
AHHH, IT SMELLS EXACTLY HOW IT DID WHEN WE WERE **TEENAGERS**.
YOU USED TO HANG OUT HERE WHEN YOU WERE TEENAGERS?
ALL THE COOL KIDS HUNG OUT AT THE MALL BACK IN THE DAY.
THEN WHAT WERE **THEY** DOING HERE?
THIS IS WHERE ME AND MOOMY HAD OUR **FIRST DATE**.
WE NEED A MALL DIRECTORY SO WE CAN FIND THE GAME STORE—
WELCOME TO THE SHADY ACRES MALL! DO YOU NEED ASSISTANCE?
AAHHH!

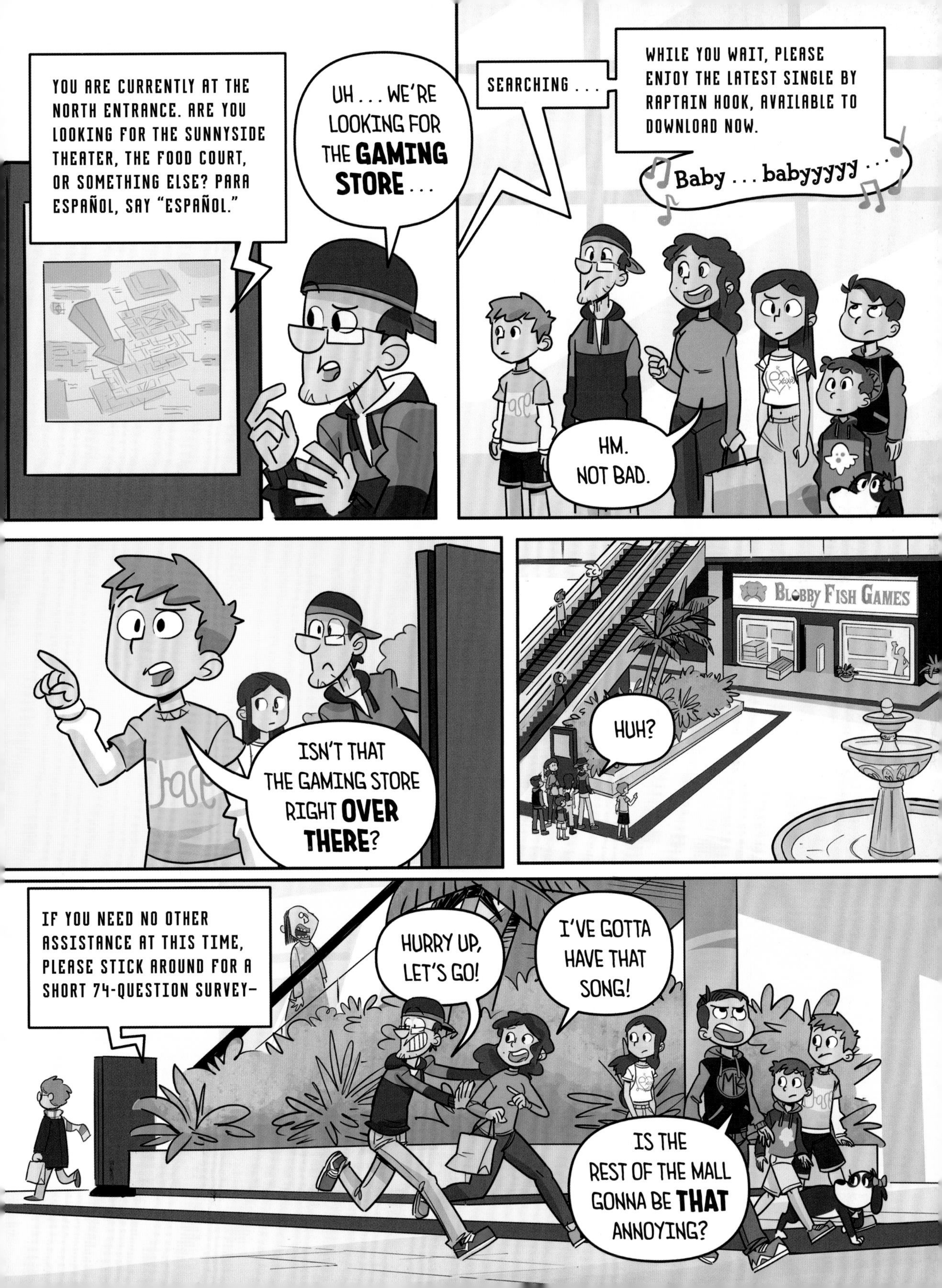
YOU ARE CURRENTLY AT THE NORTH ENTRANCE. ARE YOU LOOKING FOR THE SUNNYSIDE THEATER, THE FOOD COURT, OR SOMETHING ELSE? PARA ESPAÑOL, SAY "ESPAÑOL."
UH . . . WE'RE LOOKING FOR THE GAMING STORE . . .
SEARCHING . . .
WHILE YOU WAIT, PLEASE ENJOY THE LATEST SINGLE BY RAPTAIN HOOK, AVAILABLE TO DOWNLOAD NOW.
Baby . . . babyyyyy . . .
HM. NOT BAD.
ISN'T THAT THE GAMING STORE RIGHT OVER THERE?
BLOBBY FISH GAMES
HUH?
IF YOU NEED NO OTHER ASSISTANCE AT THIS TIME, PLEASE STICK AROUND FOR A SHORT 74-QUESTION SURVEY–
HURRY UP, LET'S GO!
I'VE GOTTA HAVE THAT SONG!
IS THE REST OF THE MALL GONNA BE THAT ANNOYING?

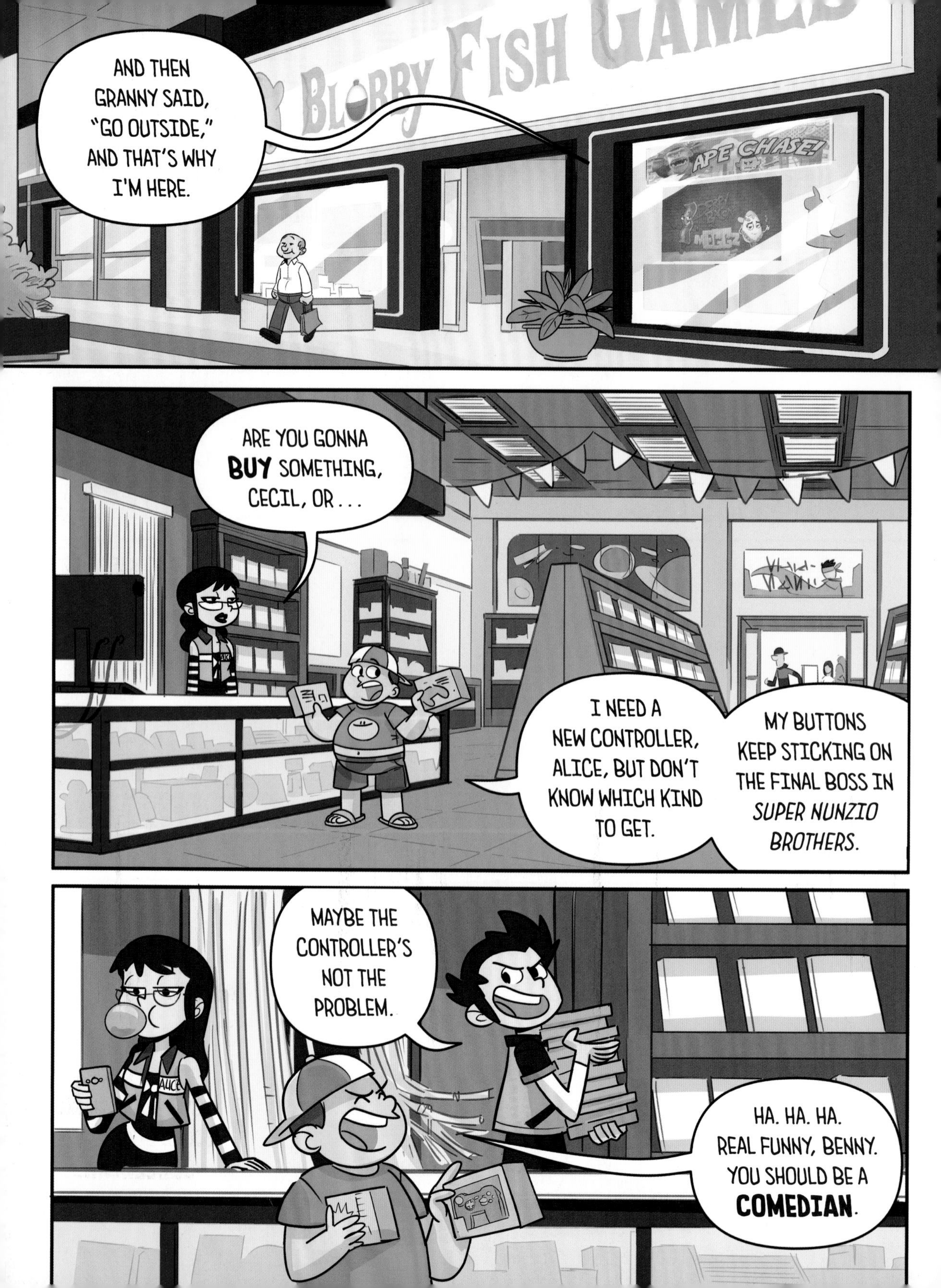
BLOBBY FISH GAMES
AND THEN GRANNY SAID, "GO OUTSIDE," AND THAT'S WHY I'M HERE.
APE CHASE!
ARE YOU GONNA **BUY** SOMETHING, CECIL, OR . . .
I NEED A NEW CONTROLLER, ALICE, BUT DON'T KNOW WHICH KIND TO GET.
MY BUTTONS KEEP STICKING ON THE FINAL BOSS IN *SUPER NUNZIO BROTHERS*.
MAYBE THE CONTROLLER'S NOT THE PROBLEM.
HA. HA. HA. REAL FUNNY, BENNY. YOU SHOULD BE A **COMEDIAN**.

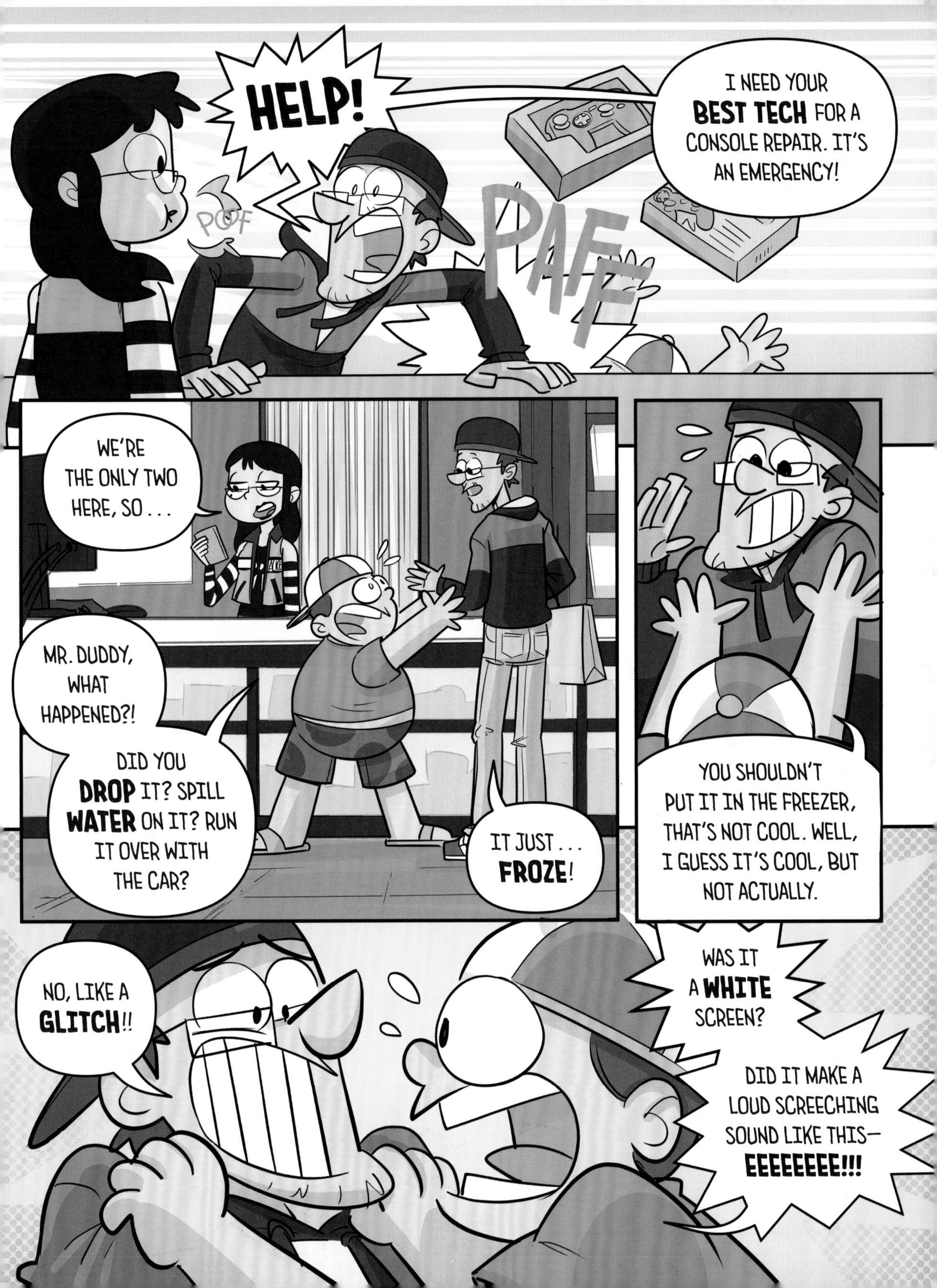
HELP!
I NEED YOUR BEST TECH FOR A CONSOLE REPAIR. IT'S AN EMERGENCY!
POOF
PAFF
WE'RE THE ONLY TWO HERE, SO . . .
MR. DUDDY, WHAT HAPPENED?!
DID YOU DROP IT? SPILL WATER ON IT? RUN IT OVER WITH THE CAR?
IT JUST . . . FROZE!
YOU SHOULDN'T PUT IT IN THE FREEZER, THAT'S NOT COOL. WELL, I GUESS IT'S COOL, BUT NOT ACTUALLY.
NO, LIKE A GLITCH!!
WAS IT A WHITE SCREEN?
DID IT MAKE A LOUD SCREECHING SOUND LIKE THIS— EEEEEEEE!!!

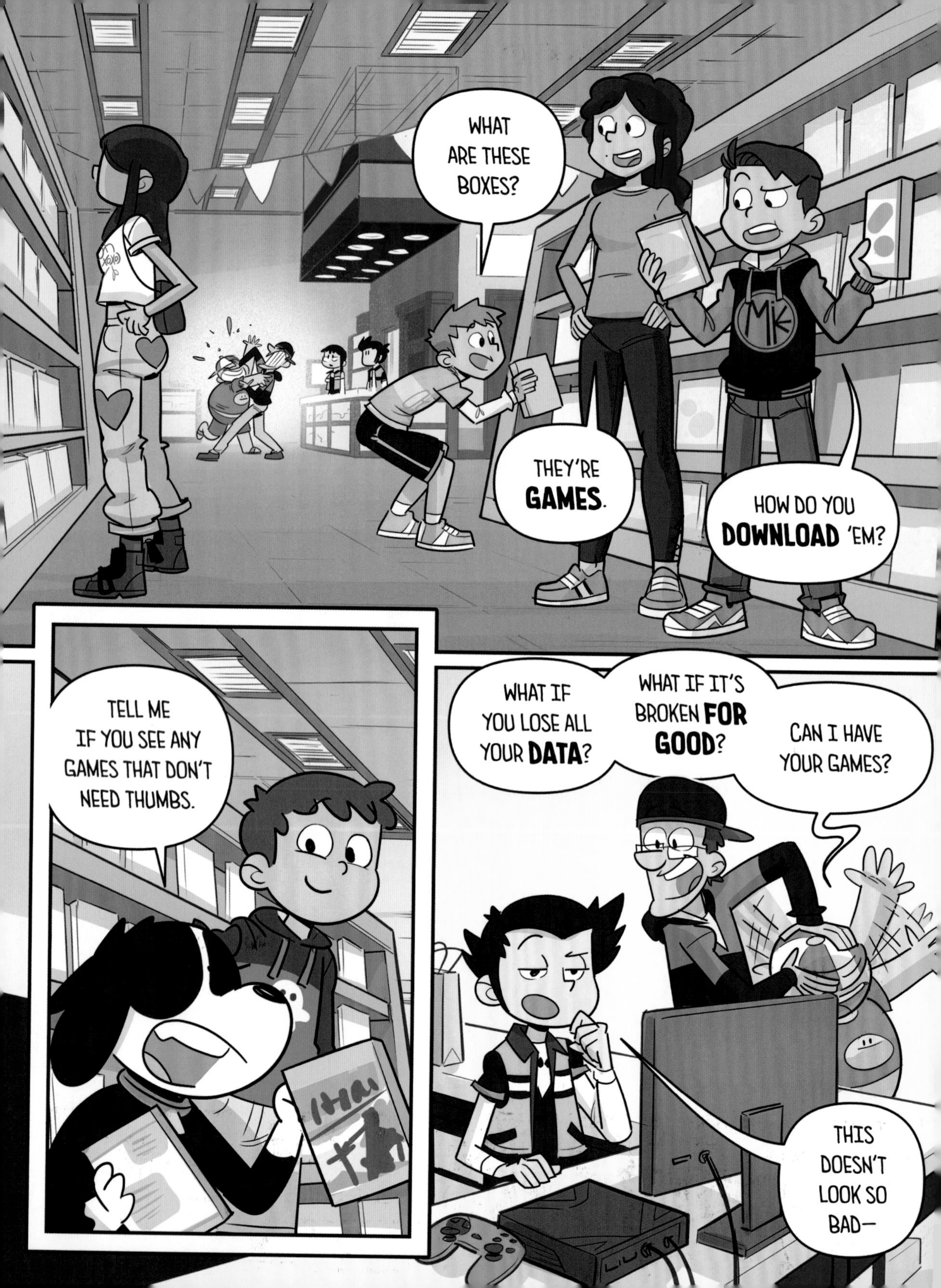
WHAT ARE THESE BOXES?
THEY'RE **GAMES**.
HOW DO YOU **DOWNLOAD** 'EM?
TELL ME IF YOU SEE ANY GAMES THAT DON'T NEED THUMBS.
WHAT IF YOU LOSE ALL YOUR **DATA**?
WHAT IF IT'S BROKEN **FOR GOOD**?
CAN I HAVE YOUR GAMES?
THIS DOESN'T LOOK SO BAD—

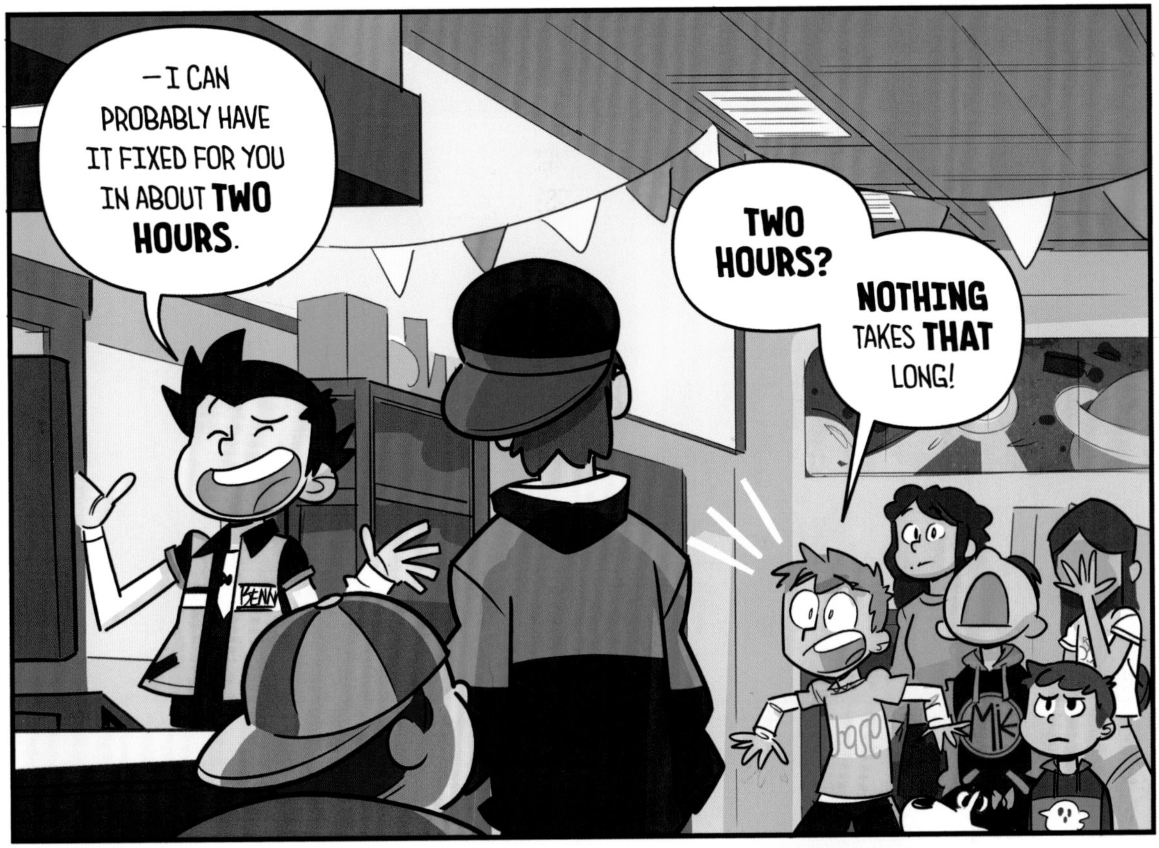
—I CAN PROBABLY HAVE IT FIXED FOR YOU IN ABOUT **TWO HOURS**.
TWO HOURS?
NOTHING TAKES **THAT** LONG!

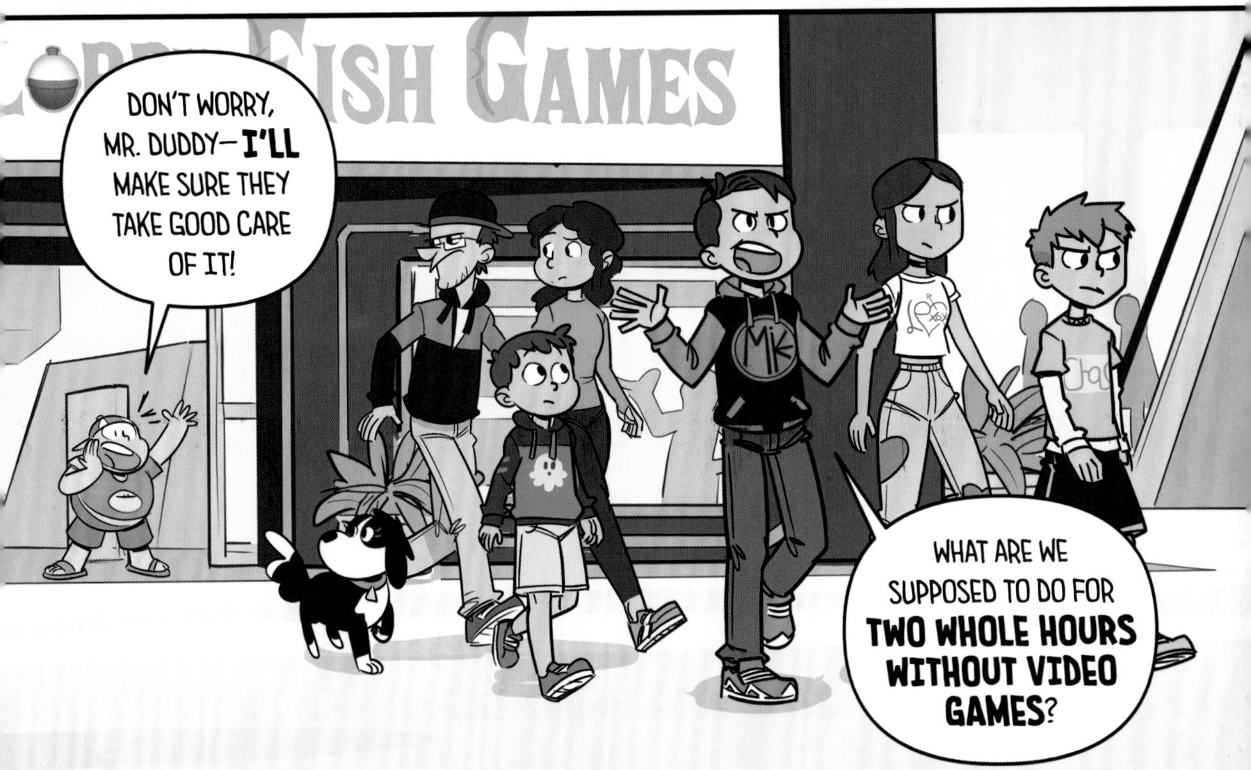
FISH GAMES
DON'T WORRY, MR. DUDDY—**I'LL** MAKE SURE THEY TAKE GOOD CARE OF IT!
WHAT ARE WE SUPPOSED TO DO FOR **TWO WHOLE HOURS WITHOUT VIDEO GAMES**?

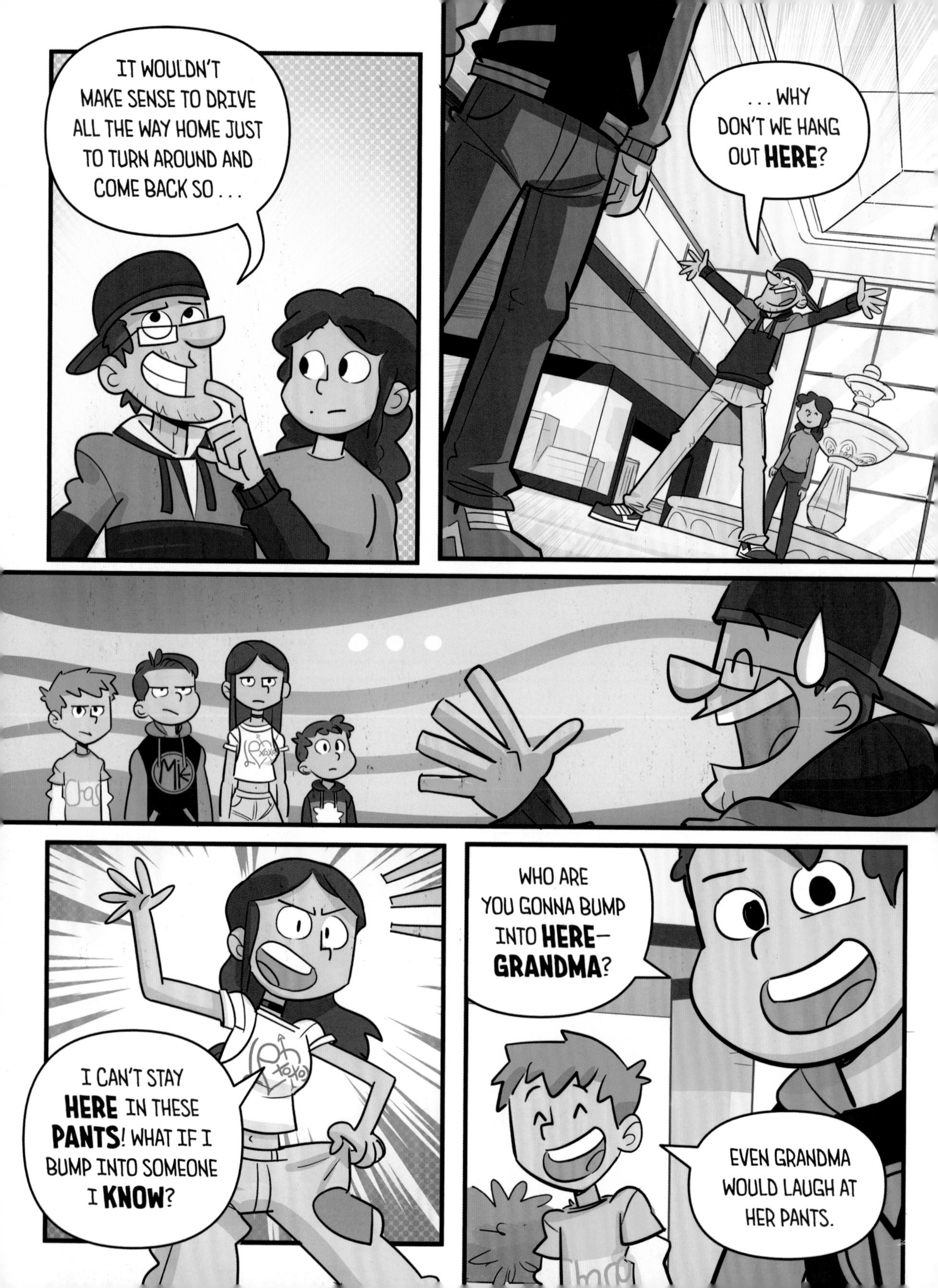
IT WOULDN'T MAKE SENSE TO DRIVE ALL THE WAY HOME JUST TO TURN AROUND AND COME BACK SO . . .
. . . WHY DON'T WE HANG OUT **HERE**?
. . .
I CAN'T STAY **HERE** IN THESE **PANTS**! WHAT IF I BUMP INTO SOMEONE I **KNOW**?
WHO ARE YOU GONNA BUMP INTO **HERE**— **GRANDMA**?
EVEN GRANDMA WOULD LAUGH AT HER PANTS.

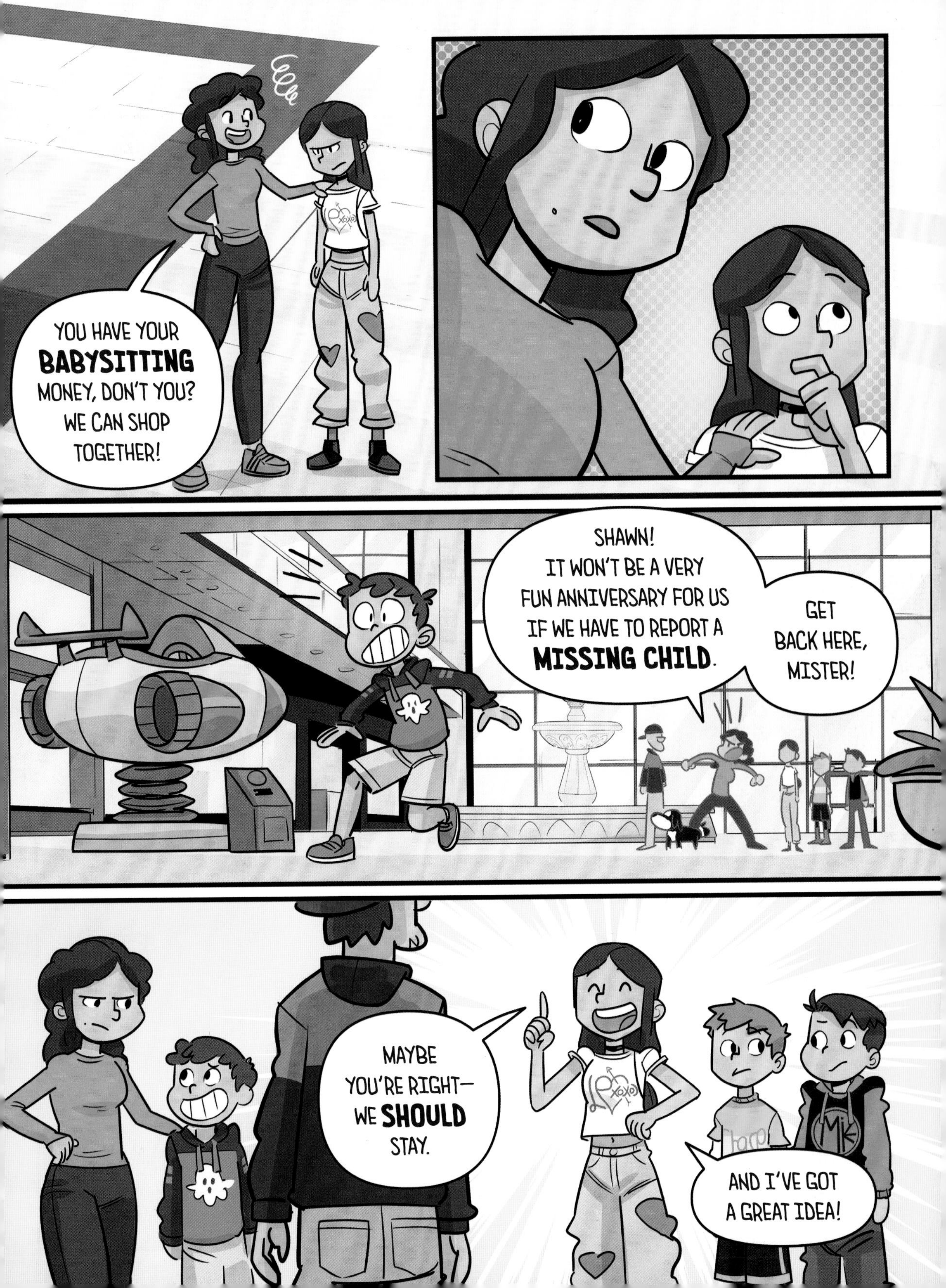
YOU HAVE YOUR BABYSITTING MONEY, DON'T YOU? WE CAN SHOP TOGETHER!
SHAWN! IT WON'T BE A VERY FUN ANNIVERSARY FOR US IF WE HAVE TO REPORT A MISSING CHILD.
GET BACK HERE, MISTER!
MAYBE YOU'RE RIGHT— WE SHOULD STAY.
AND I'VE GOT A GREAT IDEA!

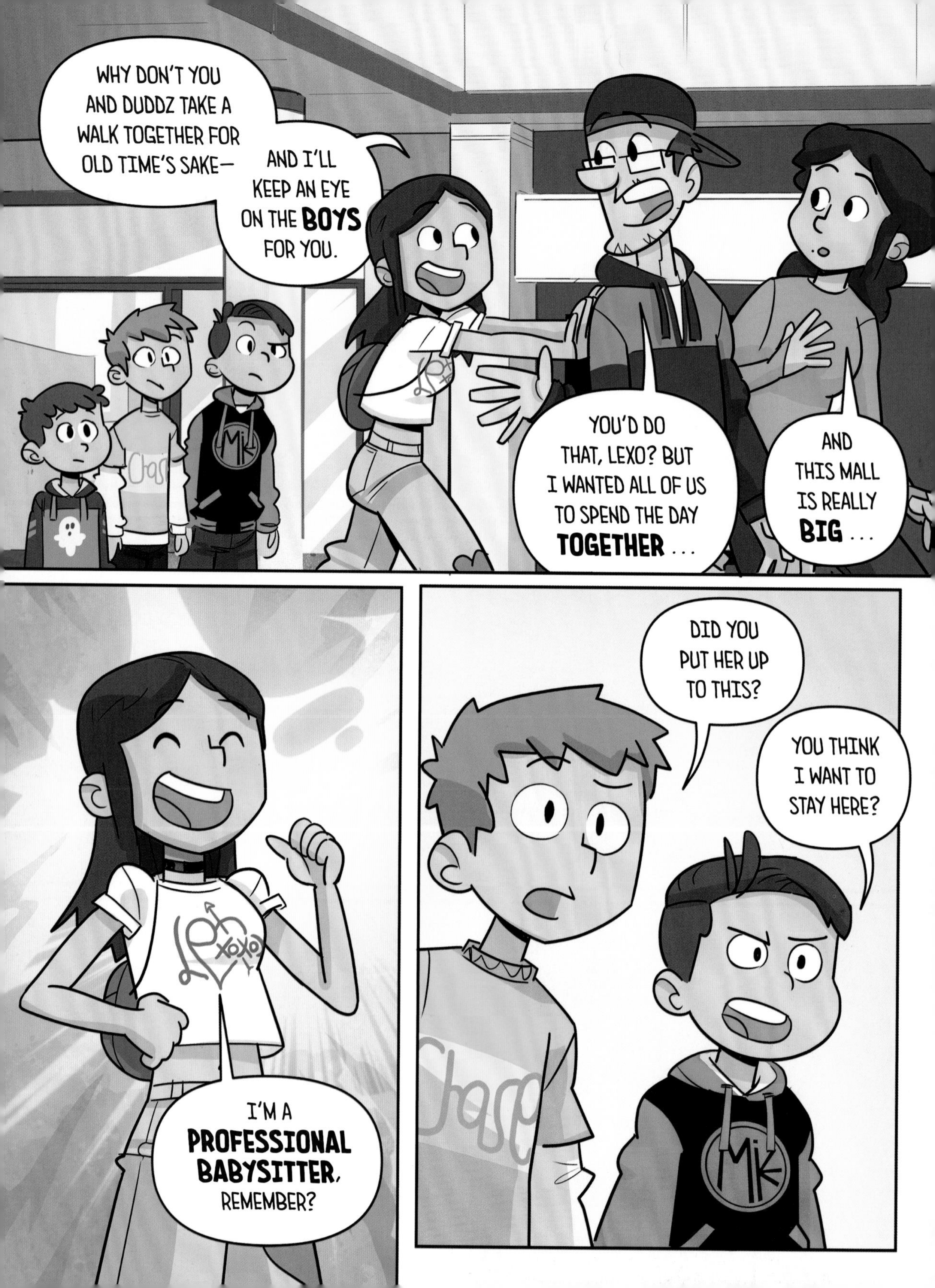
WHY DON'T YOU AND DUDDZ TAKE A WALK TOGETHER FOR OLD TIME'S SAKE—
AND I'LL KEEP AN EYE ON THE BOYS FOR YOU.
YOU'D DO THAT, LEXO? BUT I WANTED ALL OF US TO SPEND THE DAY TOGETHER . . .
AND THIS MALL IS REALLY BIG . . .
I'M A PROFESSIONAL BABYSITTER, REMEMBER?
DID YOU PUT HER UP TO THIS?
YOU THINK I WANT TO STAY HERE?

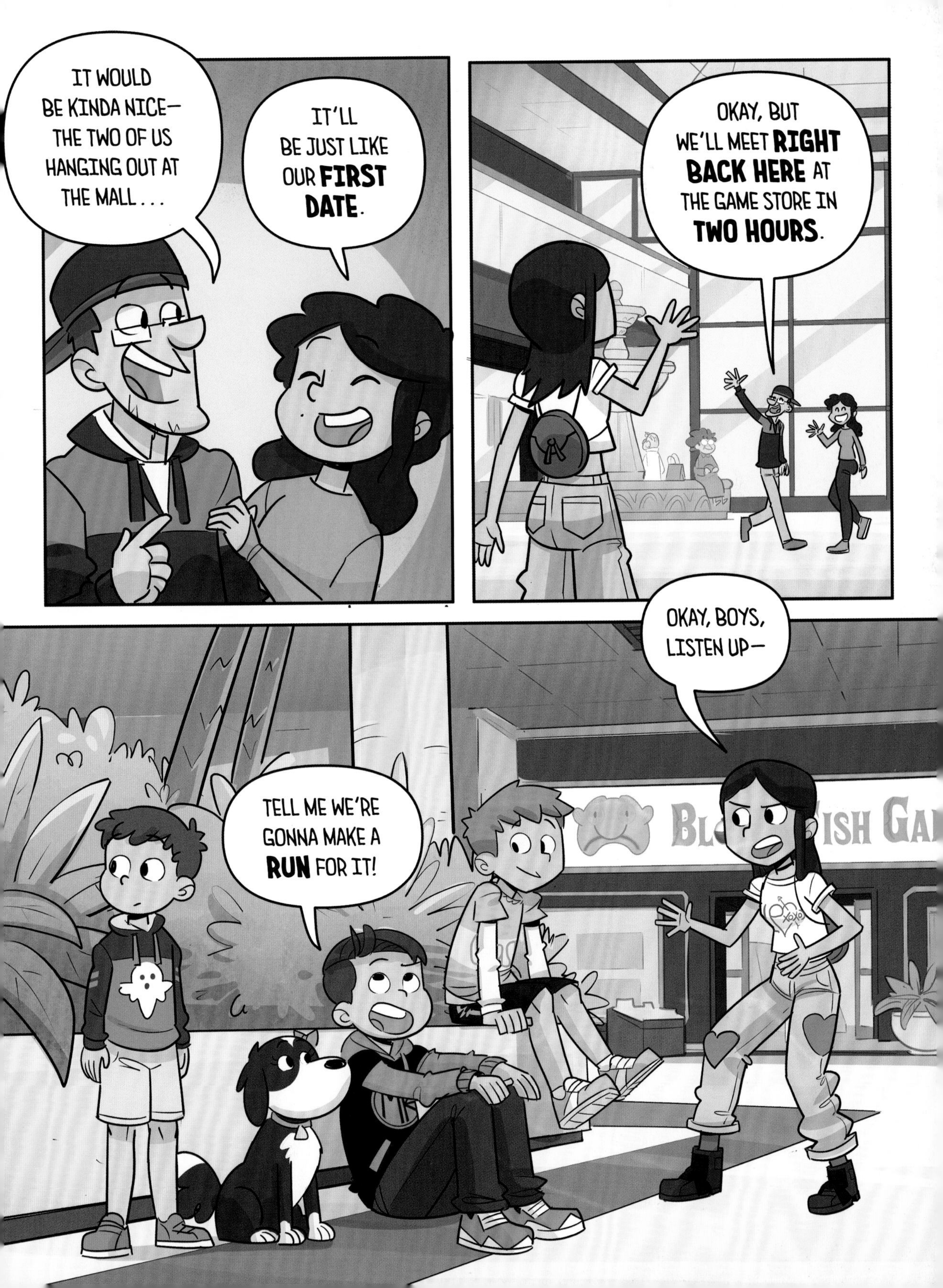
IT WOULD BE KINDA NICE— THE TWO OF US HANGING OUT AT THE MALL . . .
IT'LL BE JUST LIKE OUR FIRST DATE.
OKAY, BUT WE'LL MEET RIGHT BACK HERE AT THE GAME STORE IN TWO HOURS.
OKAY, BOYS, LISTEN UP—
TELL ME WE'RE GONNA MAKE A RUN FOR IT!

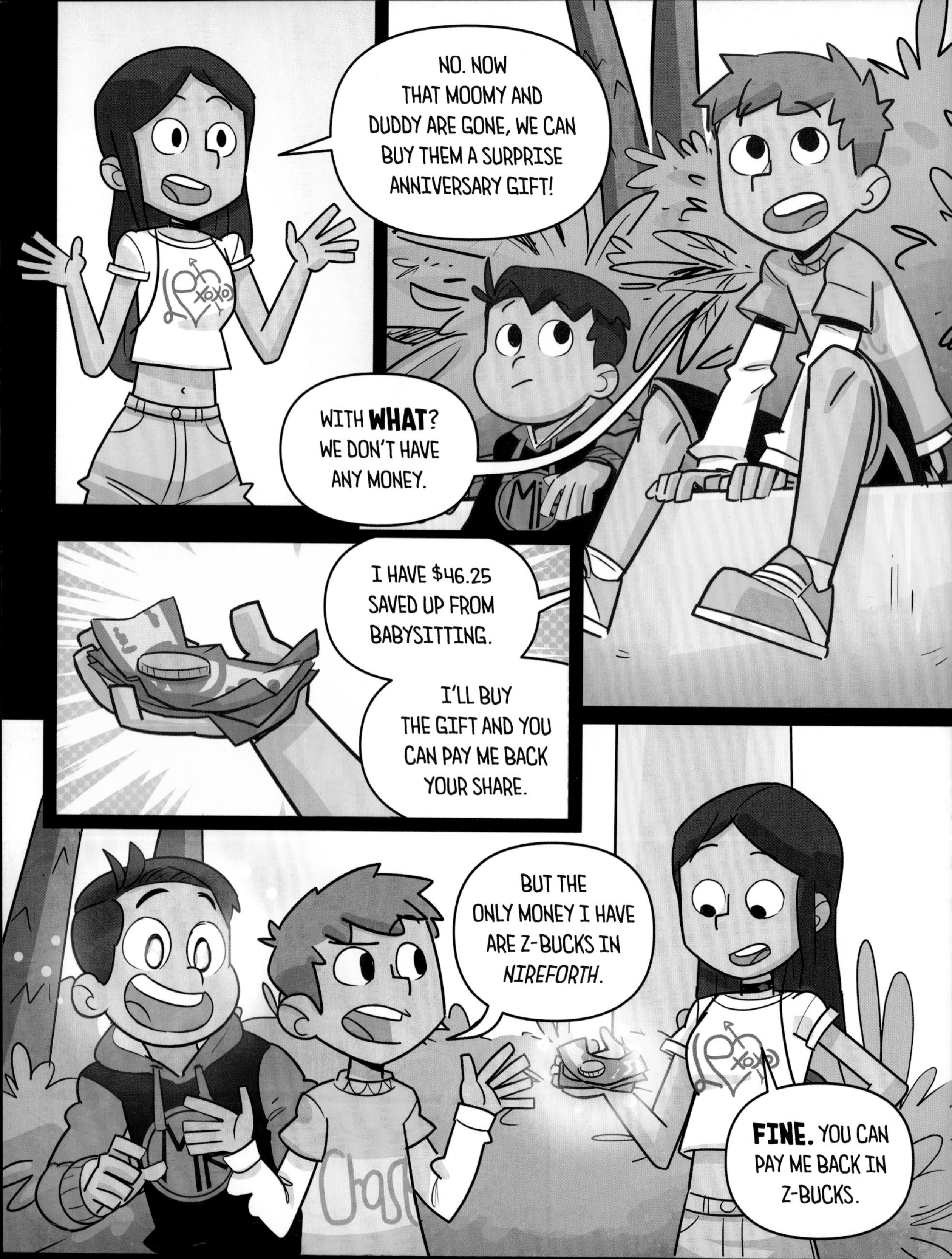

NO. NOW THAT MOOMY AND DUDDY ARE GONE, WE CAN BUY THEM A SURPRISE ANNIVERSARY GIFT!
WITH **WHAT**? WE DON'T HAVE ANY MONEY.
I HAVE $46.25 SAVED UP FROM BABYSITTING.
I'LL BUY THE GIFT AND YOU CAN PAY ME BACK YOUR SHARE.
BUT THE ONLY MONEY I HAVE ARE Z-BUCKS IN *NIREFORTH*.
FINE. YOU CAN PAY ME BACK IN Z-BUCKS.

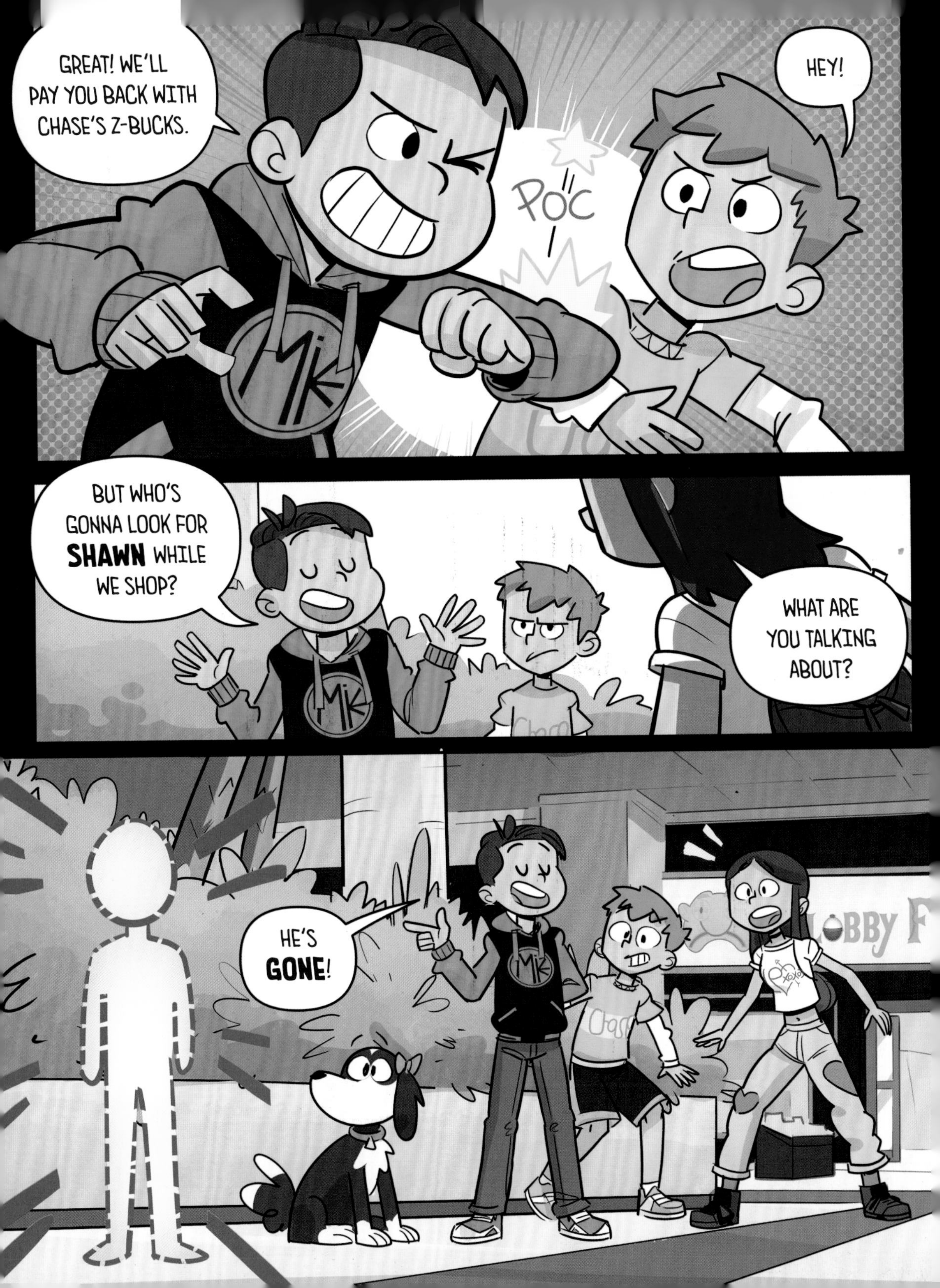
GREAT! WE'LL PAY YOU BACK WITH CHASE'S Z-BUCKS.
POC
HEY!
BUT WHO'S GONNA LOOK FOR **SHAWN** WHILE WE SHOP?
WHAT ARE YOU TALKING ABOUT?
HE'S **GONE**!
LOBBY F

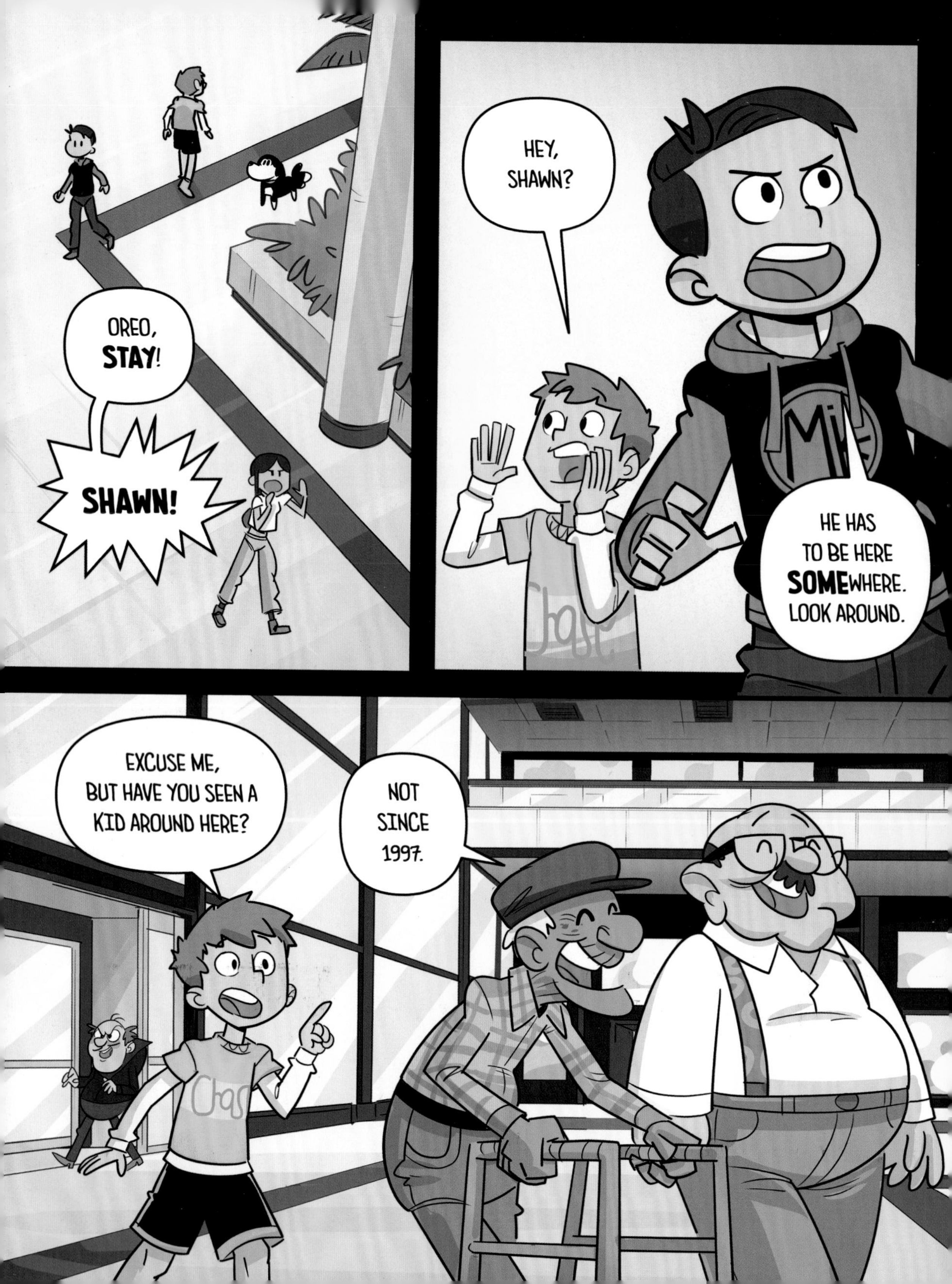
OREO, STAY!
SHAWN!
HEY, SHAWN?
HE HAS TO BE HERE SOMEWHERE. LOOK AROUND.
EXCUSE ME, BUT HAVE YOU SEEN A KID AROUND HERE?
NOT SINCE 1997.

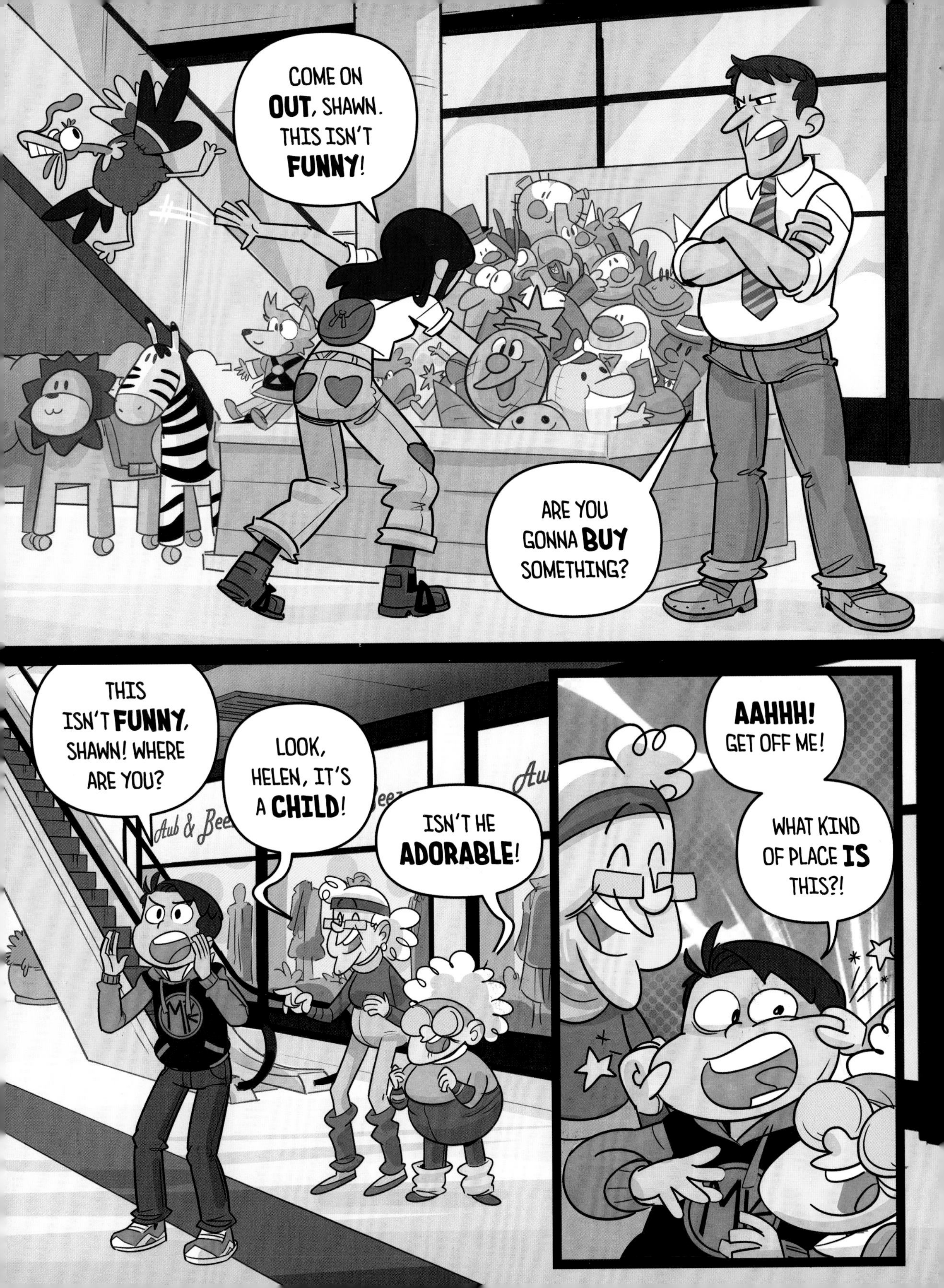
COME ON OUT, SHAWN. THIS ISN'T FUNNY!
ARE YOU GONNA BUY SOMETHING?
THIS ISN'T FUNNY, SHAWN! WHERE ARE YOU?
Aub & Bees
LOOK, HELEN, IT'S A CHILD!
ISN'T HE ADORABLE!
AAHHH! GET OFF ME!
WHAT KIND OF PLACE IS THIS?!

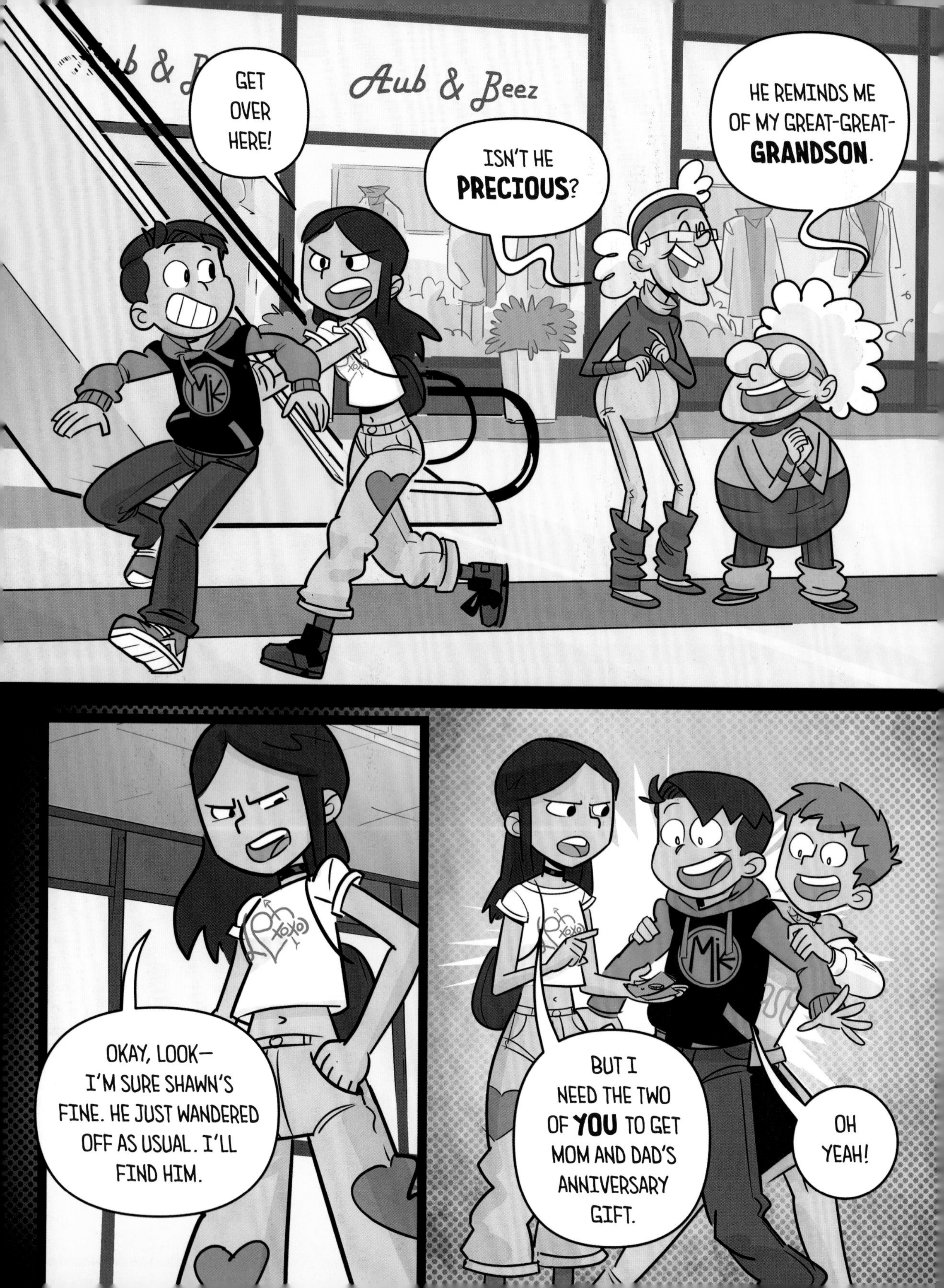
Aub & Beez
GET OVER HERE!
ISN'T HE PRECIOUS?
HE REMINDS ME OF MY GREAT-GREAT-GRANDSON.
OKAY, LOOK— I'M SURE SHAWN'S FINE. HE JUST WANDERED OFF AS USUAL. I'LL FIND HIM.
BUT I NEED THE TWO OF YOU TO GET MOM AND DAD'S ANNIVERSARY GIFT.
OH YEAH!

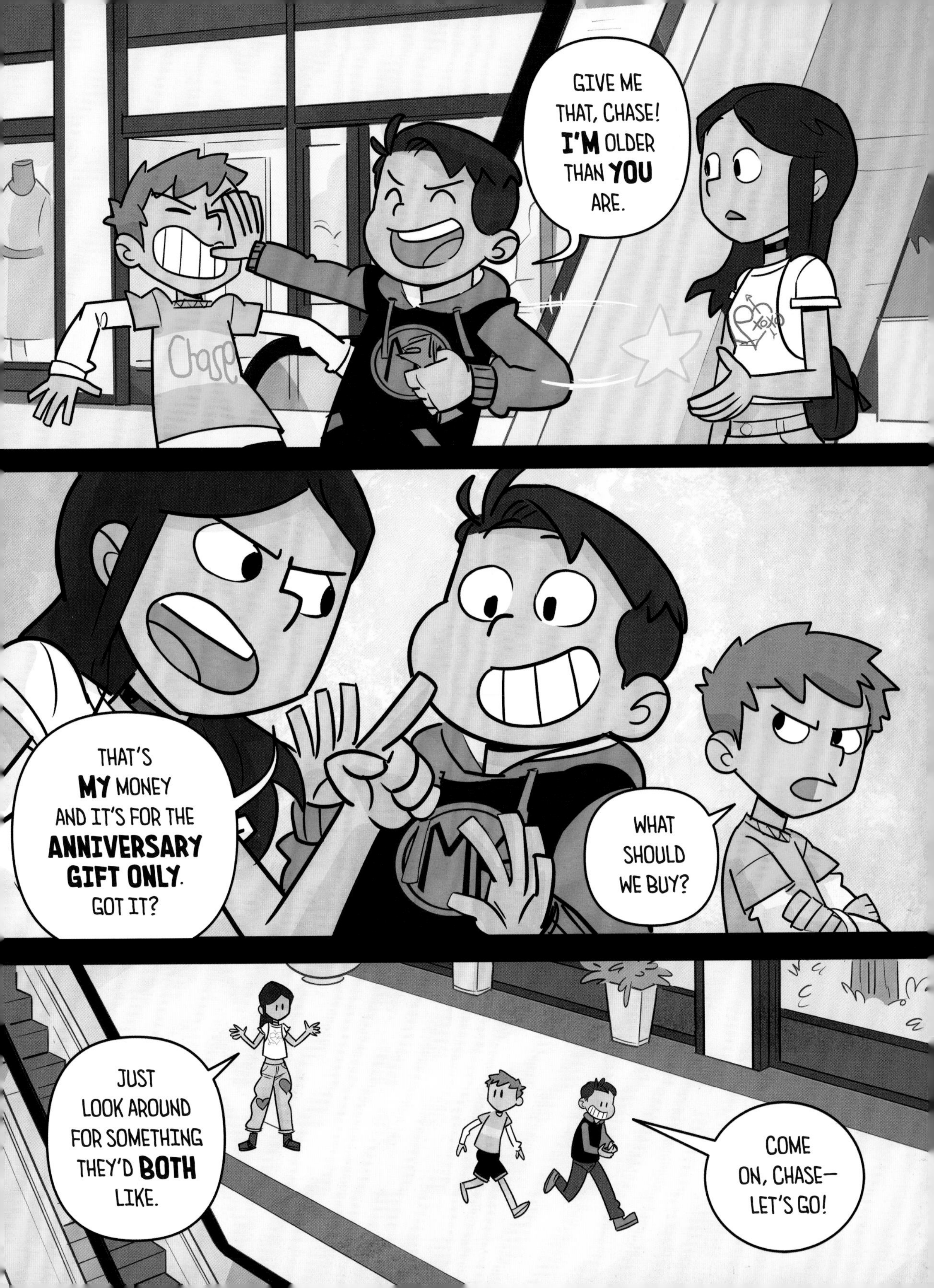
GIVE ME THAT, CHASE! **I'M** OLDER THAN **YOU** ARE.
Chase
THAT'S **MY** MONEY AND IT'S FOR THE **ANNIVERSARY GIFT ONLY**. GOT IT?
WHAT SHOULD WE BUY?
JUST LOOK AROUND FOR SOMETHING THEY'D **BOTH** LIKE.
COME ON, CHASE— LET'S GO!

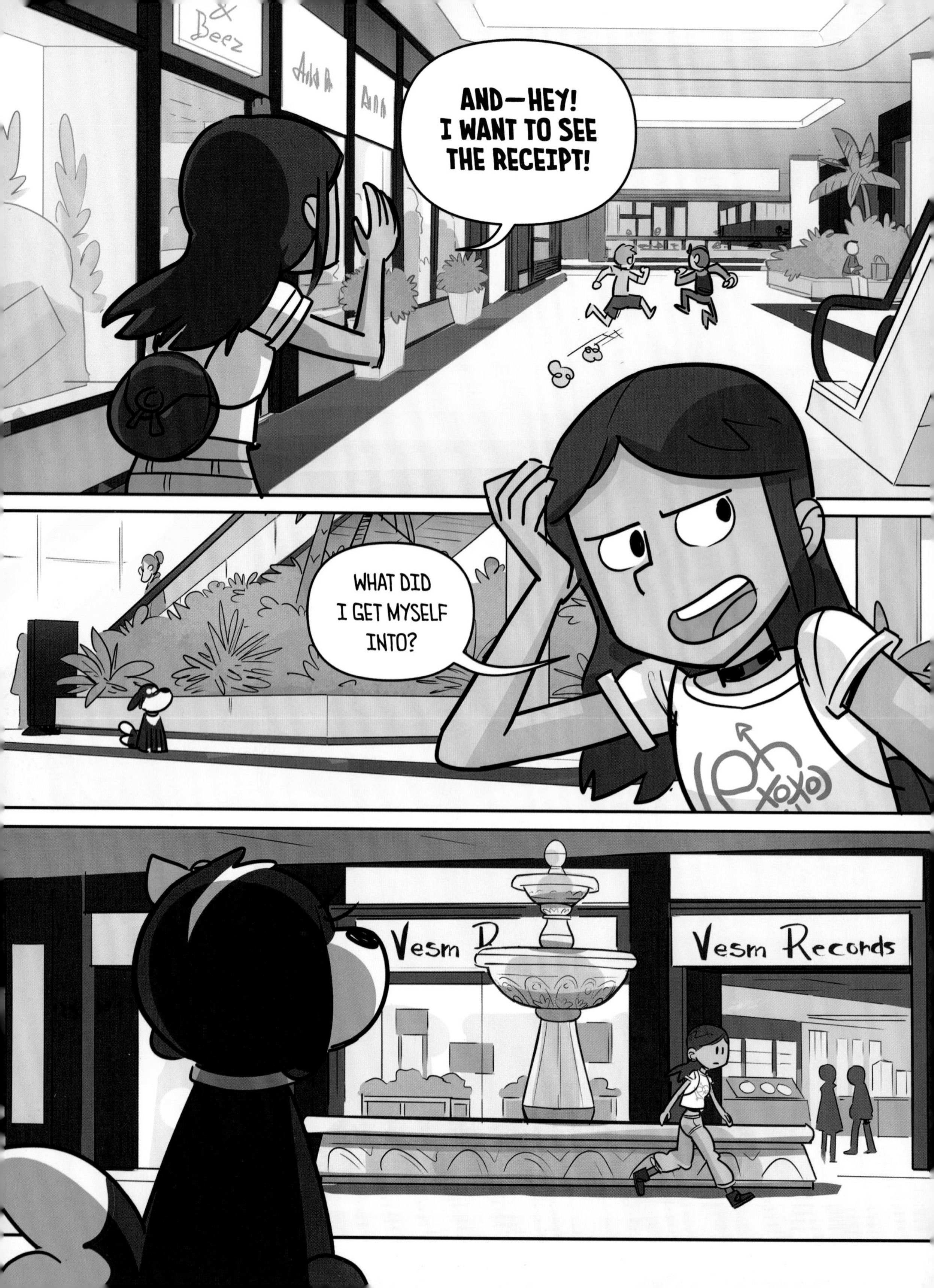
Beez
AND—HEY! I WANT TO SEE THE RECEIPT!
WHAT DID I GET MYSELF INTO?
Vesm Records

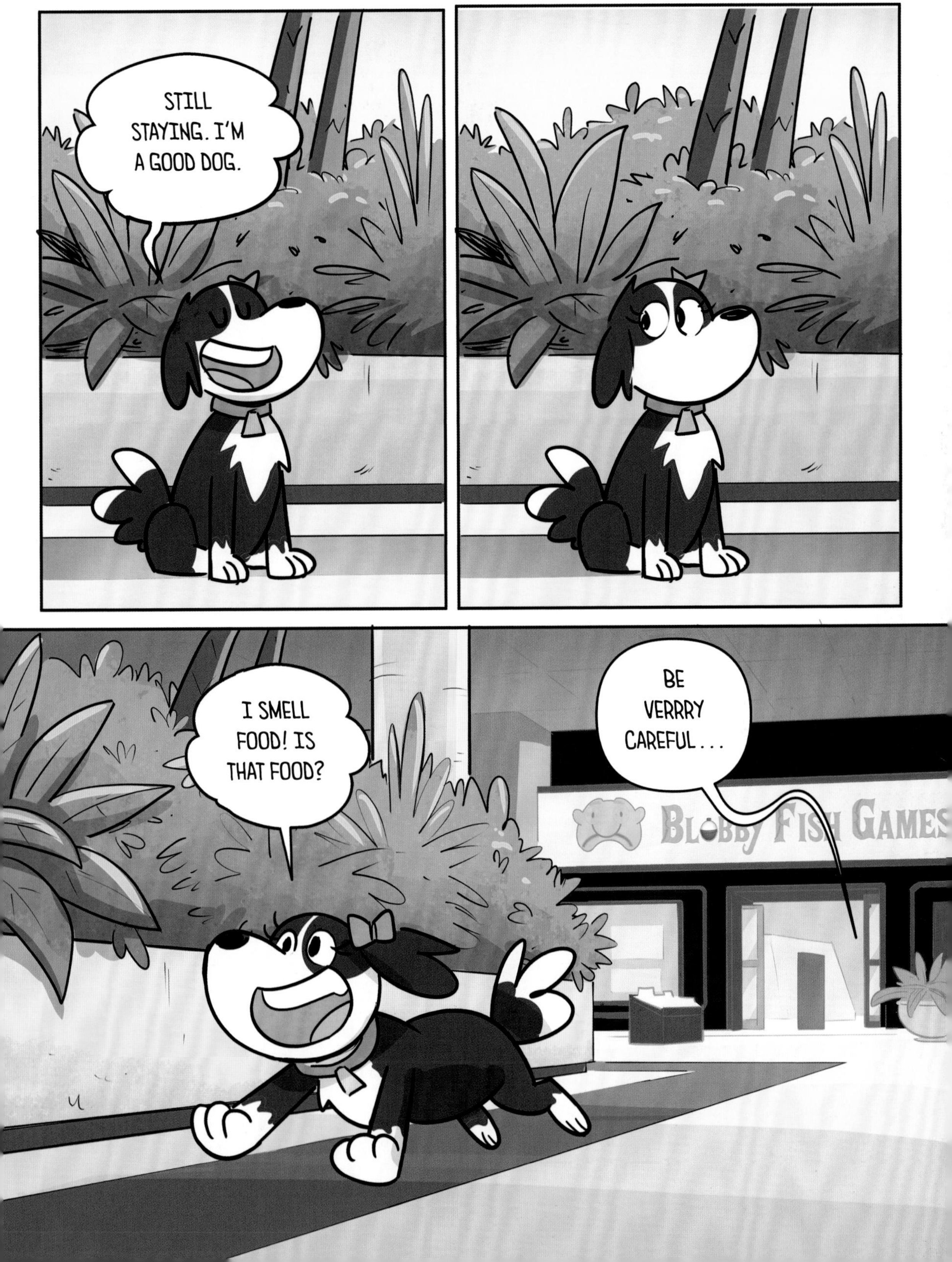
STILL STAYING. I'M A GOOD DOG.
I SMELL FOOD! IS THAT FOOD?
BE VERRRY CAREFUL . . .
BLOBBY FISH GAMES

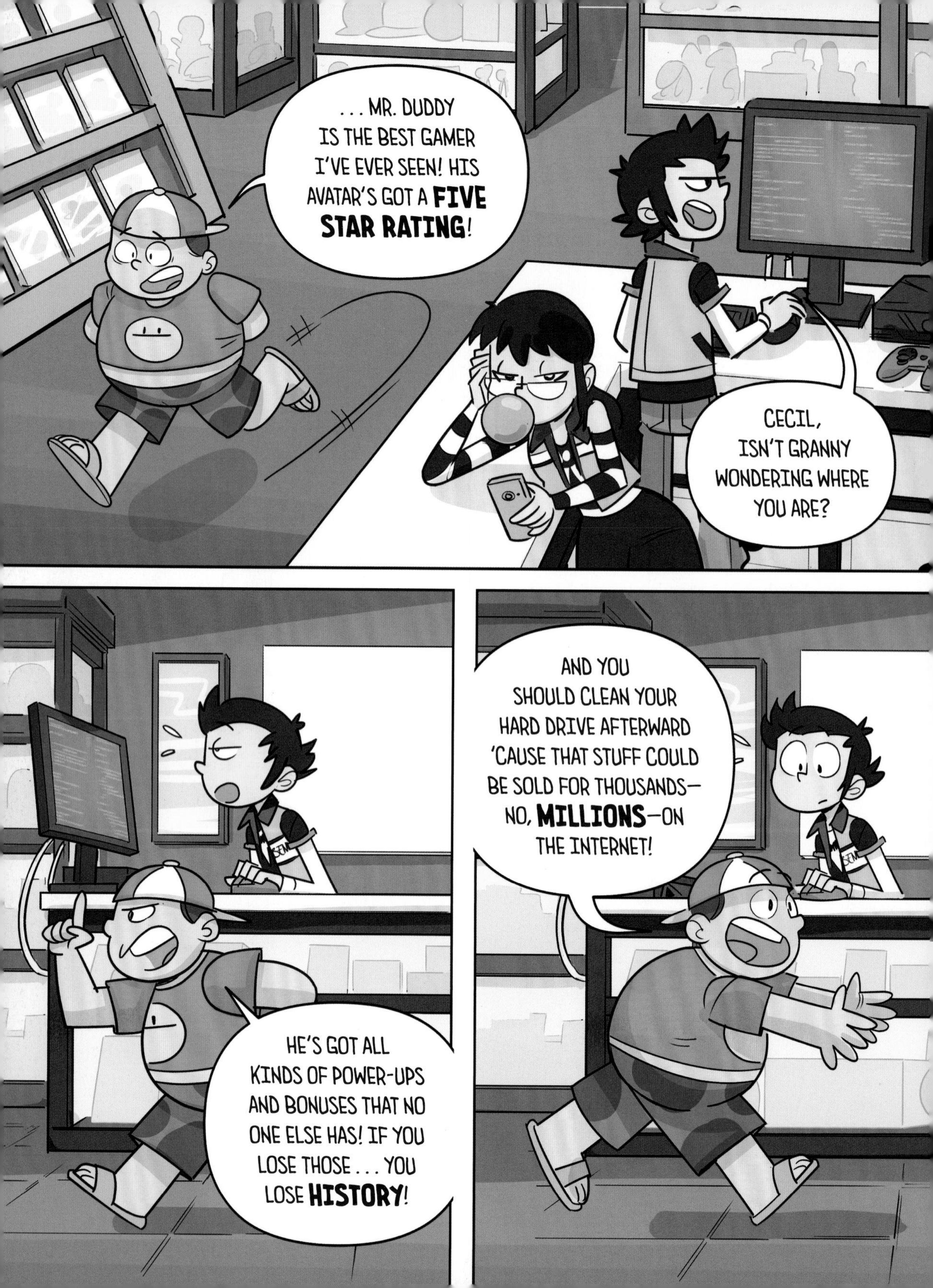
. . . MR. DUDDY IS THE BEST GAMER I'VE EVER SEEN! HIS AVATAR'S GOT A **FIVE STAR RATING**!
CECIL, ISN'T GRANNY WONDERING WHERE YOU ARE?
HE'S GOT ALL KINDS OF POWER-UPS AND BONUSES THAT NO ONE ELSE HAS! IF YOU LOSE THOSE . . . YOU LOSE **HISTORY**!
AND YOU SHOULD CLEAN YOUR HARD DRIVE AFTERWARD 'CAUSE THAT STUFF COULD BE SOLD FOR THOUSANDS—NO, **MILLIONS**—ON THE INTERNET!

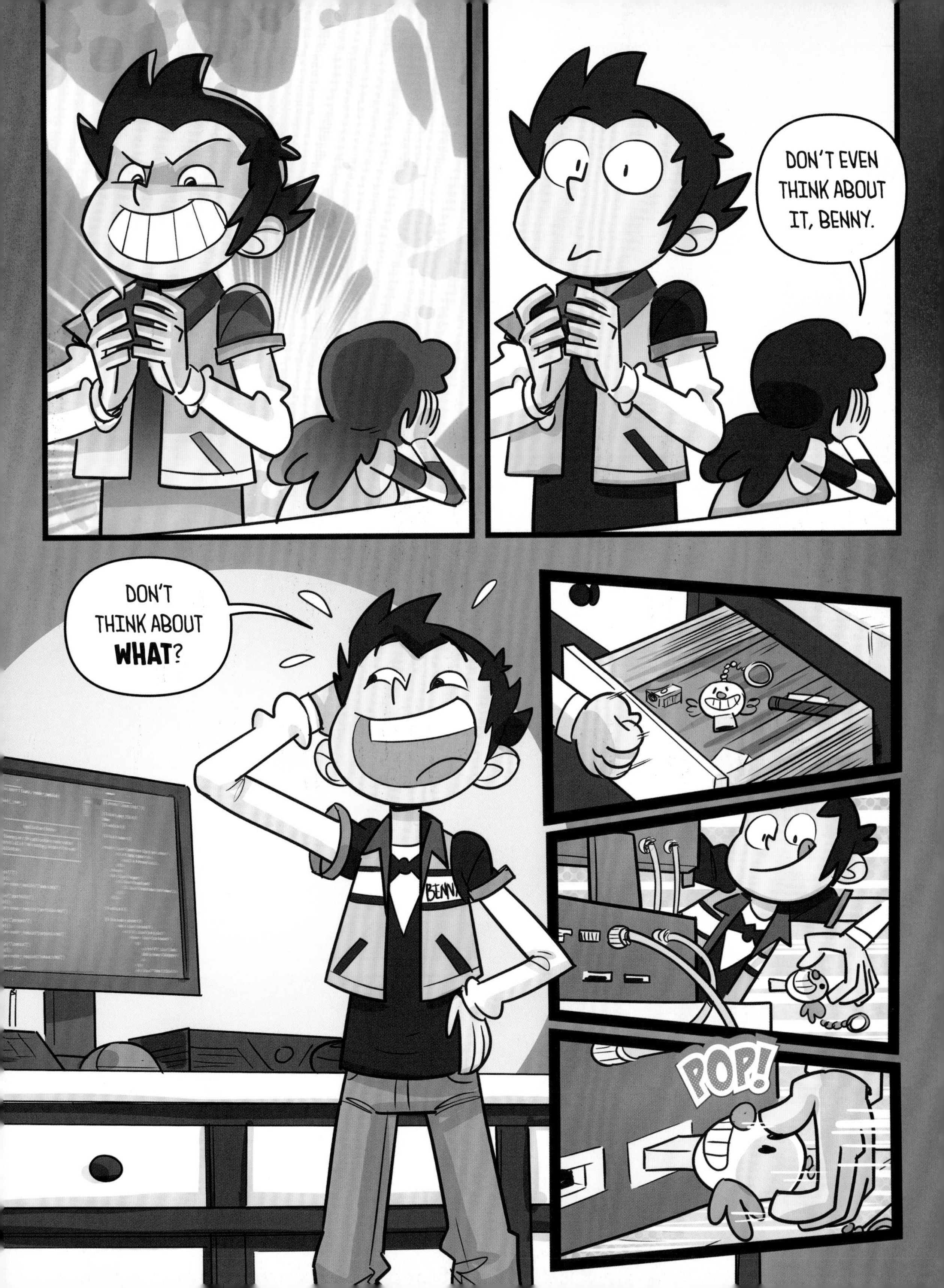
DON'T EVEN THINK ABOUT IT, BENNY.
DON'T THINK ABOUT **WHAT**?
BENNY
POP!

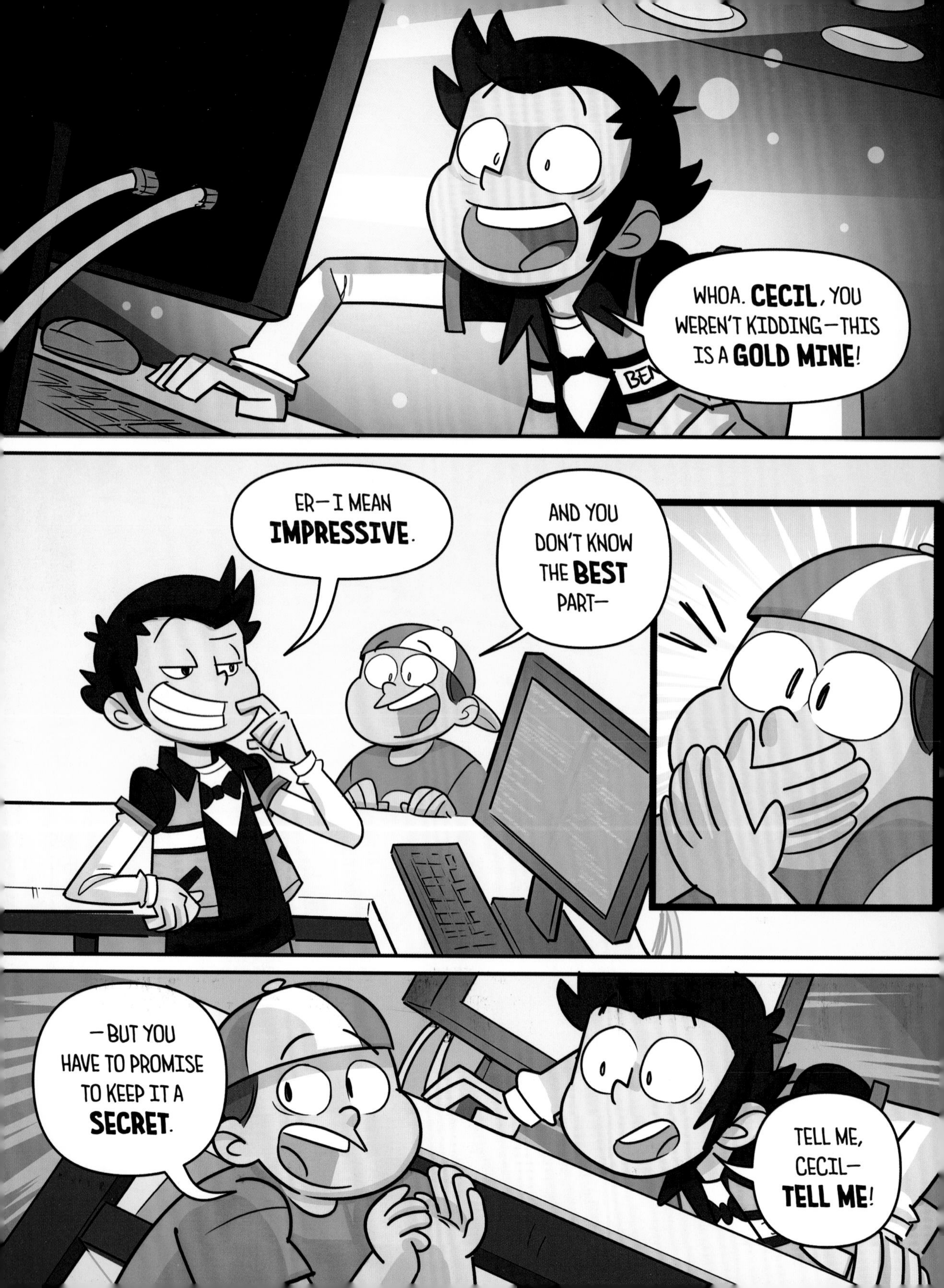
WHOA. CECIL, YOU WEREN'T KIDDING—THIS IS A GOLD MINE!
BEN
ER—I MEAN IMPRESSIVE.
AND YOU DON'T KNOW THE BEST PART—
—BUT YOU HAVE TO PROMISE TO KEEP IT A SECRET.
TELL ME, CECIL—TELL ME!

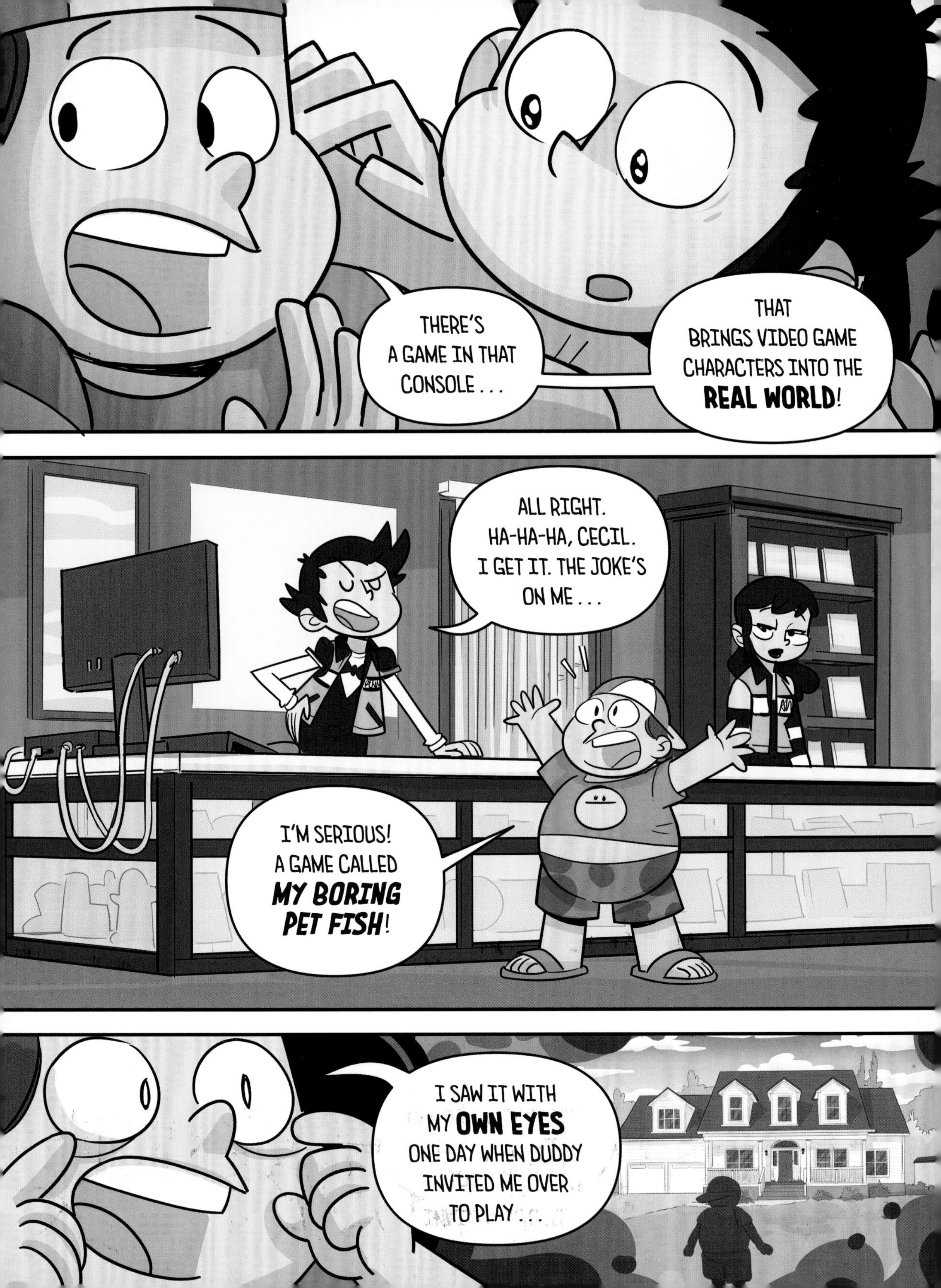

THERE'S A GAME IN THAT CONSOLE . . .
THAT BRINGS VIDEO GAME CHARACTERS INTO THE **REAL WORLD**!
ALL RIGHT. HA-HA-HA, CECIL. I GET IT. THE JOKE'S ON ME . . .
I'M SERIOUS! A GAME CALLED ***MY BORING PET FISH***!
I SAW IT WITH MY **OWN EYES** ONE DAY WHEN DUDDY INVITED ME OVER TO PLAY . . .

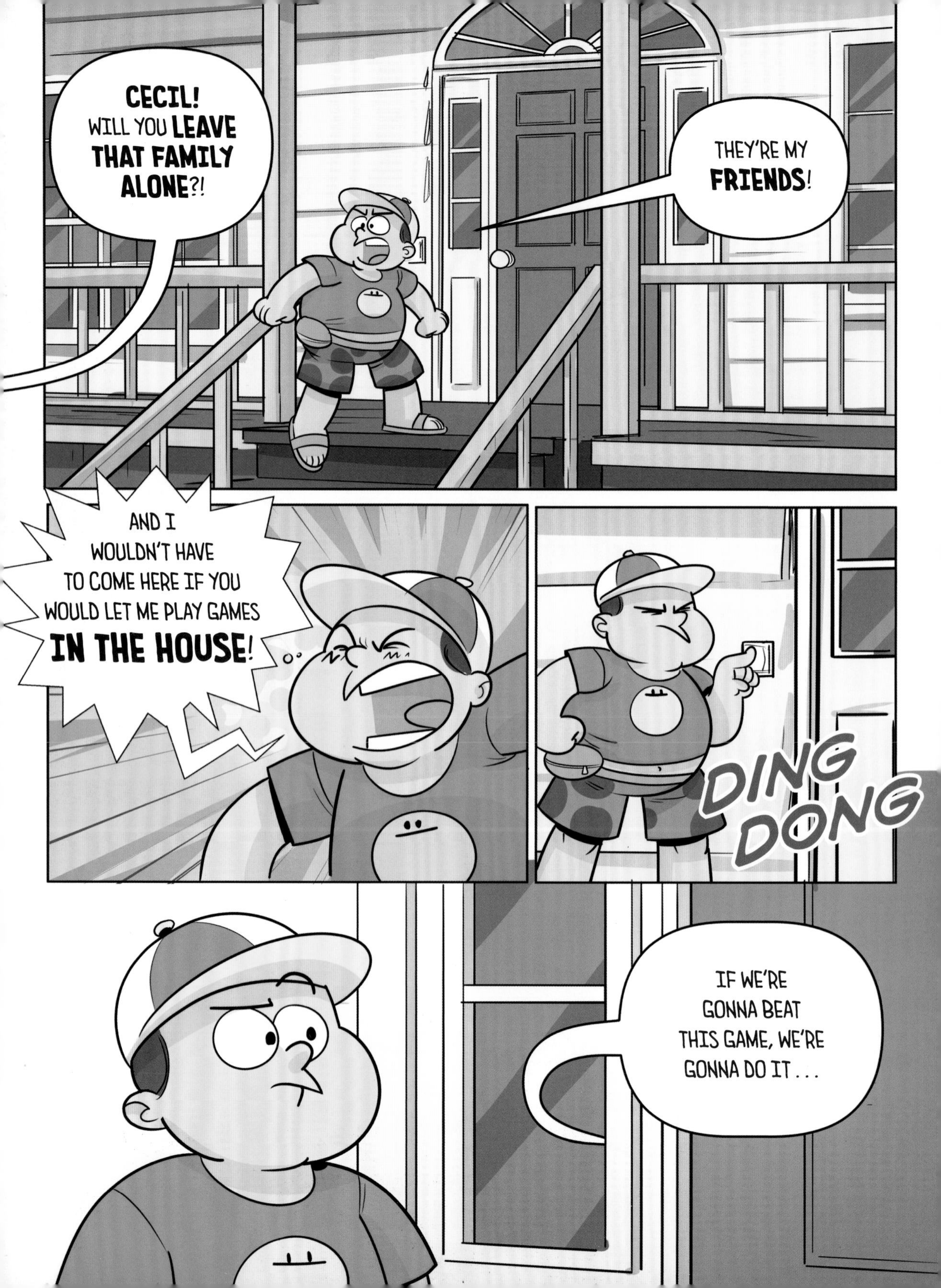
CECIL! WILL YOU LEAVE THAT FAMILY ALONE?!
THEY'RE MY FRIENDS!
AND I WOULDN'T HAVE TO COME HERE IF YOU WOULD LET ME PLAY GAMES IN THE HOUSE!
DING DONG
IF WE'RE GONNA BEAT THIS GAME, WE'RE GONNA DO IT . . .

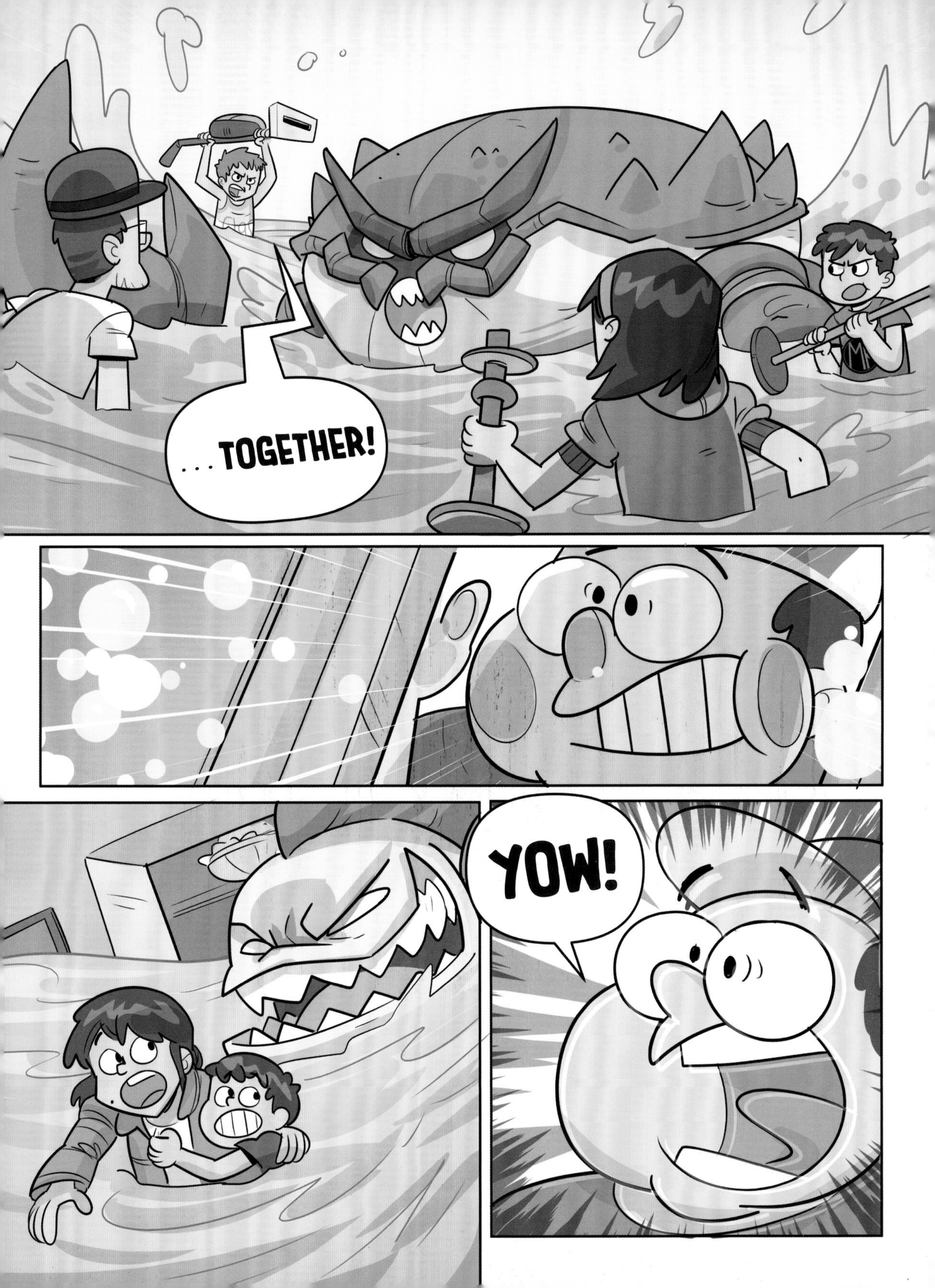
. . . TOGETHER!
YOW!

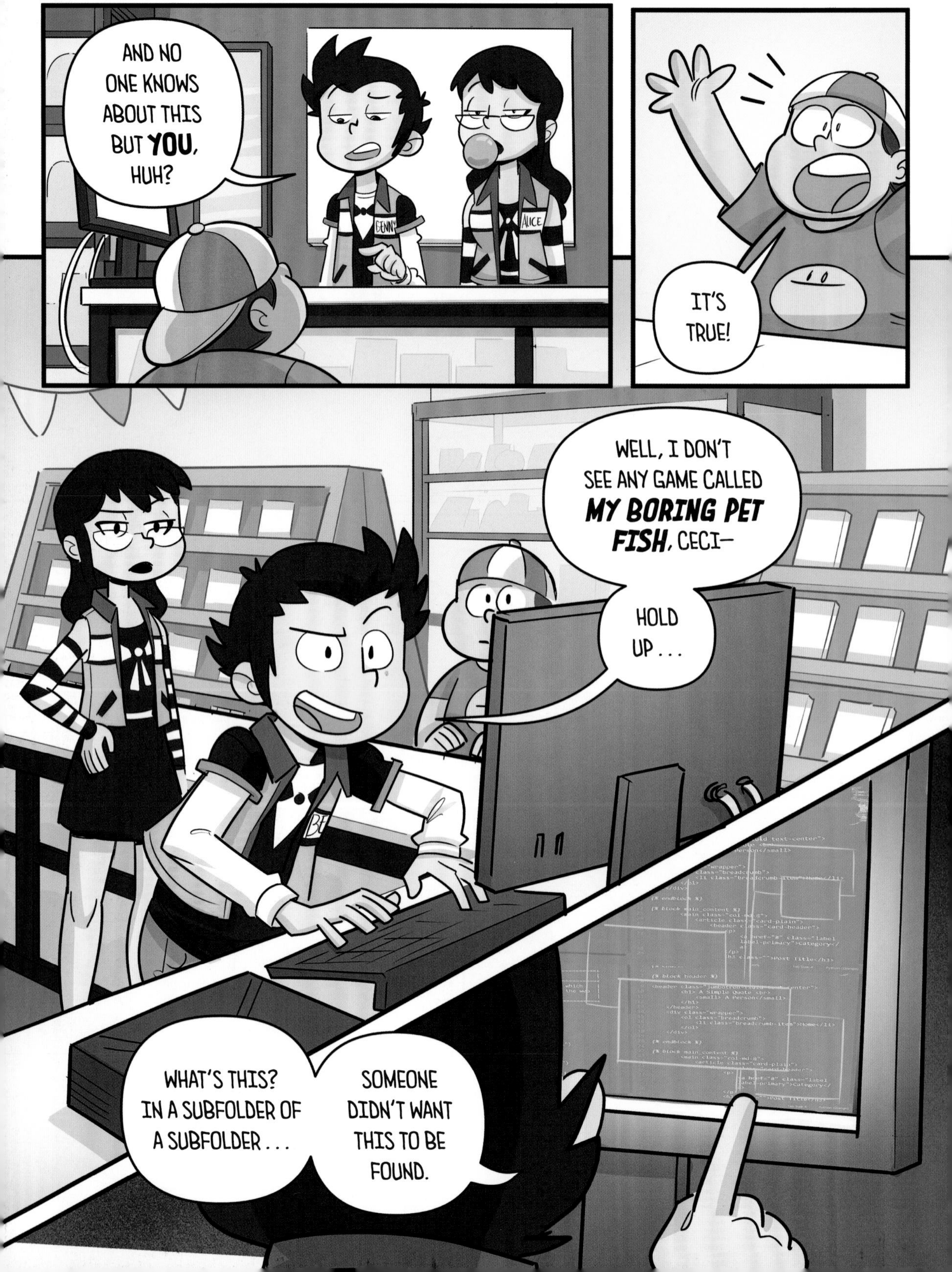
AND NO ONE KNOWS ABOUT THIS BUT **YOU**, HUH?
IT'S TRUE!
WELL, I DON'T SEE ANY GAME CALLED ***MY BORING PET FISH***, CECI—
HOLD UP . . .
WHAT'S THIS? IN A SUBFOLDER OF A SUBFOLDER . . .
SOMEONE DIDN'T WANT THIS TO BE FOUND.

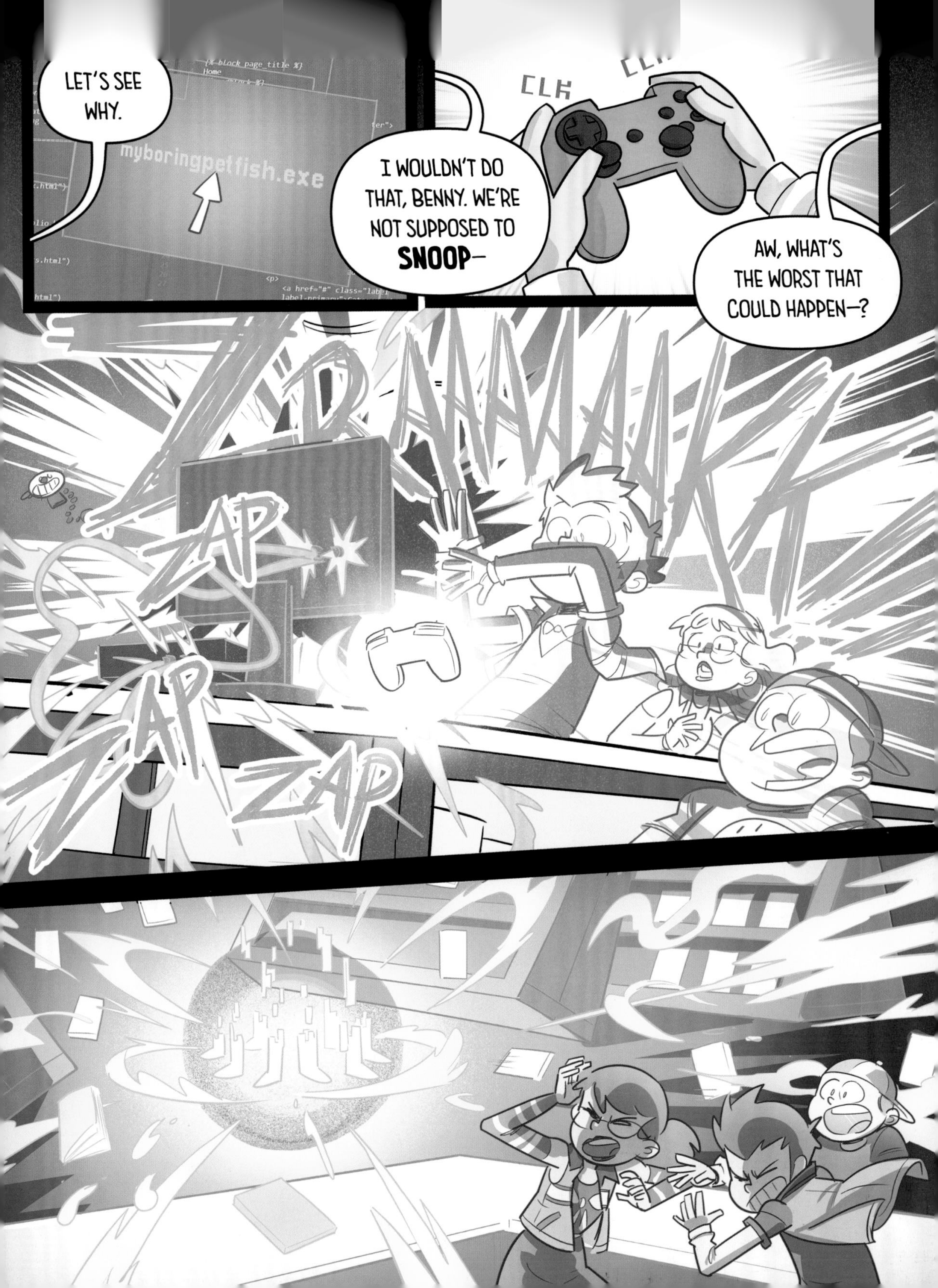
LET'S SEE WHY.
myboringpetfish.exe
CLK
CLK
I WOULDN'T DO THAT, BENNY. WE'RE NOT SUPPOSED TO **SNOOP**–
AW, WHAT'S THE WORST THAT COULD HAPPEN–?
ZRAAAAAKK
ZAP
ZAP
ZAP

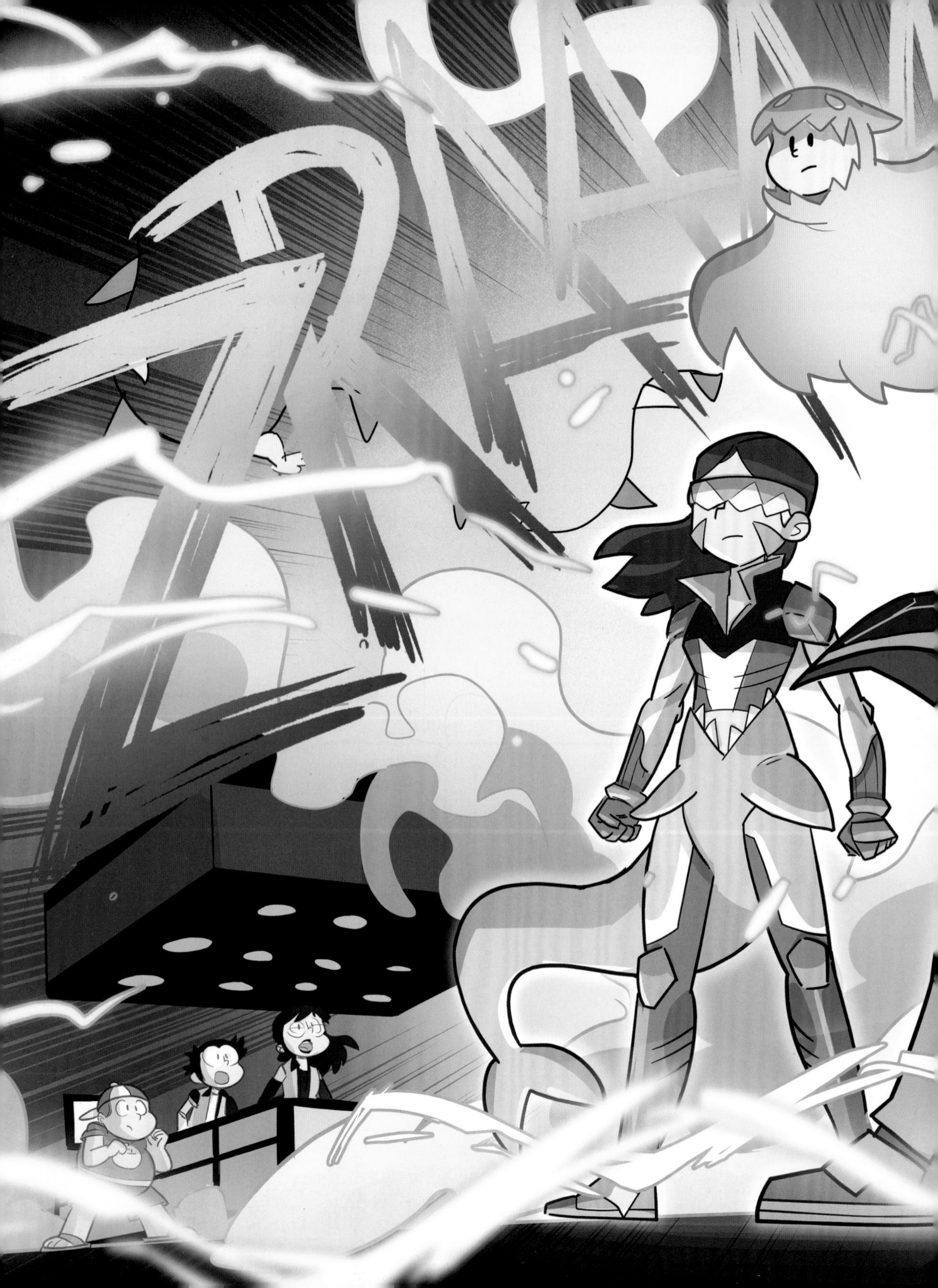

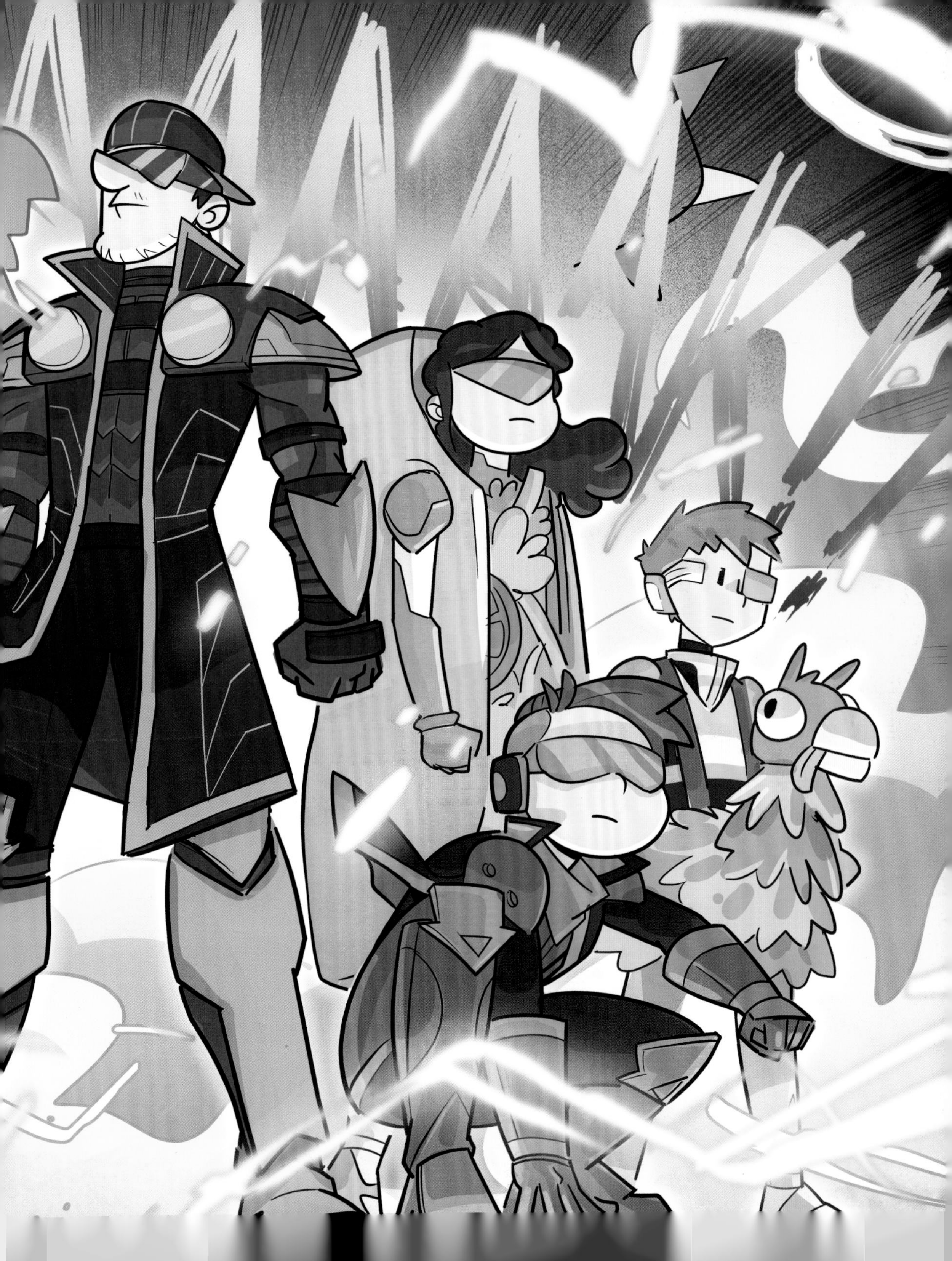

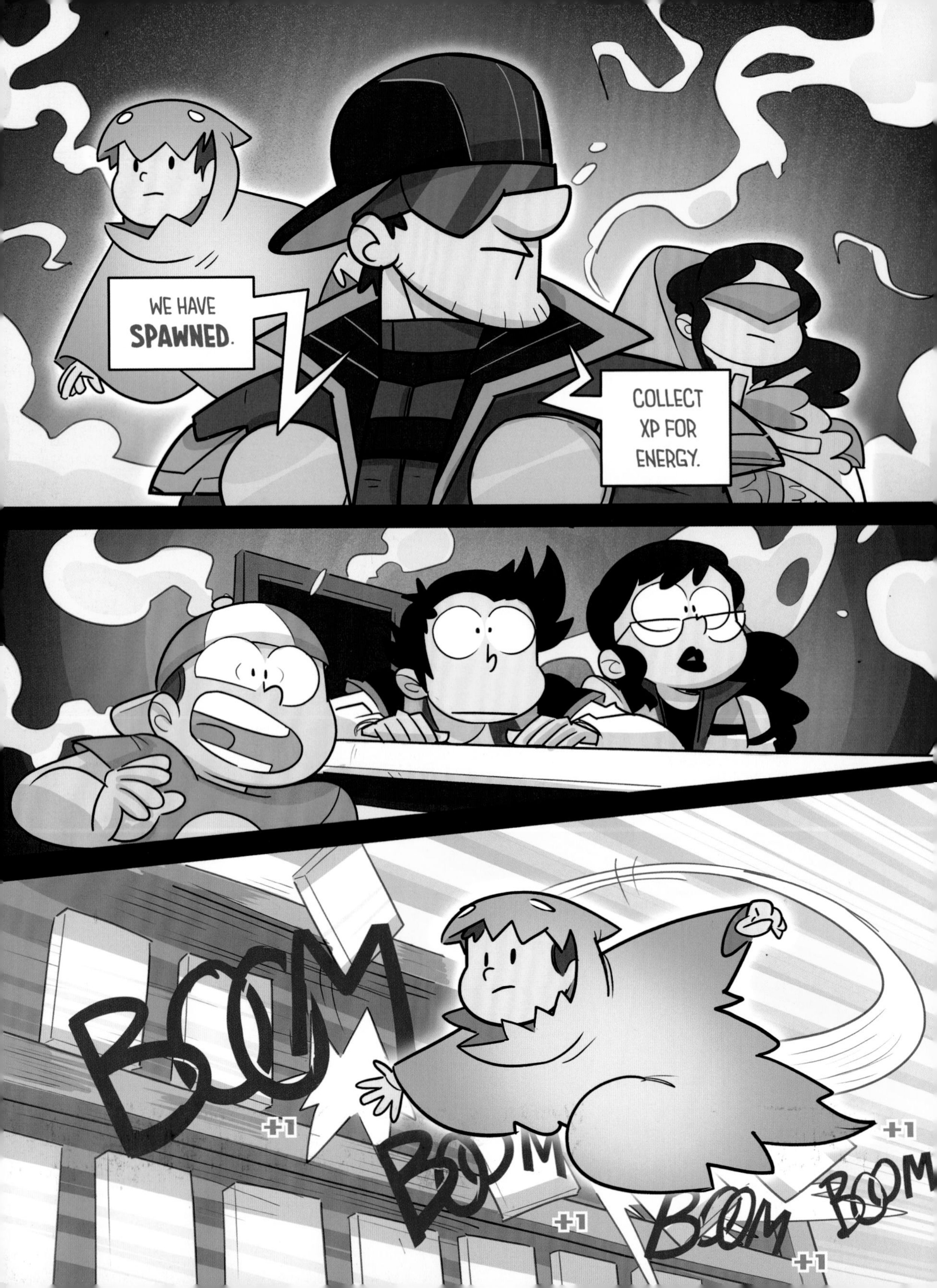
WE HAVE SPAWNED.
COLLECT XP FOR ENERGY.
BOOM
+1
BOOM
+1
BOOM
+1
BOOM
+1

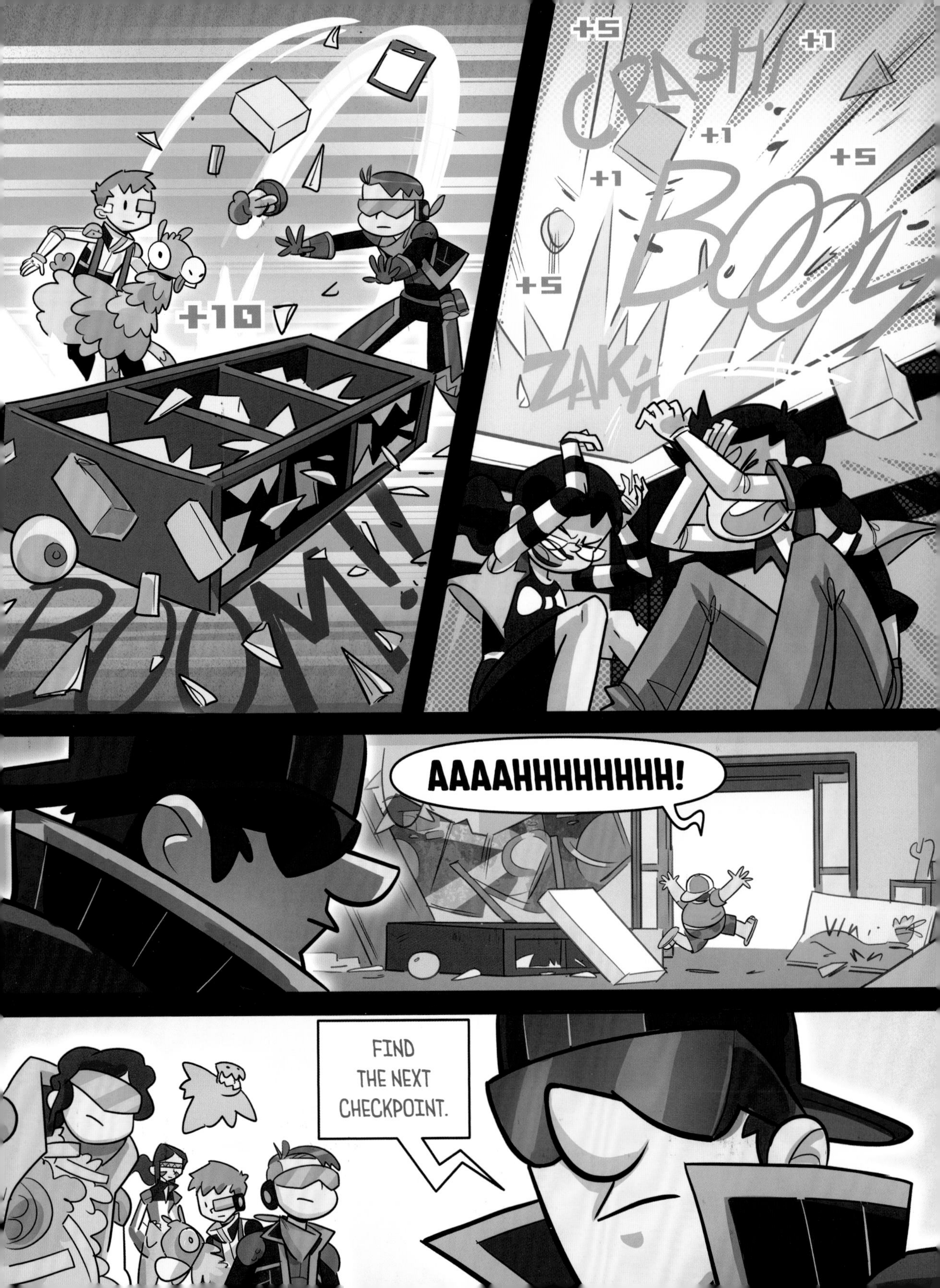
+10
BOOM!!
+5
+1
CRASH!
+1
+1
+5
BOOM
+5
ZAK!
AAAAHHHHHHHH!
FIND THE NEXT CHECKPOINT.

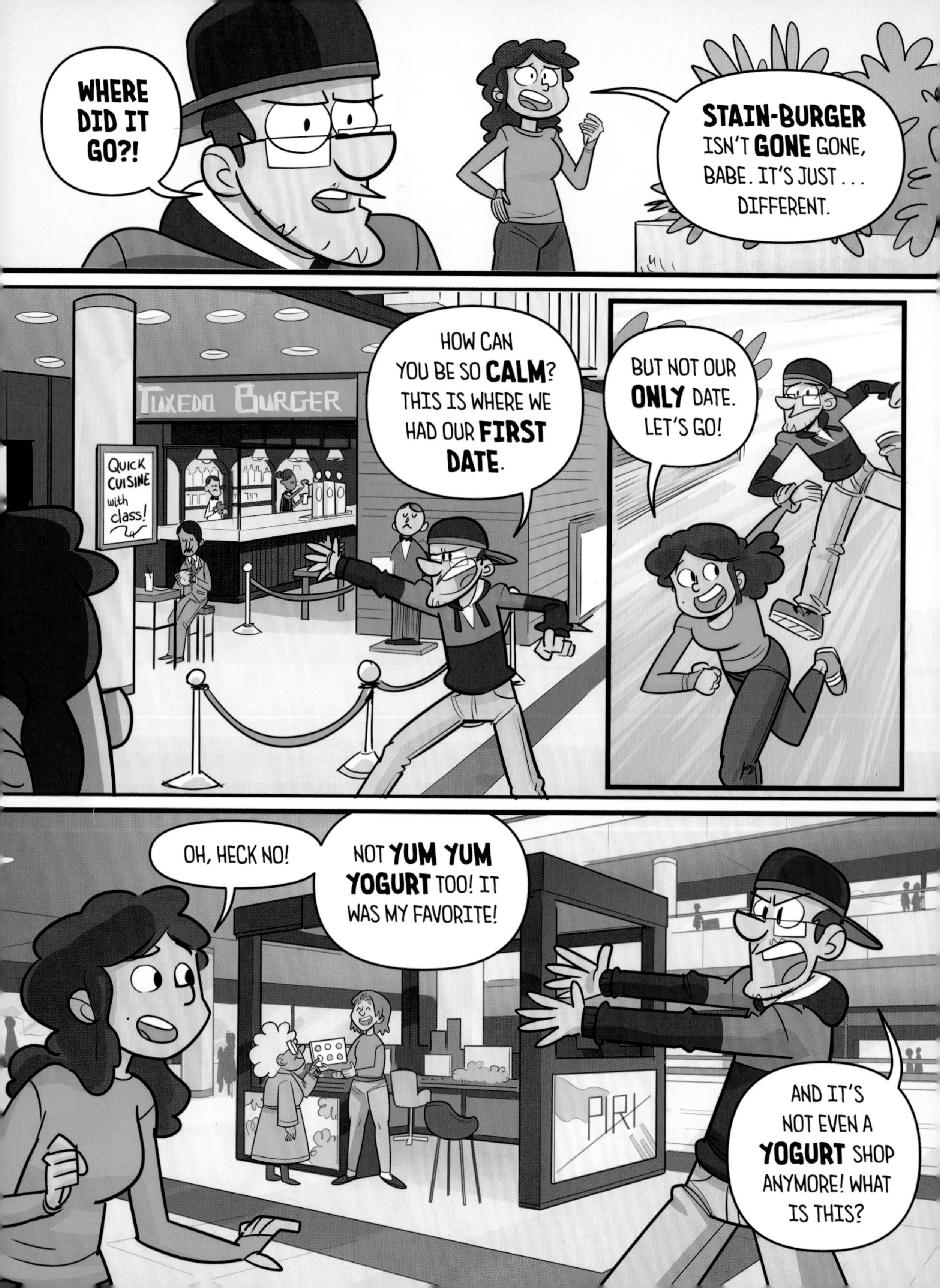
WHERE DID IT GO?!
STAIN-BURGER ISN'T GONE GONE, BABE. IT'S JUST . . . DIFFERENT.
TUXEDO BURGER
QUICK CUISINE with class!
HOW CAN YOU BE SO CALM? THIS IS WHERE WE HAD OUR FIRST DATE.
BUT NOT OUR ONLY DATE. LET'S GO!
OH, HECK NO!
NOT YUM YUM YOGURT TOO! IT WAS MY FAVORITE!
AND IT'S NOT EVEN A YOGURT SHOP ANYMORE! WHAT IS THIS?

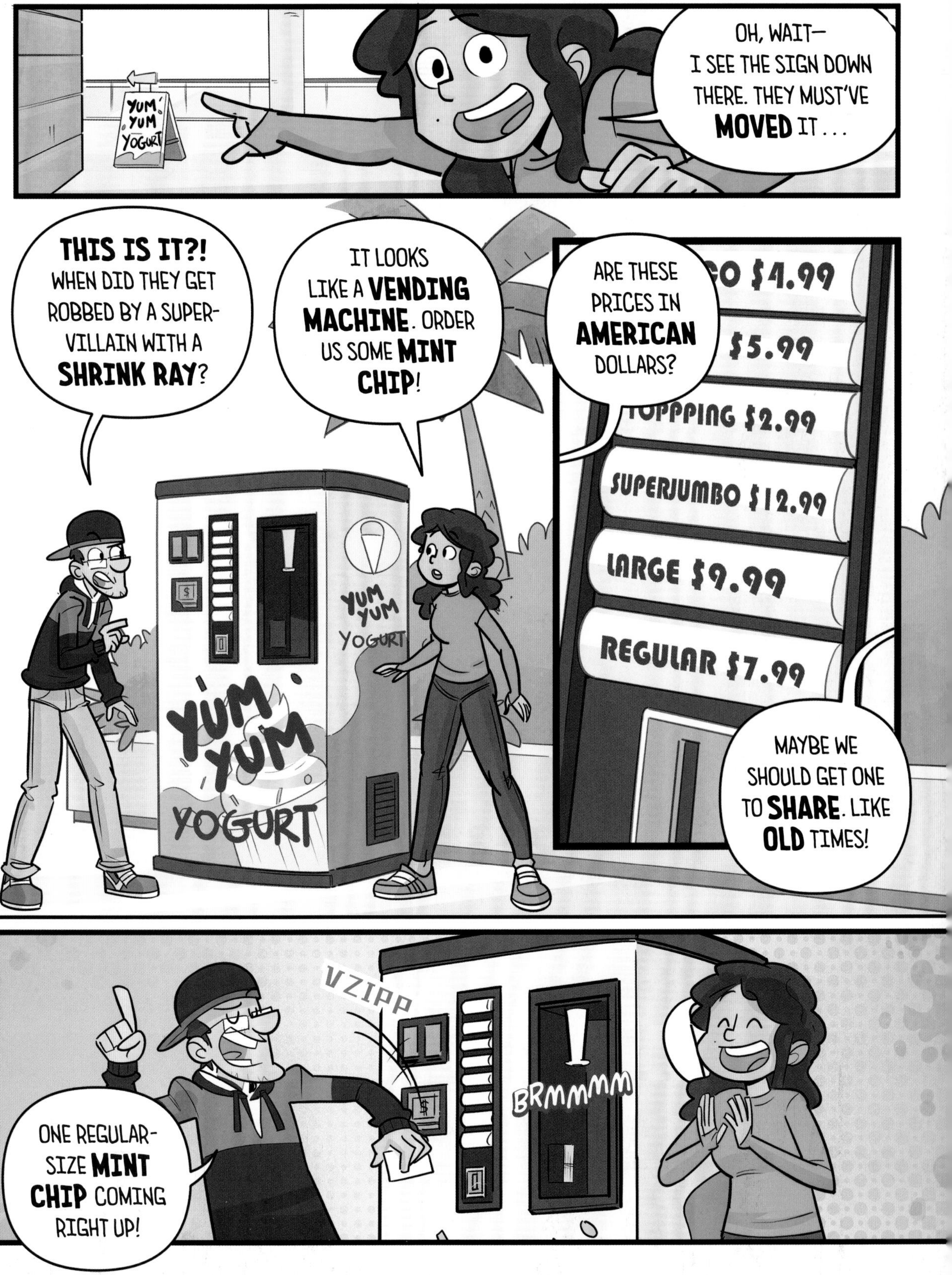
YUM YUM YOGURT
OH, WAIT— I SEE THE SIGN DOWN THERE. THEY MUST'VE **MOVED** IT . . .
THIS IS IT?! WHEN DID THEY GET ROBBED BY A SUPER-VILLAIN WITH A **SHRINK RAY**?
IT LOOKS LIKE A **VENDING MACHINE**. ORDER US SOME **MINT CHIP**!
YUM YUM YOGURT
YUM YUM YOGURT
ARE THESE PRICES IN **AMERICAN** DOLLARS?
$4.99
$5.99
$2.99
SUPERJUMBO $12.99
LARGE $9.99
REGULAR $7.99
MAYBE WE SHOULD GET ONE TO **SHARE**. LIKE **OLD** TIMES!
VZIPP
BRMMMM
ONE REGULAR-SIZE **MINT CHIP** COMING RIGHT UP!

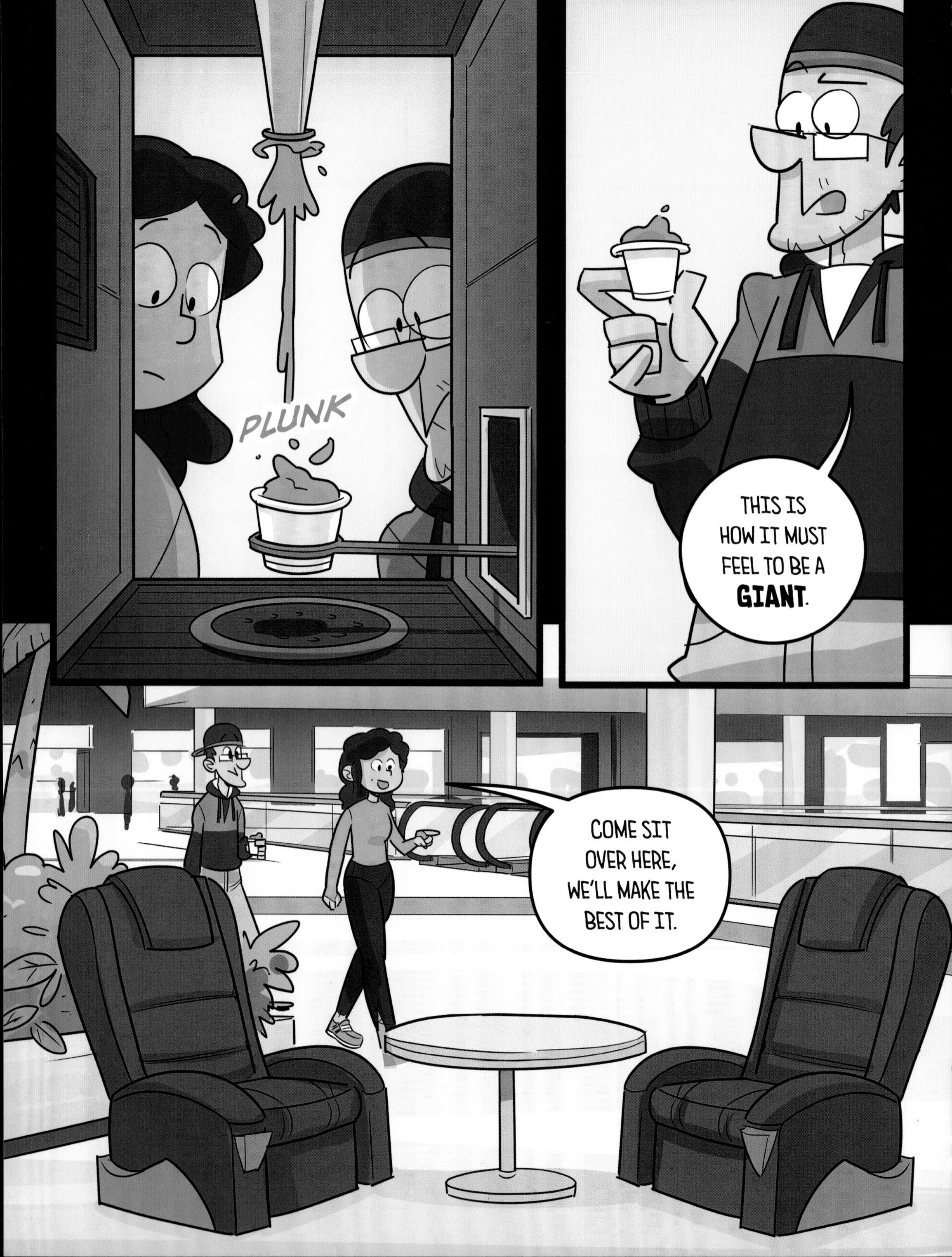
PLUNK
THIS IS HOW IT MUST FEEL TO BE A **GIANT**.
COME SIT OVER HERE, WE'LL MAKE THE BEST OF IT.

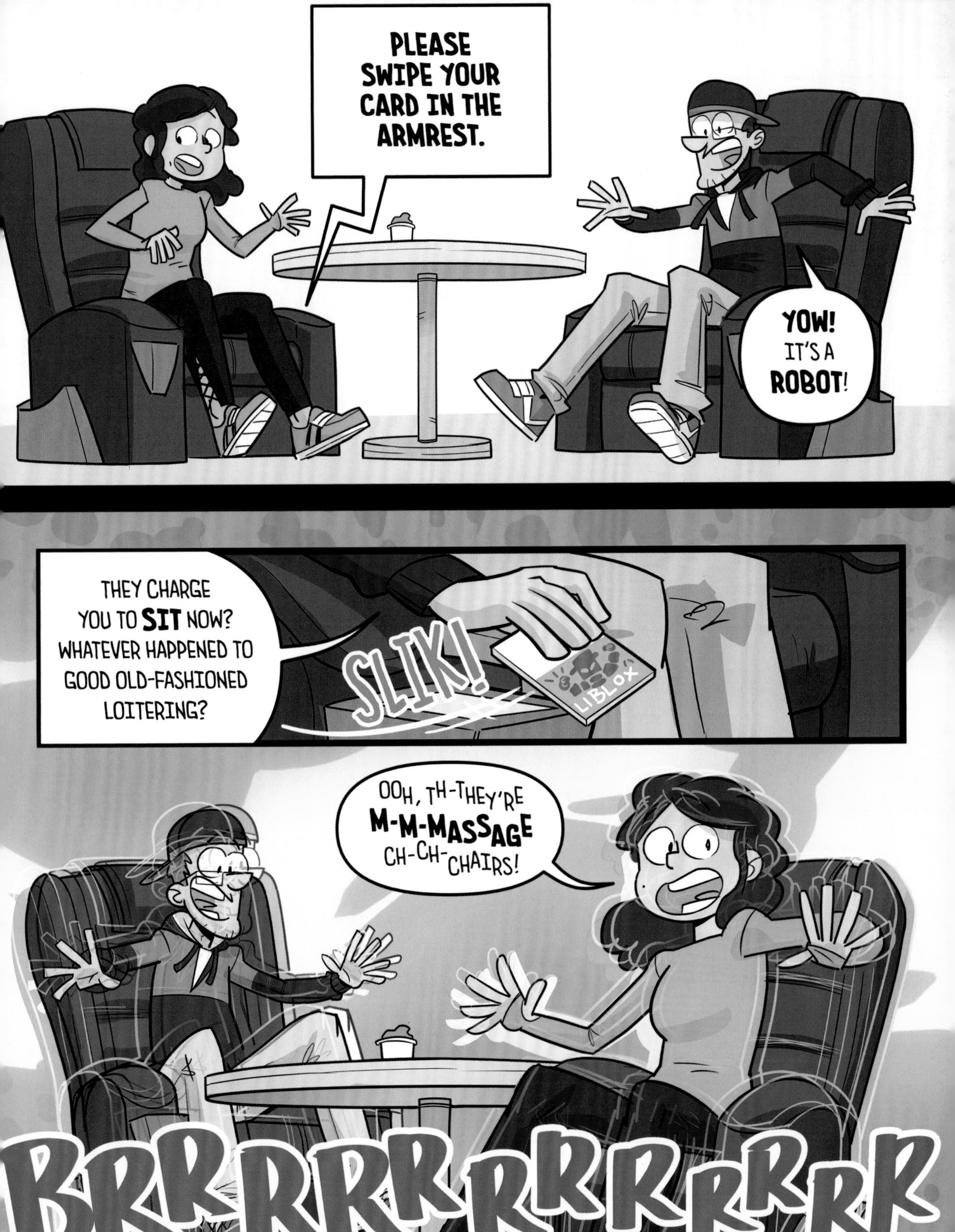
PLEASE SWIPE YOUR CARD IN THE ARMREST.
YOW! IT'S A ROBOT!
THEY CHARGE YOU TO SIT NOW? WHATEVER HAPPENED TO GOOD OLD-FASHIONED LOITERING?
SLIK!
LIBLOX
OOH, TH-THEY'RE M-M-MASSAGE CH-CH-CHAIRS!
BRRRRRRRRRRRR

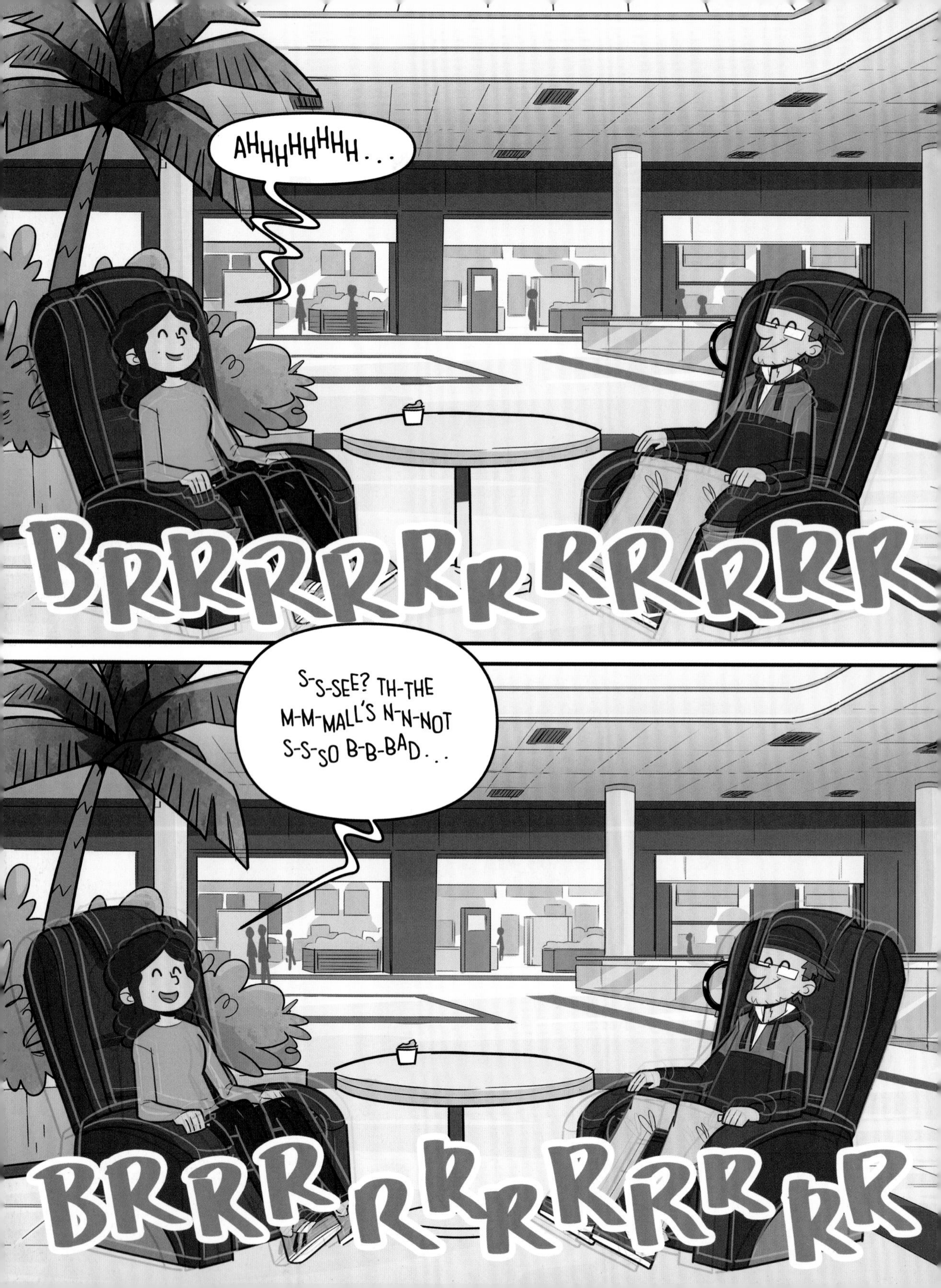

AHHHHHHHH...
BRRRRRRRRRRR
S-S-SEE? TH-THE M-M-MALL'S N-N-NOT S-S-SO B-B-BAD...
BRRRRRRRRRRR

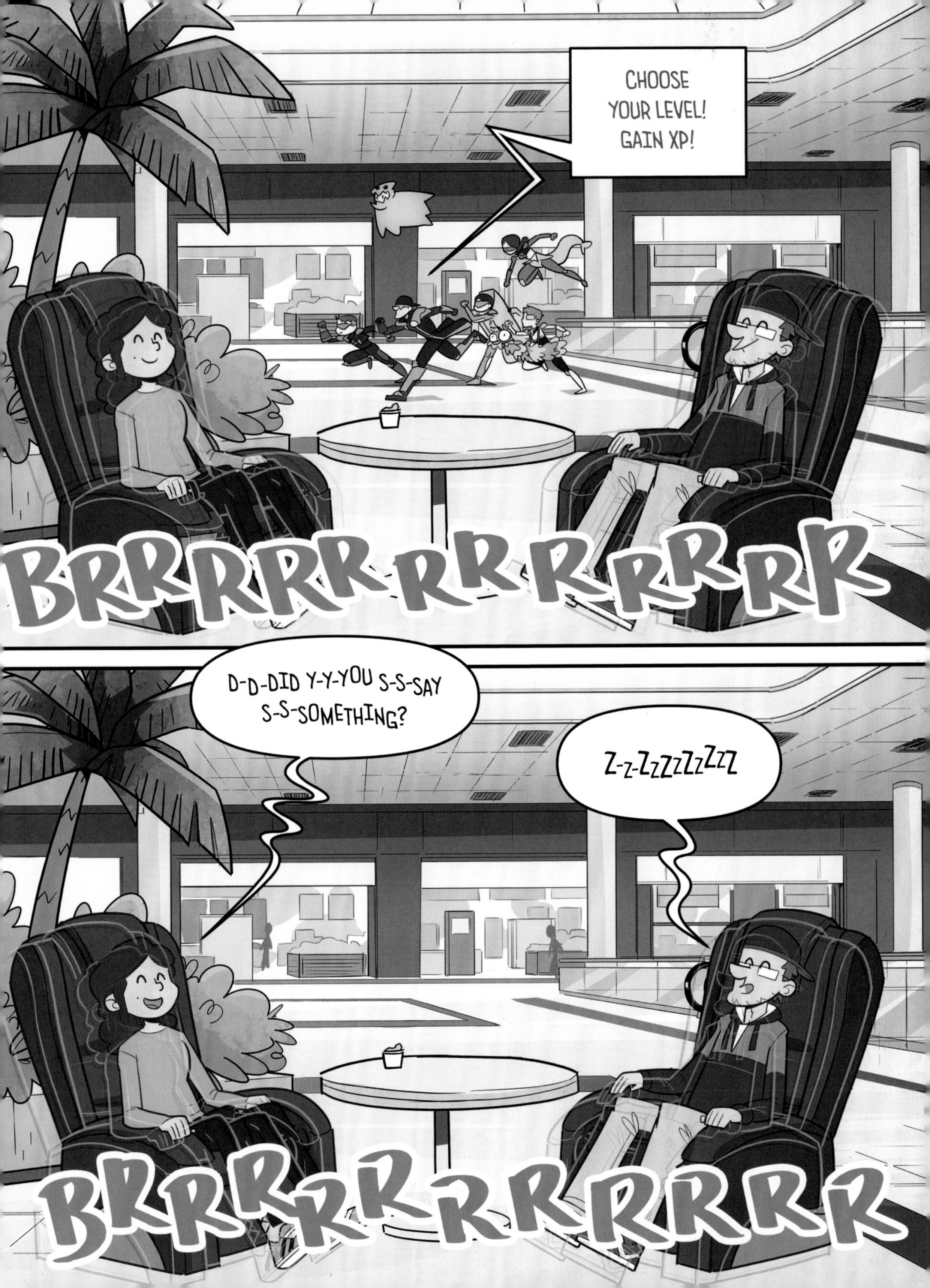
CHOOSE YOUR LEVEL! GAIN XP!
BRRRRRRRRRRRR
D-D-DID Y-Y-YOU S-S-SAY S-S-SOMETHING?
Z-z-ZzZzZzZzz
BRRRRRRRRRRR

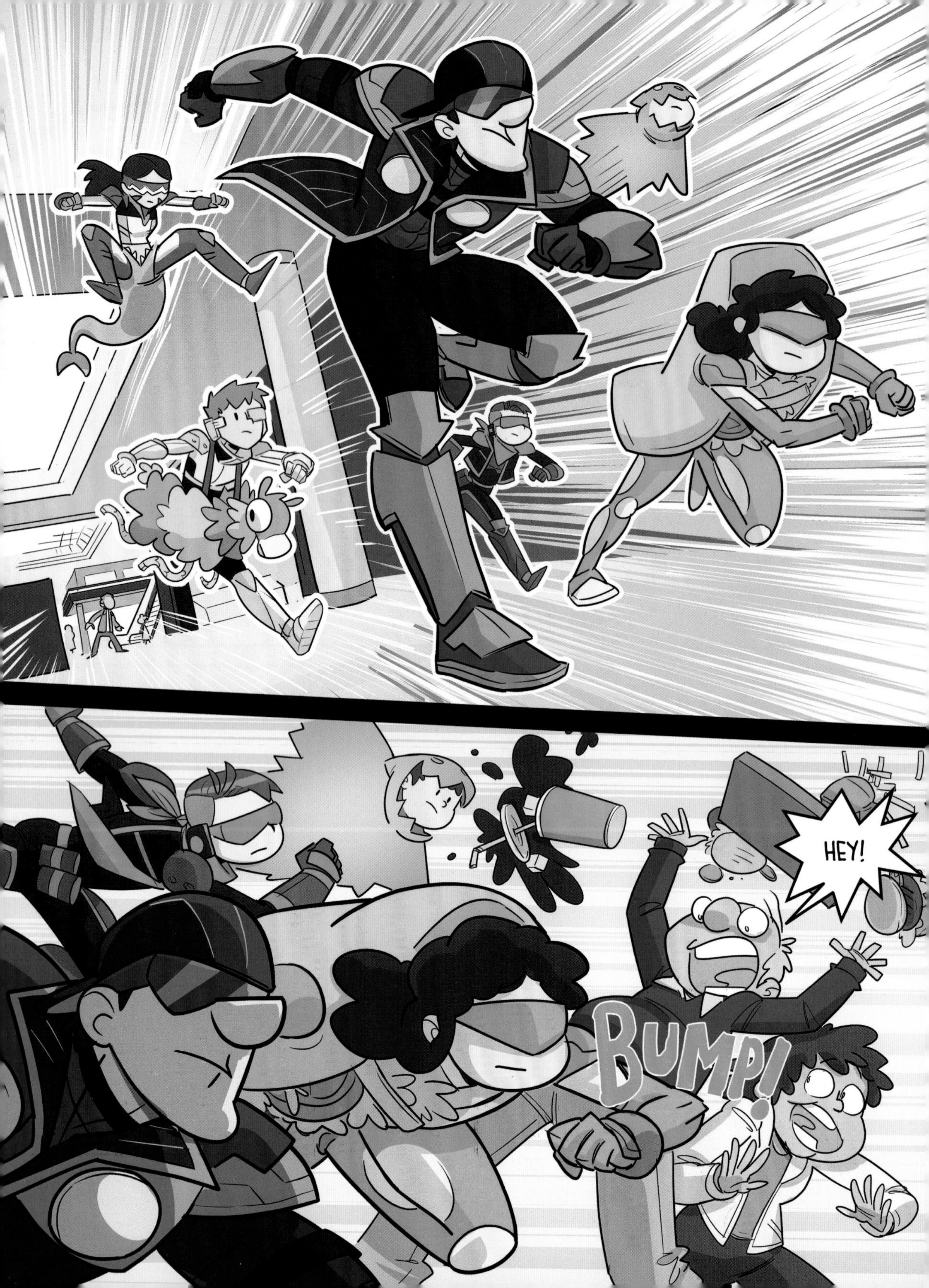
HEY!
BUMP!

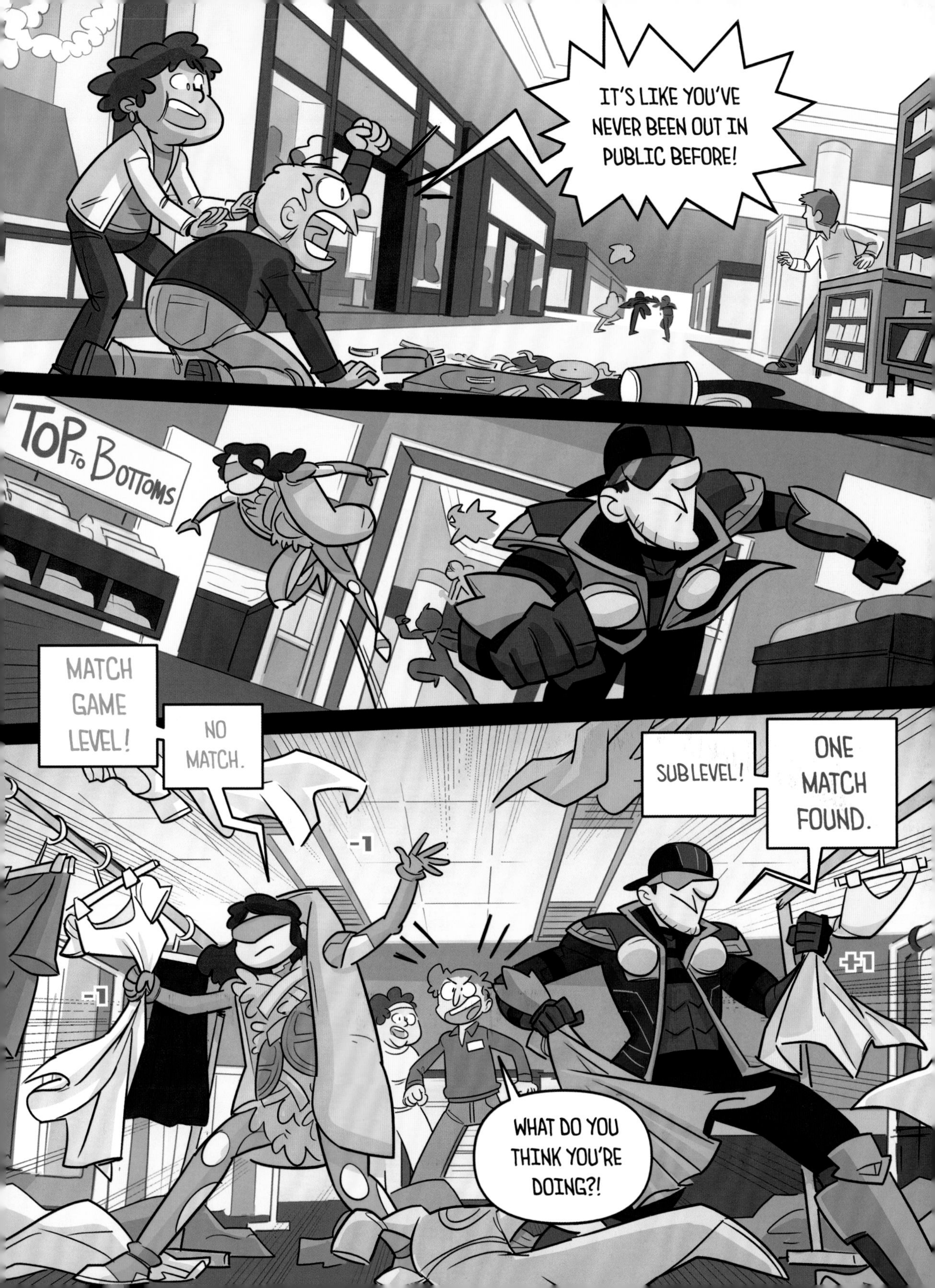
IT'S LIKE YOU'VE NEVER BEEN OUT IN PUBLIC BEFORE!
TOP TO BOTTOMS
MATCH GAME LEVEL!
NO MATCH.
SUB LEVEL!
ONE MATCH FOUND.
-1
-1
+1
WHAT DO YOU THINK YOU'RE DOING?!

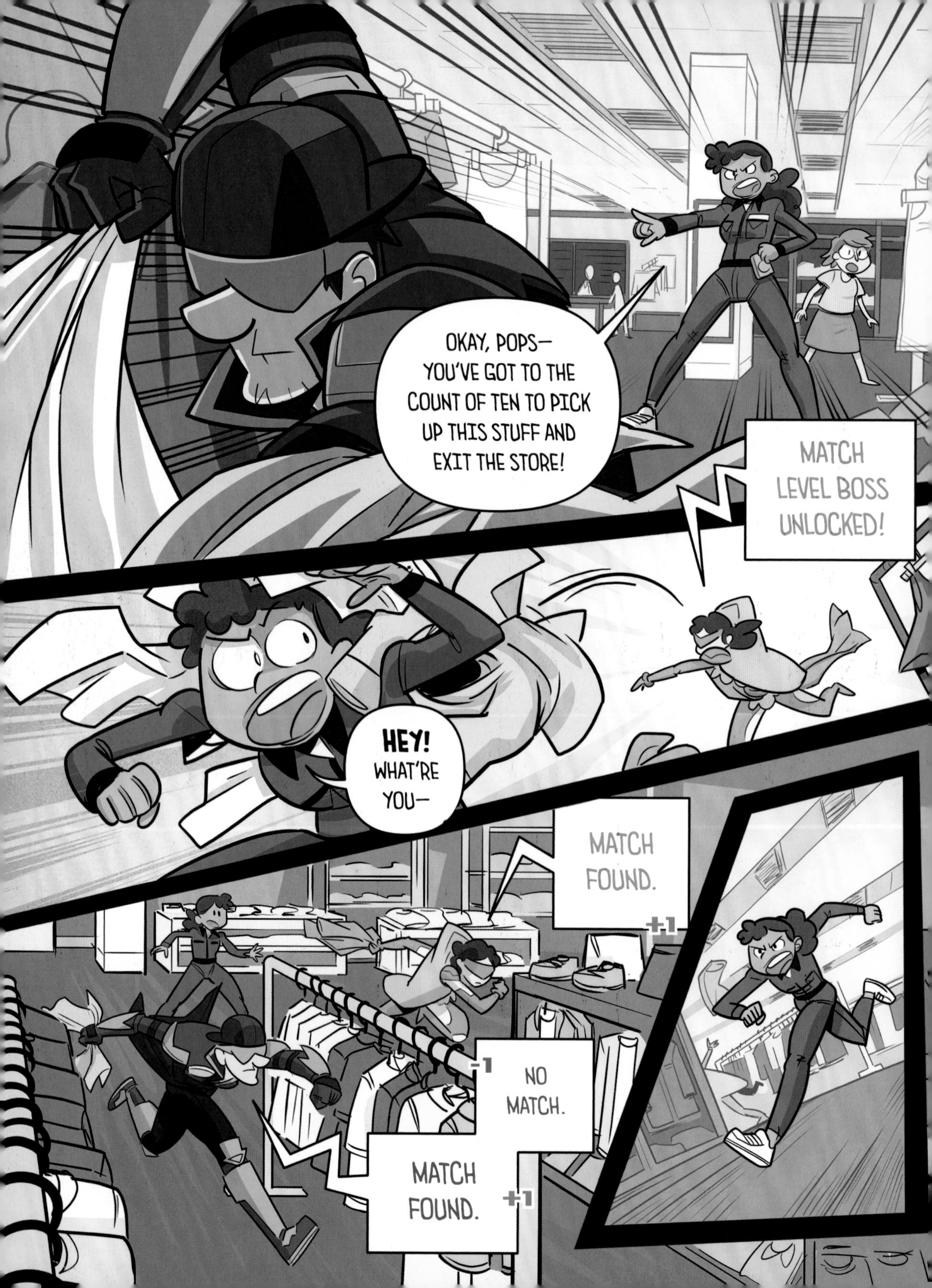
OKAY, POPS— YOU'VE GOT TO THE COUNT OF TEN TO PICK UP THIS STUFF AND EXIT THE STORE!
MATCH LEVEL BOSS UNLOCKED!
HEY! WHAT'RE YOU—
MATCH FOUND.
+1
-1
NO MATCH.
MATCH FOUND.
+1

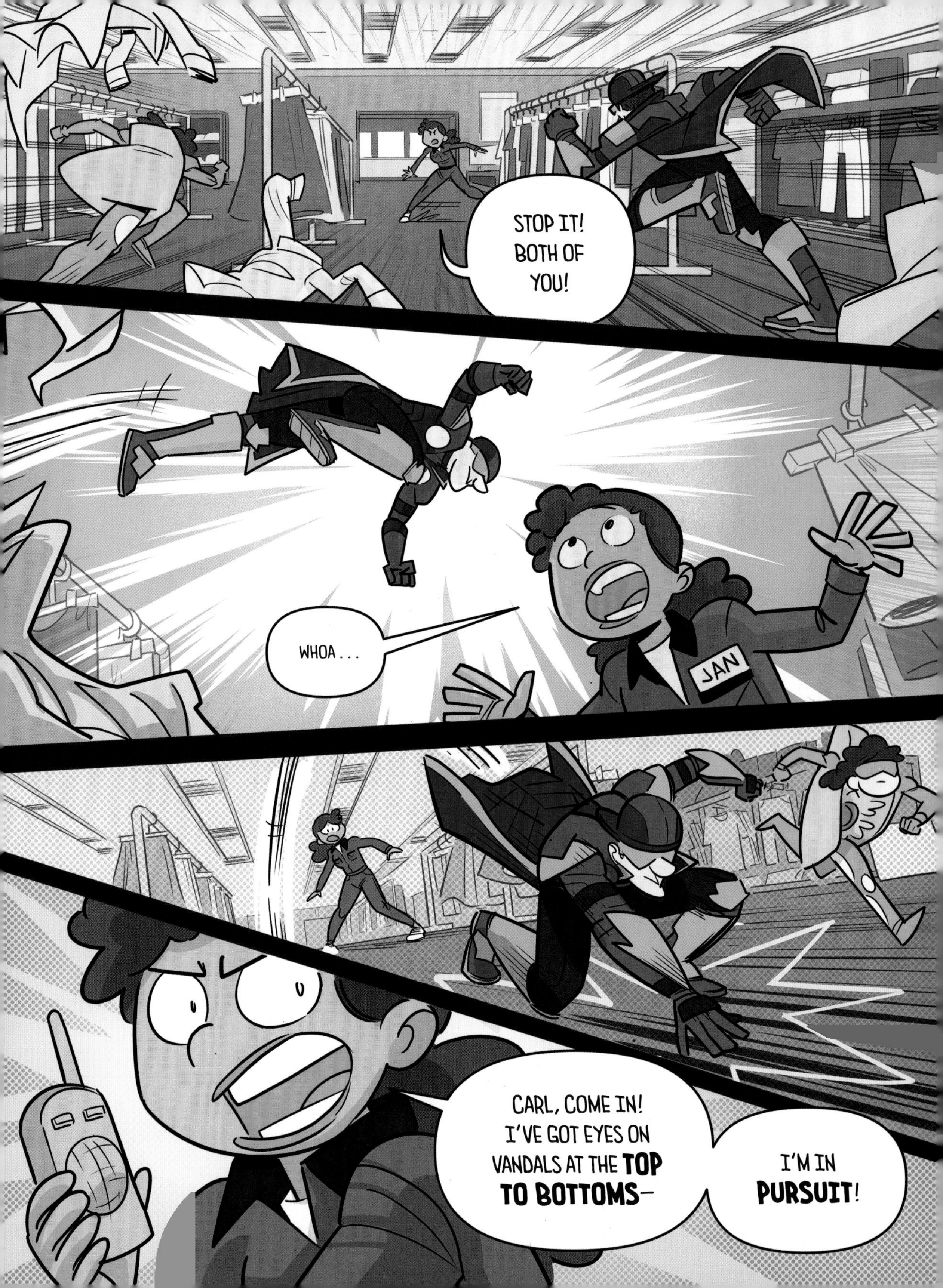
STOP IT! BOTH OF YOU!
WHOA . . .
JAN
CARL, COME IN! I'VE GOT EYES ON VANDALS AT THE **TOP TO BOTTOMS**—
I'M IN **PURSUIT**!

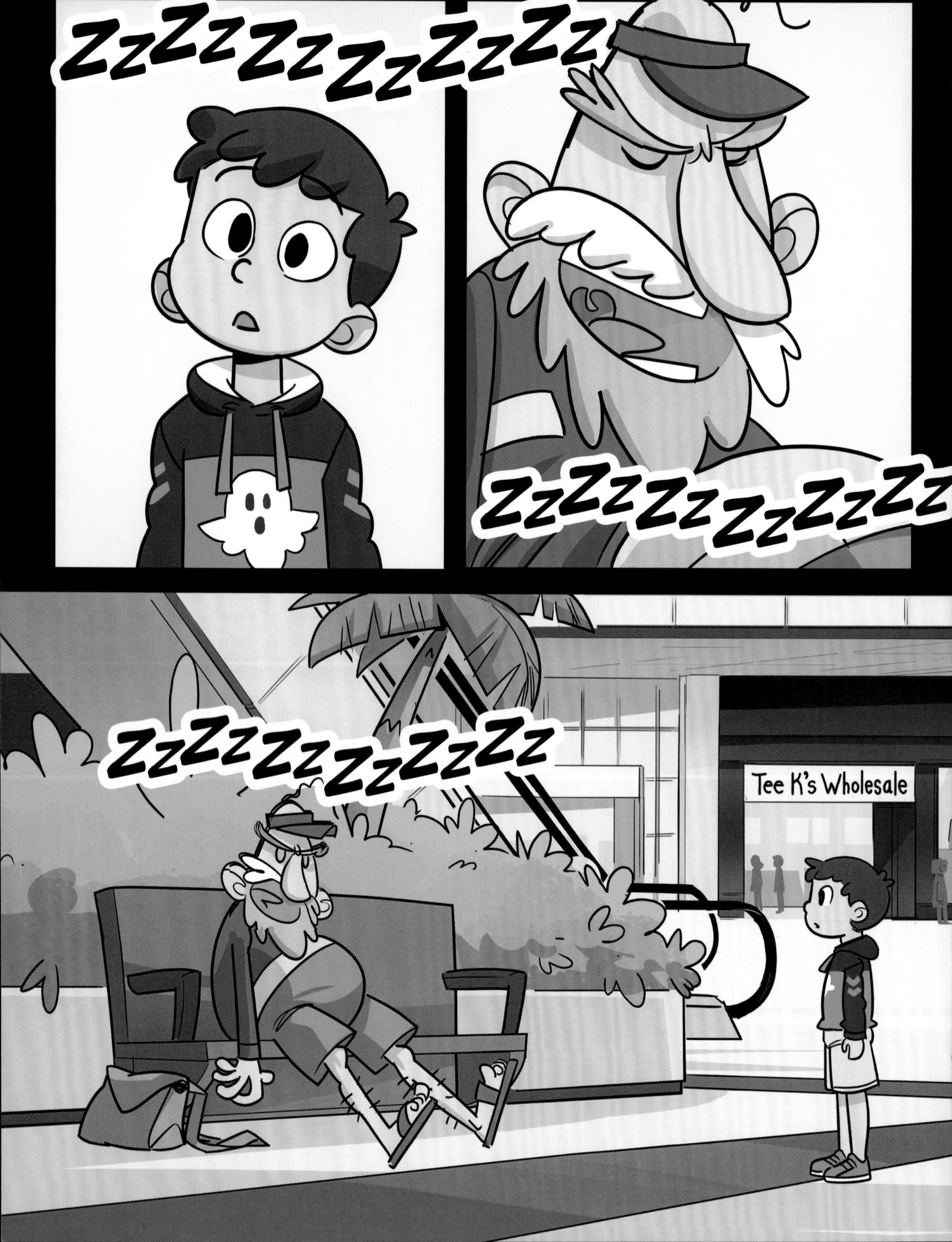

ZzZzZzZzZzZz
ZzZzZzZzZzZz
ZzZzZzZzZzZz
Tee K's Wholesale

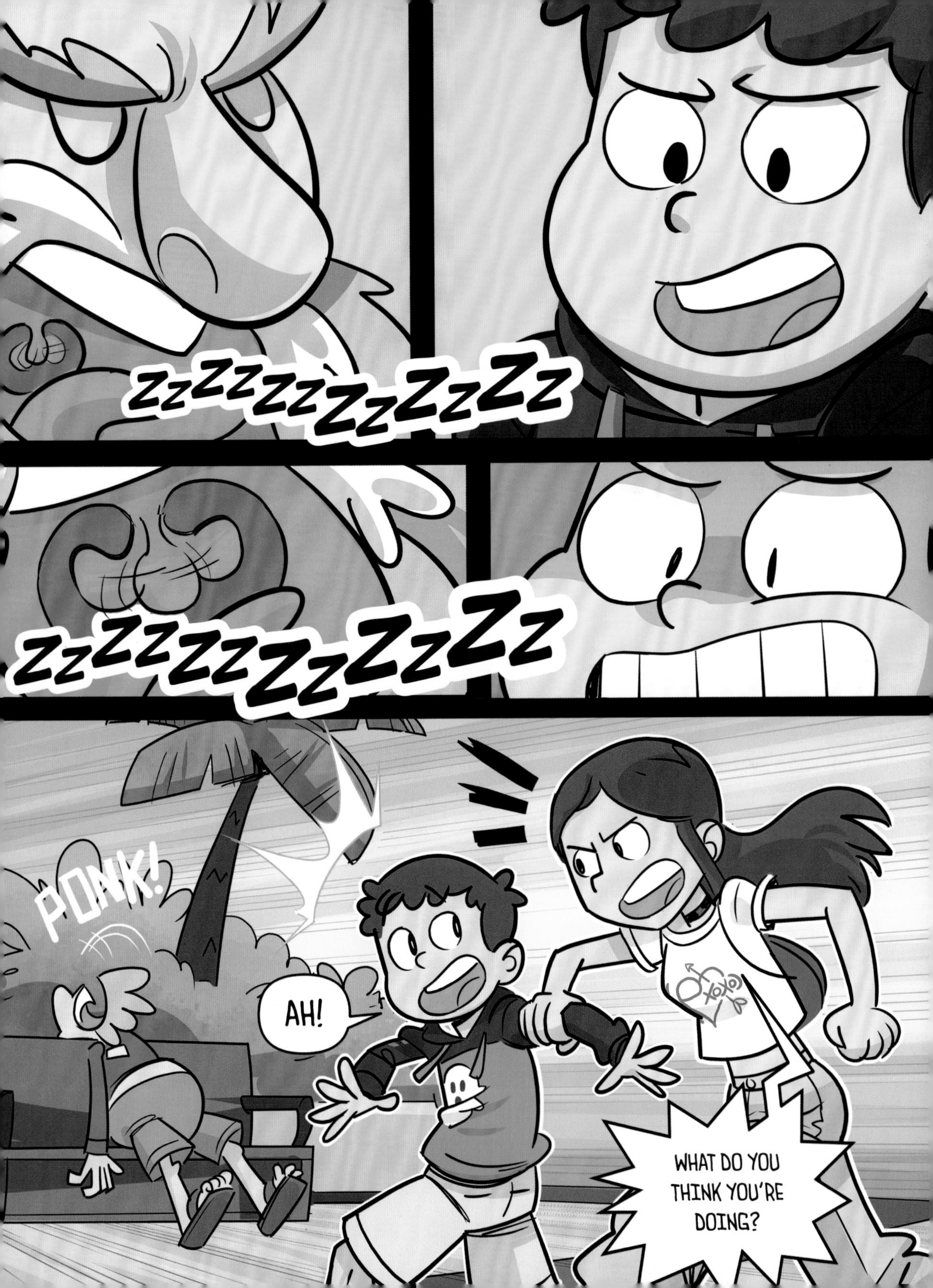

ZzZzZzZzZzZz
ZzZzZzZzZzZz
PONK!
AH!
WHAT DO YOU THINK YOU'RE DOING?

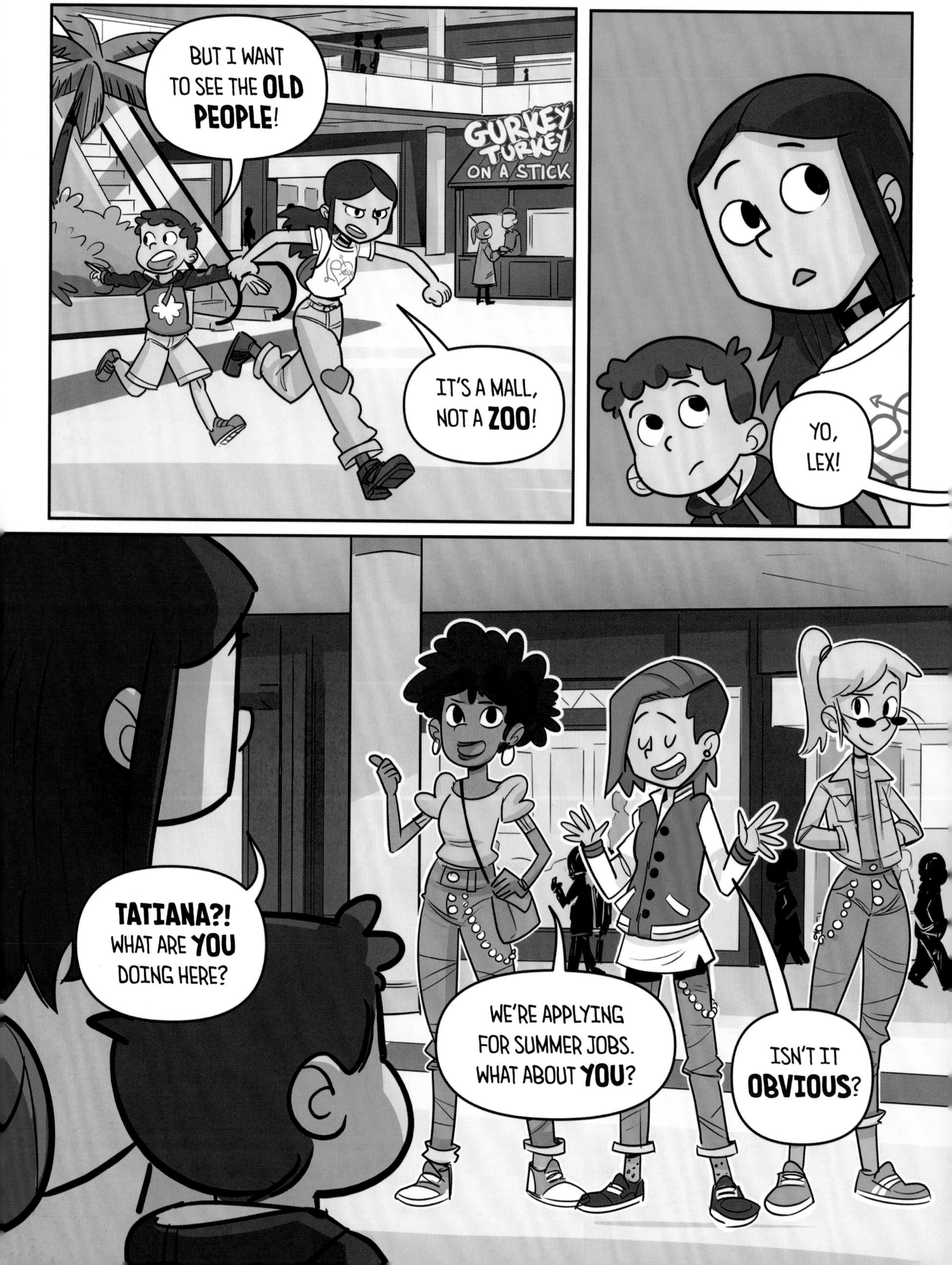
BUT I WANT TO SEE THE **OLD PEOPLE**!
GURKEY TURKEY ON A STICK
IT'S A MALL, NOT A **ZOO**!
YO, LEX!
TATIANA?! WHAT ARE **YOU** DOING HERE?
WE'RE APPLYING FOR SUMMER JOBS. WHAT ABOUT **YOU**?
ISN'T IT **OBVIOUS**?

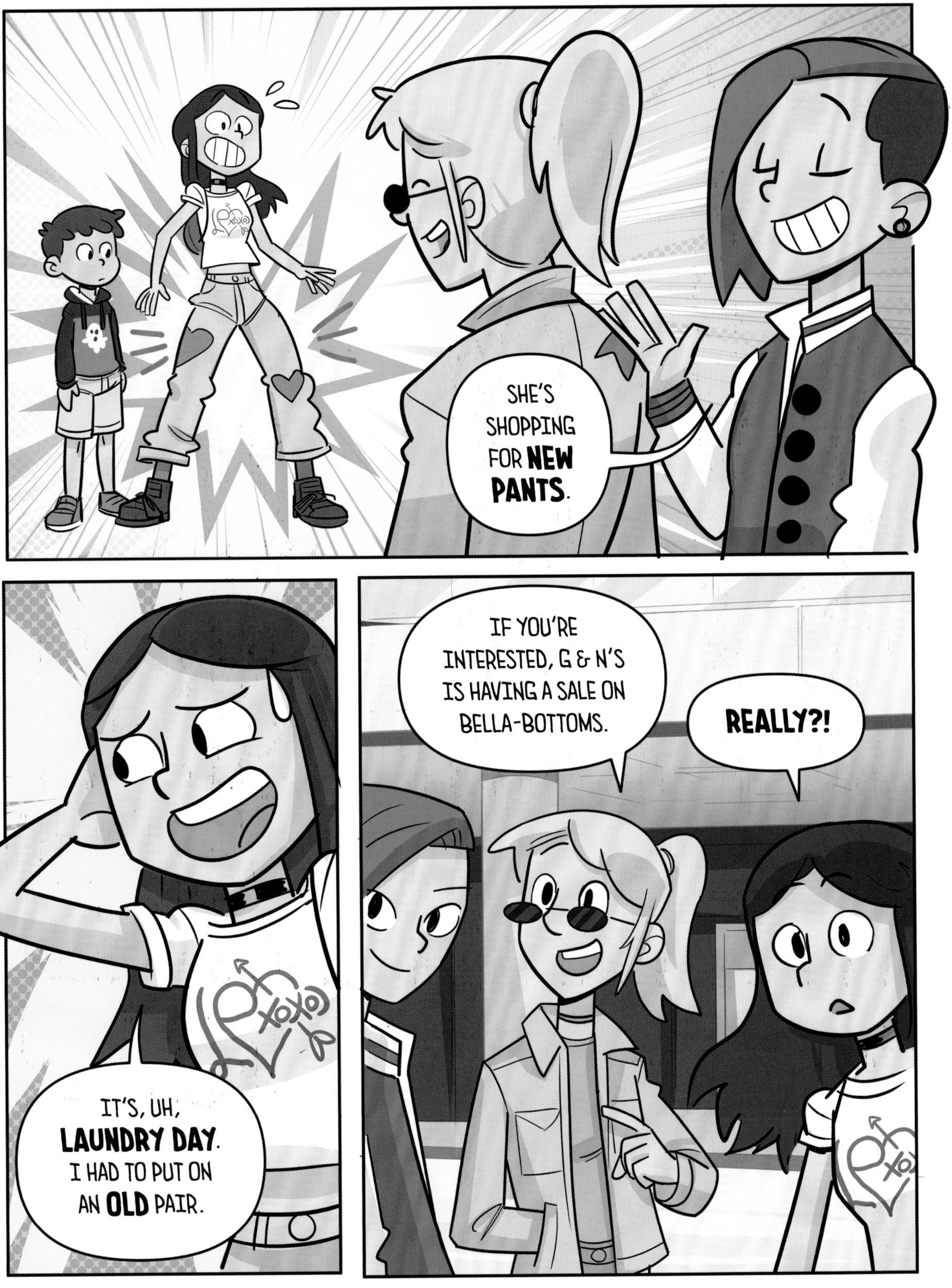
SHE'S SHOPPING FOR NEW PANTS.
IT'S, UH, LAUNDRY DAY. I HAD TO PUT ON AN OLD PAIR.
IF YOU'RE INTERESTED, G & N'S IS HAVING A SALE ON BELLA-BOTTOMS.
REALLY?!

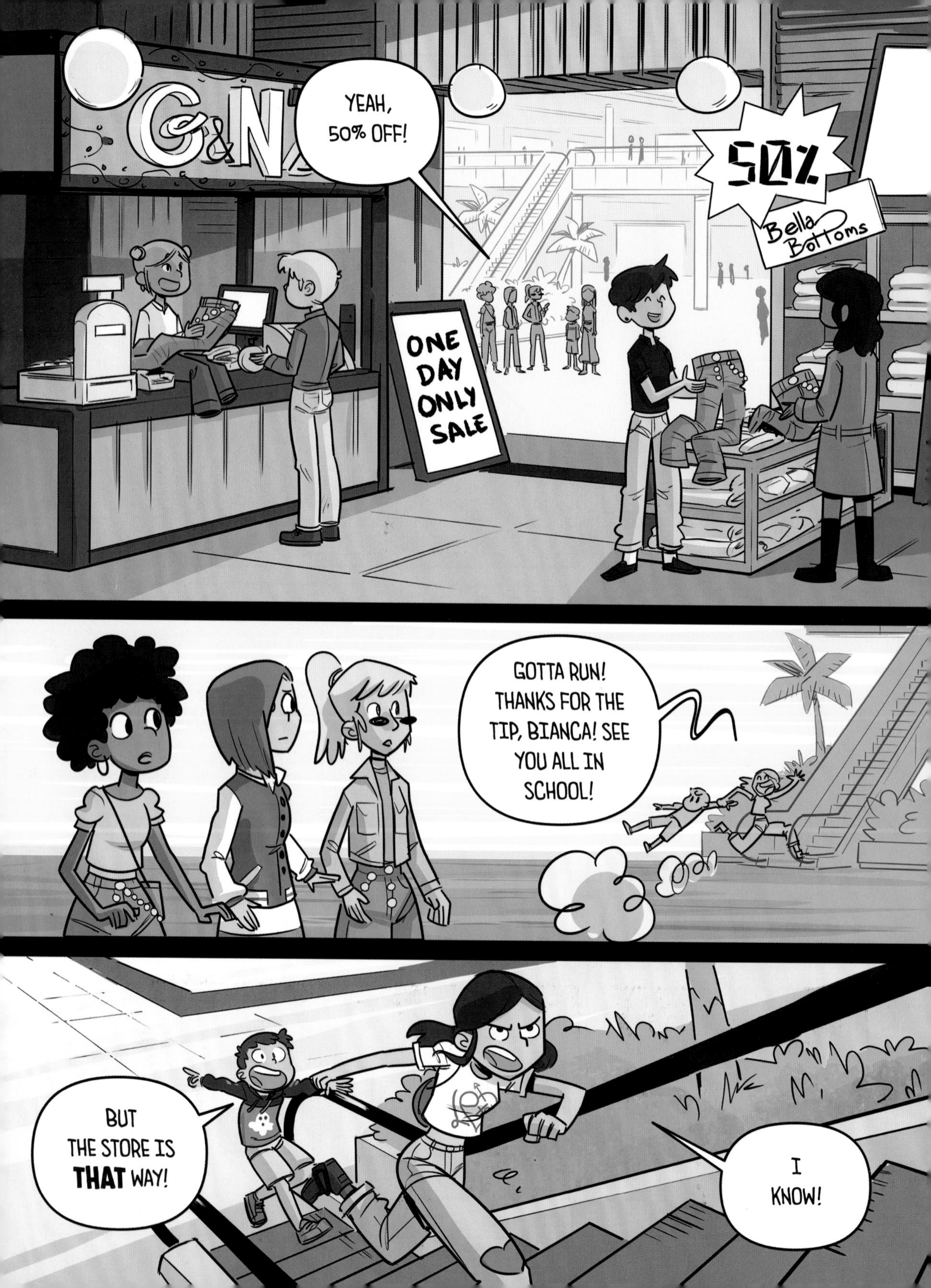
G&N
YEAH, 50% OFF!
50%
Bella Bottoms
ONE DAY ONLY SALE
GOTTA RUN! THANKS FOR THE TIP, BIANCA! SEE YOU ALL IN SCHOOL!
BUT THE STORE IS **THAT** WAY!
I KNOW!

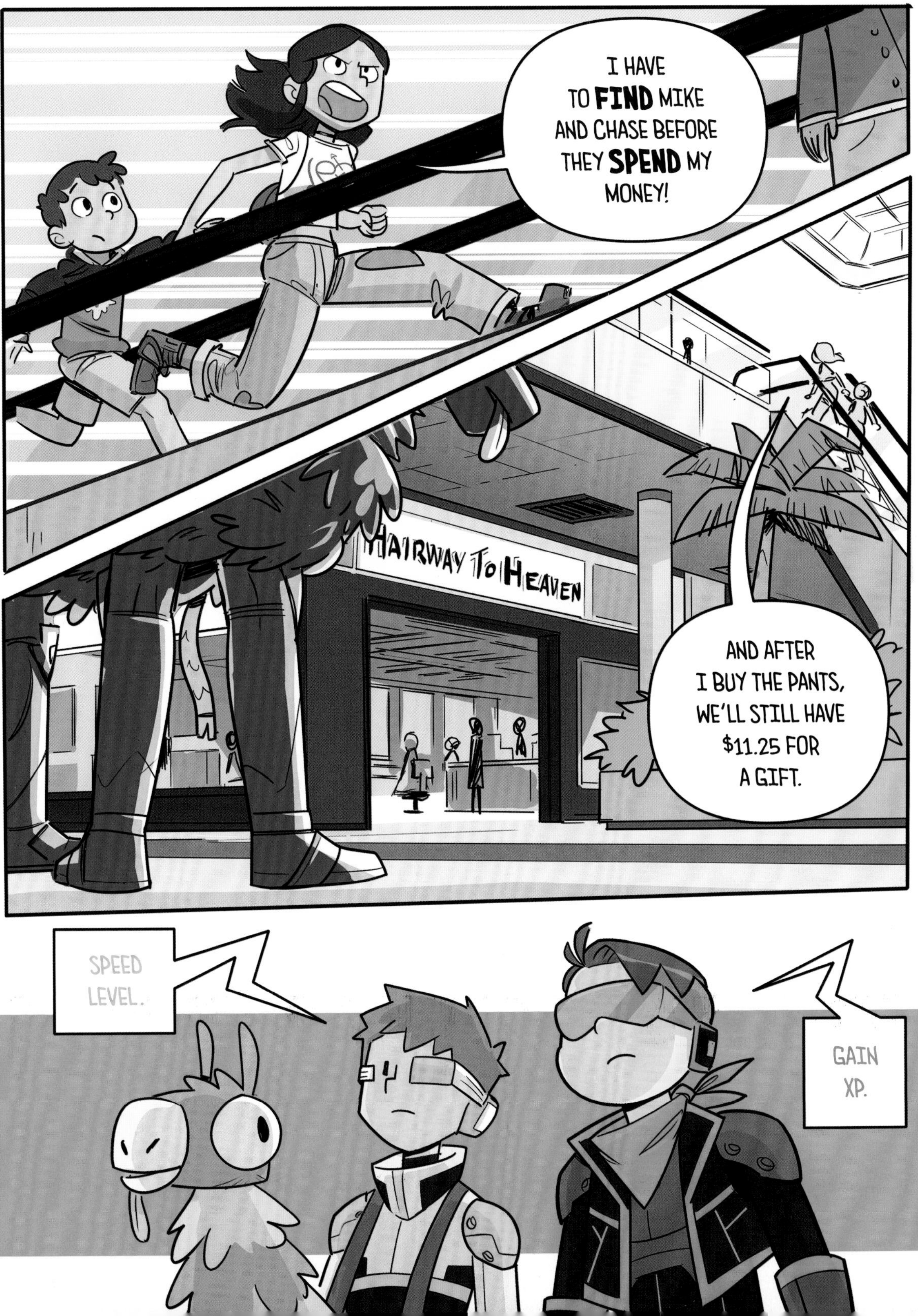
I HAVE TO FIND MIKE AND CHASE BEFORE THEY SPEND MY MONEY!
HAIRWAY TO HEAVEN
AND AFTER I BUY THE PANTS, WE'LL STILL HAVE $11.25 FOR A GIFT.
SPEED LEVEL.
GAIN XP.

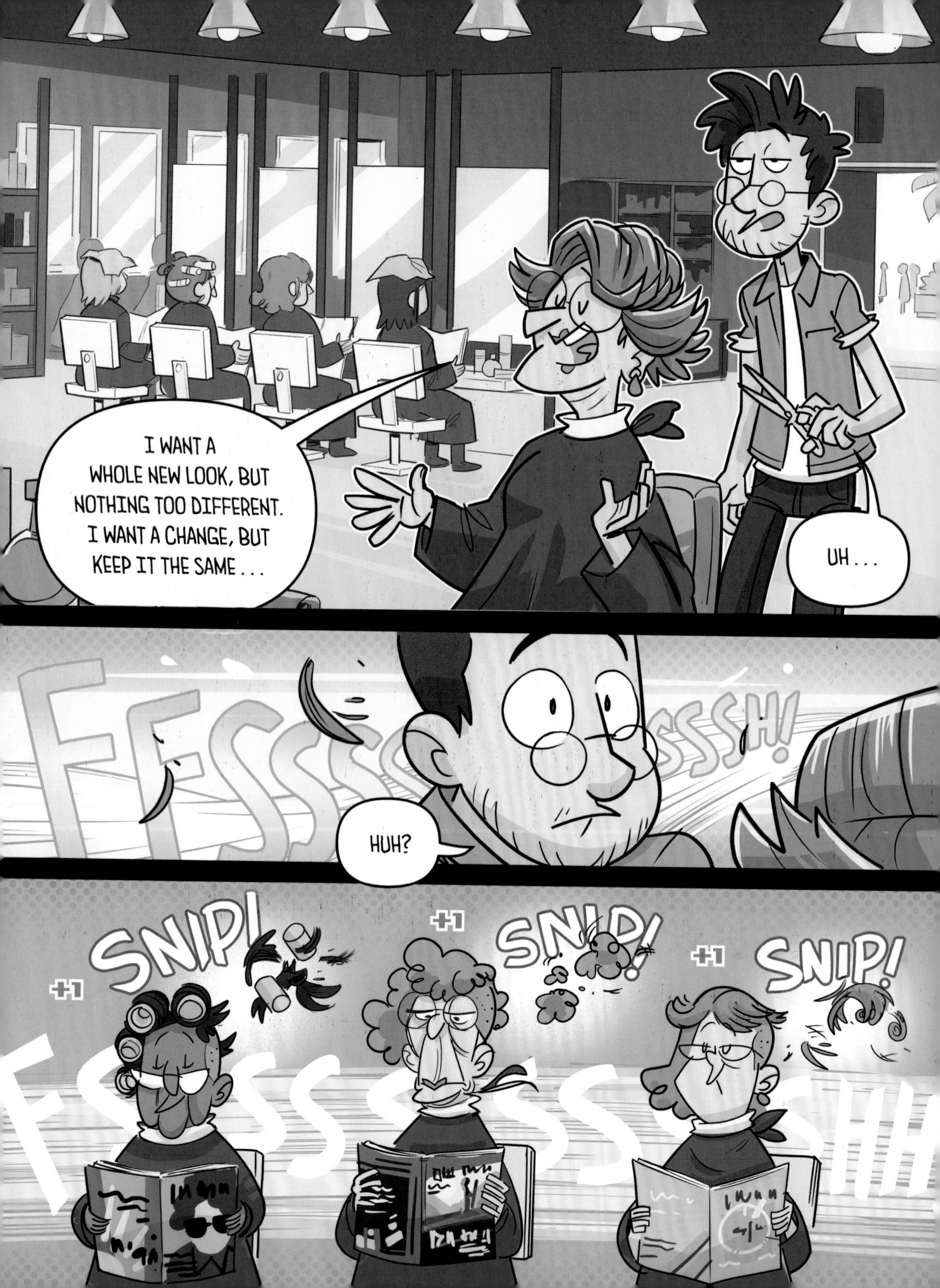
I WANT A WHOLE NEW LOOK, BUT NOTHING TOO DIFFERENT. I WANT A CHANGE, BUT KEEP IT THE SAME . . .
UH . . .
FFSSSSSSSH!
HUH?
SNIP!
+1
SNIP!
+1
SNIP!
+1
FSSSSSSSHH

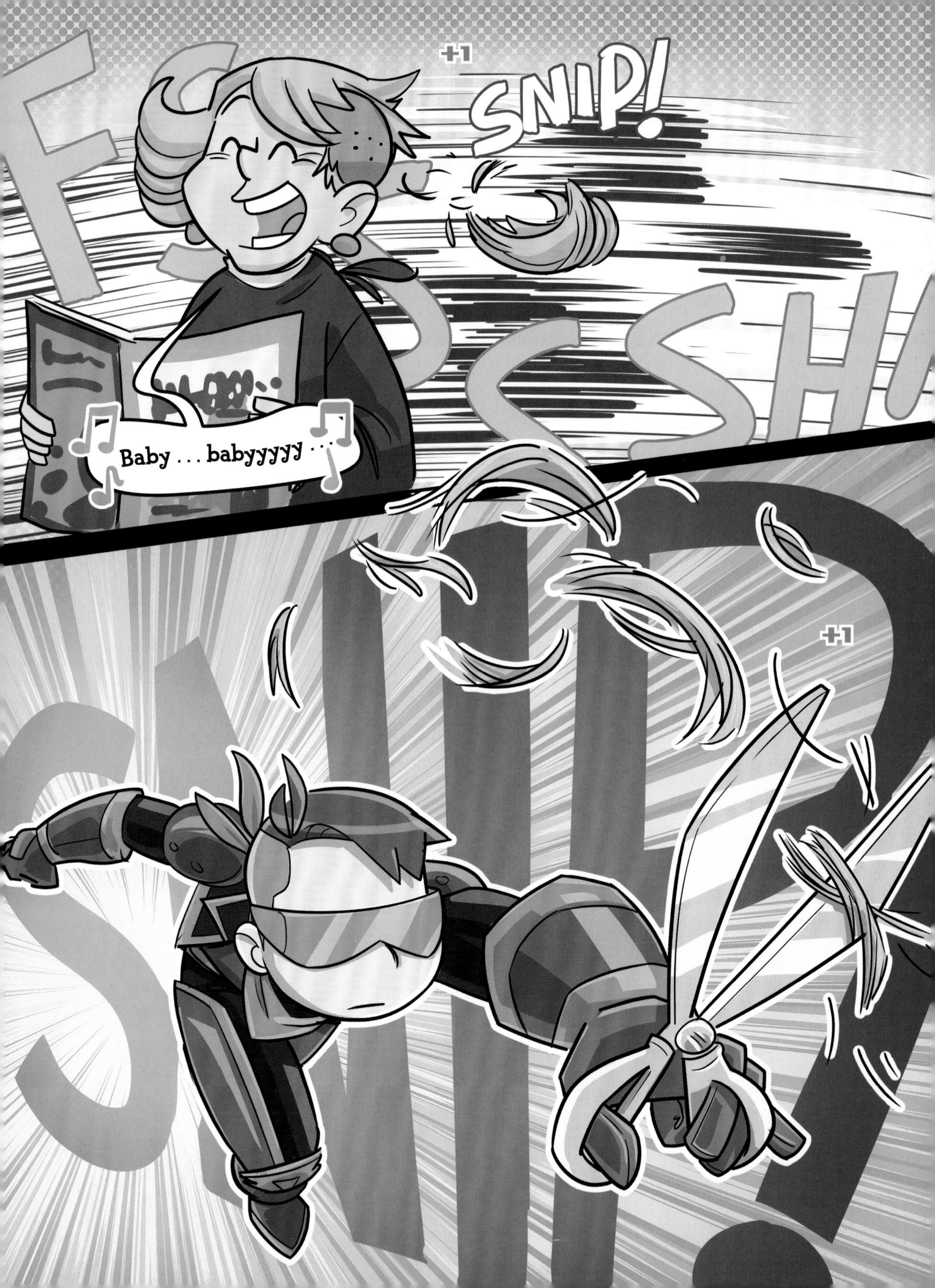
+1
SNIP!
Baby . . . babyyyyy . . .
+1

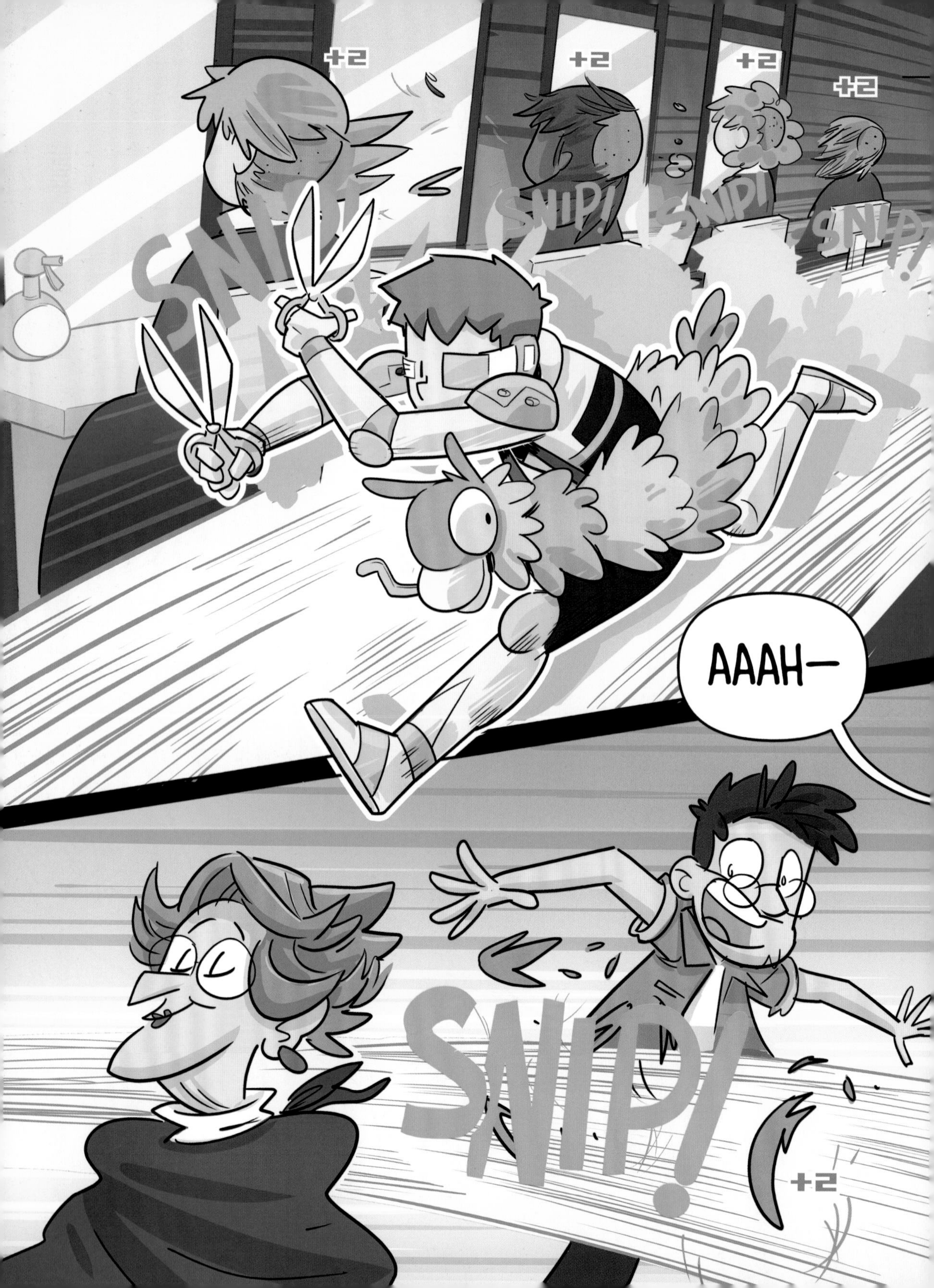
+2
+2
+2
+2
SNIP!
SNIP!
SNIP!
SNIP!
AAAH—
SNIP!
+2

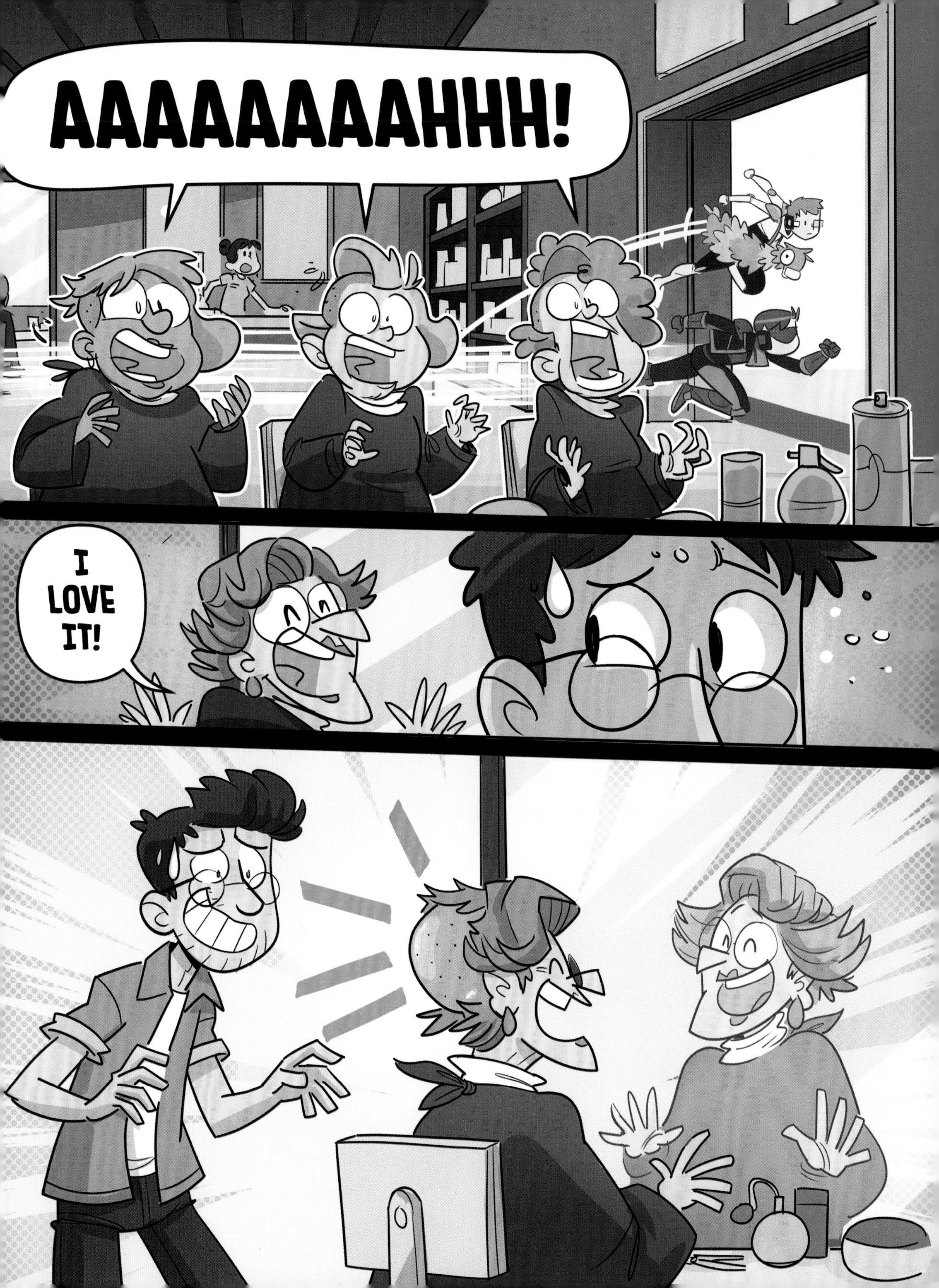
AAAAAAAAAHHH!
I LOVE IT!

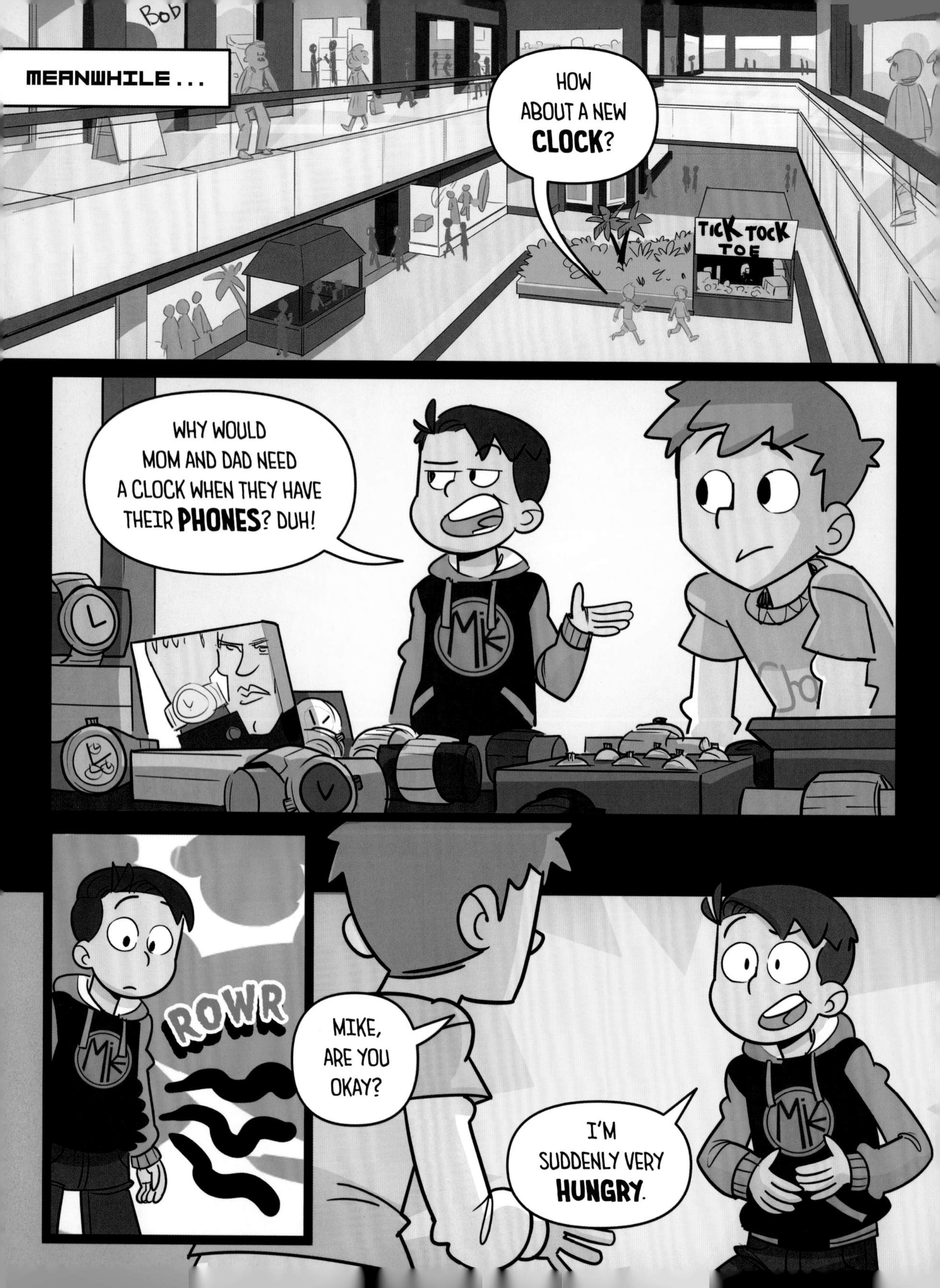
MEANWHILE . . .
Bob
HOW ABOUT A NEW CLOCK?
TICK TOCK TOE
WHY WOULD MOM AND DAD NEED A CLOCK WHEN THEY HAVE THEIR PHONES? DUH!
ROWR
MIKE, ARE YOU OKAY?
I'M SUDDENLY VERY HUNGRY.

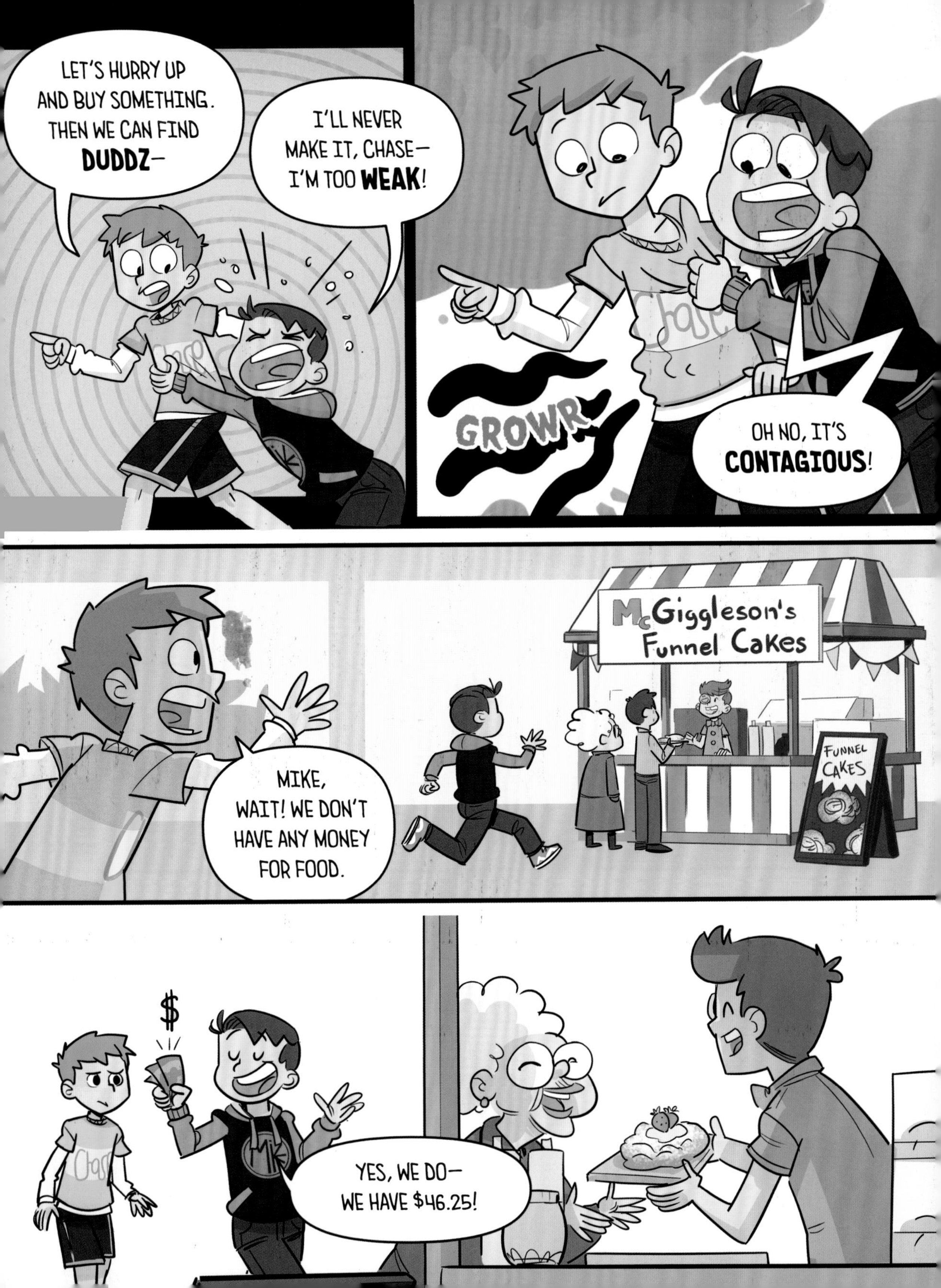
LET'S HURRY UP AND BUY SOMETHING. THEN WE CAN FIND **DUDDZ**—
I'LL NEVER MAKE IT, CHASE—I'M TOO **WEAK**!
GROWR
OH NO, IT'S **CONTAGIOUS**!
McGiggleson's Funnel Cakes
FUNNEL CAKES
MIKE, WAIT! WE DON'T HAVE ANY MONEY FOR FOOD.
$
YES, WE DO—WE HAVE $46.25!

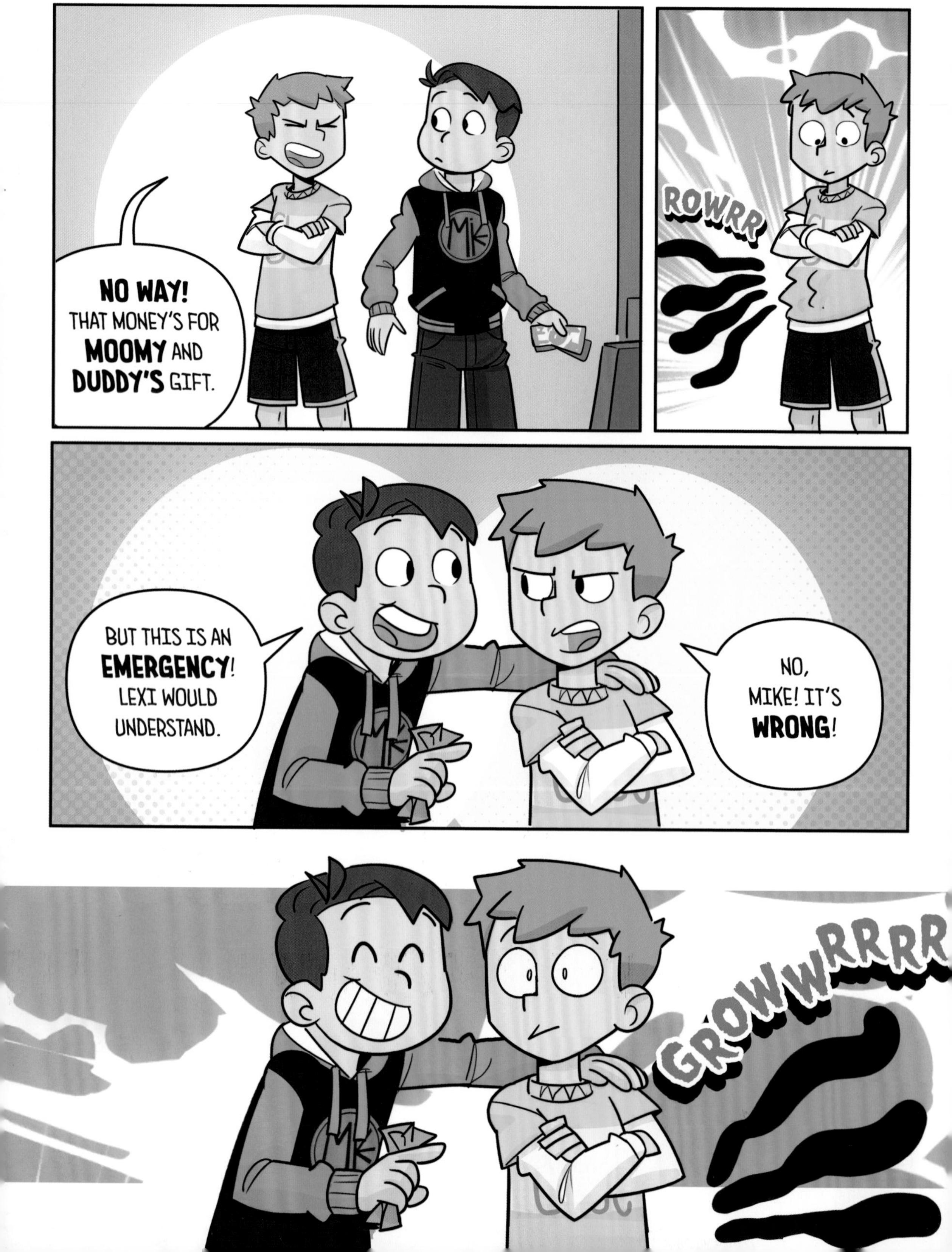
NO WAY! THAT MONEY'S FOR MOOMY AND DUDDY'S GIFT.
ROWRR
BUT THIS IS AN EMERGENCY! LEXI WOULD UNDERSTAND.
NO, MIKE! IT'S WRONG!
GROWWRRRRR

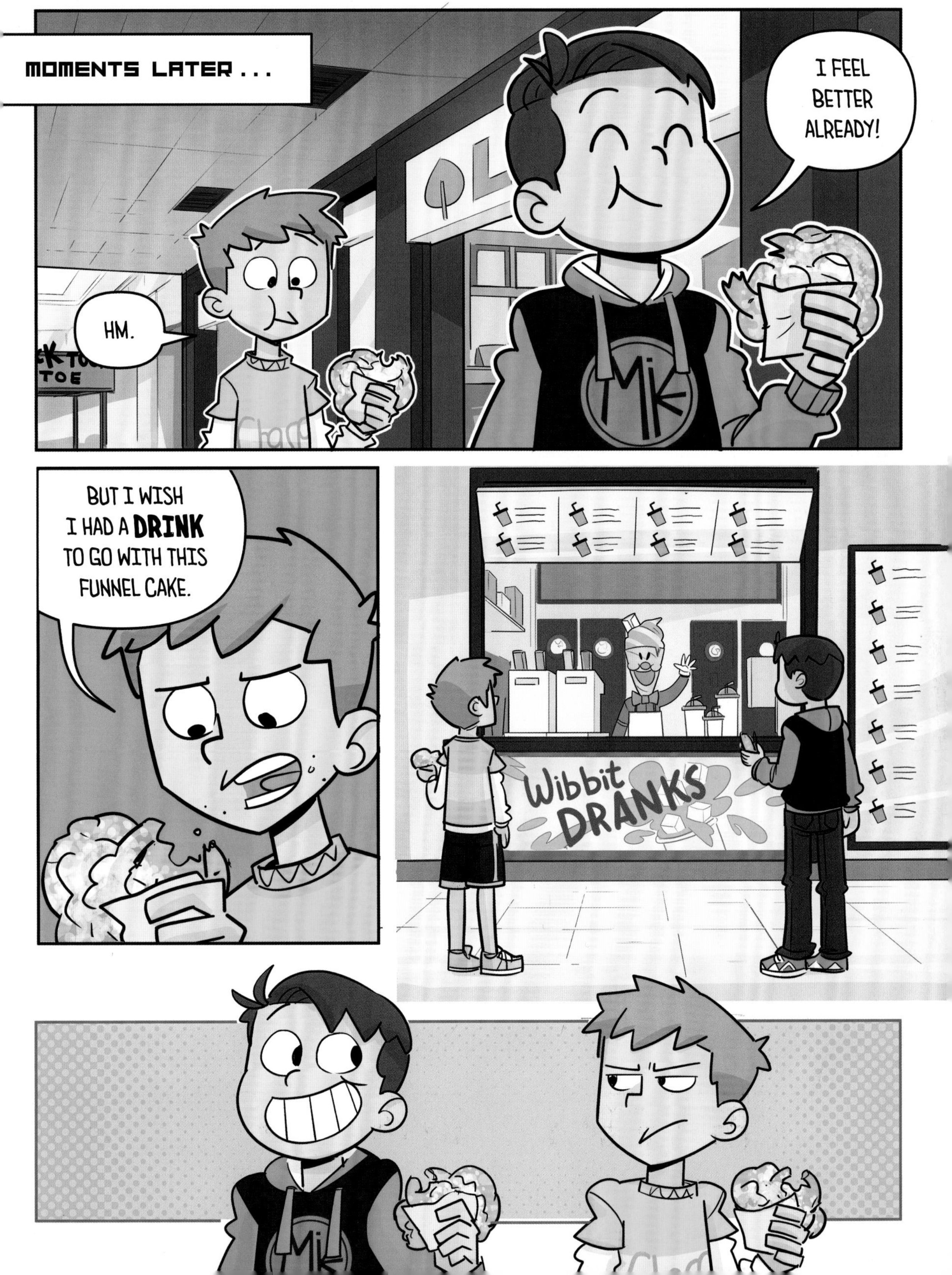
MOMENTS LATER . . .
I FEEL BETTER ALREADY!
HM.
BUT I WISH I HAD A **DRINK** TO GO WITH THIS FUNNEL CAKE.
Wibbit DRANKS

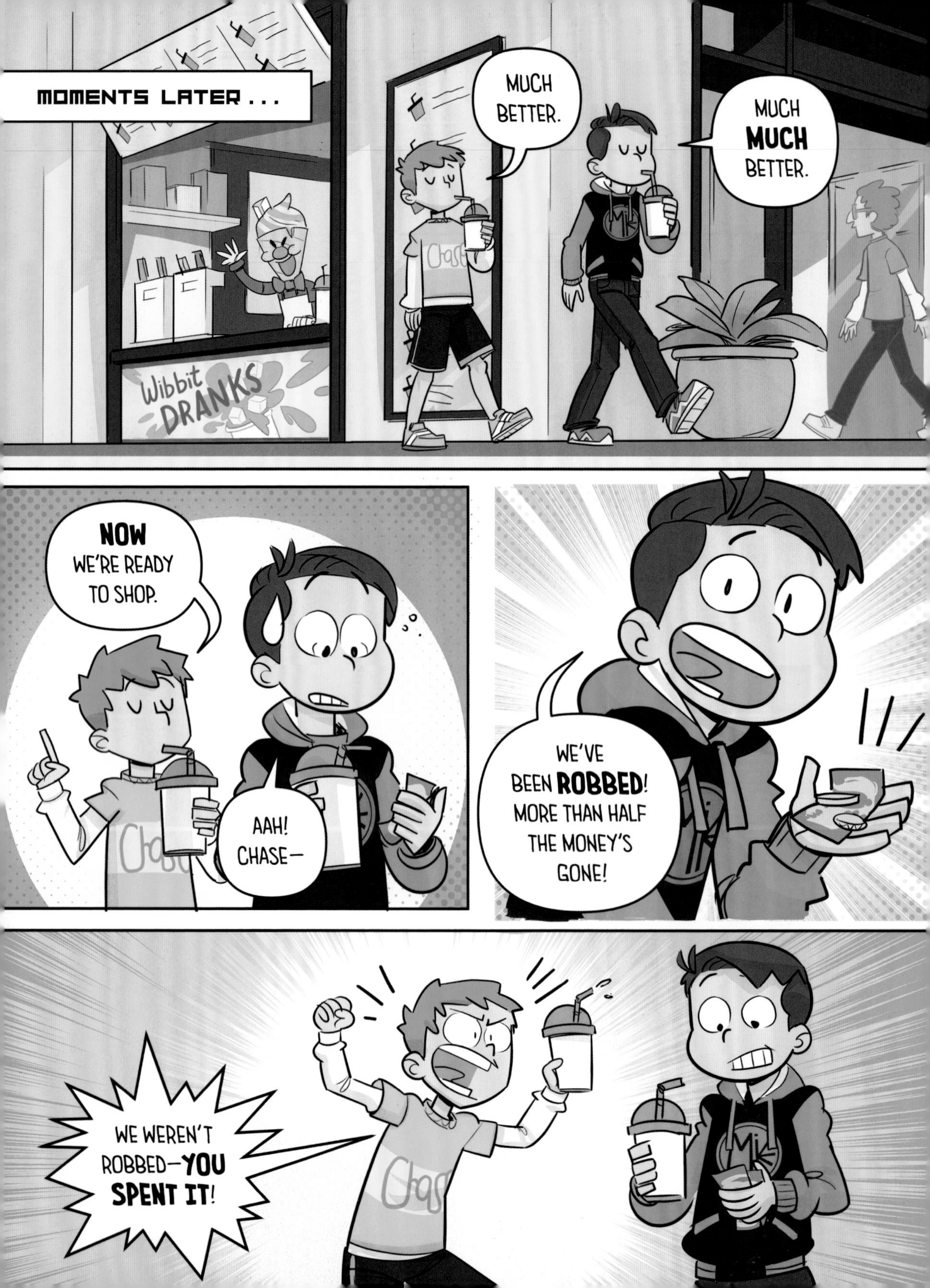
MOMENTS LATER . . .
Wibbit DRANKS
MUCH BETTER.
MUCH **MUCH** BETTER.
NOW WE'RE READY TO SHOP.
AAH! CHASE—
WE'VE BEEN **ROBBED**! MORE THAN HALF THE MONEY'S GONE!
WE WEREN'T ROBBED—**YOU SPENT IT**!

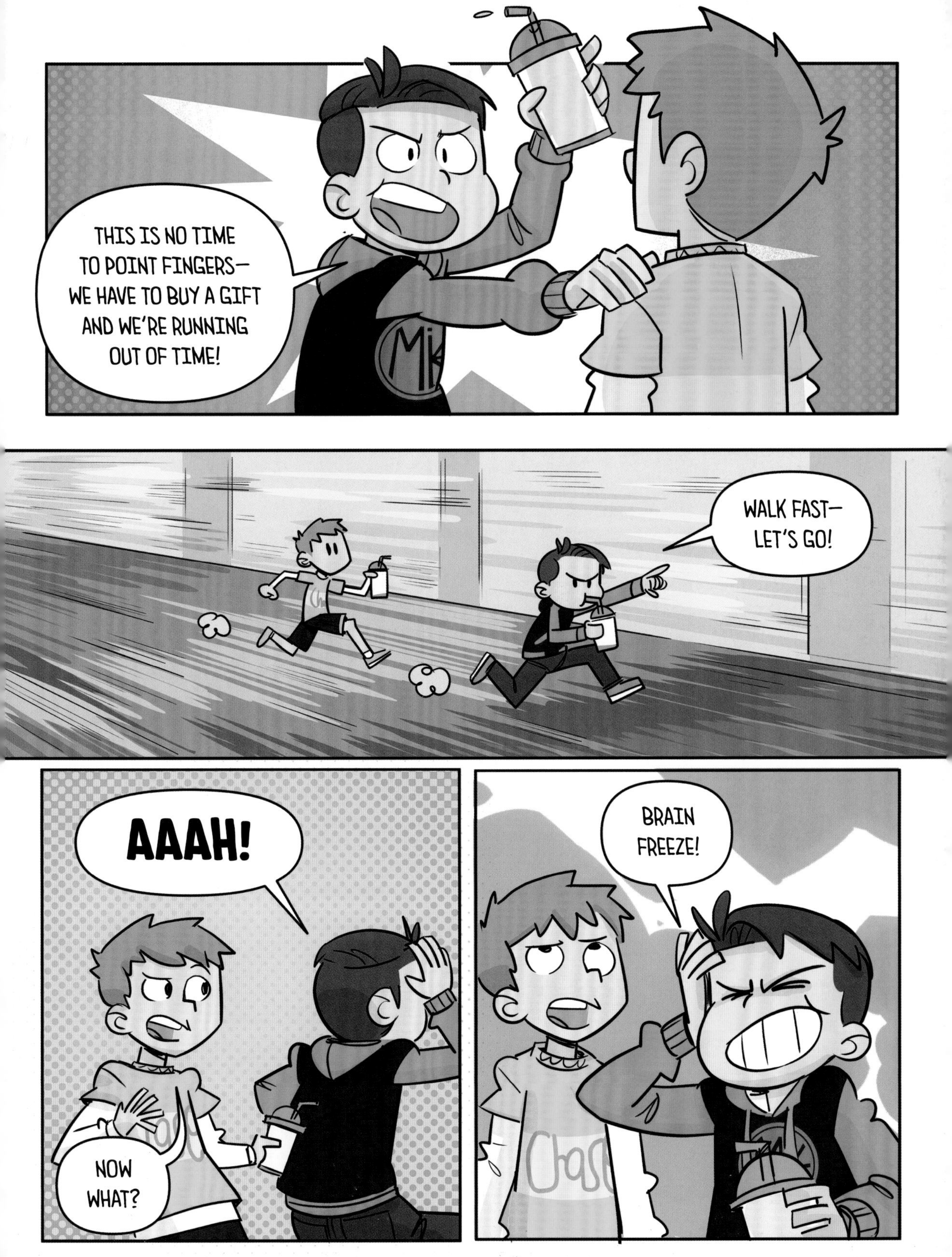
THIS IS NO TIME TO POINT FINGERS— WE HAVE TO BUY A GIFT AND WE'RE RUNNING OUT OF TIME!
WALK FAST— LET'S GO!
AAAH!
NOW WHAT?
BRAIN FREEZE!

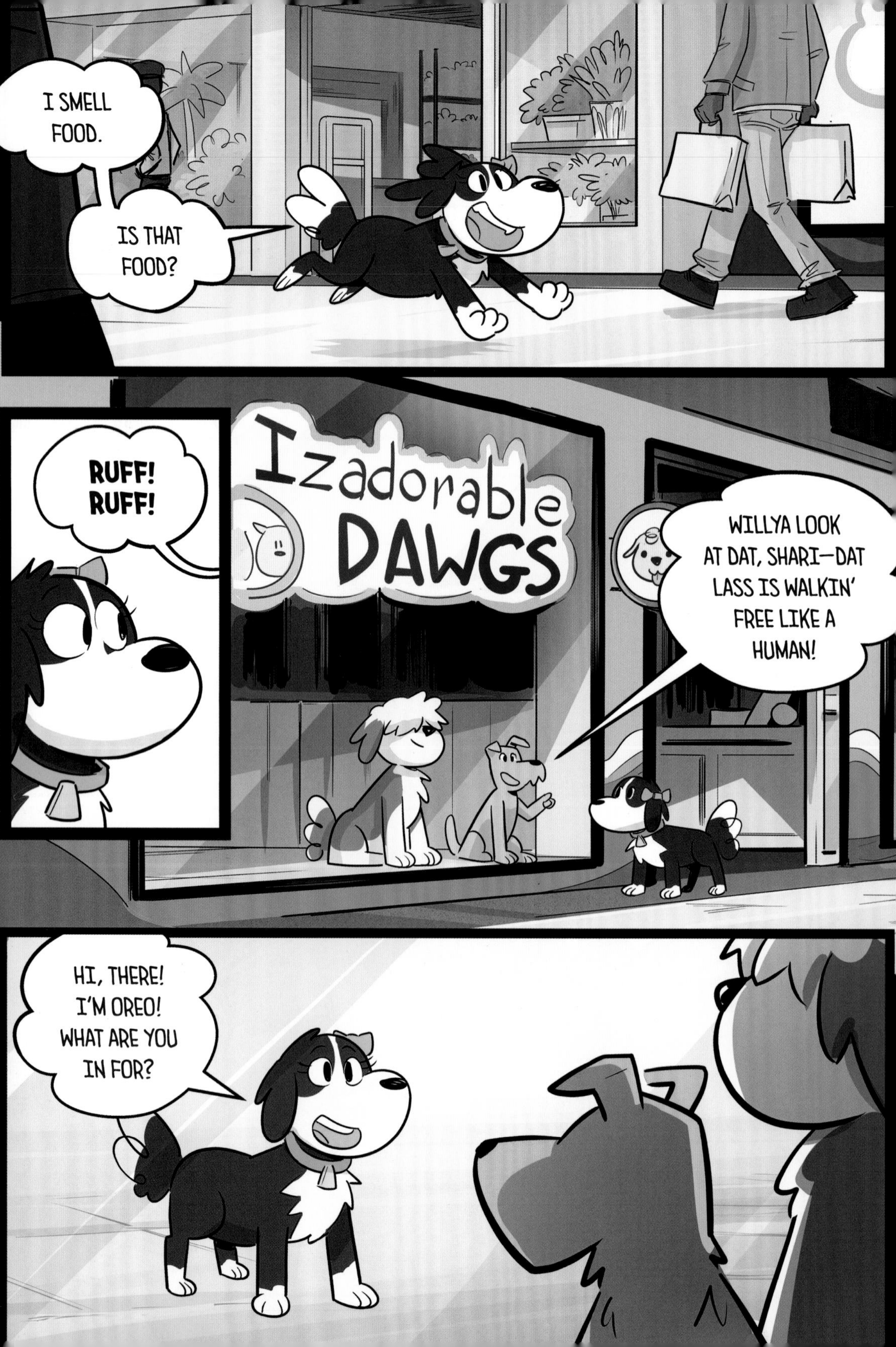

I SMELL FOOD.
IS THAT FOOD?
RUFF! RUFF!
Izadorable DAWGS
WILLYA LOOK AT DAT, SHARI—DAT LASS IS WALKIN' FREE LIKE A HUMAN!
HI, THERE! I'M OREO! WHAT ARE YOU IN FOR?

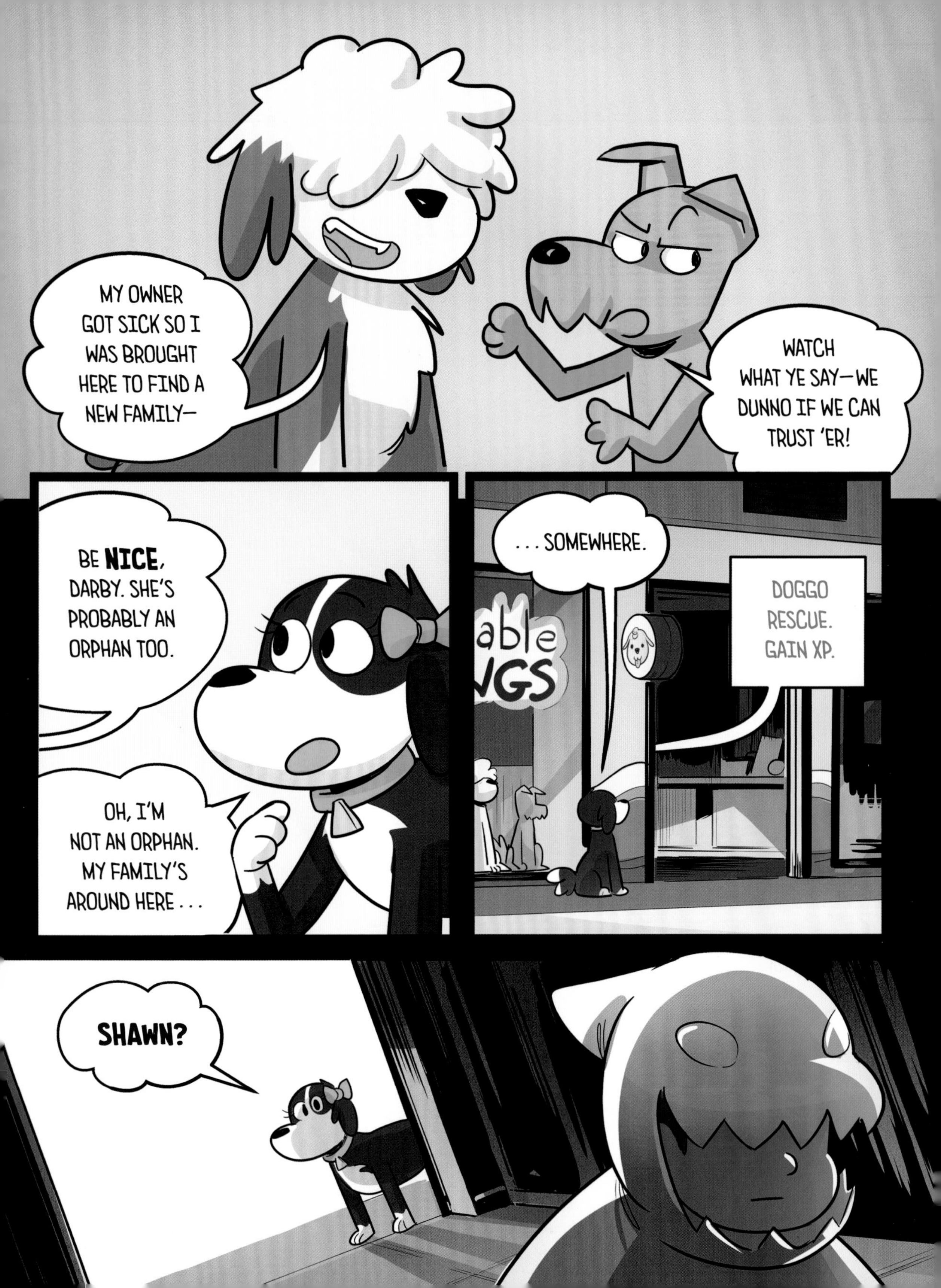

MY OWNER GOT SICK SO I WAS BROUGHT HERE TO FIND A NEW FAMILY—
WATCH WHAT YE SAY—WE DUNNO IF WE CAN TRUST 'ER!
BE NICE, DARBY. SHE'S PROBABLY AN ORPHAN TOO.
OH, I'M NOT AN ORPHAN. MY FAMILY'S AROUND HERE . . .
. . . SOMEWHERE.
DOGGO RESCUE. GAIN XP.
SHAWN?

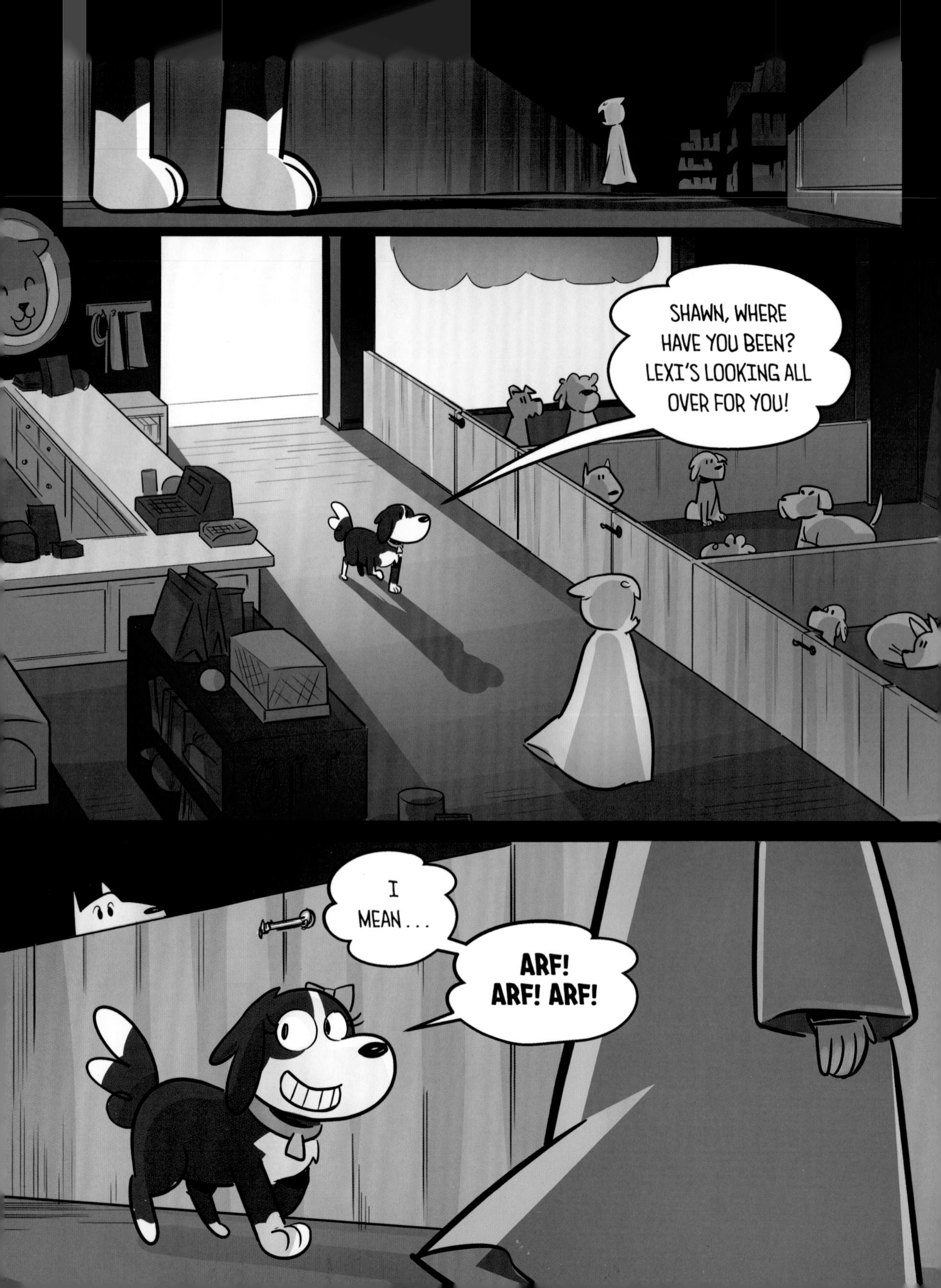
SHAWN, WHERE HAVE YOU BEEN? LEXI'S LOOKING ALL OVER FOR YOU!
I MEAN . . .
ARF! ARF! ARF!

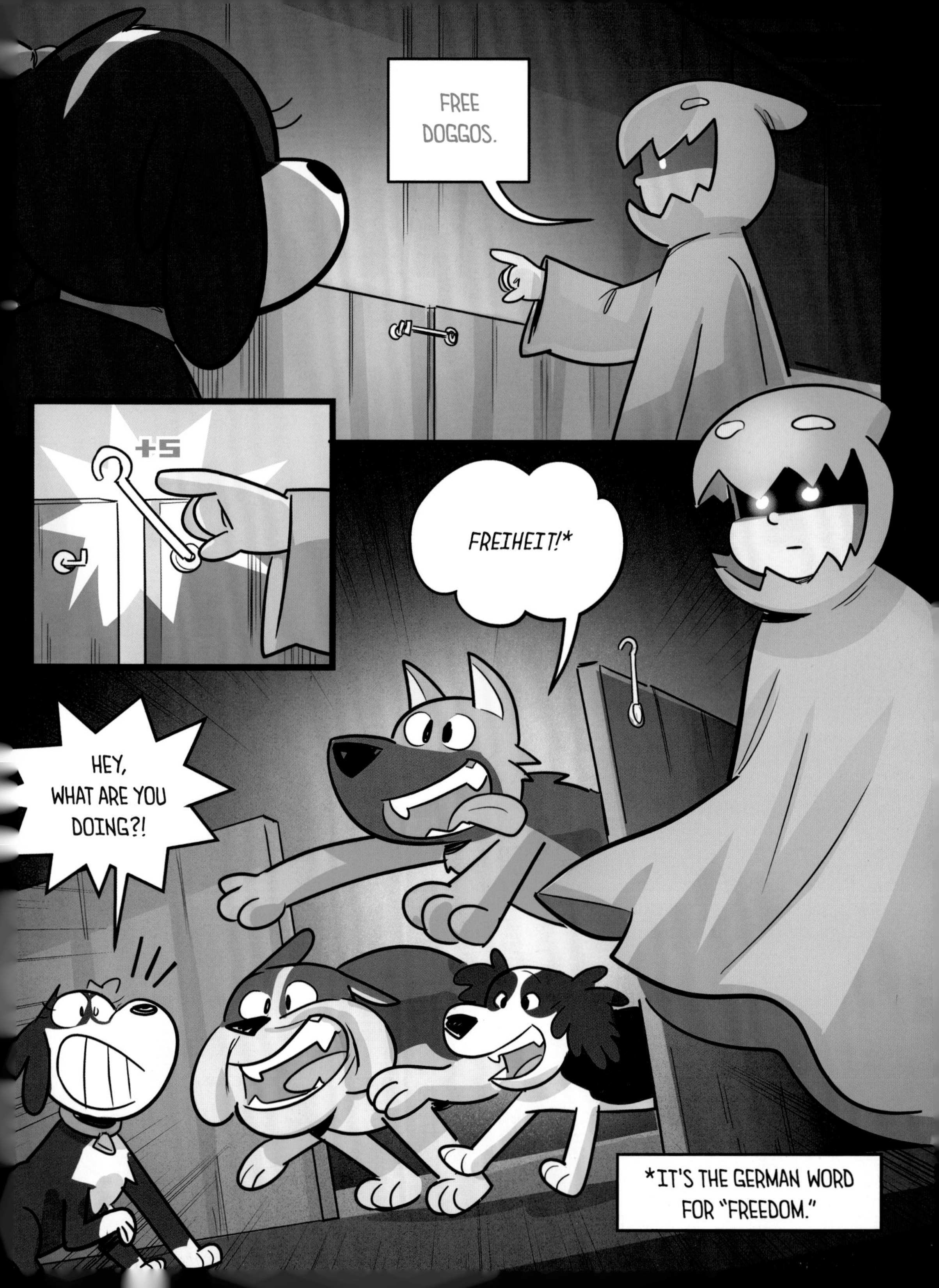
FREE DOGGOS.
+5
FREIHEIT!*
HEY, WHAT ARE YOU DOING?!
*IT'S THE GERMAN WORD FOR "FREEDOM."

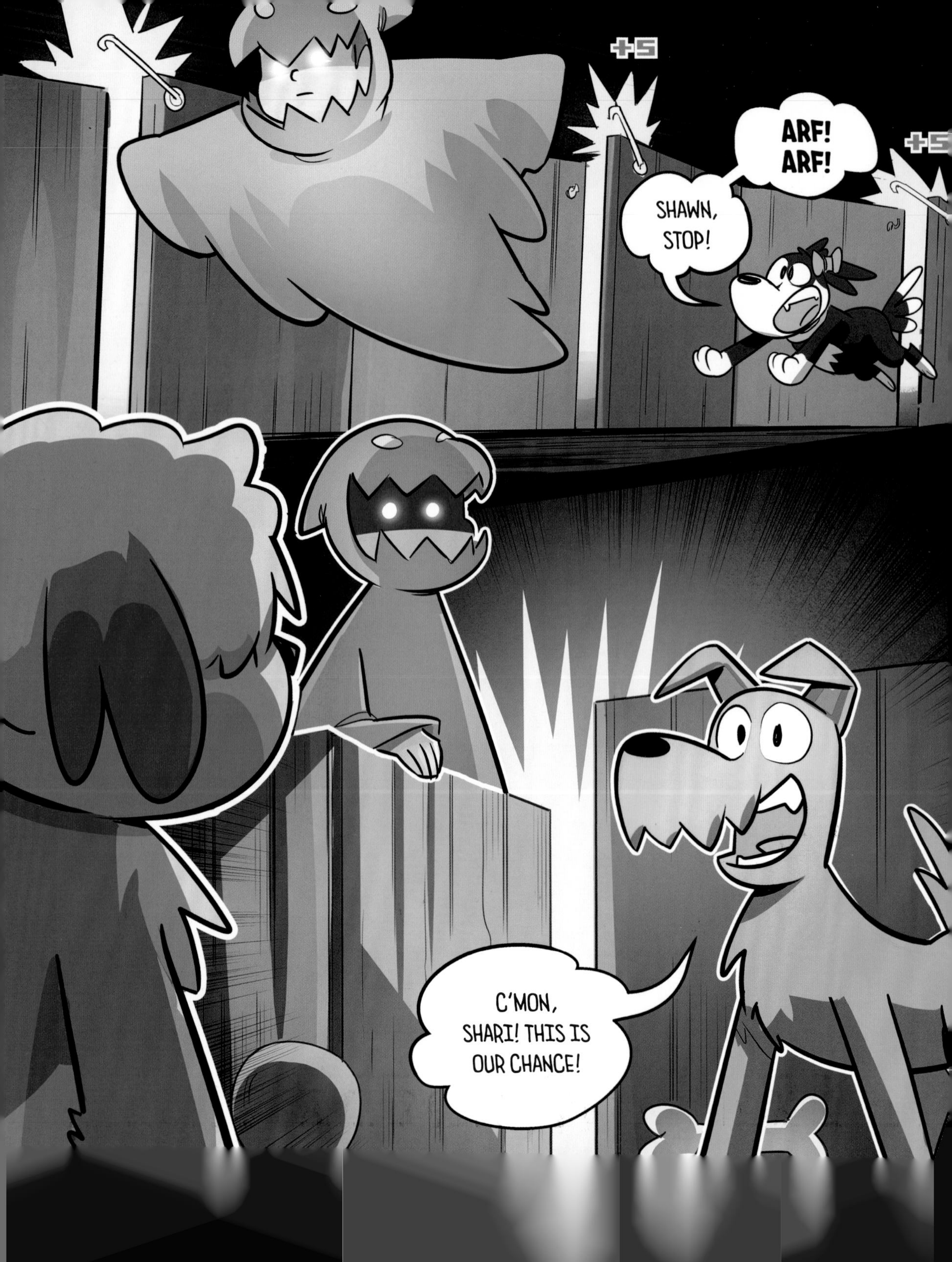
+5
+5
ARF! ARF!
SHAWN, STOP!
C'MON, SHARI! THIS IS OUR CHANCE!

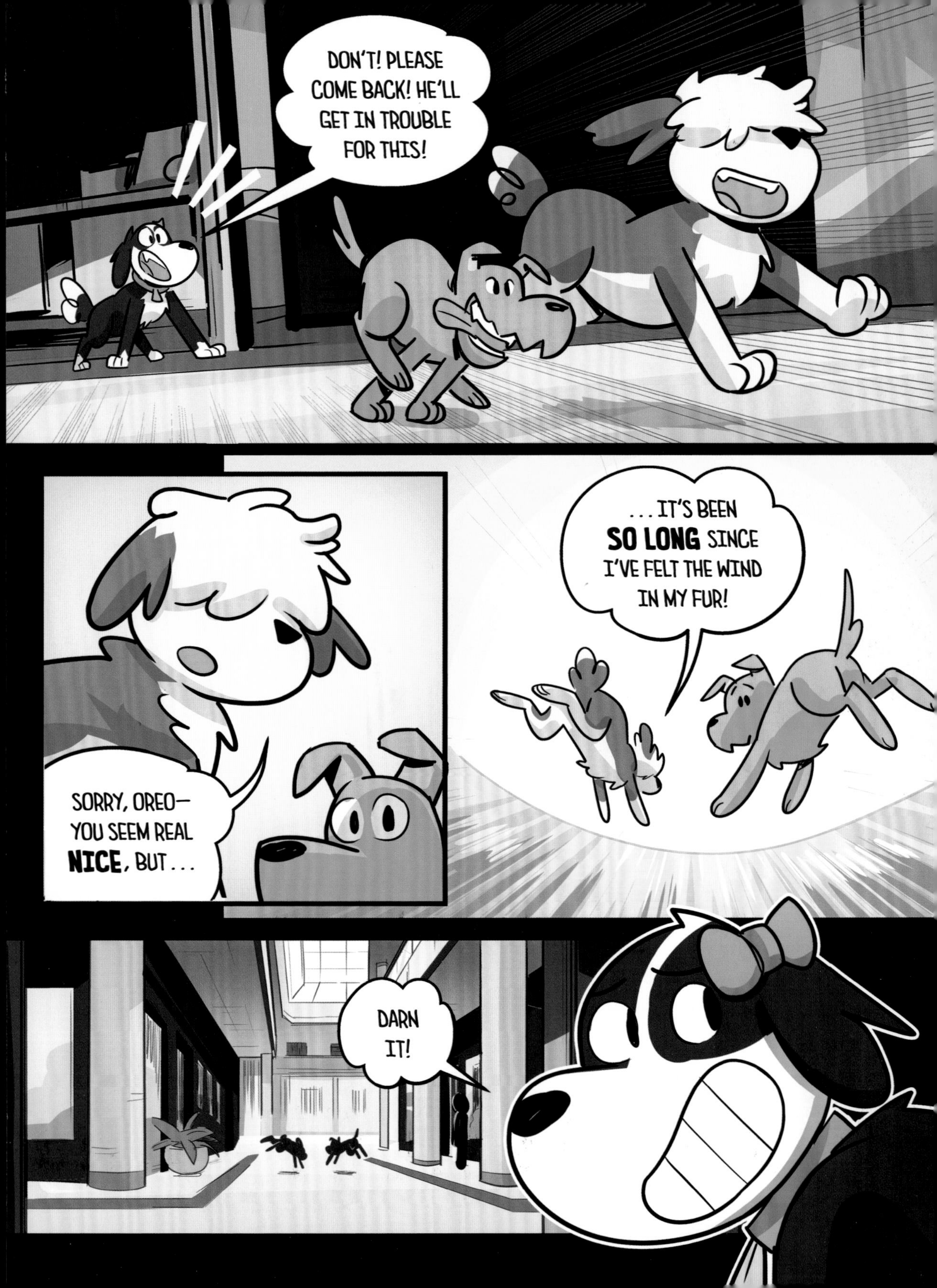
DON'T! PLEASE COME BACK! HE'LL GET IN TROUBLE FOR THIS!
SORRY, OREO— YOU SEEM REAL NICE, BUT . . .
. . . IT'S BEEN SO LONG SINCE I'VE FELT THE WIND IN MY FUR!
DARN IT!

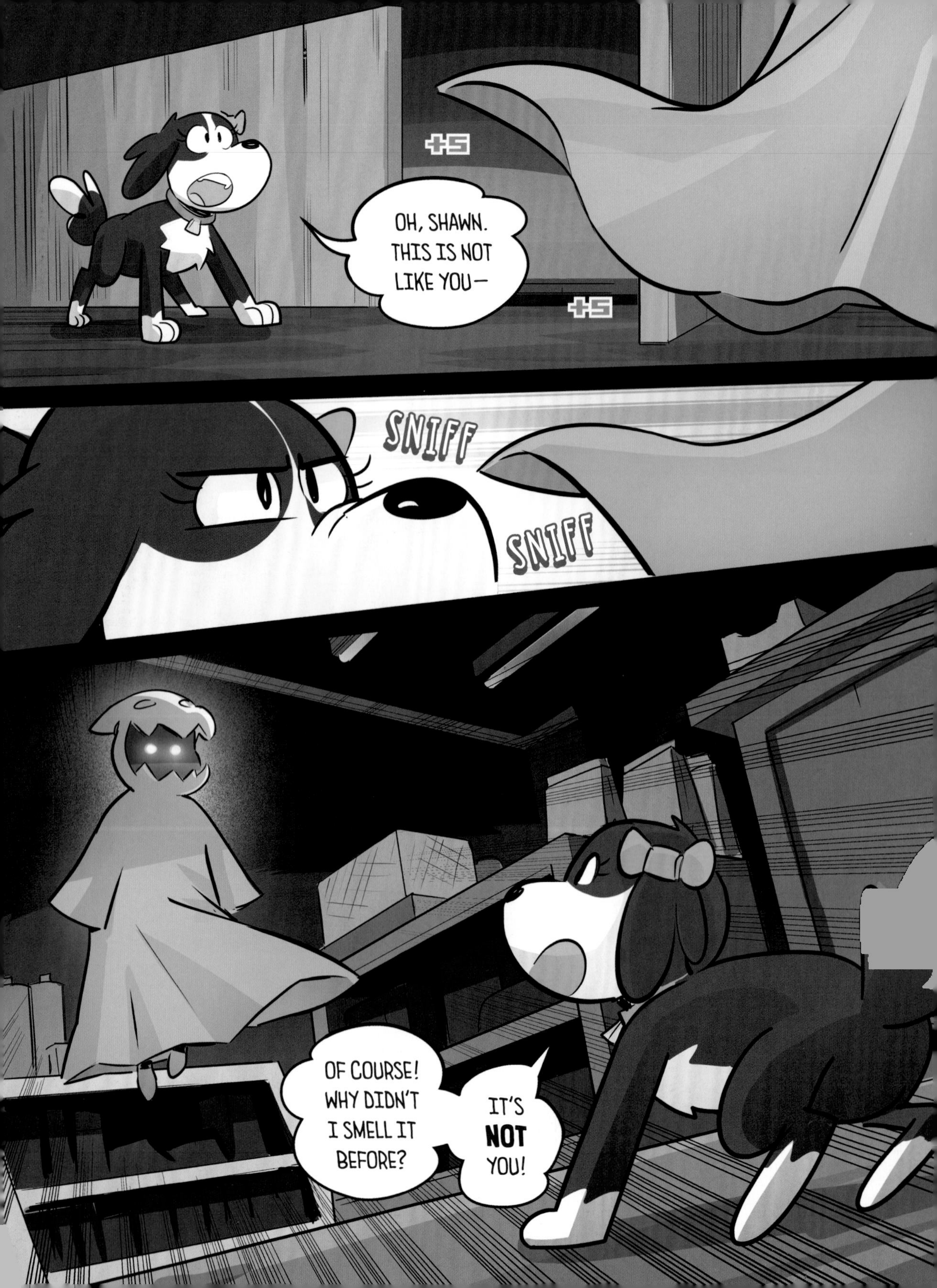
+5
OH, SHAWN. THIS IS NOT LIKE YOU—
+5
SNIFF
SNIFF
OF COURSE! WHY DIDN'T I SMELL IT BEFORE?
IT'S **NOT** YOU!

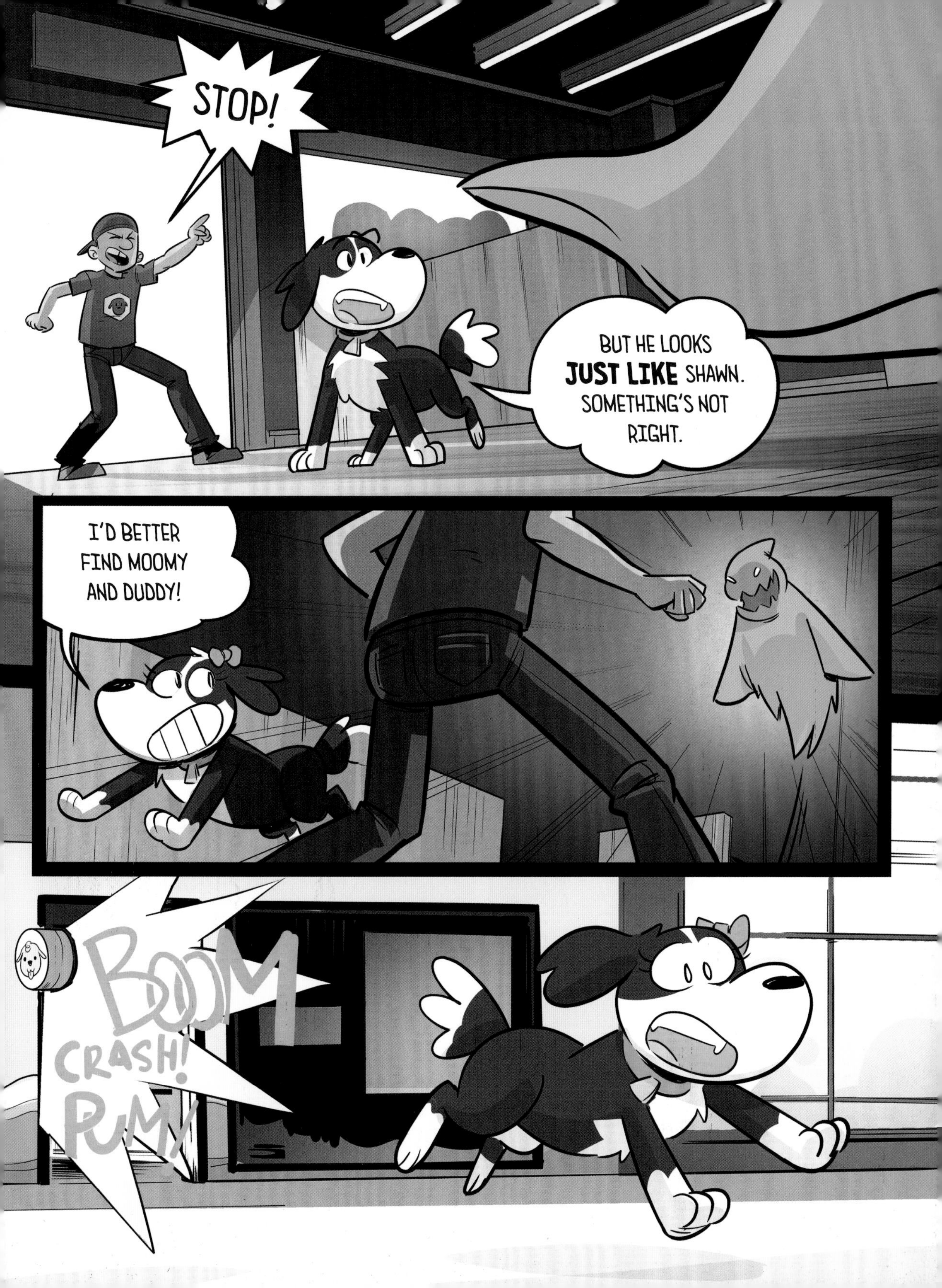
STOP!
BUT HE LOOKS **JUST LIKE** SHAWN. SOMETHING'S NOT RIGHT.
I'D BETTER FIND MOOMY AND DUDDY!
BOOM
CRASH!
PUM!

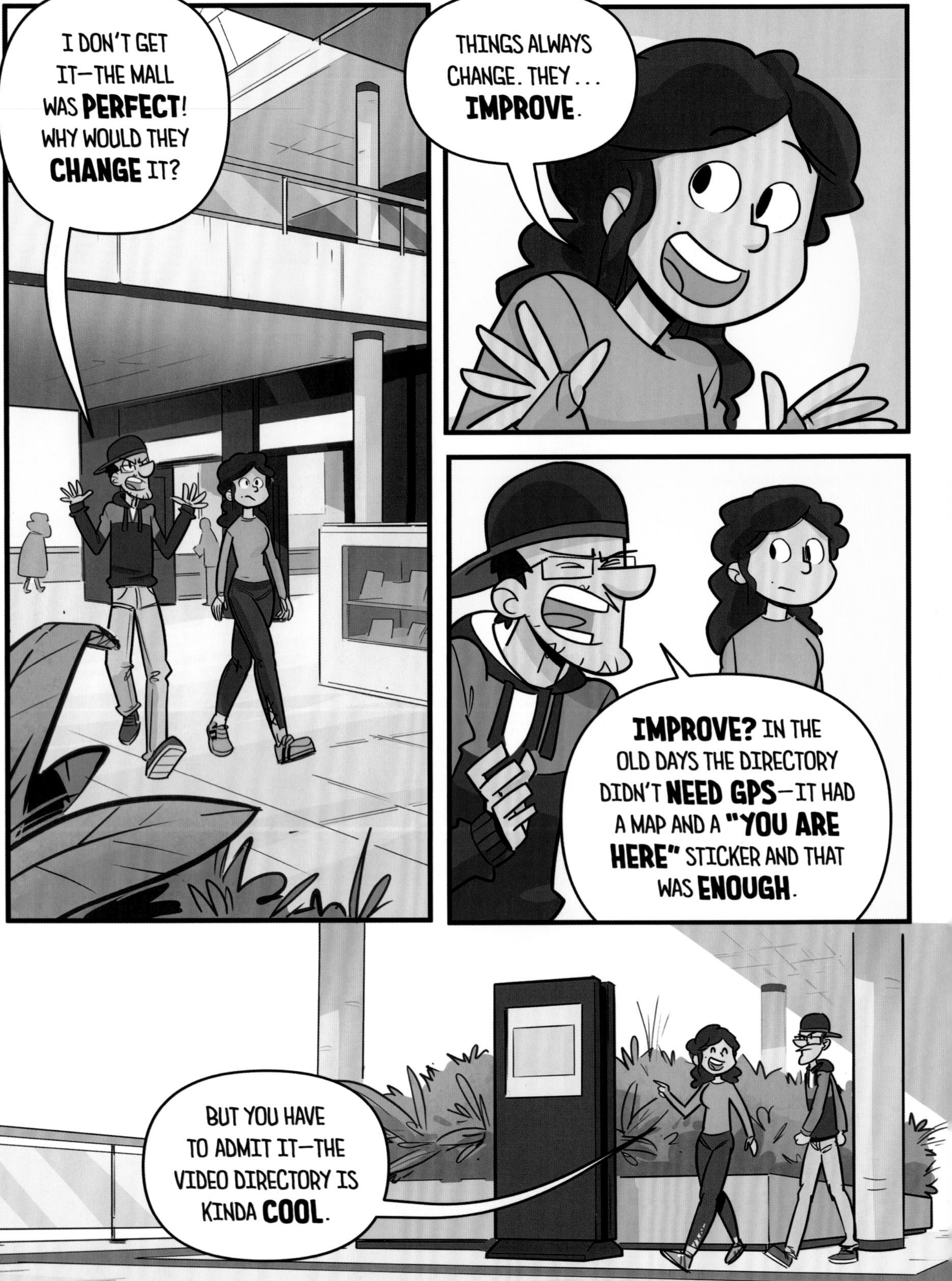
I DON'T GET IT—THE MALL WAS **PERFECT**! WHY WOULD THEY **CHANGE** IT?
THINGS ALWAYS CHANGE. THEY . . . **IMPROVE**.
IMPROVE? IN THE OLD DAYS THE DIRECTORY DIDN'T **NEED GPS**—IT HAD A MAP AND A **"YOU ARE HERE"** STICKER AND THAT WAS **ENOUGH**.
BUT YOU HAVE TO ADMIT IT—THE VIDEO DIRECTORY IS KINDA **COOL**.

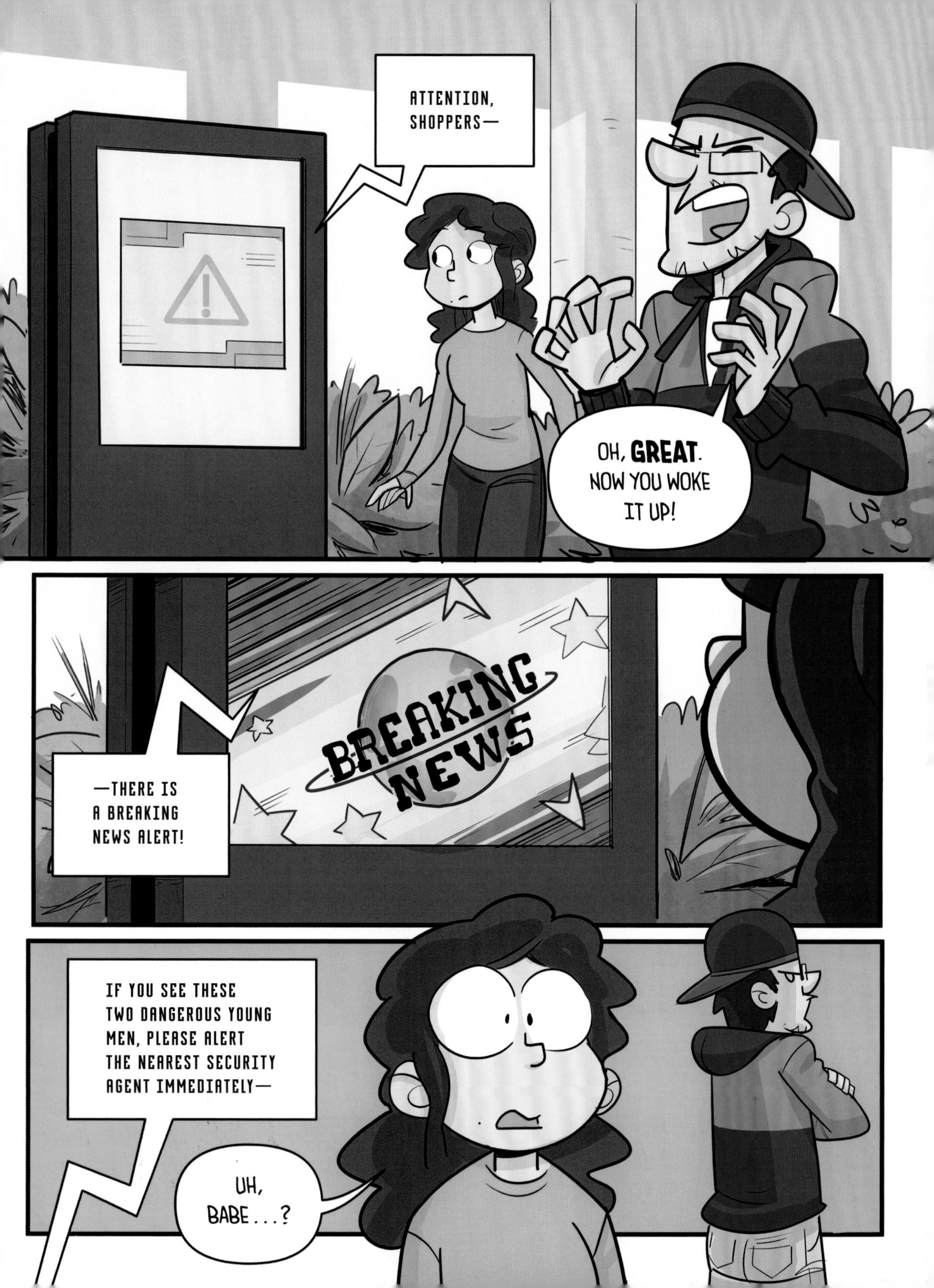
ATTENTION, SHOPPERS—
OH, **GREAT**. NOW YOU WOKE IT UP!
BREAKING NEWS
—THERE IS A BREAKING NEWS ALERT!
IF YOU SEE THESE TWO DANGEROUS YOUNG MEN, PLEASE ALERT THE NEAREST SECURITY AGENT IMMEDIATELY—
UH, BABE . . . ?

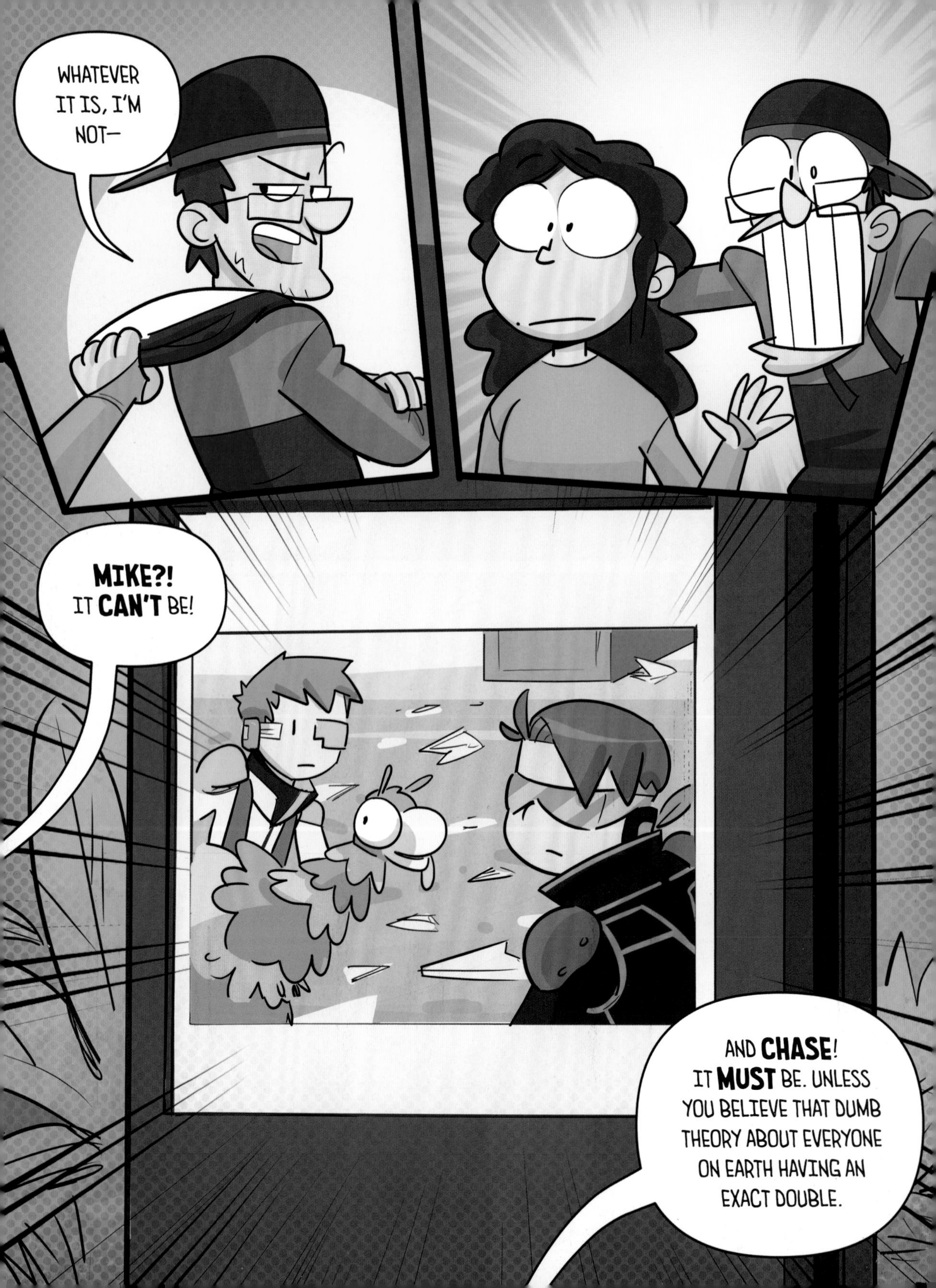
WHATEVER IT IS, I'M NOT—
MIKE?! IT CAN'T BE!
AND CHASE! IT MUST BE. UNLESS YOU BELIEVE THAT DUMB THEORY ABOUT EVERYONE ON EARTH HAVING AN EXACT DOUBLE.

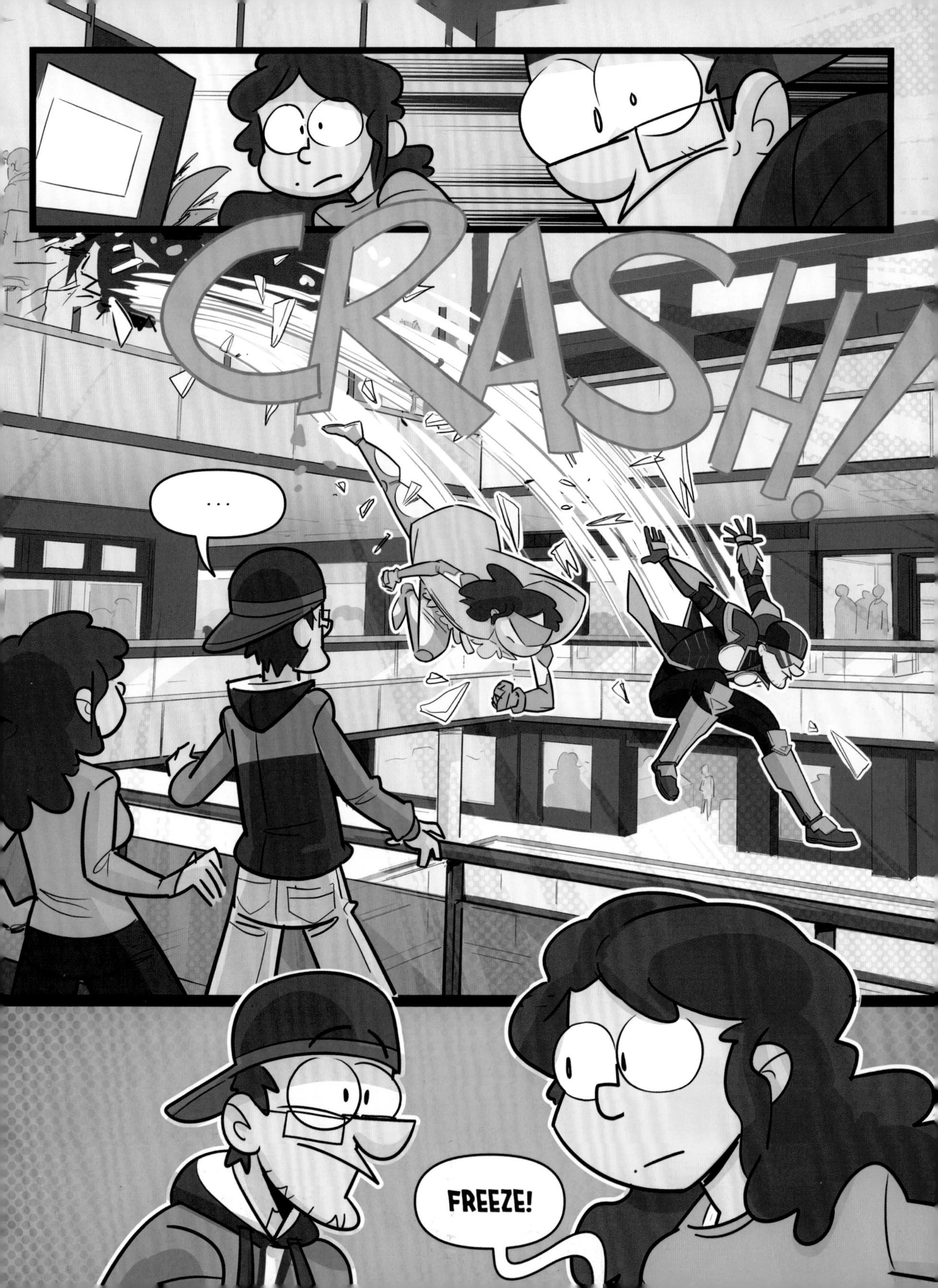
CRASH!
...
FREEZE!

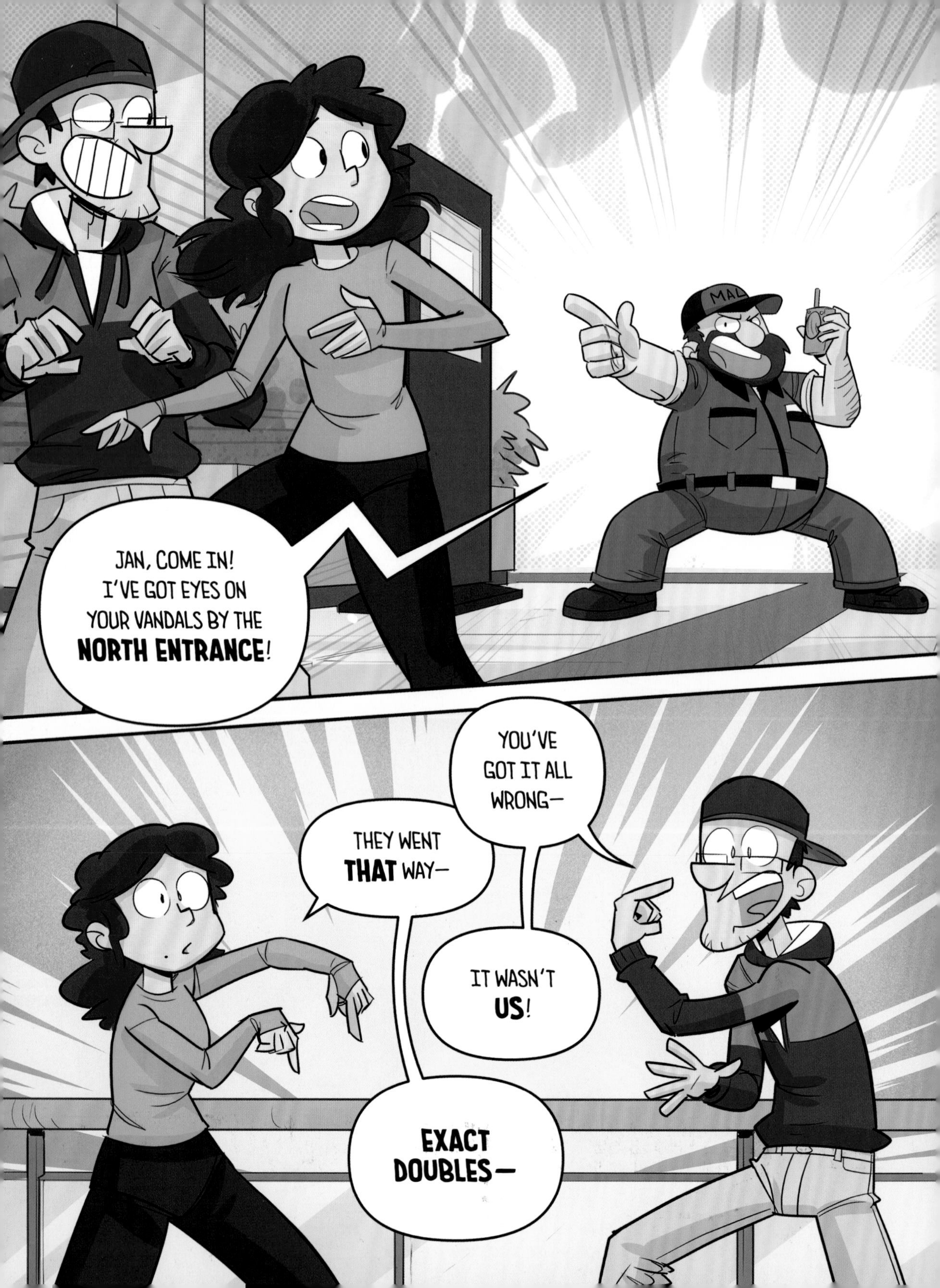

JAN, COME IN! I'VE GOT EYES ON YOUR VANDALS BY THE **NORTH ENTRANCE**!
YOU'VE GOT IT ALL WRONG—
THEY WENT **THAT** WAY—
IT WASN'T **US**!
EXACT DOUBLES—

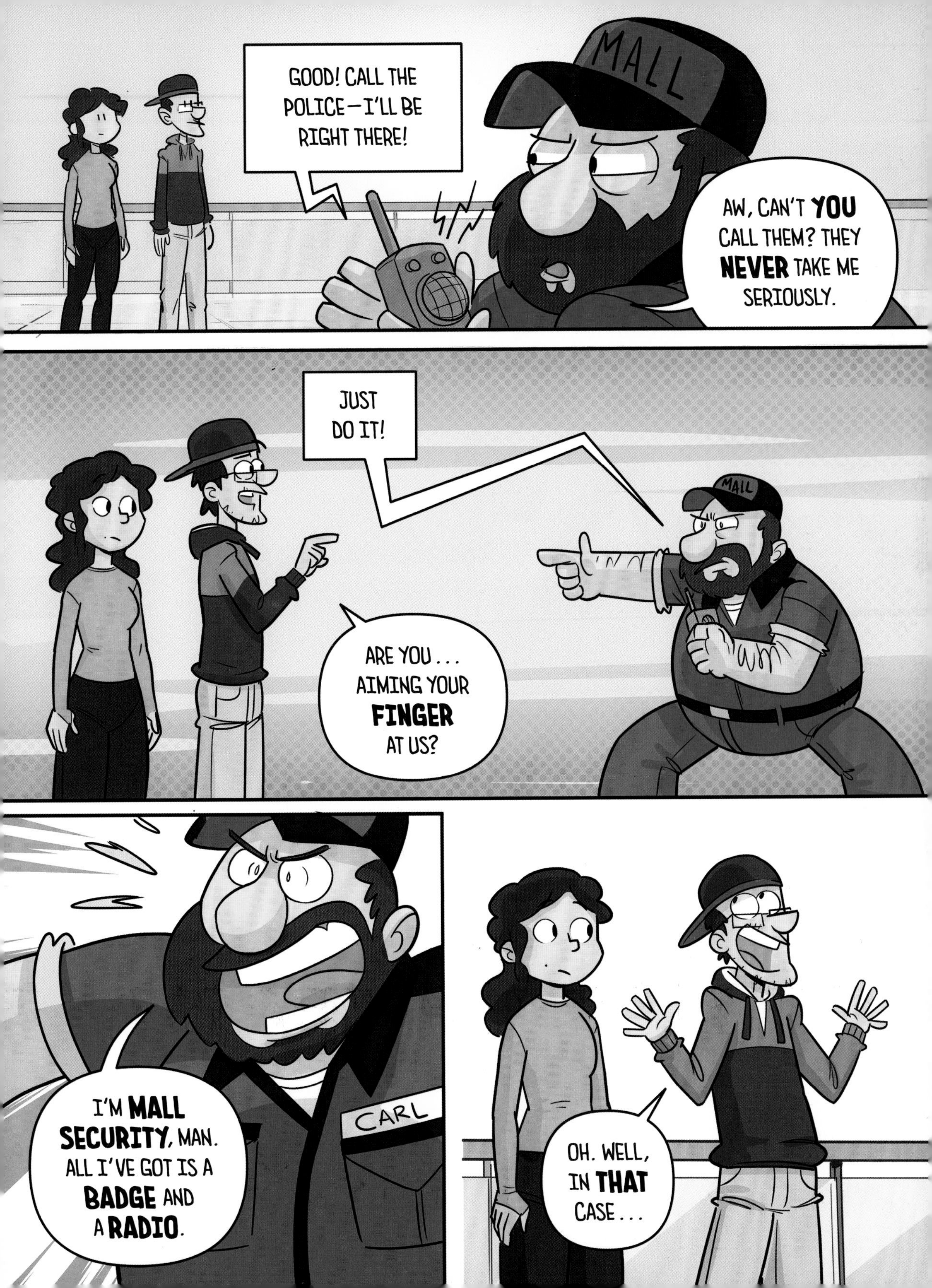
MALL
GOOD! CALL THE POLICE—I'LL BE RIGHT THERE!
AW, CAN'T **YOU** CALL THEM? THEY **NEVER** TAKE ME SERIOUSLY.
JUST DO IT!
MALL
ARE YOU . . . AIMING YOUR **FINGER** AT US?
I'M **MALL SECURITY**, MAN. ALL I'VE GOT IS A **BADGE** AND A **RADIO**.
CARL
OH. WELL, IN **THAT** CASE . . .

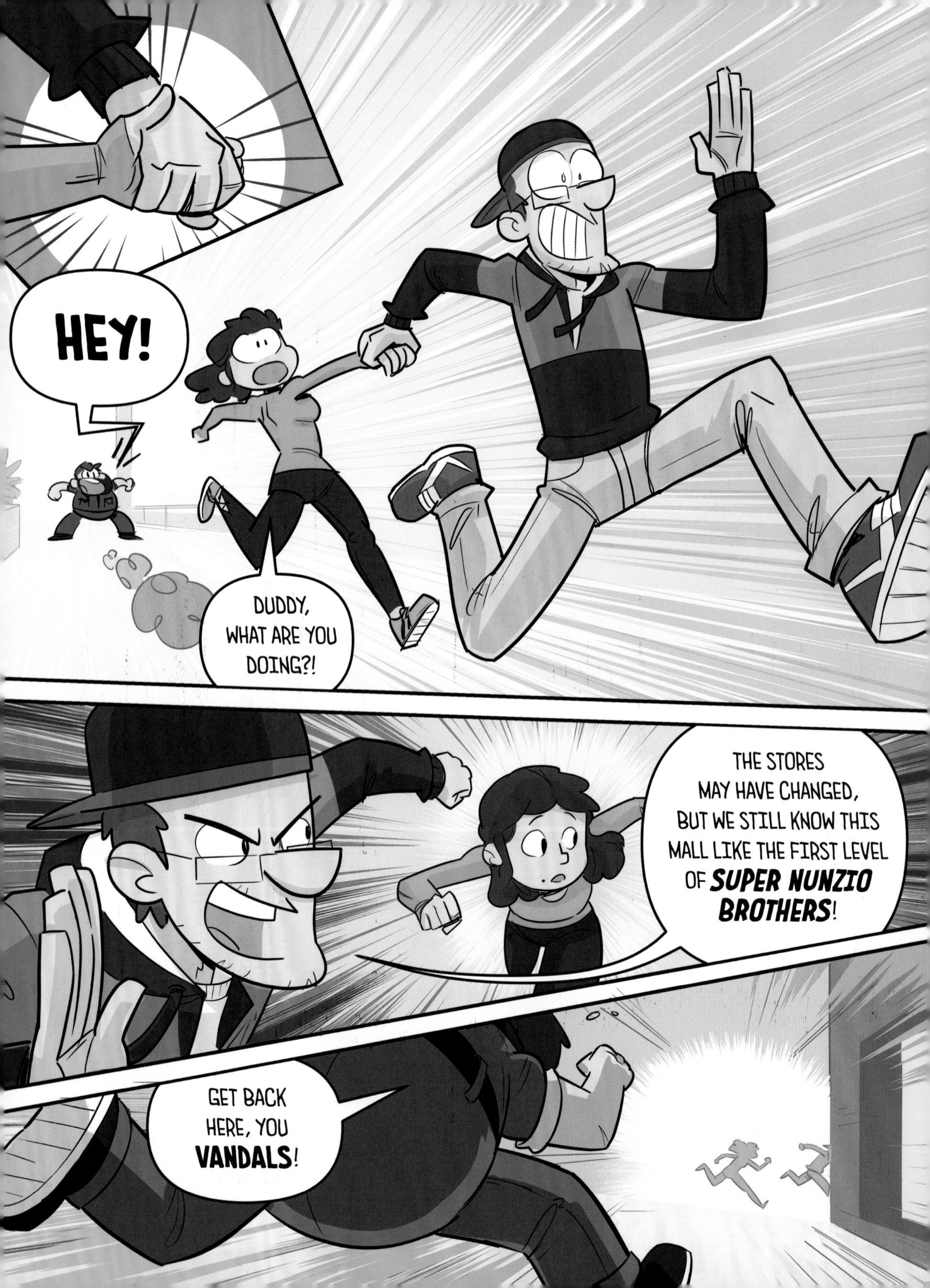
HEY!
DUDDY, WHAT ARE YOU DOING?!
THE STORES MAY HAVE CHANGED, BUT WE STILL KNOW THIS MALL LIKE THE FIRST LEVEL OF **SUPER NUNZIO BROTHERS**!
GET BACK HERE, YOU **VANDALS**!

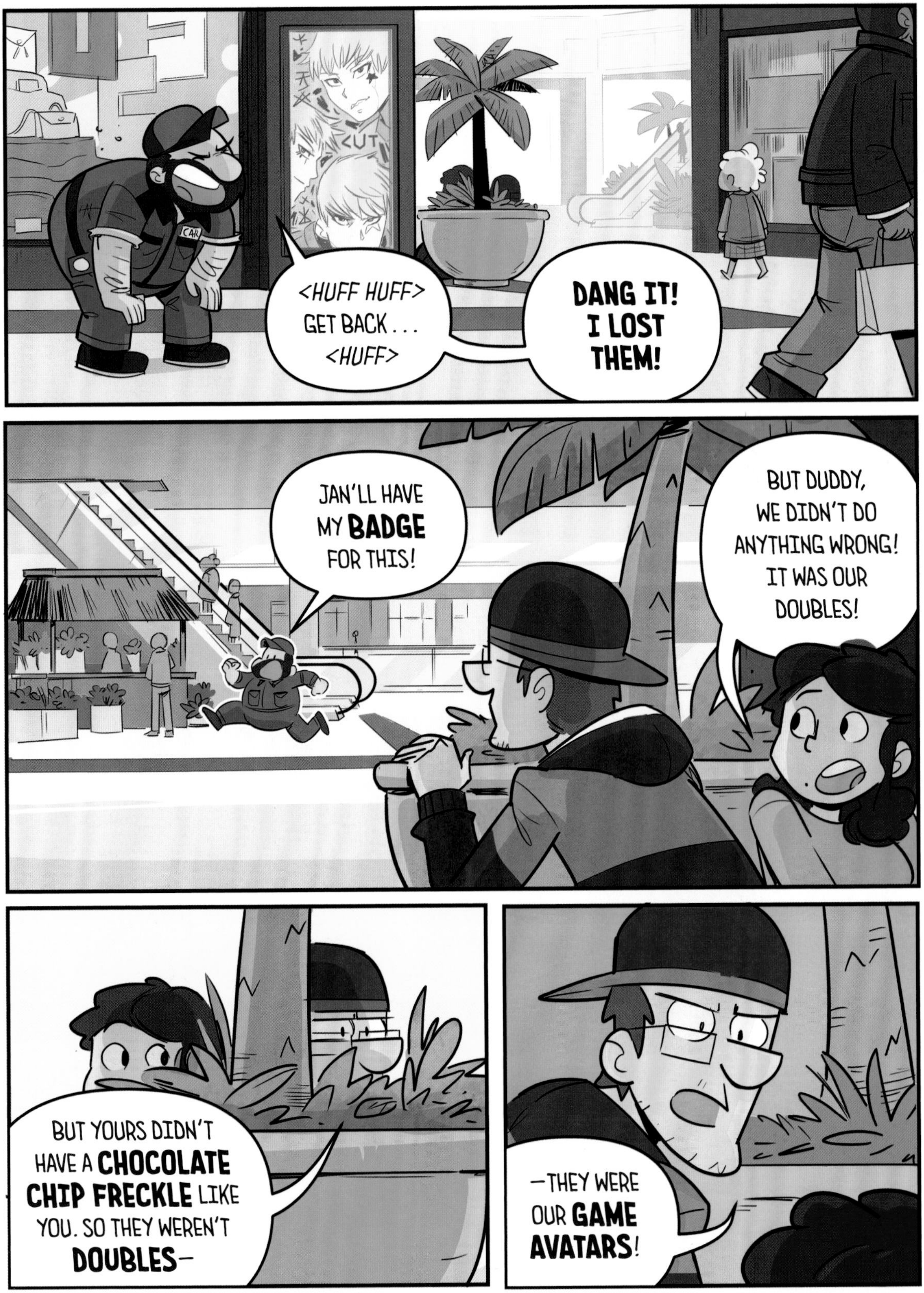
<HUFF HUFF> GET BACK . . . <HUFF>
DANG IT! I LOST THEM!
JAN'LL HAVE MY BADGE FOR THIS!
BUT DUDDY, WE DIDN'T DO ANYTHING WRONG! IT WAS OUR DOUBLES!
BUT YOURS DIDN'T HAVE A CHOCOLATE CHIP FRECKLE LIKE YOU. SO THEY WEREN'T DOUBLES—
—THEY WERE OUR GAME AVATARS!

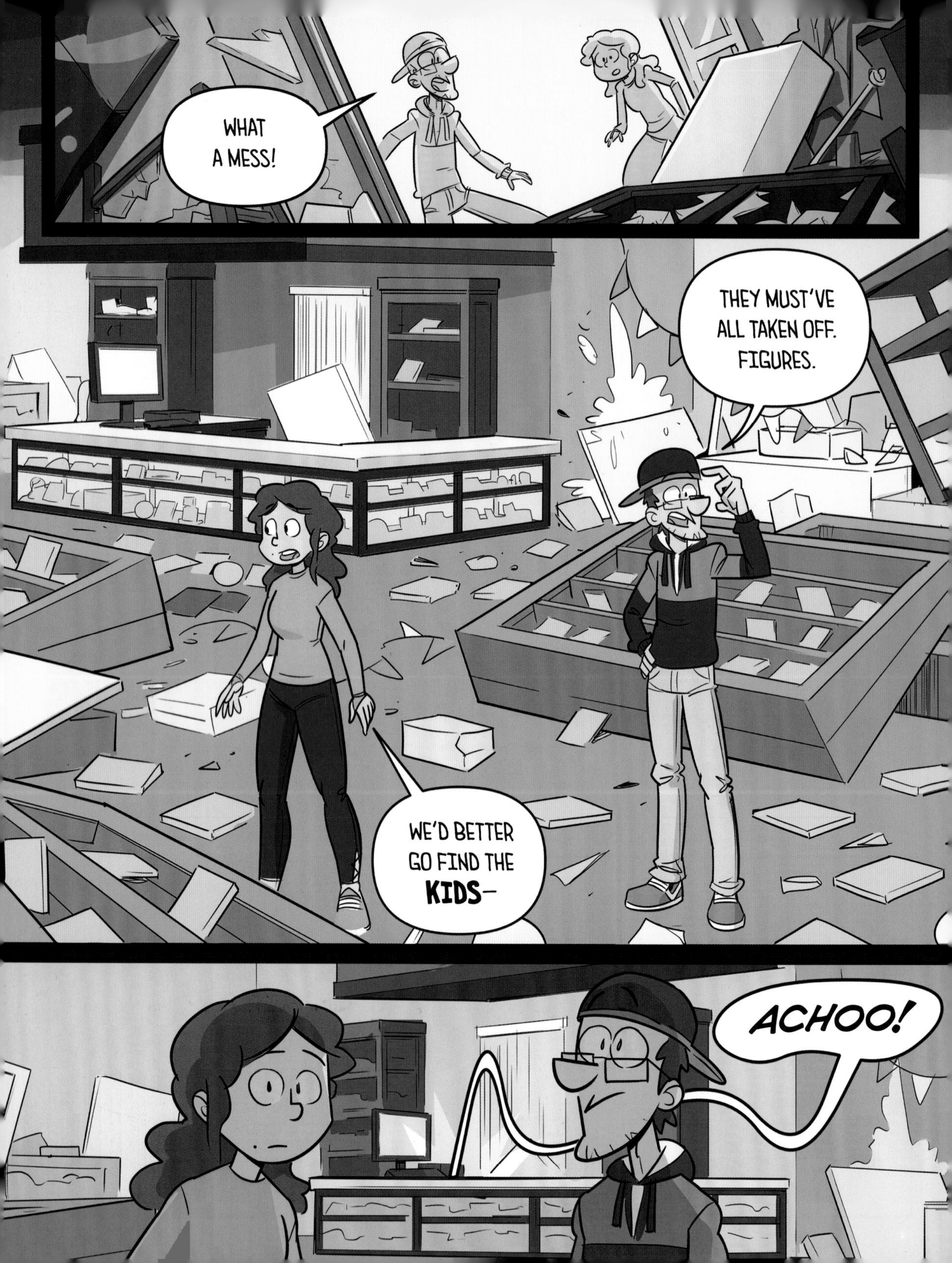
WHAT A MESS!
THEY MUST'VE ALL TAKEN OFF. FIGURES.
WE'D BETTER GO FIND THE **KIDS**—
ACHOO!

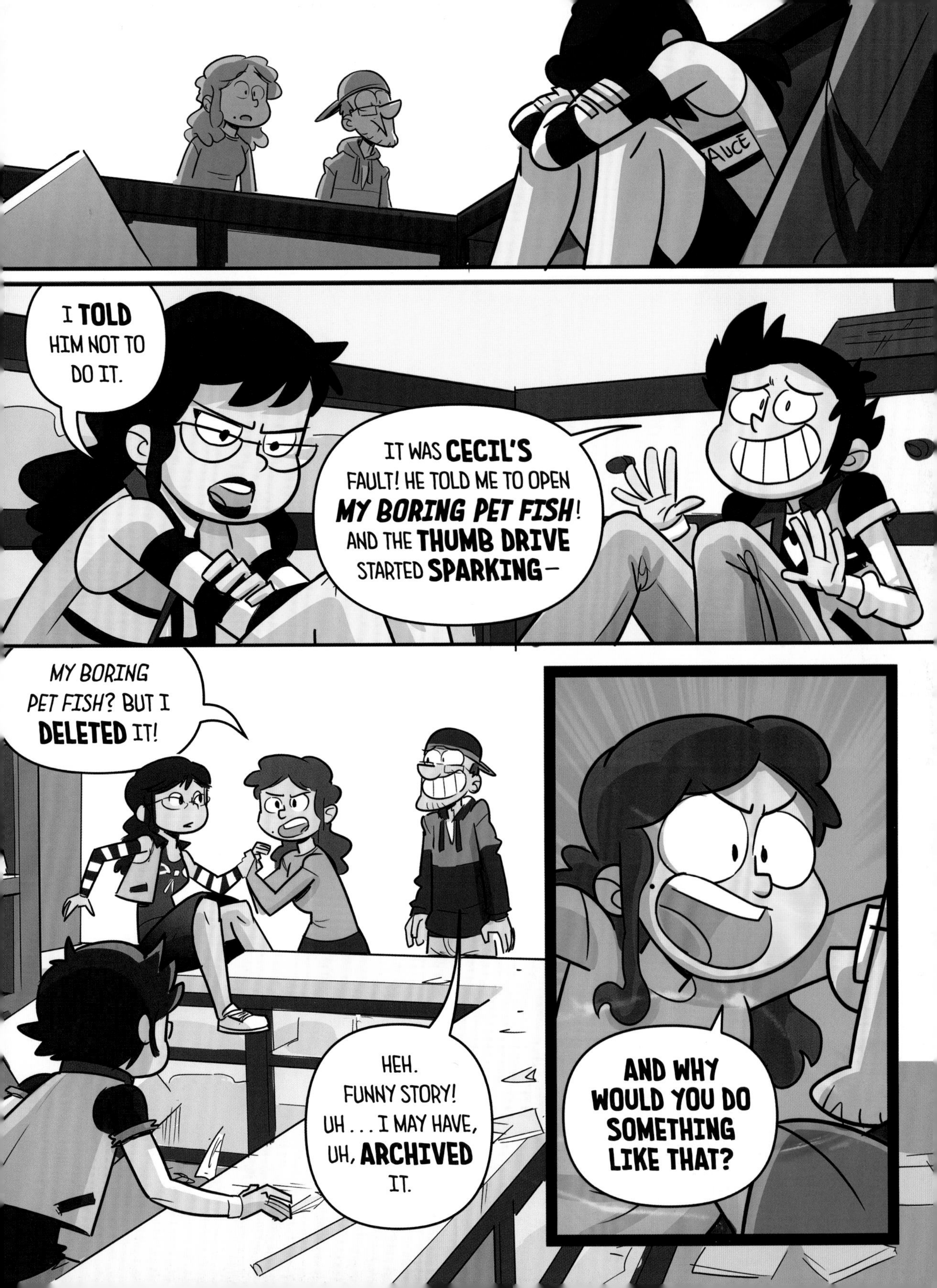

ALICE
I TOLD HIM NOT TO DO IT.
IT WAS CECIL'S FAULT! HE TOLD ME TO OPEN MY BORING PET FISH! AND THE THUMB DRIVE STARTED SPARKING—
MY BORING PET FISH? BUT I DELETED IT!
HEH. FUNNY STORY! UH . . . I MAY HAVE, UH, ARCHIVED IT.
AND WHY WOULD YOU DO SOMETHING LIKE THAT?

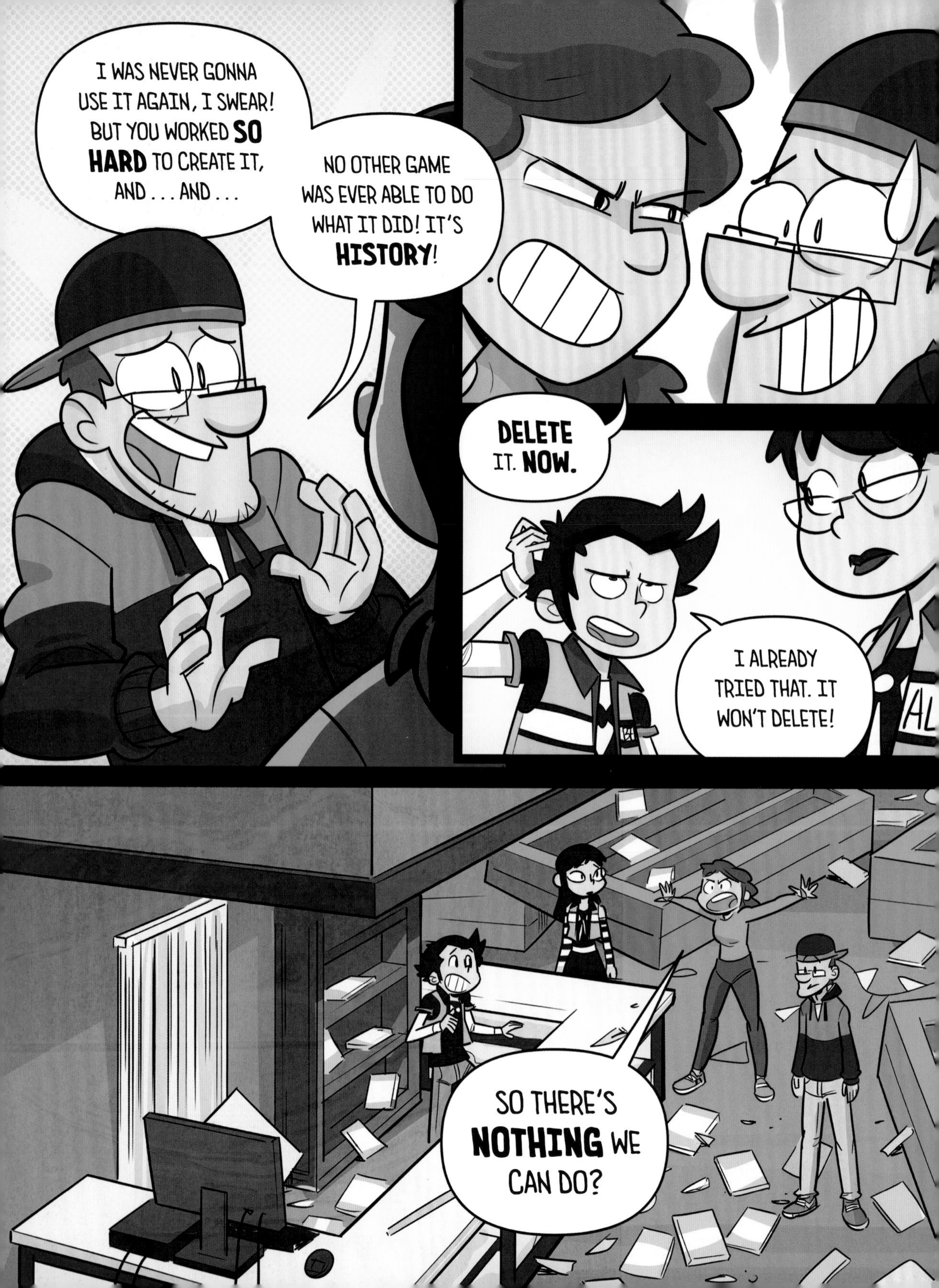
I WAS NEVER GONNA USE IT AGAIN, I SWEAR! BUT YOU WORKED **SO HARD** TO CREATE IT, AND . . . AND . . .
NO OTHER GAME WAS EVER ABLE TO DO WHAT IT DID! IT'S **HISTORY**!
DELETE IT. **NOW.**
I ALREADY TRIED THAT. IT WON'T DELETE!
SO THERE'S **NOTHING** WE CAN DO?

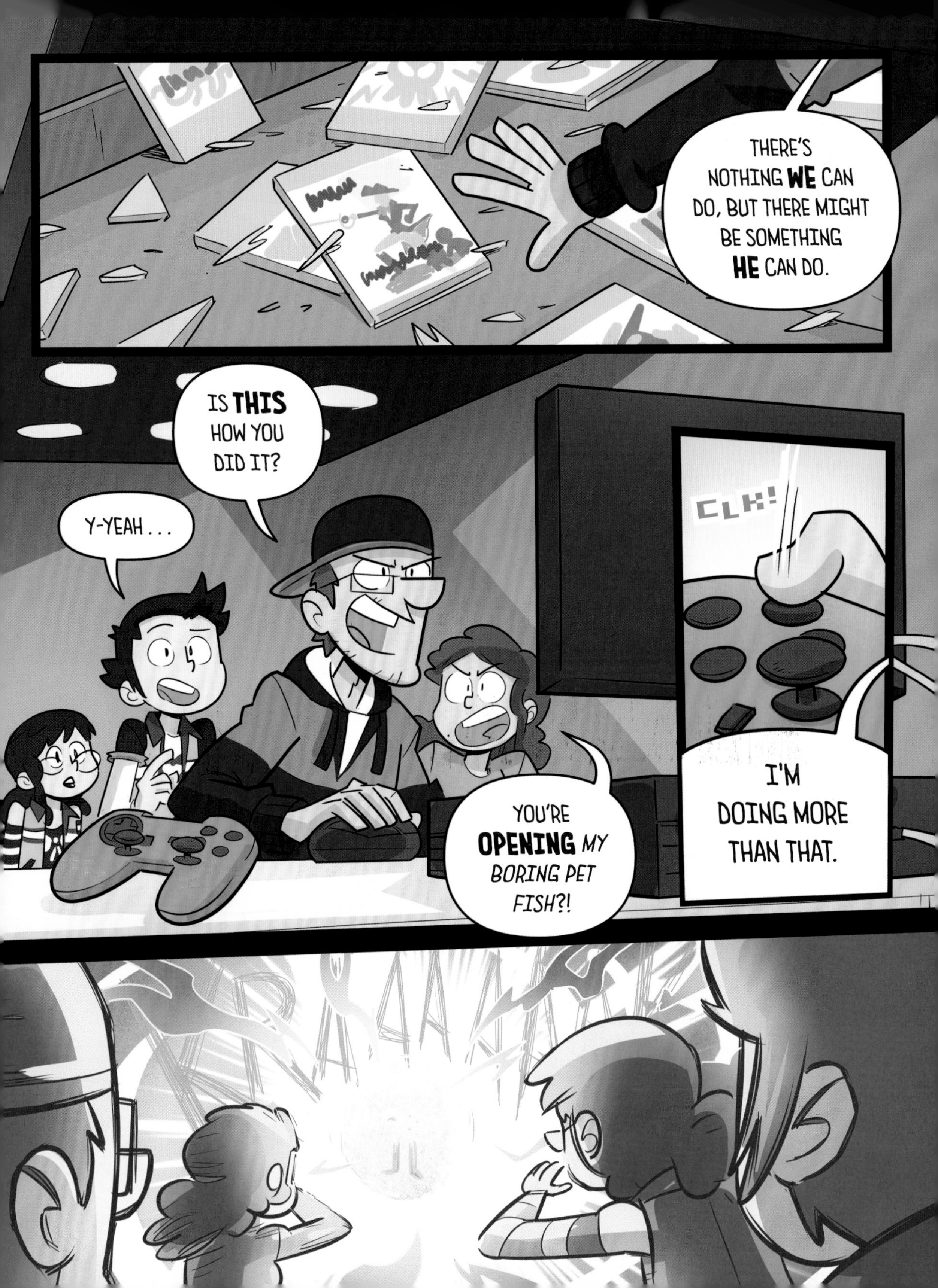
THERE'S NOTHING **WE** CAN DO, BUT THERE MIGHT BE SOMETHING **HE** CAN DO.
IS **THIS** HOW YOU DID IT?
Y-YEAH . . .
CLK!
YOU'RE **OPENING** *MY BORING PET FISH?!*
I'M DOING MORE THAN THAT.

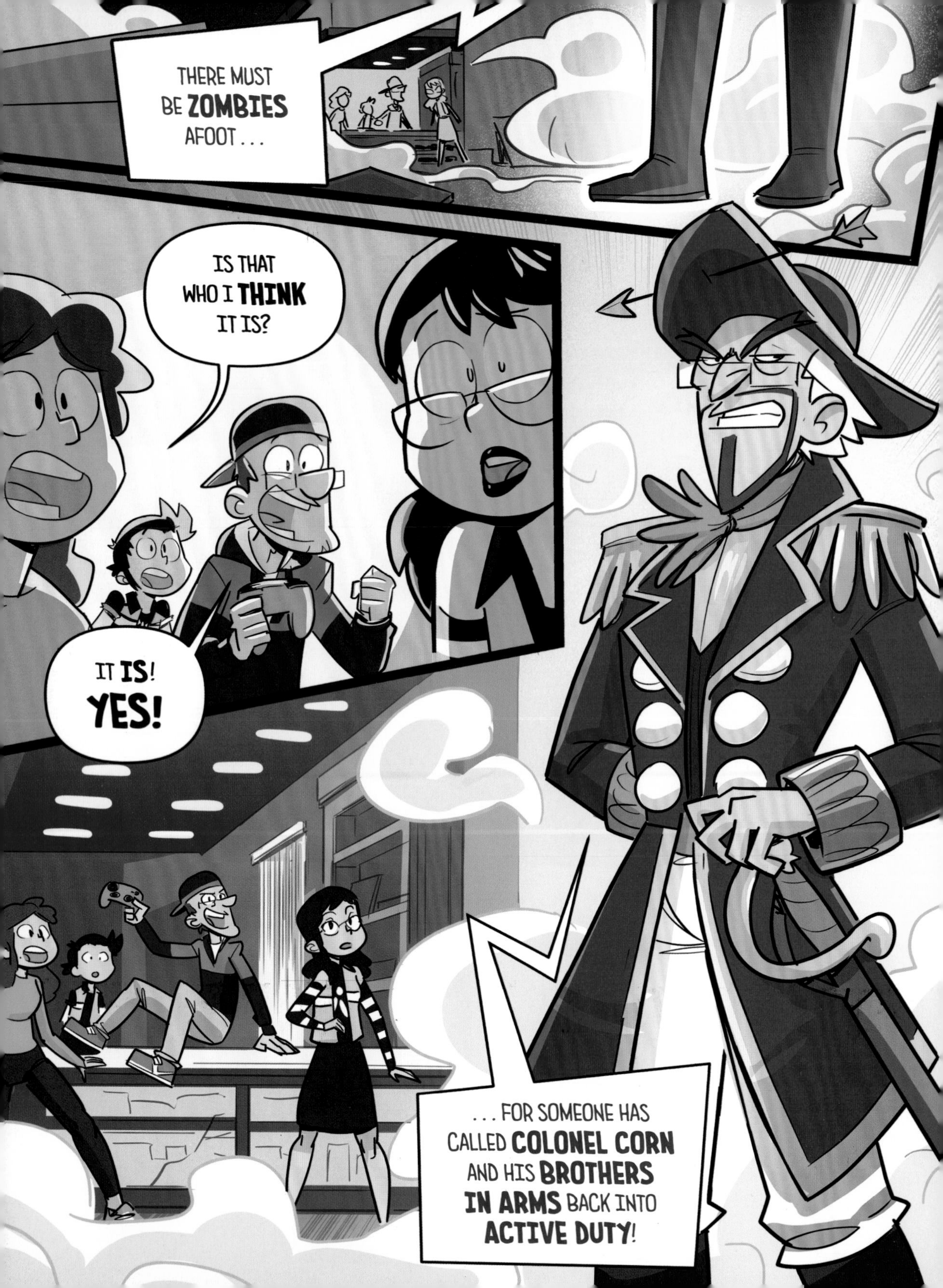
THERE MUST BE ZOMBIES AFOOT . . .
IS THAT WHO I THINK IT IS?
IT IS! YES!
. . . FOR SOMEONE HAS CALLED COLONEL CORN AND HIS BROTHERS IN ARMS BACK INTO ACTIVE DUTY!

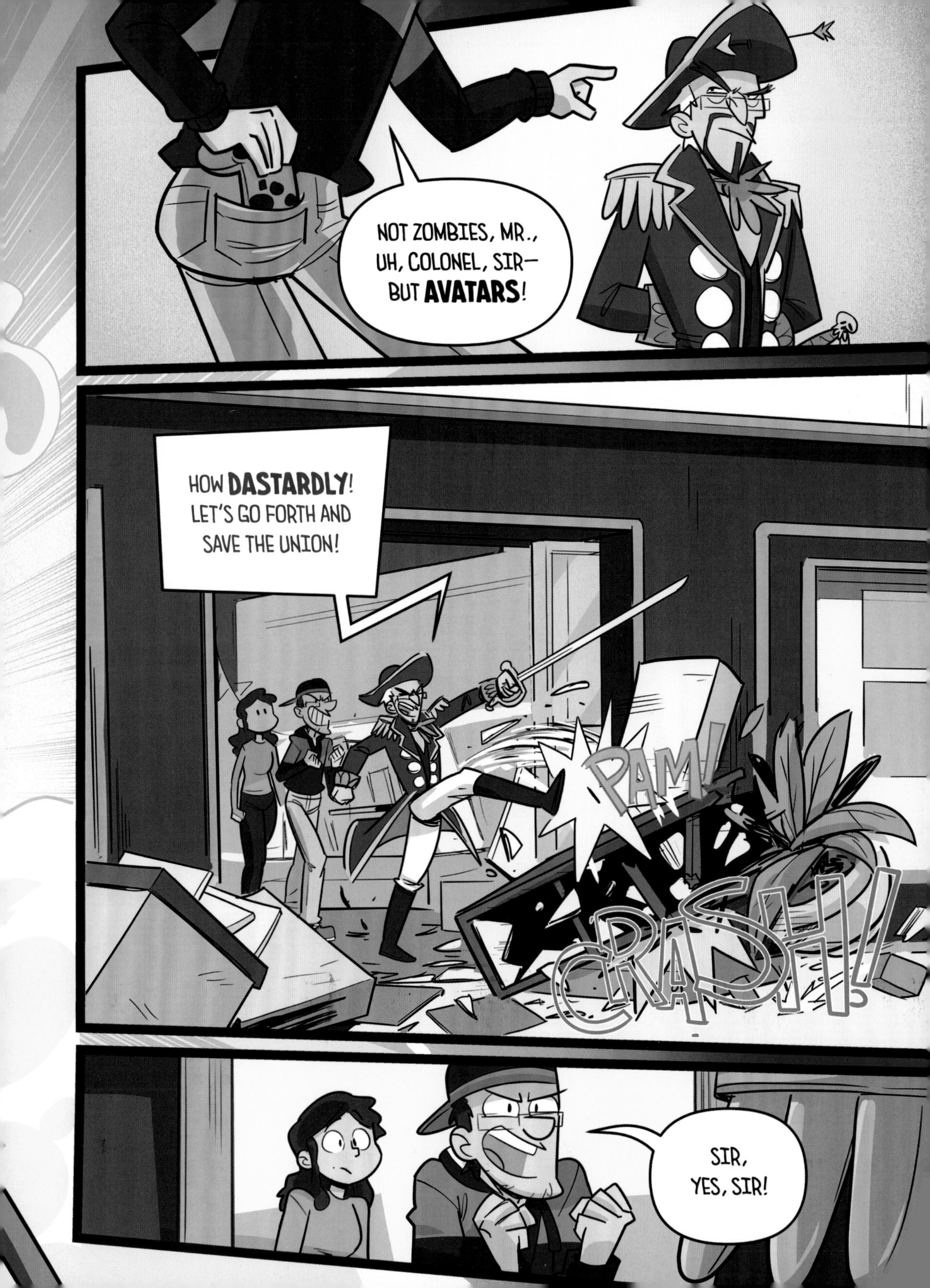
NOT ZOMBIES, MR., UH, COLONEL, SIR—BUT **AVATARS**!
HOW **DASTARDLY**! LET'S GO FORTH AND SAVE THE UNION!
PAM!
CRASH!
SIR, YES, SIR!

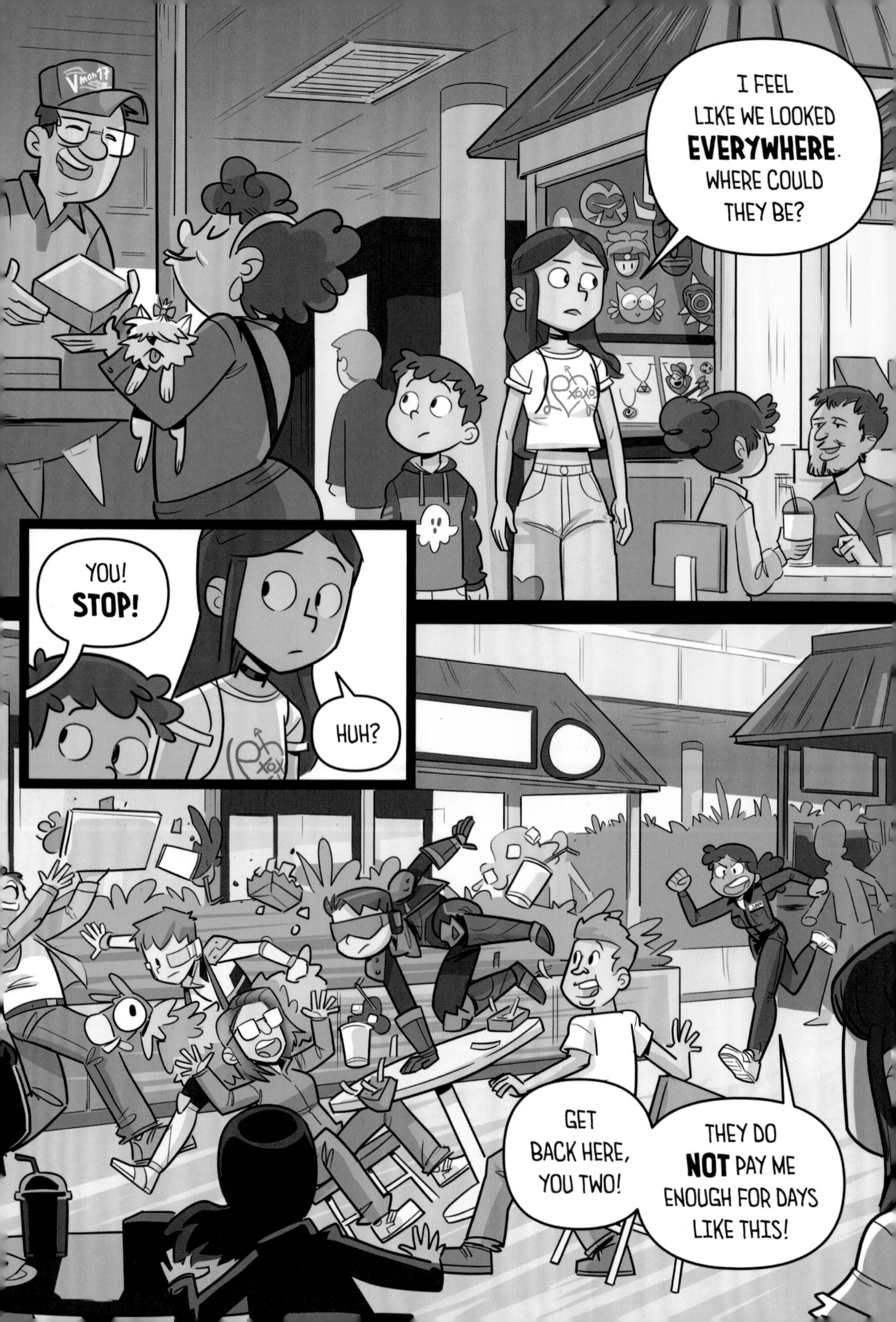
I FEEL LIKE WE LOOKED **EVERYWHERE**. WHERE COULD THEY BE?
YOU! **STOP!**
HUH?
GET BACK HERE, YOU TWO!
THEY DO **NOT** PAY ME ENOUGH FOR DAYS LIKE THIS!

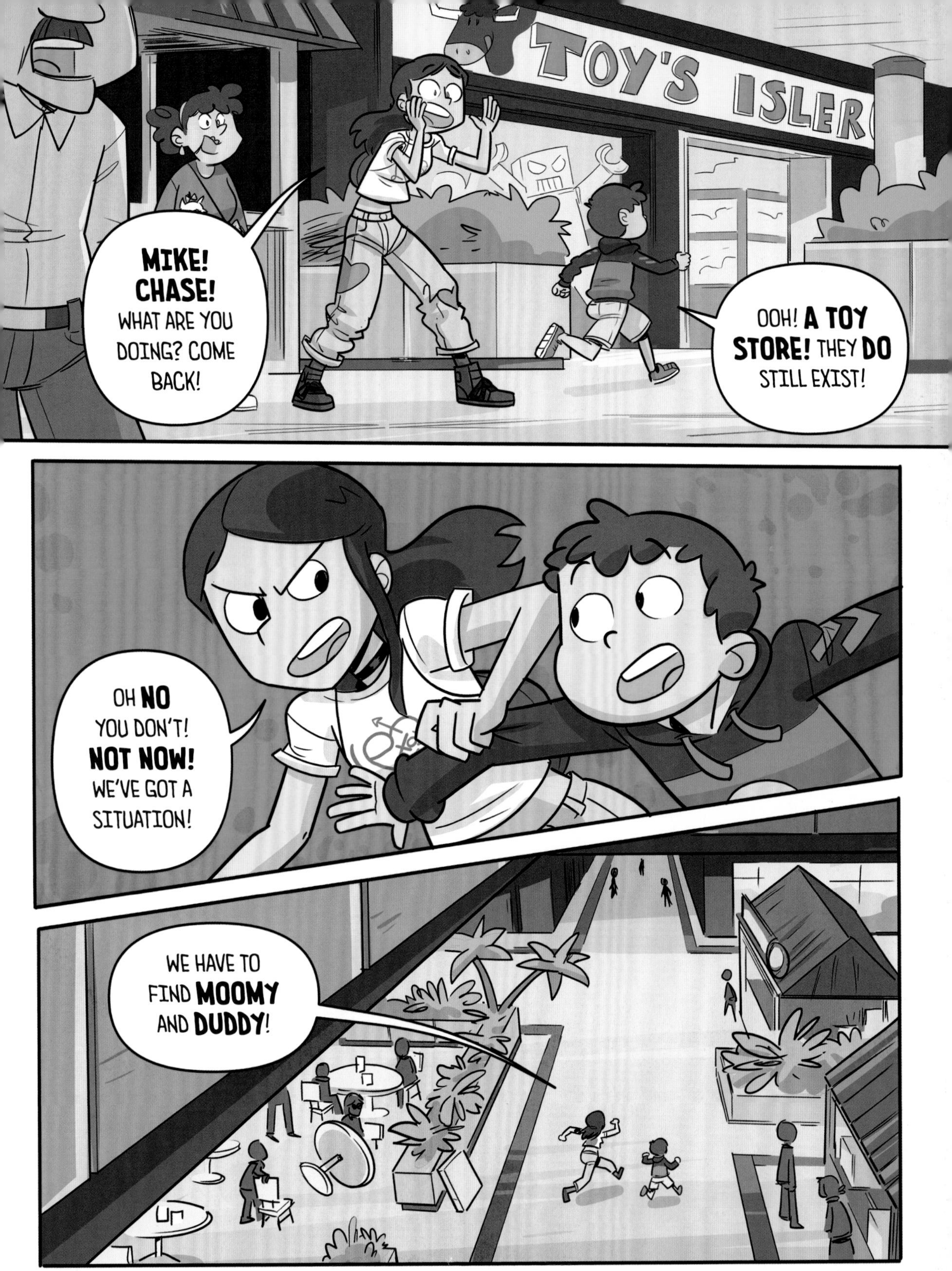
TOY'S ISLER
MIKE! CHASE! WHAT ARE YOU DOING? COME BACK!
OOH! A TOY STORE! THEY DO STILL EXIST!
OH NO YOU DON'T! NOT NOW! WE'VE GOT A SITUATION!
WE HAVE TO FIND MOOMY AND DUDDY!

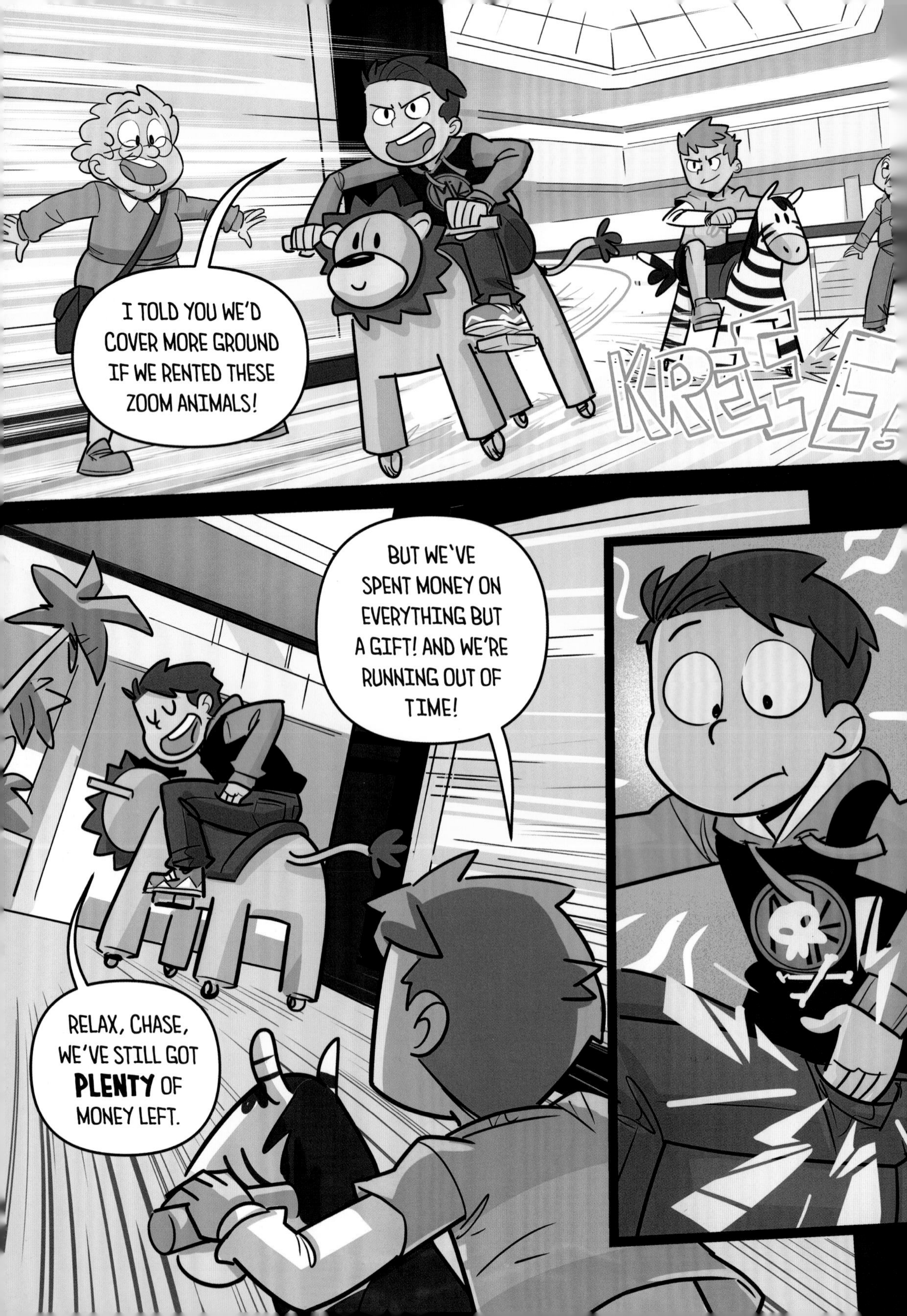
I TOLD YOU WE'D COVER MORE GROUND IF WE RENTED THESE ZOOM ANIMALS!
KREEE
BUT WE'VE SPENT MONEY ON EVERYTHING BUT A GIFT! AND WE'RE RUNNING OUT OF TIME!
RELAX, CHASE, WE'VE STILL GOT **PLENTY** OF MONEY LEFT.

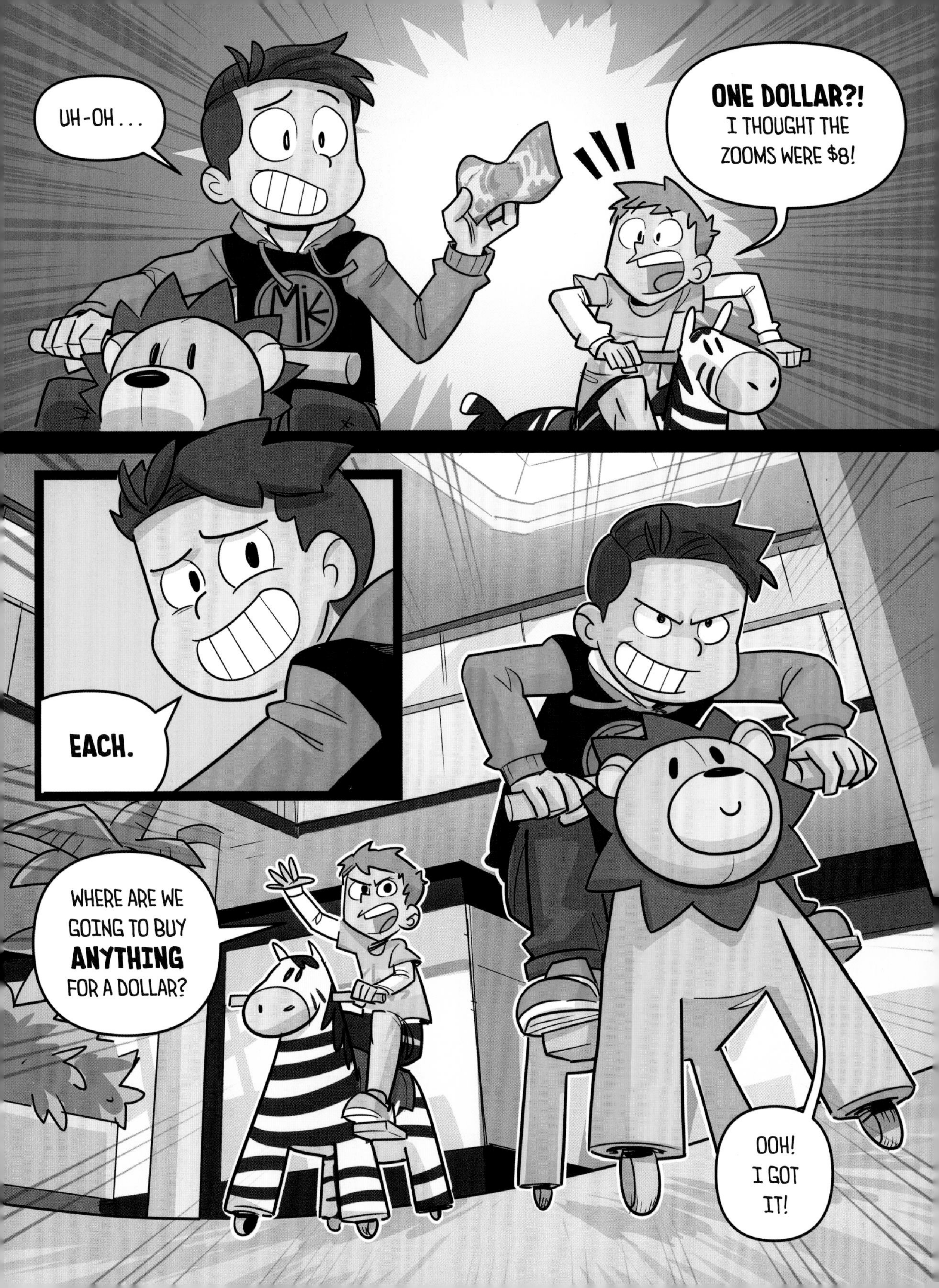

UH-OH . . .
ONE DOLLAR?! I THOUGHT THE ZOOMS WERE $8!
EACH.
WHERE ARE WE GOING TO BUY ANYTHING FOR A DOLLAR?
OOH! I GOT IT!

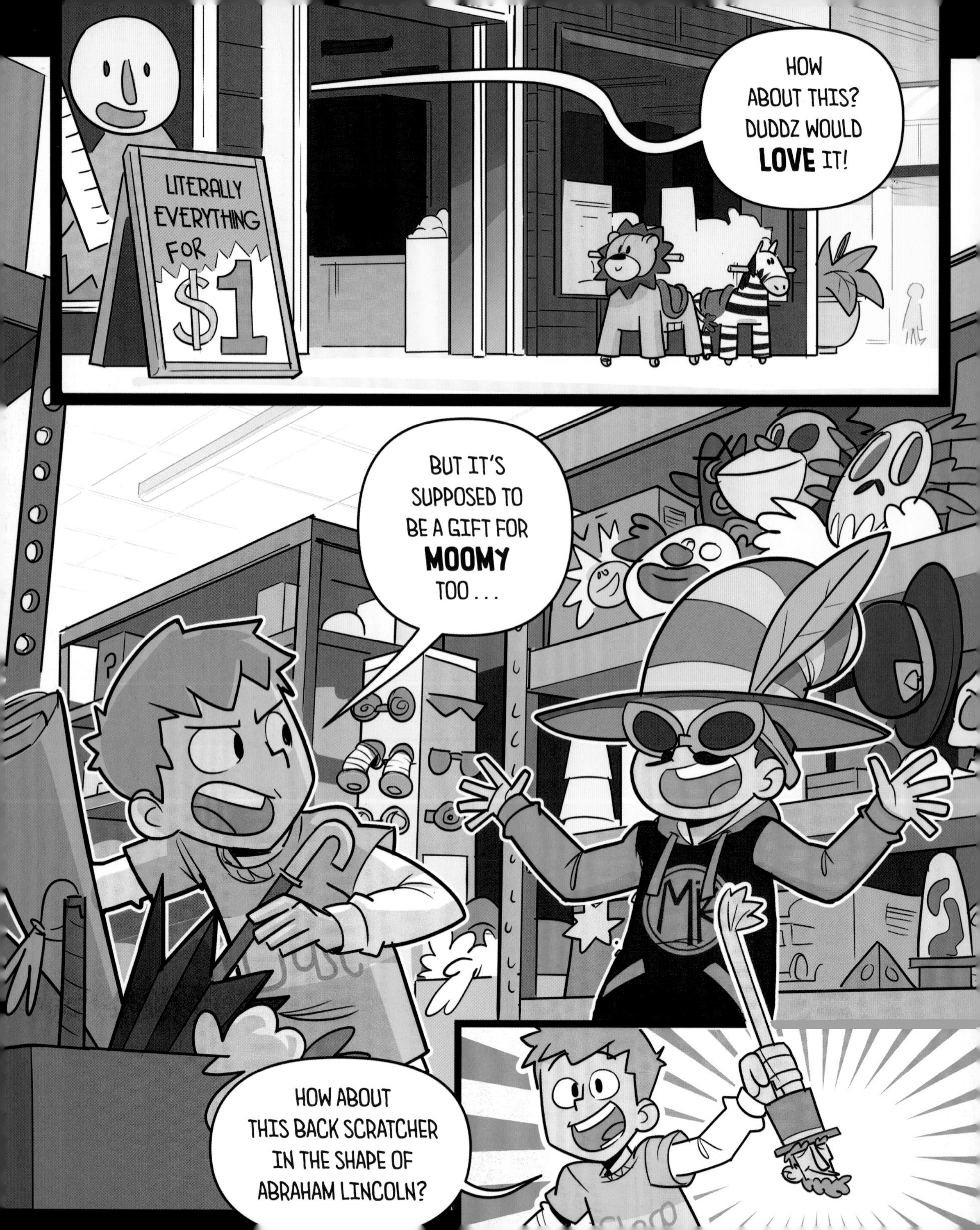
LITERALLY EVERYTHING FOR $1
HOW ABOUT THIS? DUDDZ WOULD **LOVE** IT!
BUT IT'S SUPPOSED TO BE A GIFT FOR **MOOMY** TOO . . .
HOW ABOUT THIS BACK SCRATCHER IN THE SHAPE OF ABRAHAM LINCOLN?

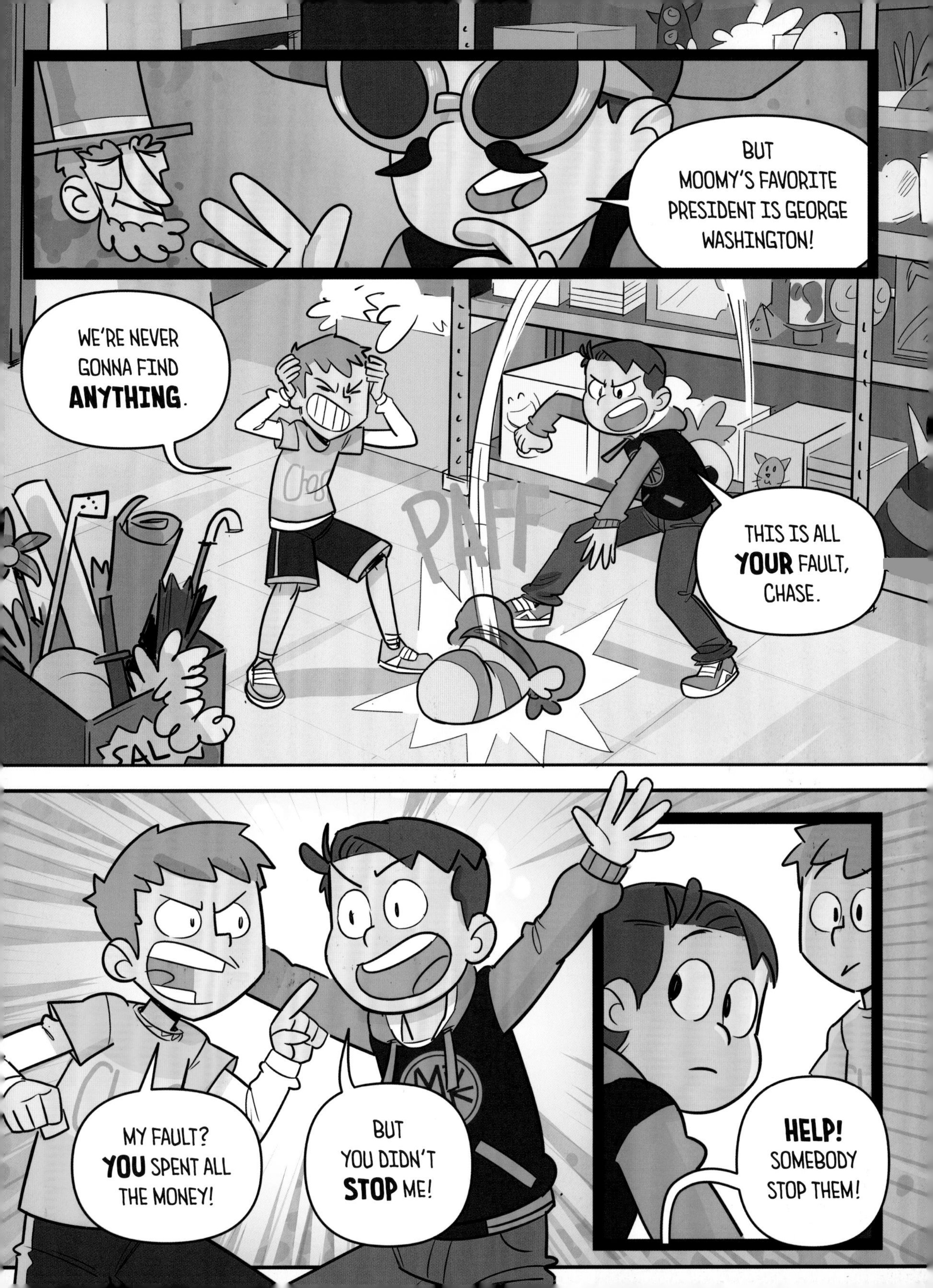
BUT MOOMY'S FAVORITE PRESIDENT IS GEORGE WASHINGTON!
WE'RE NEVER GONNA FIND **ANYTHING**.
PAFF
THIS IS ALL **YOUR** FAULT, CHASE.
MY FAULT? **YOU** SPENT ALL THE MONEY!
BUT YOU DIDN'T **STOP** ME!
HELP! SOMEBODY STOP THEM!

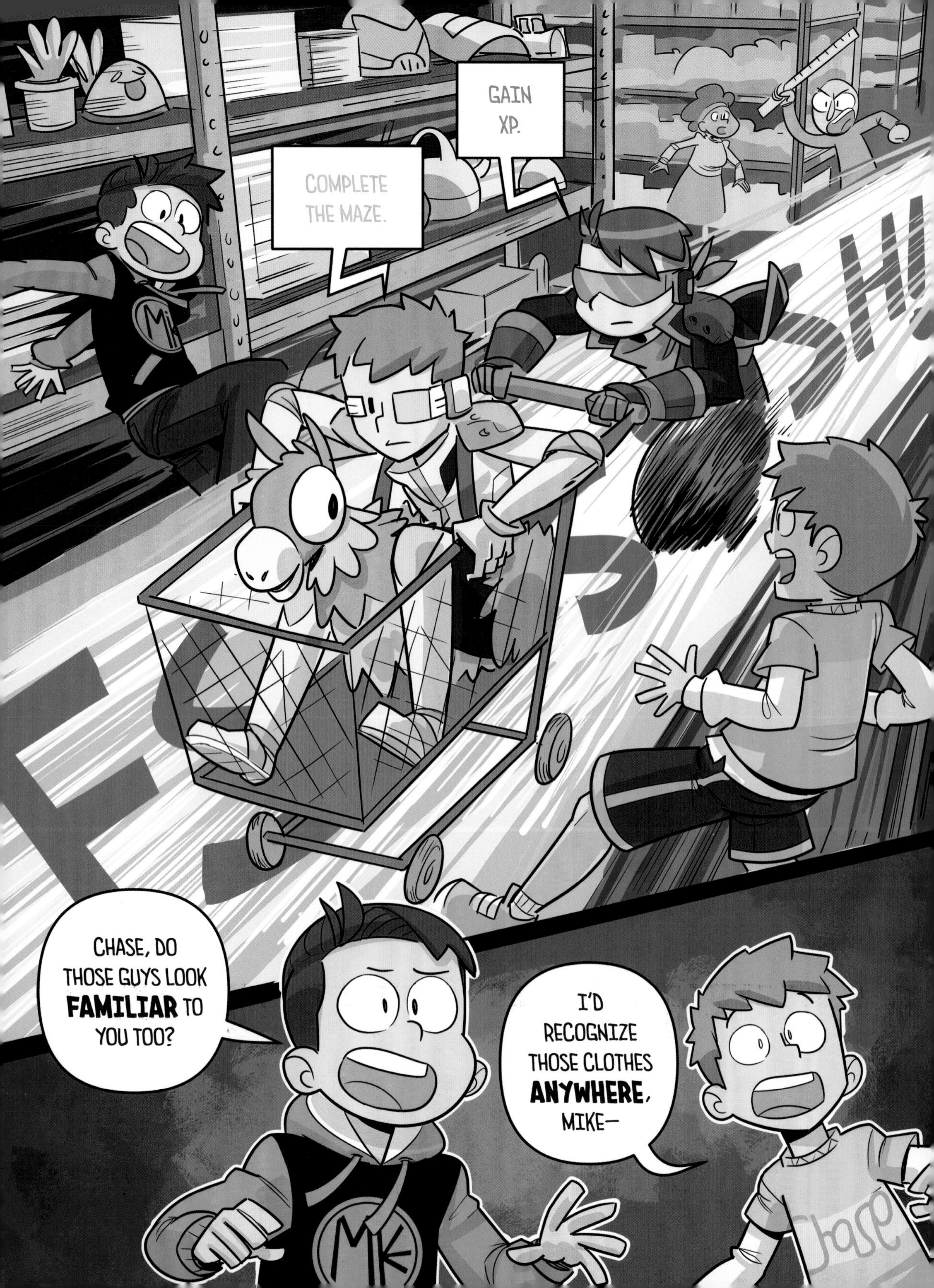
COMPLETE THE MAZE.
GAIN XP.
CHASE, DO THOSE GUYS LOOK **FAMILIAR** TO YOU TOO?
I'D RECOGNIZE THOSE CLOTHES **ANYWHERE**, MIKE—
MK
Chase

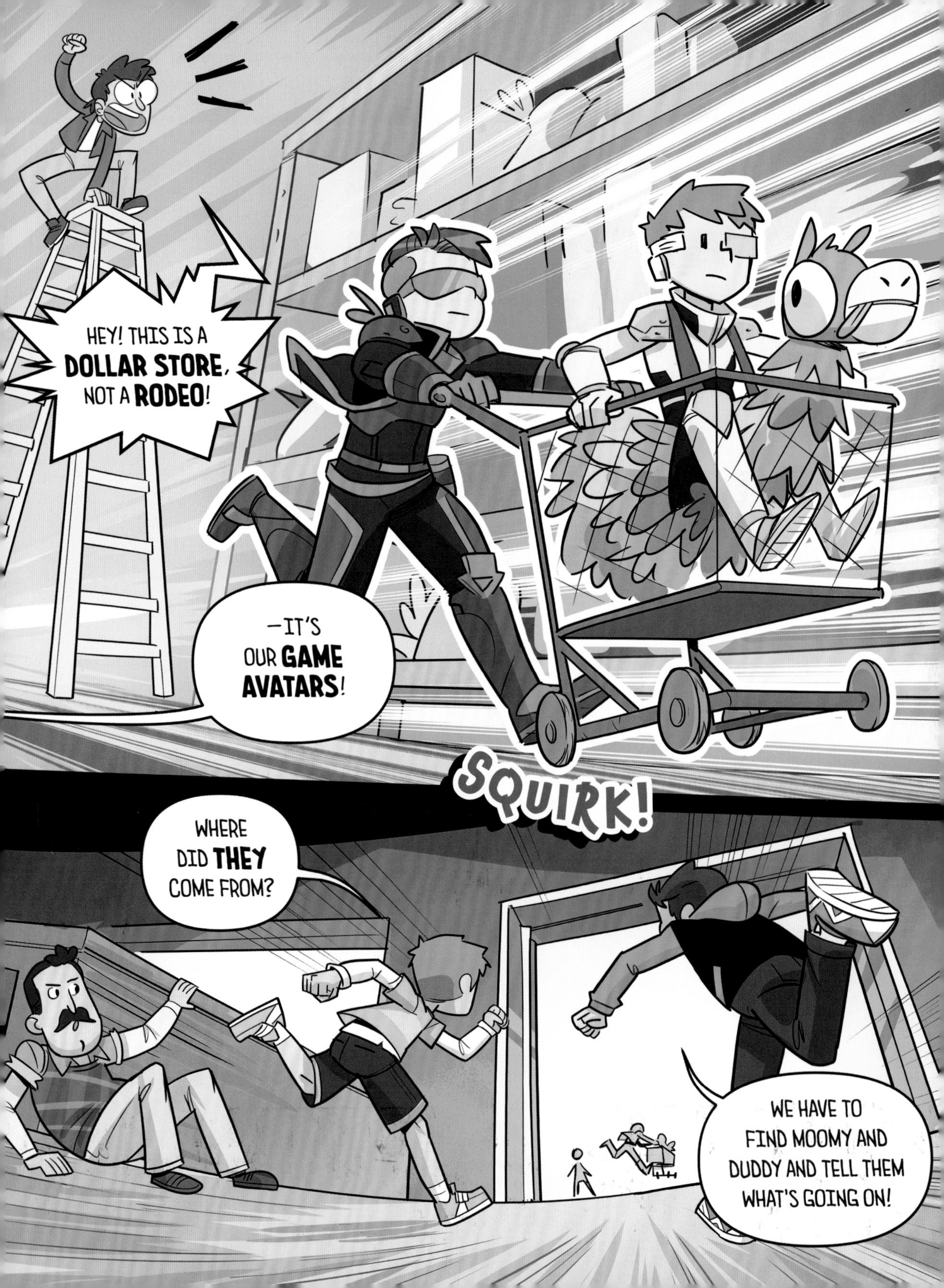
HEY! THIS IS A DOLLAR STORE, NOT A RODEO!
—IT'S OUR GAME AVATARS!
SQUIRK!
WHERE DID THEY COME FROM?
WE HAVE TO FIND MOOMY AND DUDDY AND TELL THEM WHAT'S GOING ON!

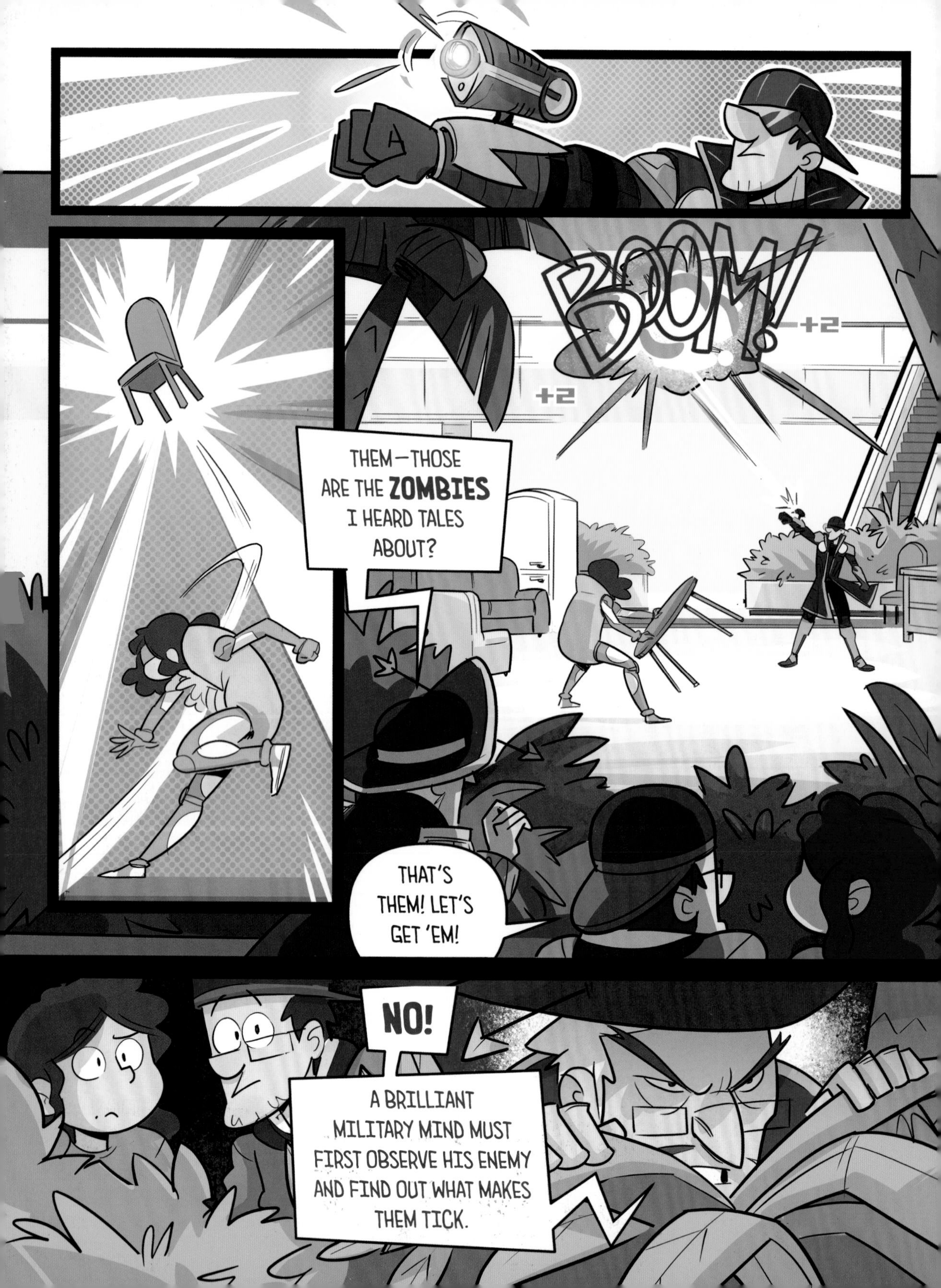
BOOM!
+2
+2
THEM—THOSE ARE THE ZOMBIES I HEARD TALES ABOUT?
THAT'S THEM! LET'S GET 'EM!
NO!
A BRILLIANT MILITARY MIND MUST FIRST OBSERVE HIS ENEMY AND FIND OUT WHAT MAKES THEM TICK.

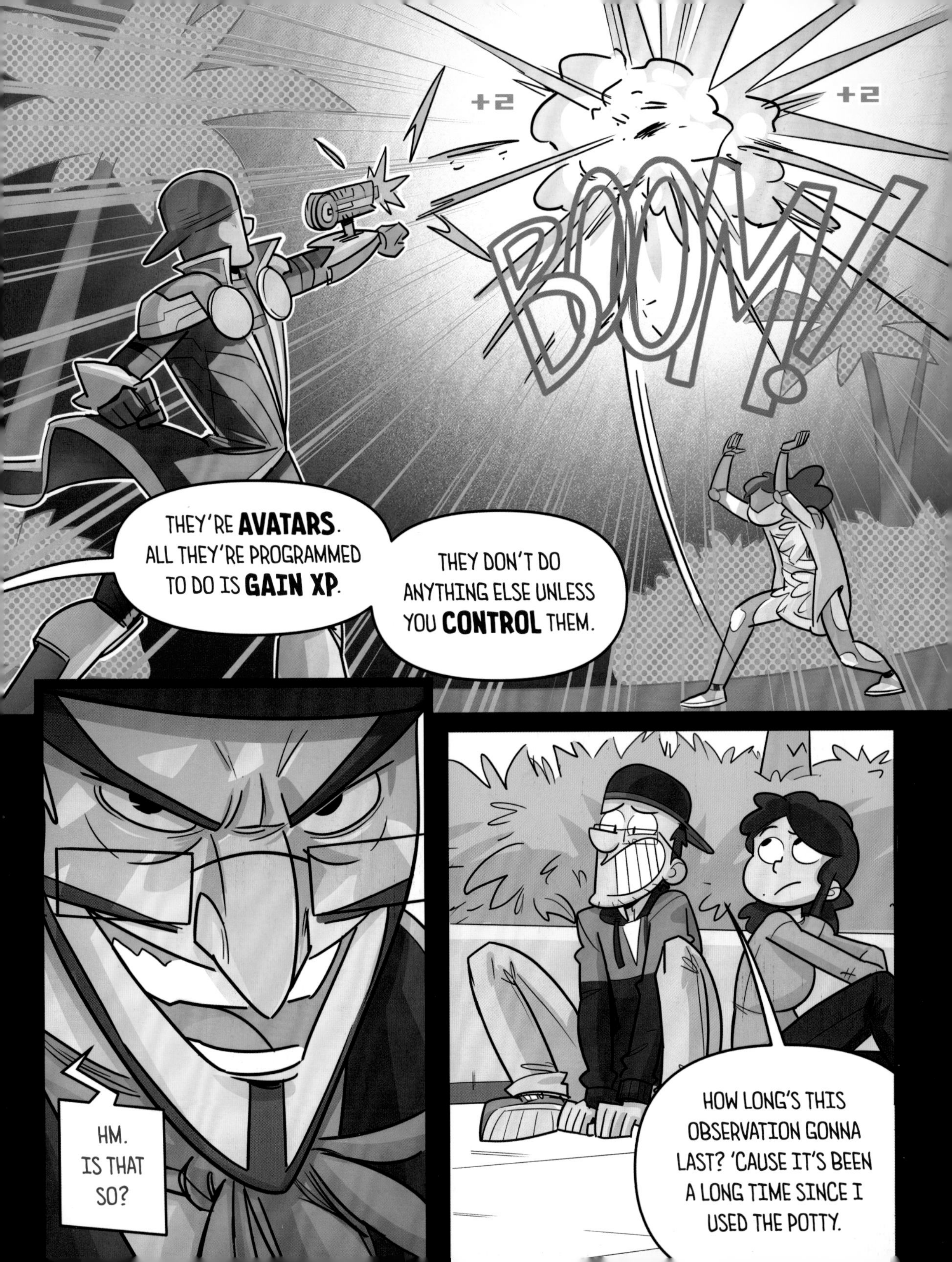
+2
+2
BOOM!
THEY'RE **AVATARS**. ALL THEY'RE PROGRAMMED TO DO IS **GAIN XP**.
THEY DON'T DO ANYTHING ELSE UNLESS YOU **CONTROL** THEM.
HM. IS THAT SO?
HOW LONG'S THIS OBSERVATION GONNA LAST? 'CAUSE IT'S BEEN A LONG TIME SINCE I USED THE POTTY.

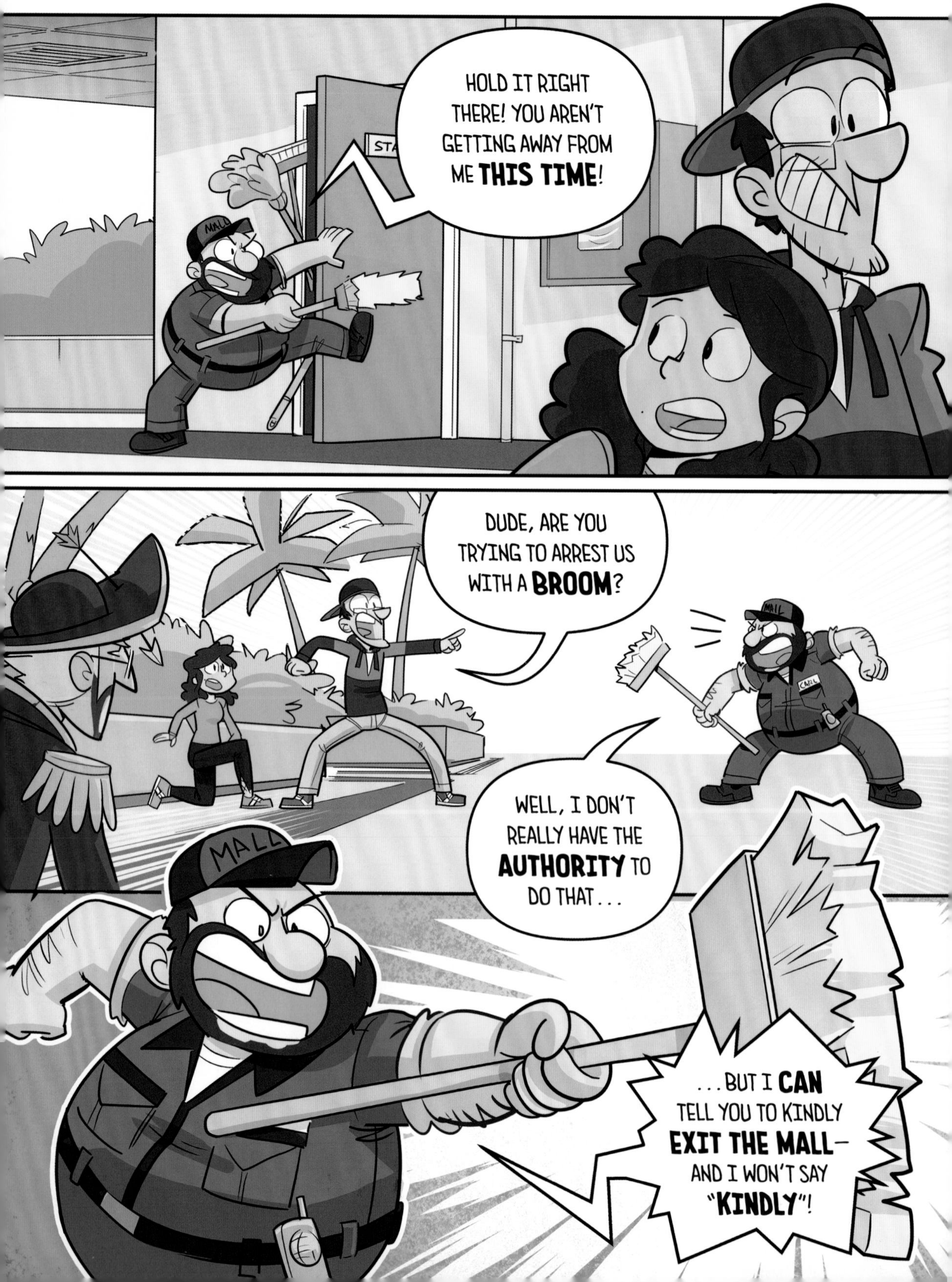

HOLD IT RIGHT THERE! YOU AREN'T GETTING AWAY FROM ME **THIS TIME**!
DUDE, ARE YOU TRYING TO ARREST US WITH A **BROOM**?
WELL, I DON'T REALLY HAVE THE **AUTHORITY** TO DO THAT . . .
. . . BUT I **CAN** TELL YOU TO KINDLY **EXIT THE MALL**— AND I WON'T SAY "**KINDLY**"!

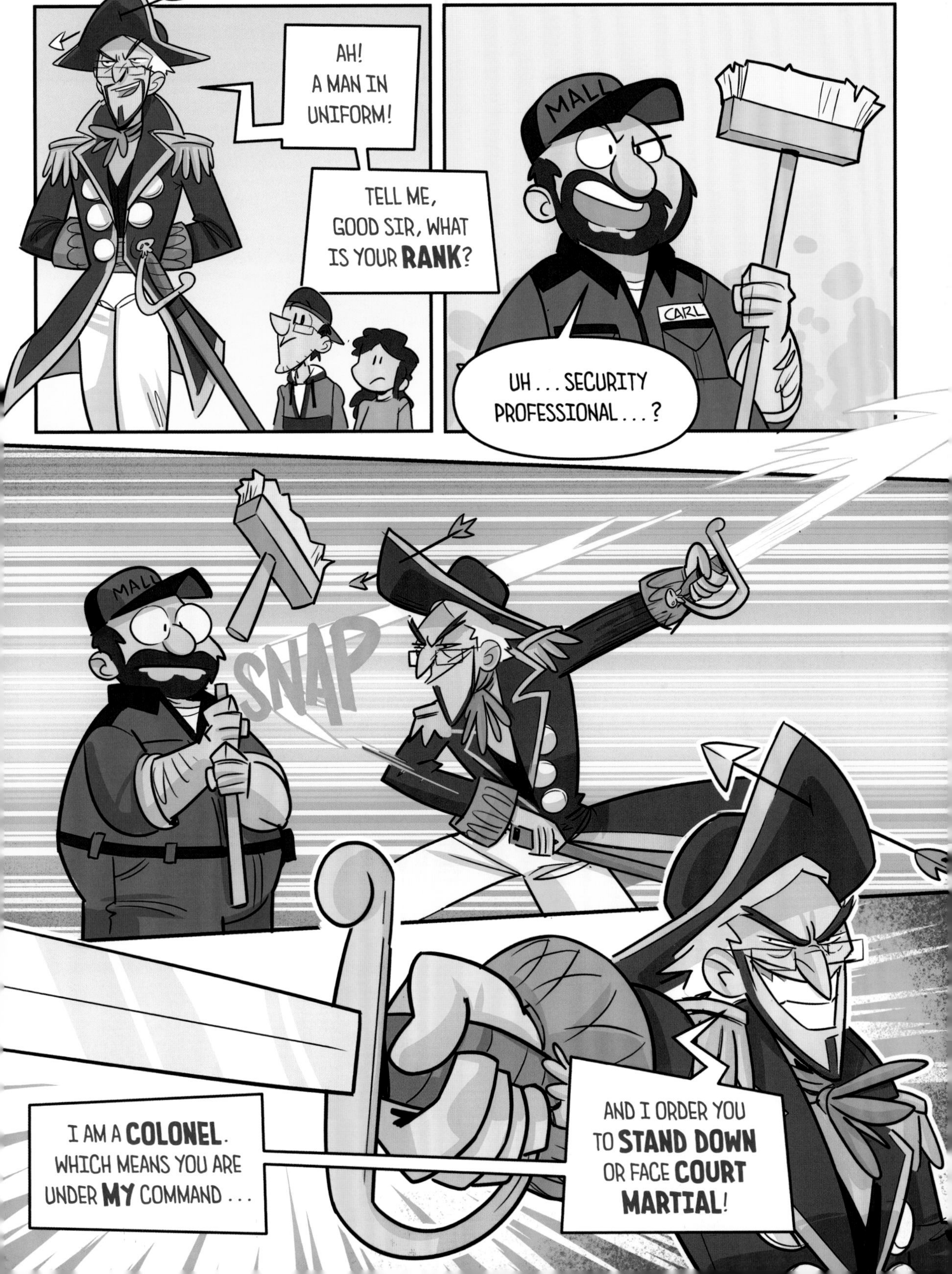

AH! A MAN IN UNIFORM!
TELL ME, GOOD SIR, WHAT IS YOUR **RANK**?
MALL
CARL
UH . . . SECURITY PROFESSIONAL . . . ?
MALL
SNAP
I AM A **COLONEL**. WHICH MEANS YOU ARE UNDER **MY** COMMAND . . .
AND I ORDER YOU TO **STAND DOWN** OR FACE **COURT MARTIAL**!

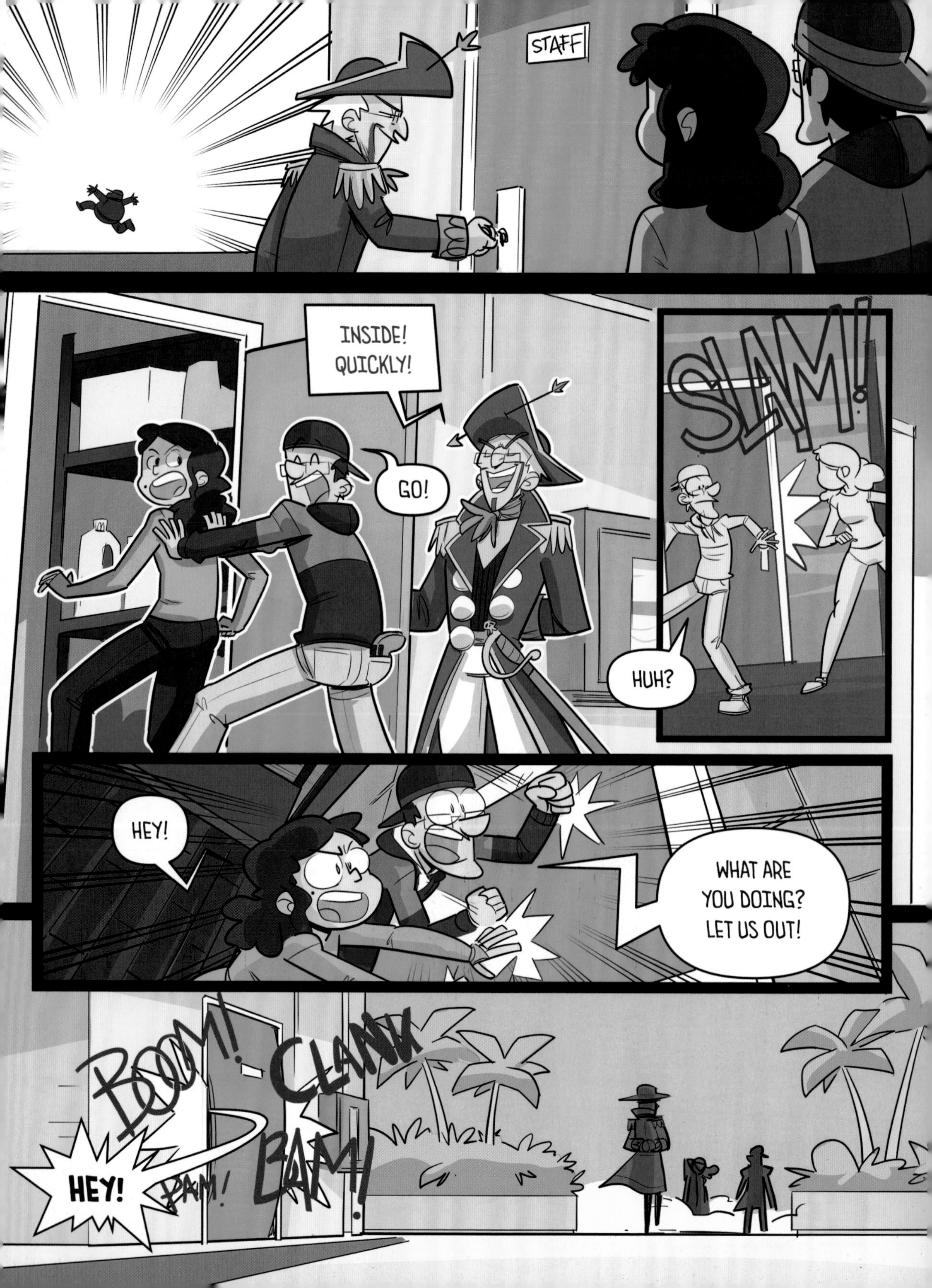
STAFF
INSIDE! QUICKLY!
GO!
SLAM!
HUH?
HEY!
WHAT ARE YOU DOING? LET US OUT!
BOOM!
CLANK
HEY!
BAM!
BAM!

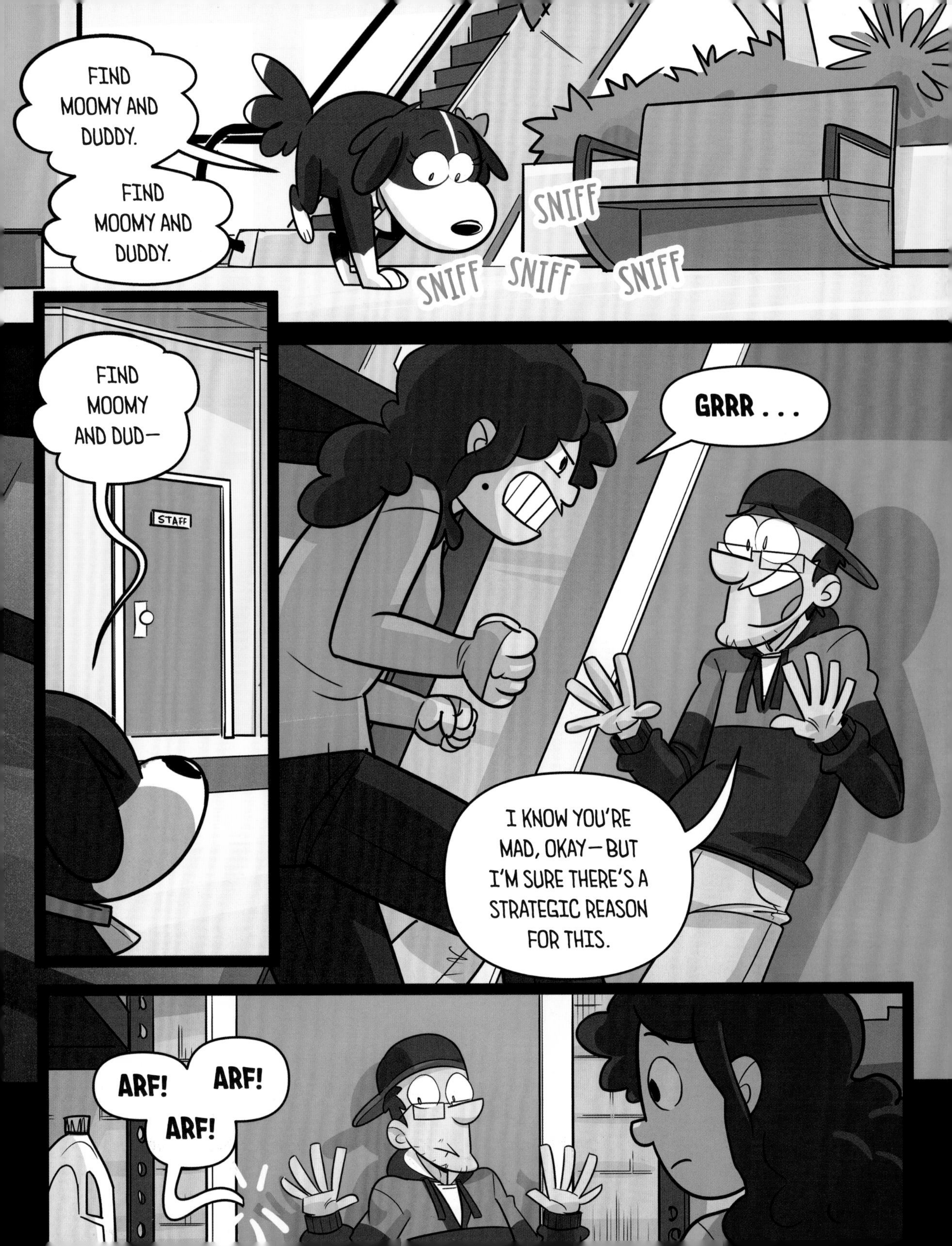
FIND MOOMY AND DUDDY.
FIND MOOMY AND DUDDY.
SNIFF
SNIFF
SNIFF
SNIFF
FIND MOOMY AND DUD—
STAFF
GRRR . . .
I KNOW YOU'RE MAD, OKAY—BUT I'M SURE THERE'S A STRATEGIC REASON FOR THIS.
ARF!
ARF!
ARF!

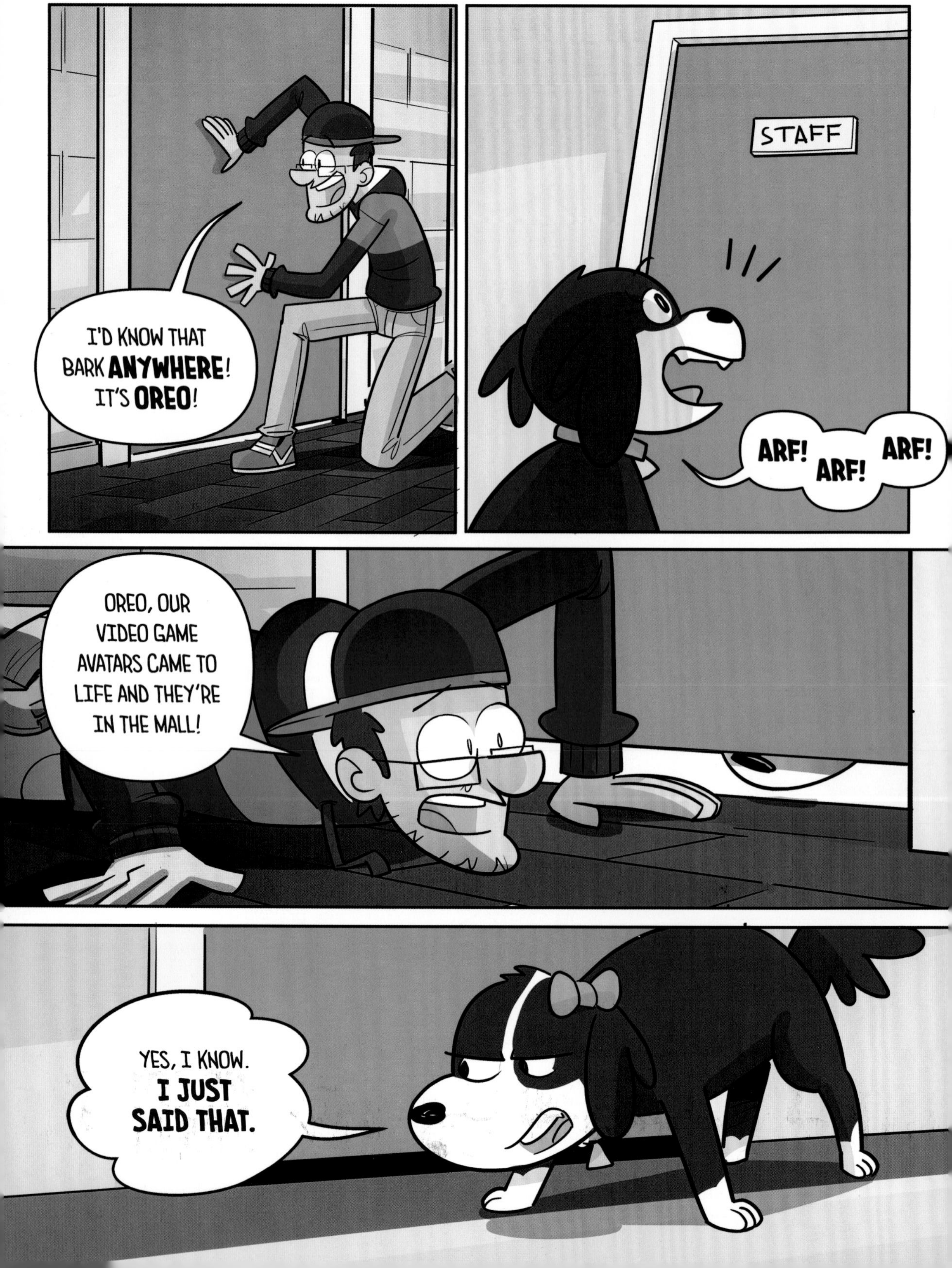
I'D KNOW THAT BARK **ANYWHERE**! IT'S **OREO**!
STAFF
ARF! ARF! ARF!
OREO, OUR VIDEO GAME AVATARS CAME TO LIFE AND THEY'RE IN THE MALL!
YES, I KNOW. **I JUST SAID THAT.**

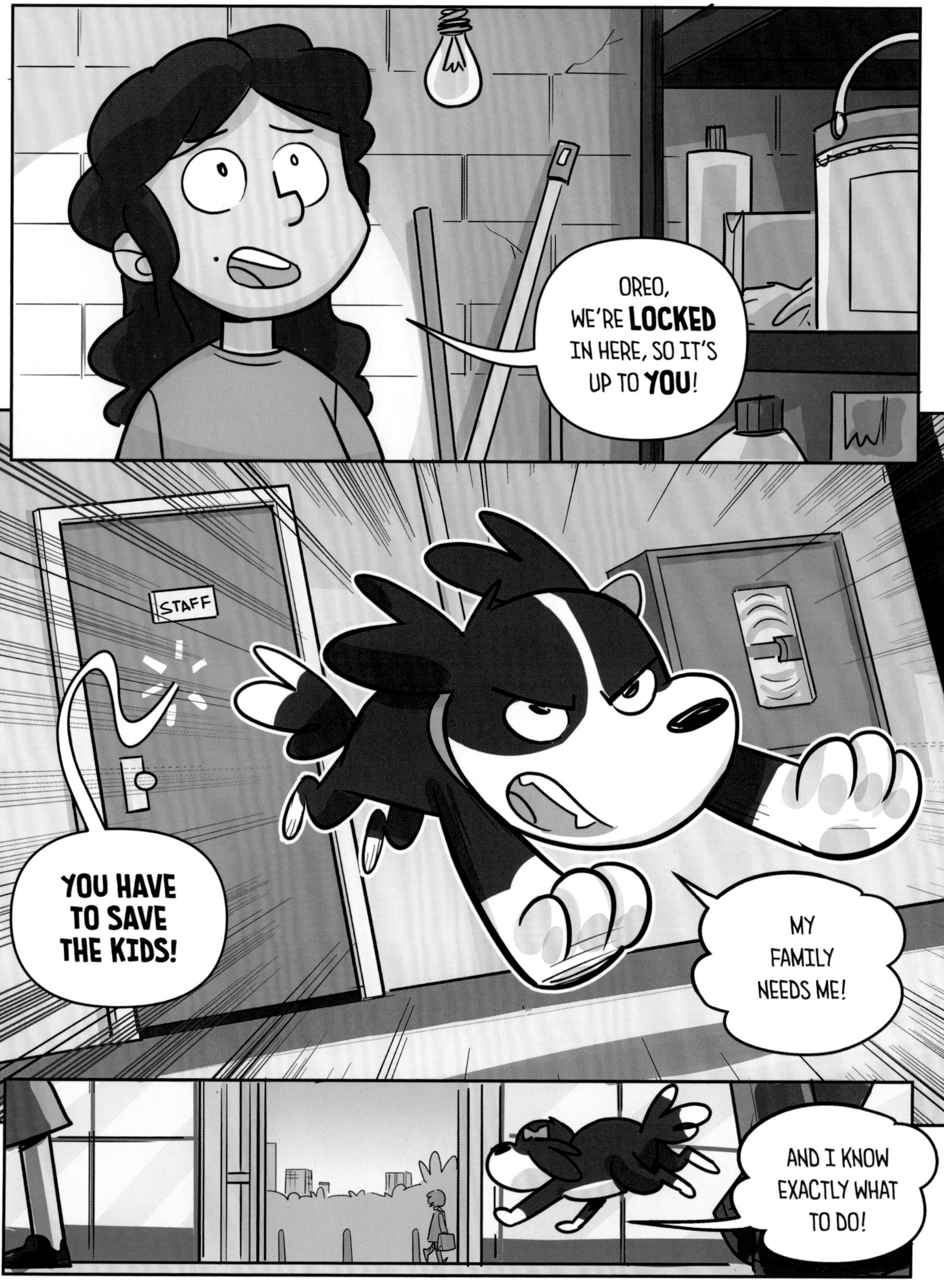
OREO, WE'RE **LOCKED** IN HERE, SO IT'S UP TO **YOU**!
STAFF
YOU HAVE TO SAVE THE KIDS!
MY FAMILY NEEDS ME!
AND I KNOW EXACTLY WHAT TO DO!

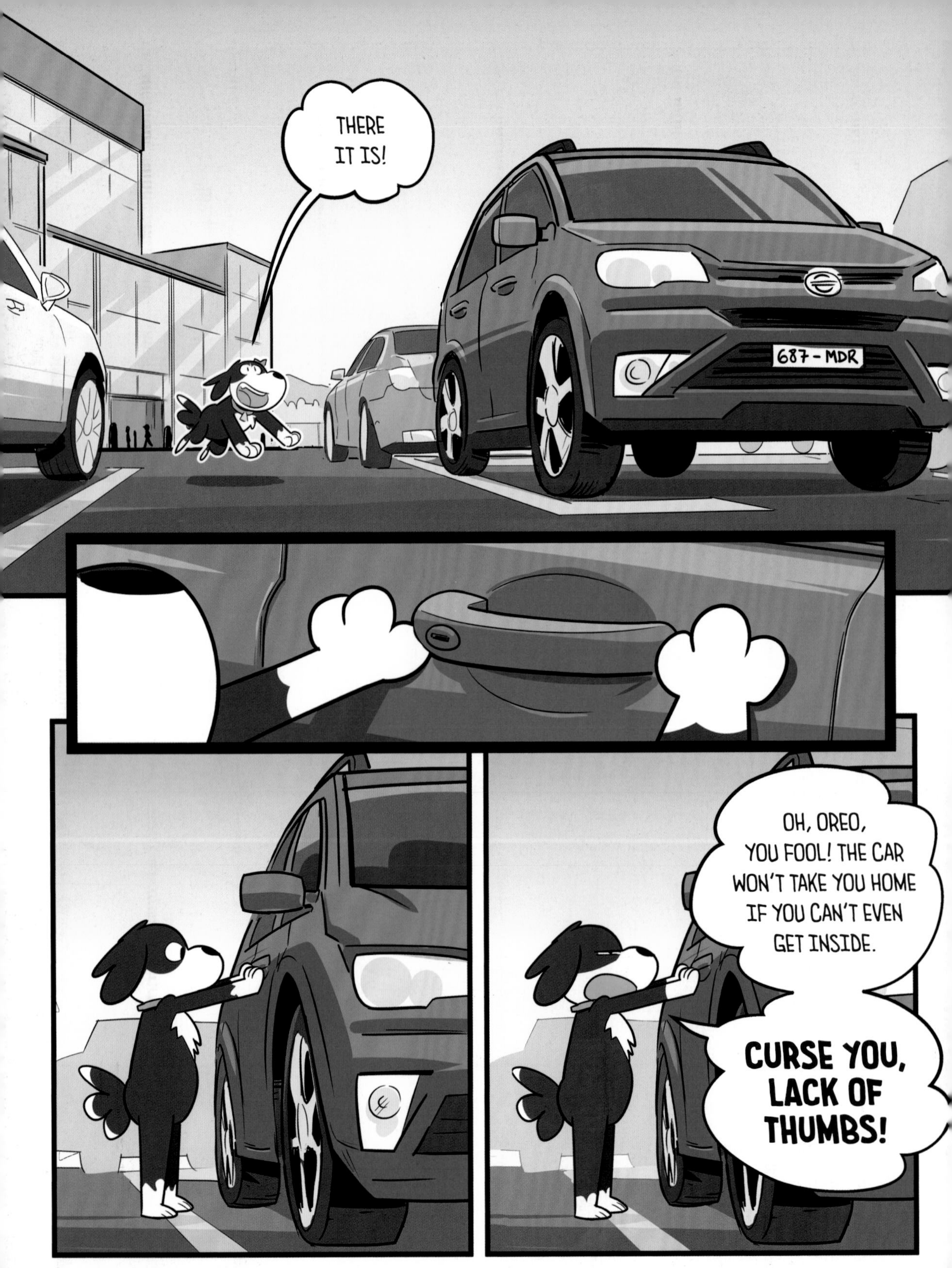
THERE IT IS!
687 - MDR
OH, OREO, YOU FOOL! THE CAR WON'T TAKE YOU HOME IF YOU CAN'T EVEN GET INSIDE.
CURSE YOU, LACK OF THUMBS!

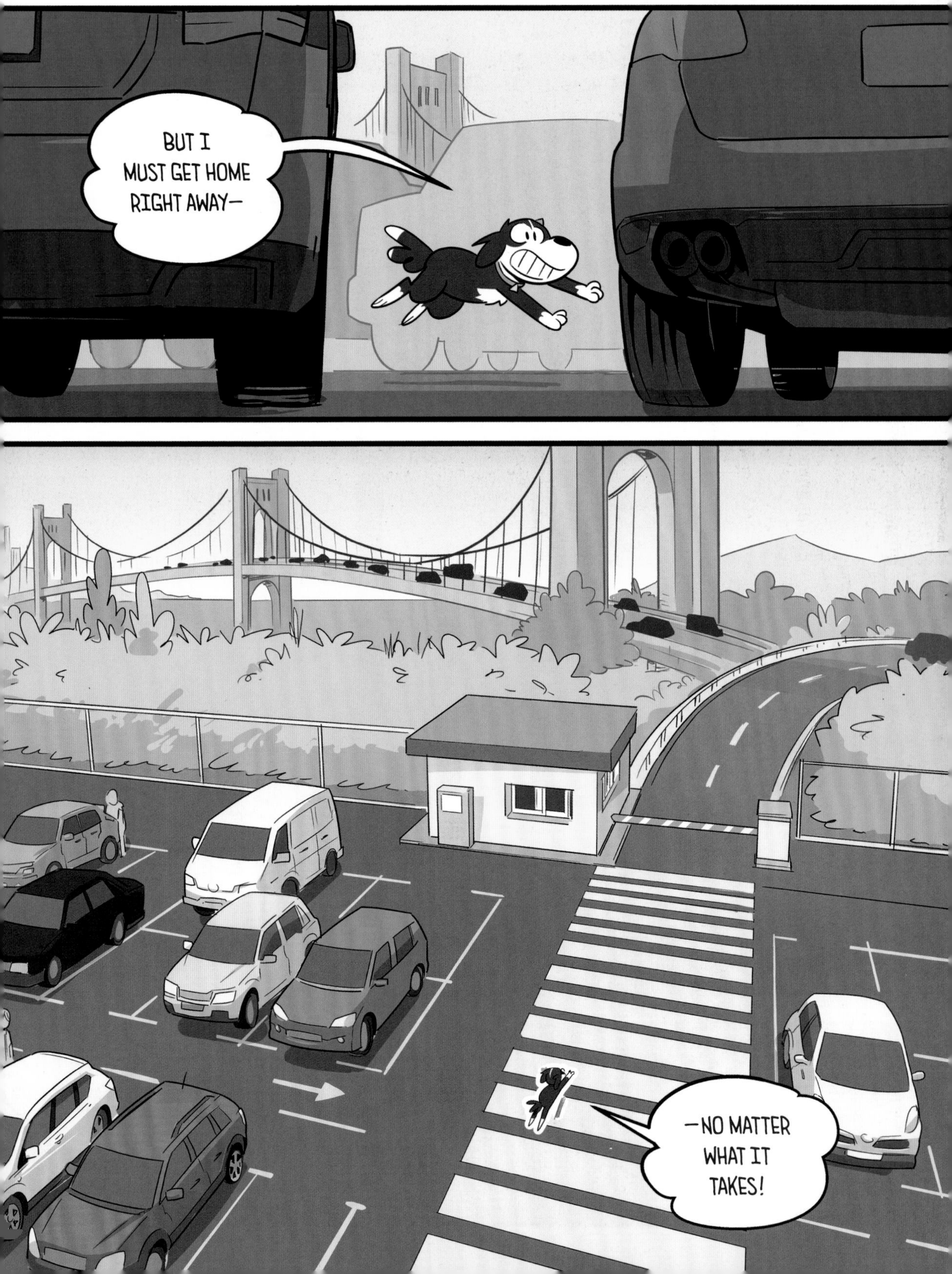
BUT I MUST GET HOME RIGHT AWAY—
—NO MATTER WHAT IT TAKES!

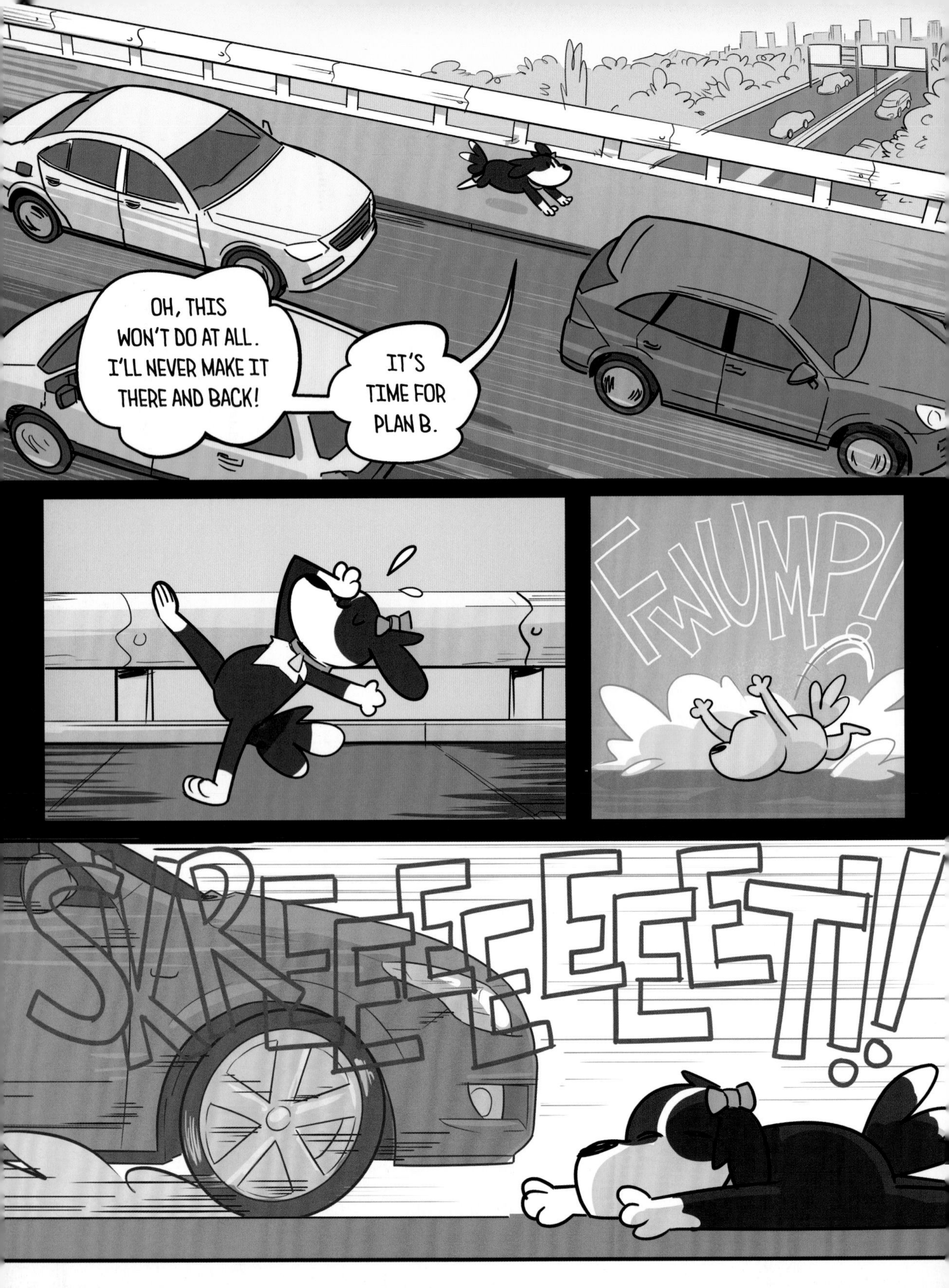
OH, THIS WON'T DO AT ALL. I'LL NEVER MAKE IT THERE AND BACK!
IT'S TIME FOR PLAN B.
FWUMP!
SKREEEEEEET!!

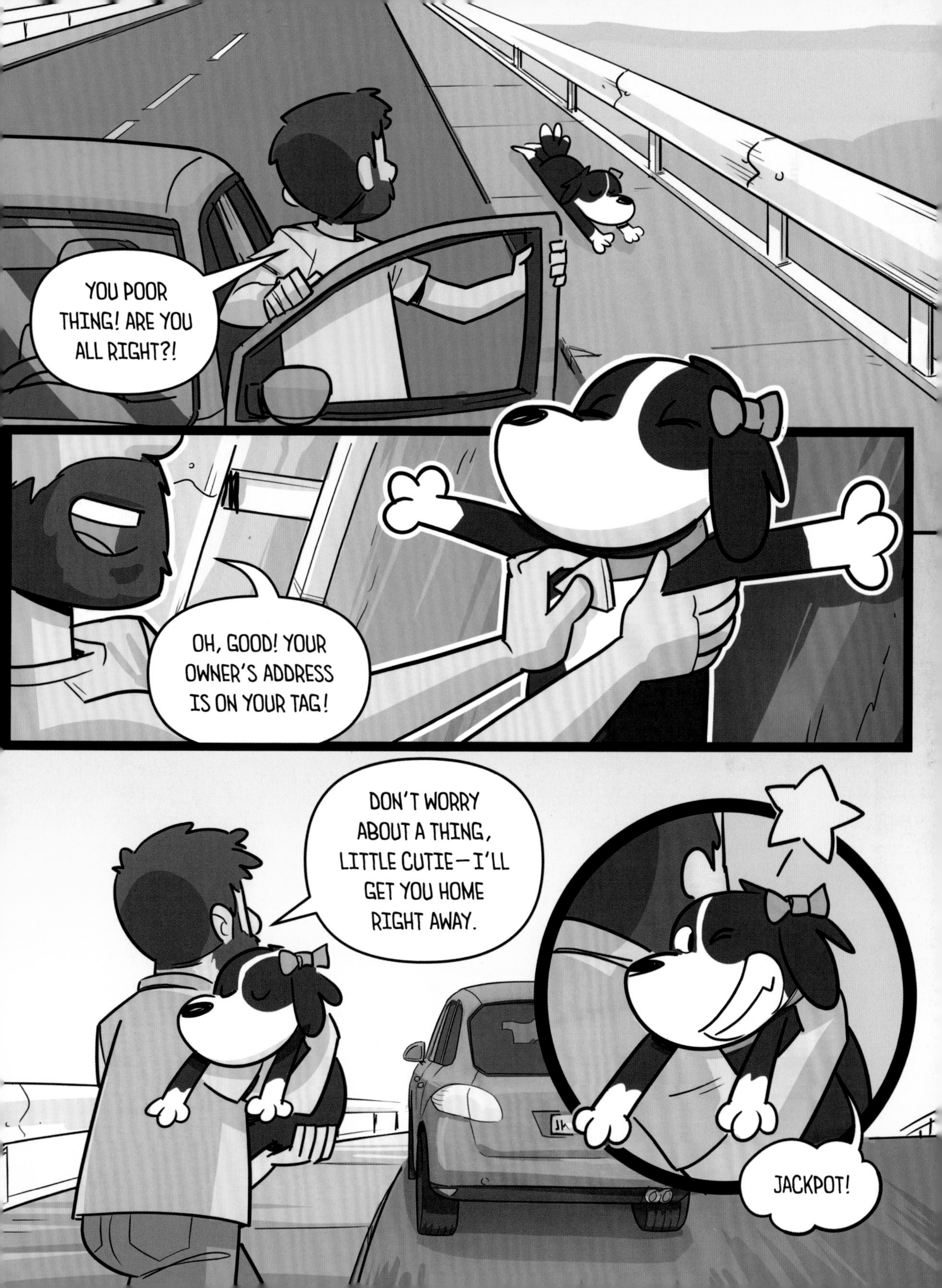
YOU POOR THING! ARE YOU ALL RIGHT?!
OH, GOOD! YOUR OWNER'S ADDRESS IS ON YOUR TAG!
DON'T WORRY ABOUT A THING, LITTLE CUTIE—I'LL GET YOU HOME RIGHT AWAY.
JACKPOT!

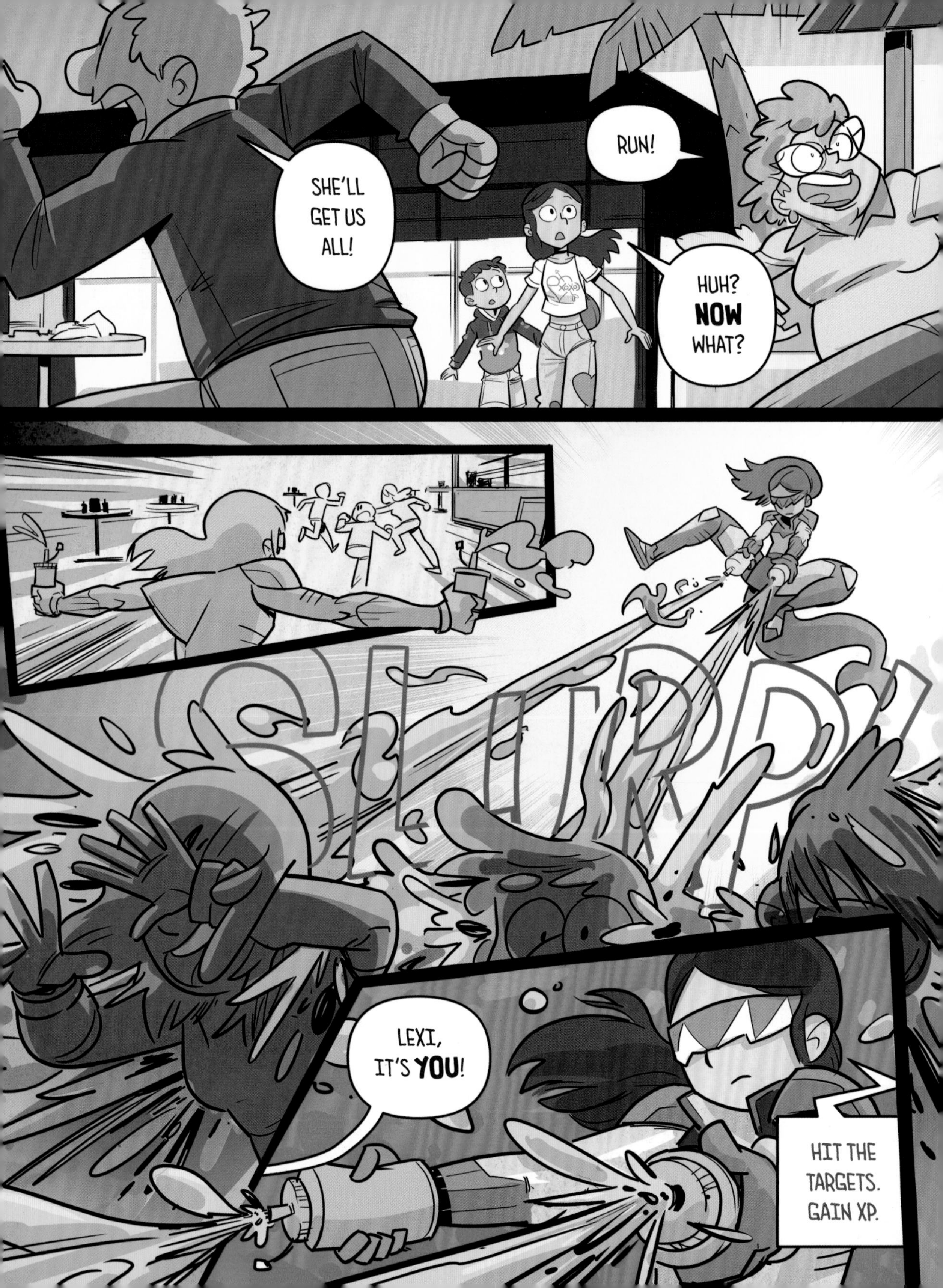
SHE'LL GET US ALL!
RUN!
HUH? **NOW** WHAT?
SLURP!
LEXI, IT'S **YOU**!
HIT THE TARGETS. GAIN XP.

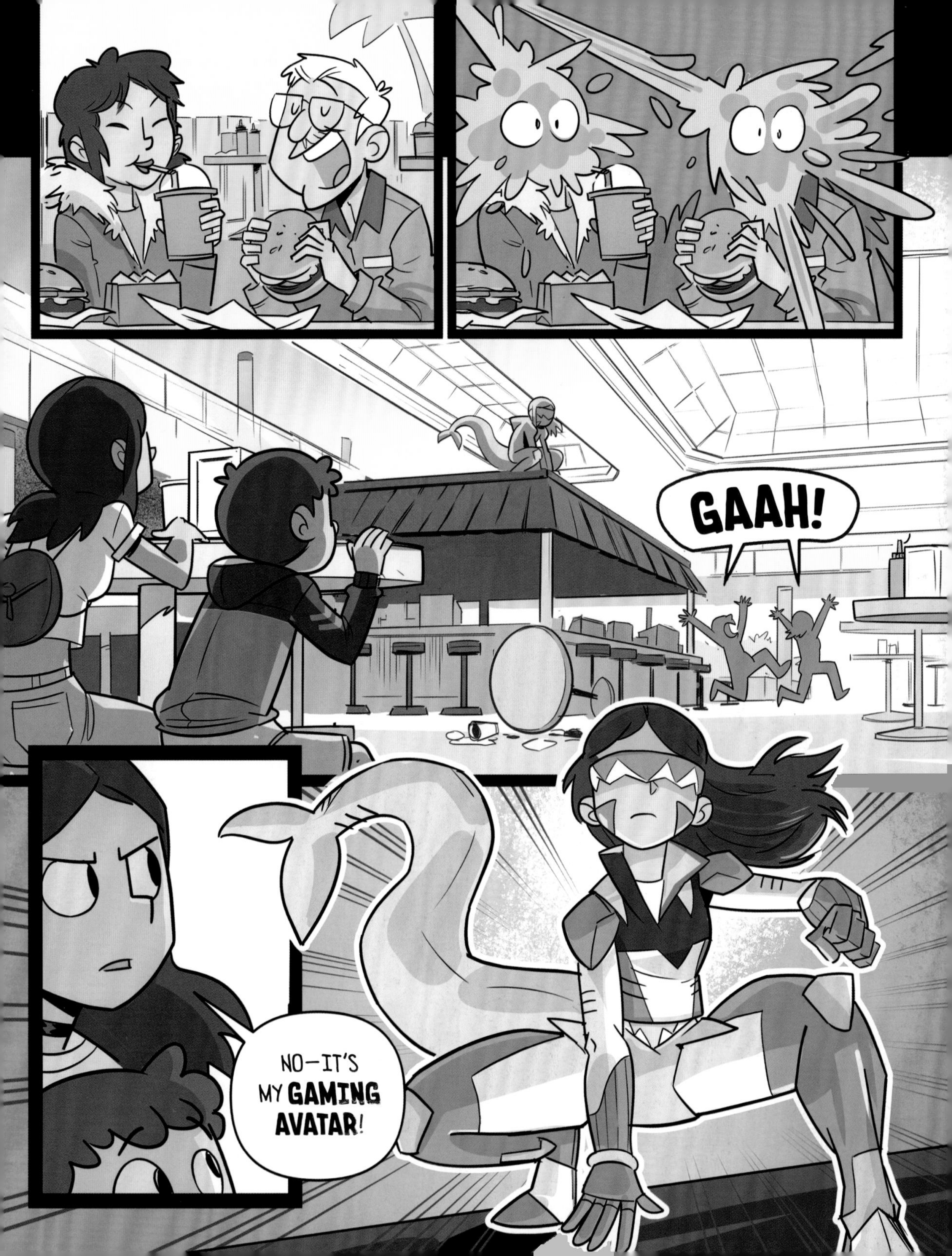
GAAH!
NO—IT'S MY GAMING AVATAR!

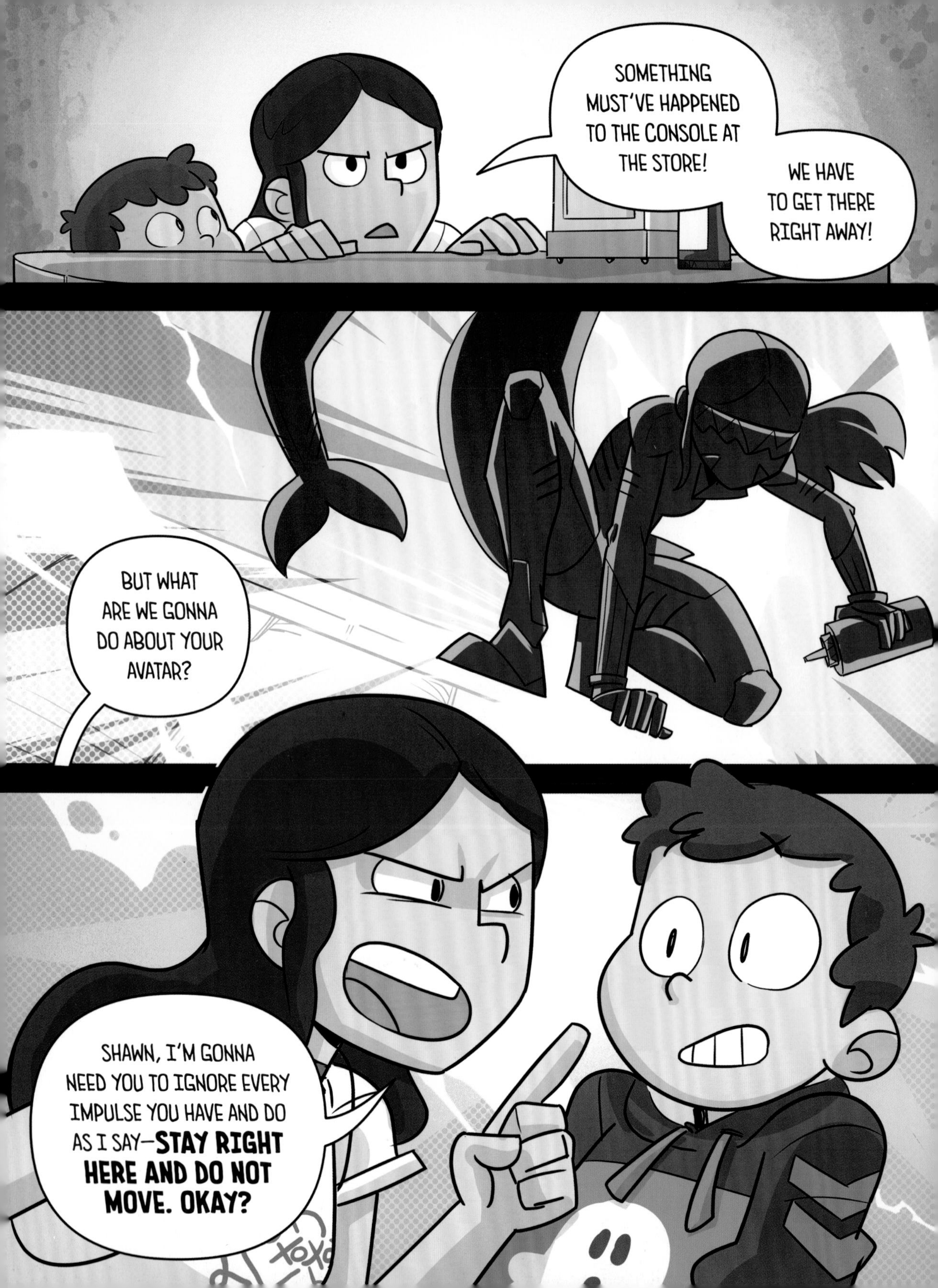
SOMETHING MUST'VE HAPPENED TO THE CONSOLE AT THE STORE!
WE HAVE TO GET THERE RIGHT AWAY!
BUT WHAT ARE WE GONNA DO ABOUT YOUR AVATAR?
SHAWN, I'M GONNA NEED YOU TO IGNORE EVERY IMPULSE YOU HAVE AND DO AS I SAY—STAY RIGHT HERE AND DO NOT MOVE. OKAY?

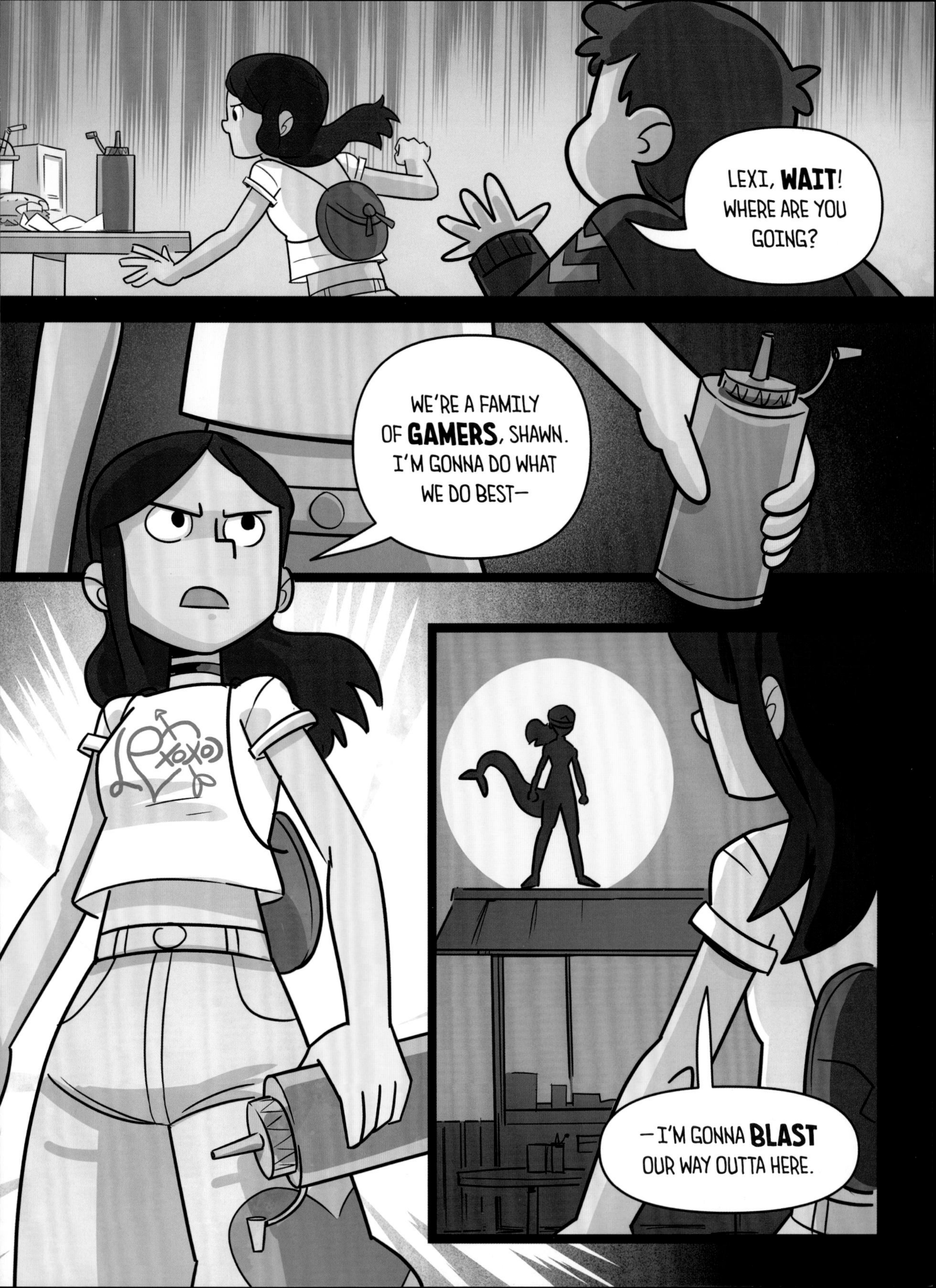
LEXI, WAIT! WHERE ARE YOU GOING?
WE'RE A FAMILY OF GAMERS, SHAWN. I'M GONNA DO WHAT WE DO BEST—
XOXO
—I'M GONNA BLAST OUR WAY OUTTA HERE.

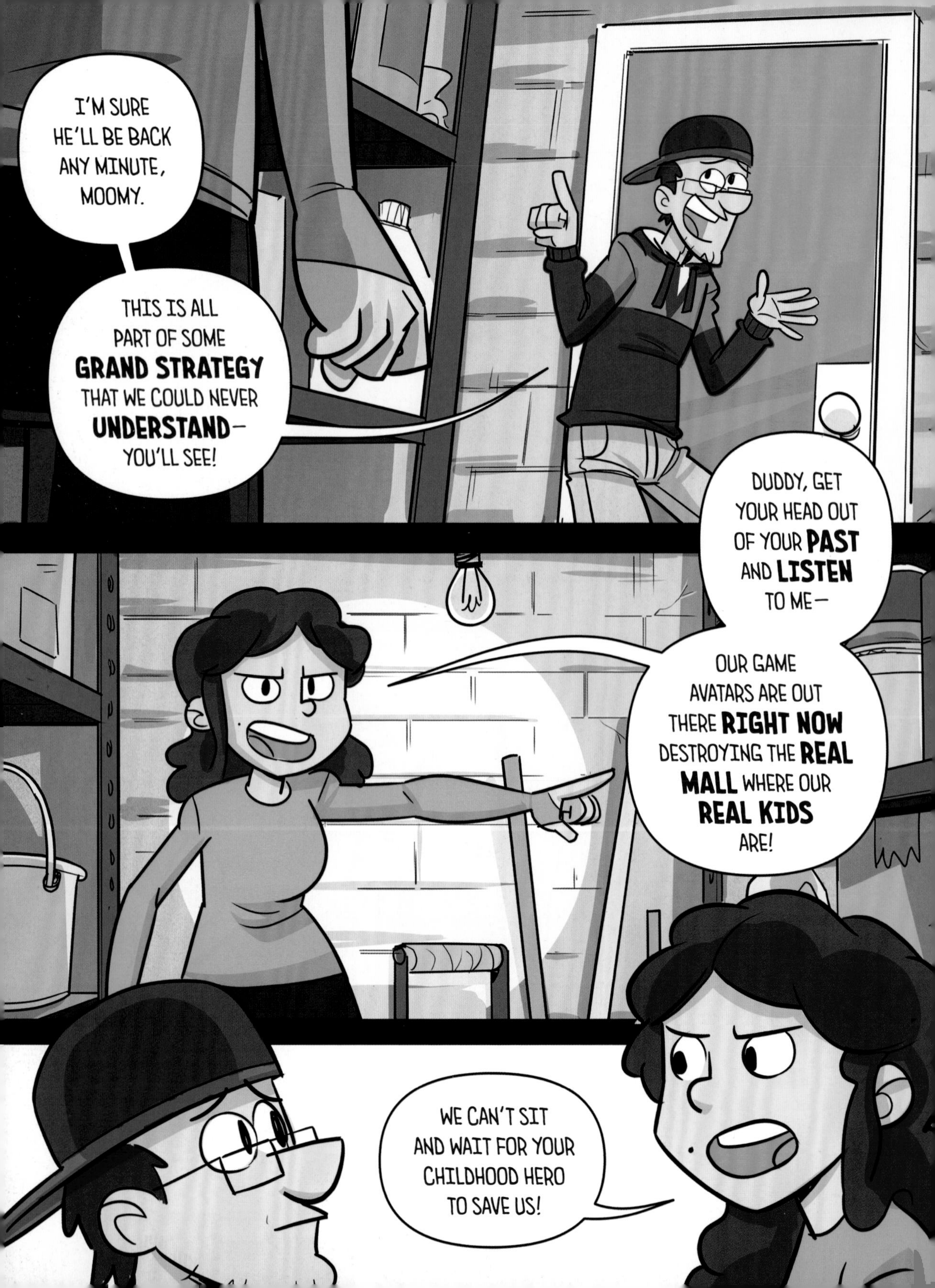
I'M SURE HE'LL BE BACK ANY MINUTE, MOOMY.
THIS IS ALL PART OF SOME **GRAND STRATEGY** THAT WE COULD NEVER **UNDERSTAND**— YOU'LL SEE!
DUDDY, GET YOUR HEAD OUT OF YOUR **PAST** AND **LISTEN** TO ME—
OUR GAME AVATARS ARE OUT THERE **RIGHT NOW** DESTROYING THE **REAL MALL** WHERE OUR **REAL KIDS** ARE!
WE CAN'T SIT AND WAIT FOR YOUR CHILDHOOD HERO TO SAVE US!

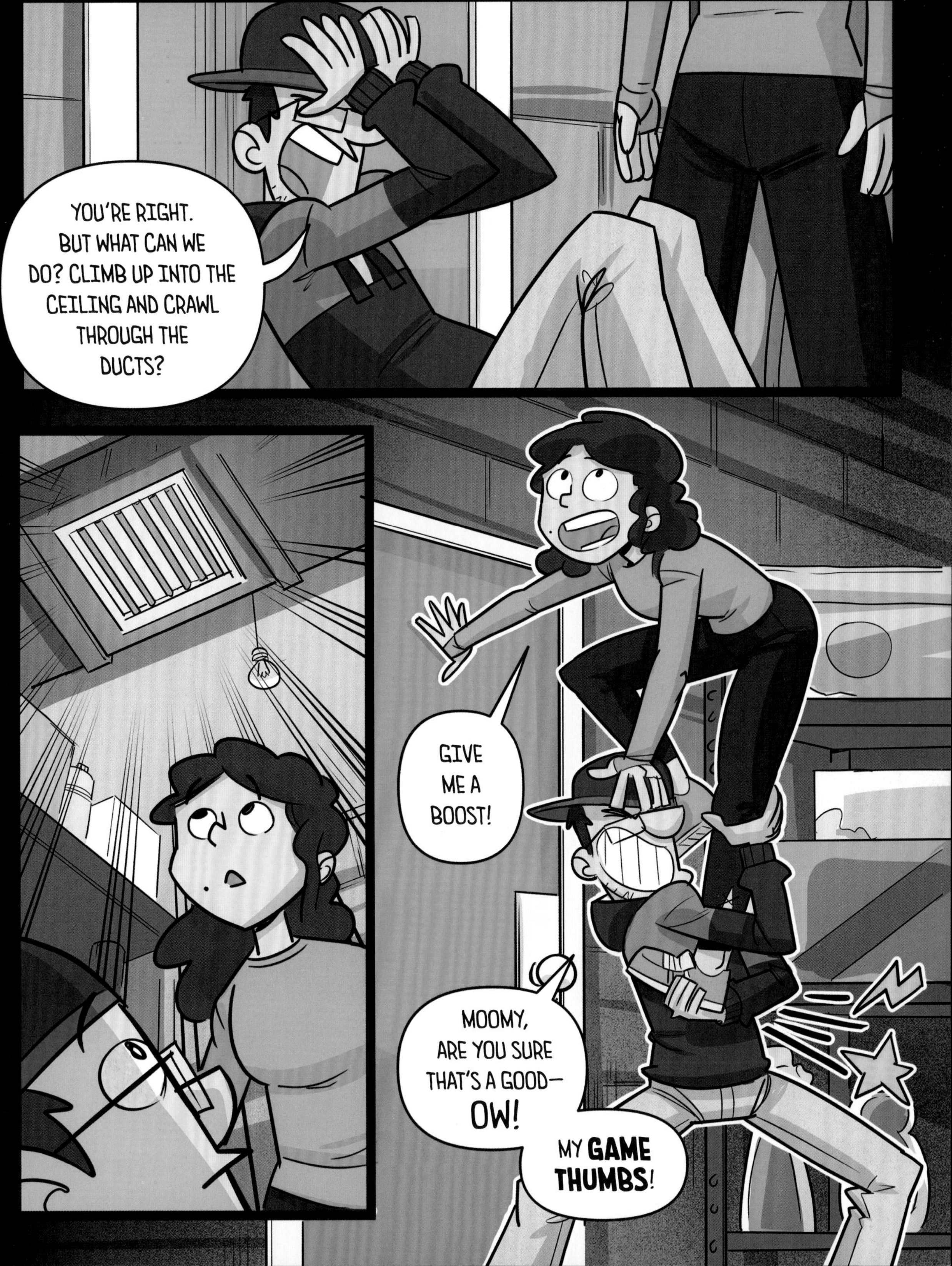
YOU'RE RIGHT. BUT WHAT CAN WE DO? CLIMB UP INTO THE CEILING AND CRAWL THROUGH THE DUCTS?
GIVE ME A BOOST!
MOOMY, ARE YOU SURE THAT'S A GOOD— OW!
MY **GAME THUMBS**!

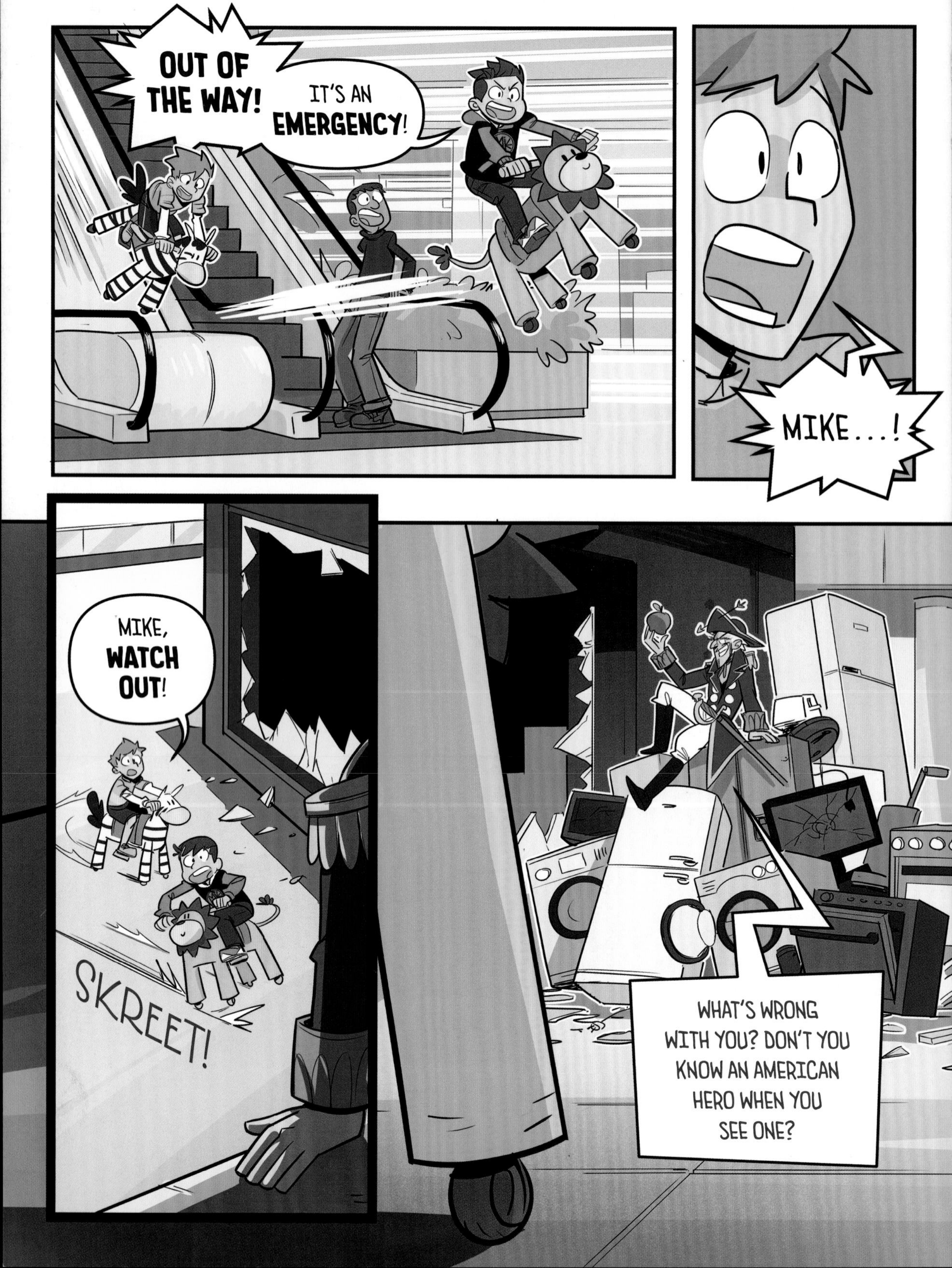

OUT OF THE WAY!
IT'S AN EMERGENCY!
MIKE...!
MIKE, WATCH OUT!
SKREET!
WHAT'S WRONG WITH YOU? DON'T YOU KNOW AN AMERICAN HERO WHEN YOU SEE ONE?

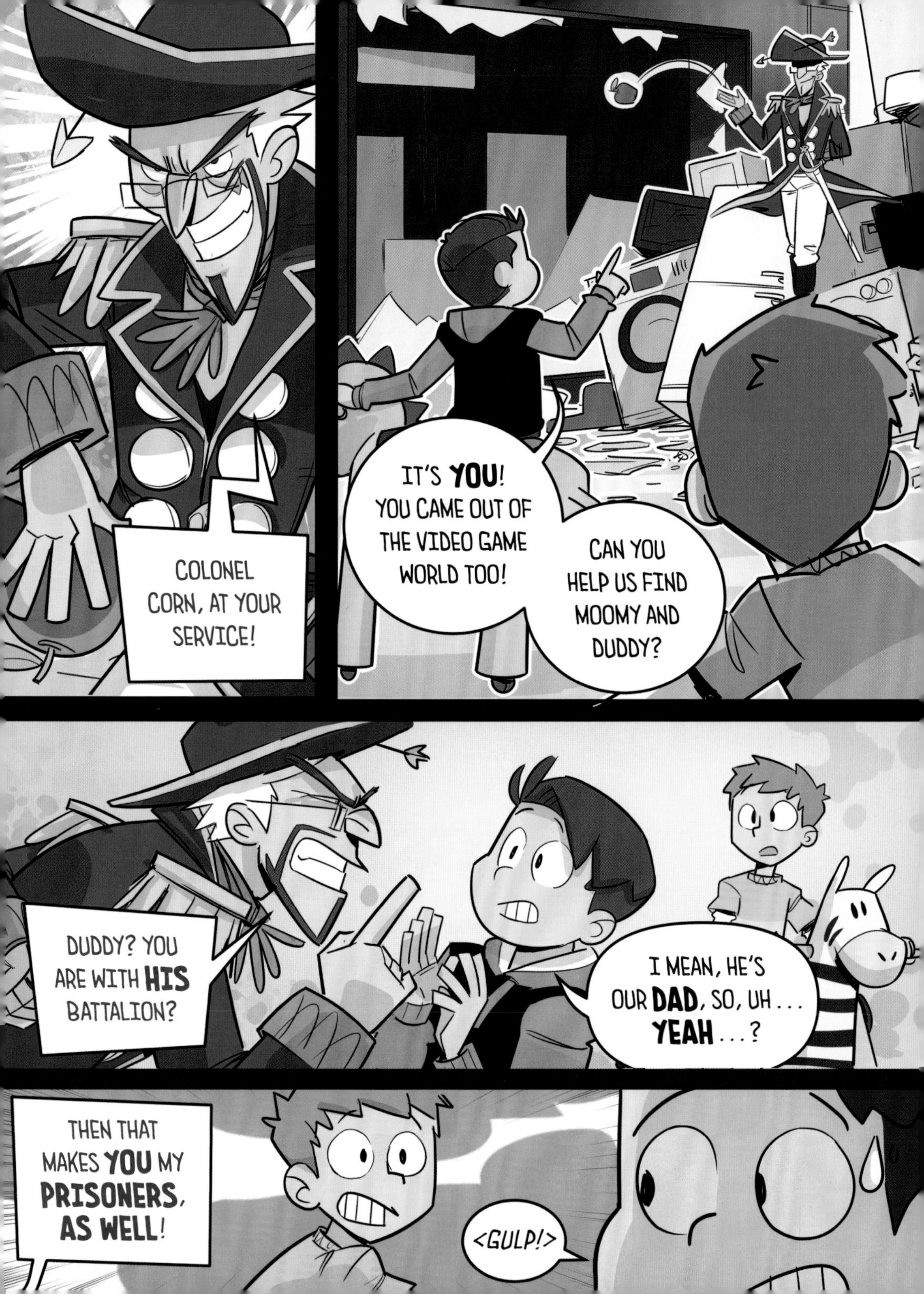
COLONEL CORN, AT YOUR SERVICE!
IT'S YOU! YOU CAME OUT OF THE VIDEO GAME WORLD TOO!
CAN YOU HELP US FIND MOOMY AND DUDDY?
DUDDY? YOU ARE WITH HIS BATTALION?
I MEAN, HE'S OUR DAD, SO, UH . . . YEAH . . . ?
THEN THAT MAKES YOU MY PRISONERS, AS WELL!
<GULP!>

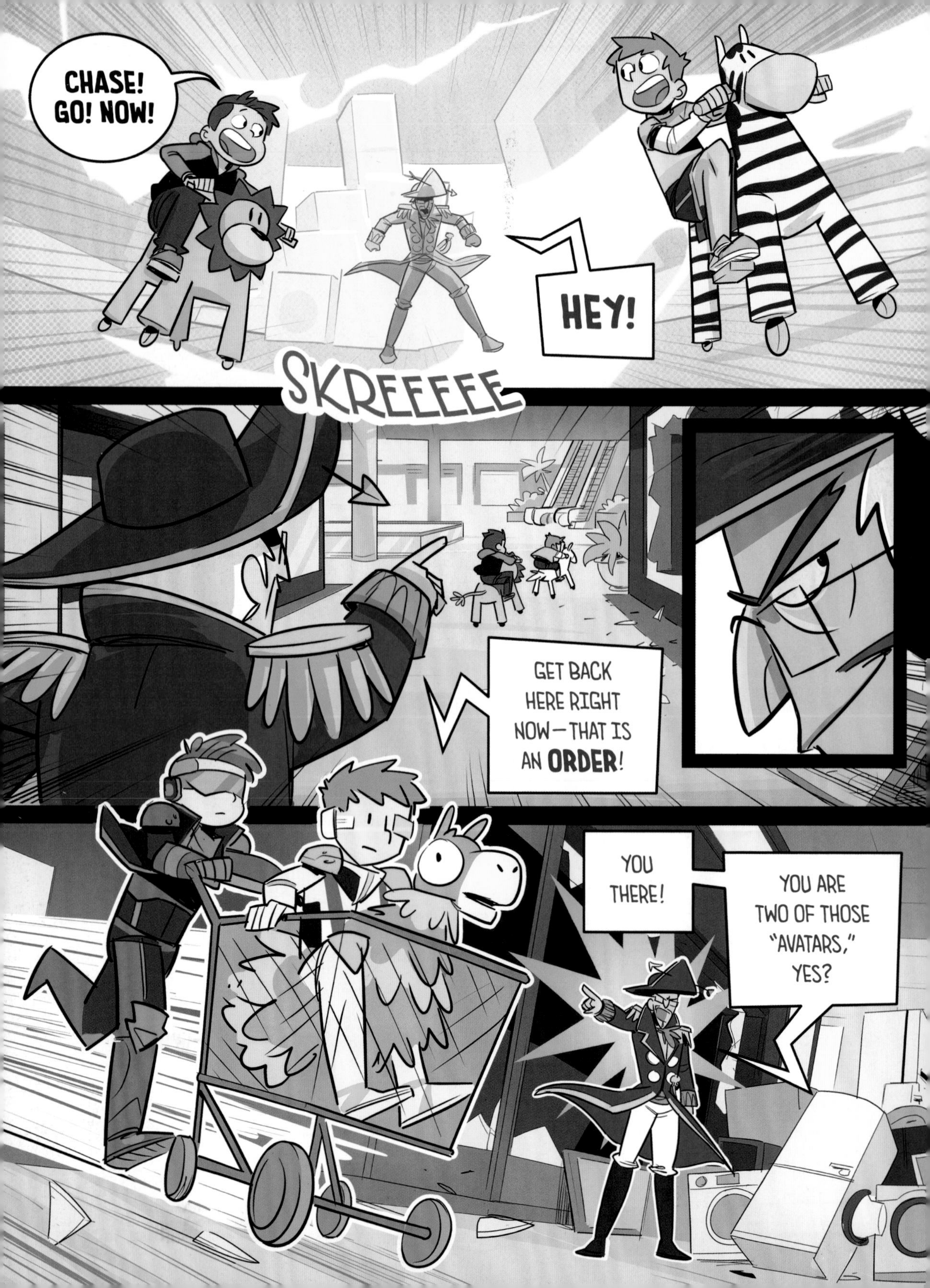
CHASE! GO! NOW!
HEY!
SKREEEEE
GET BACK HERE RIGHT NOW—THAT IS AN **ORDER**!
YOU THERE!
YOU ARE TWO OF THOSE "AVATARS," YES?

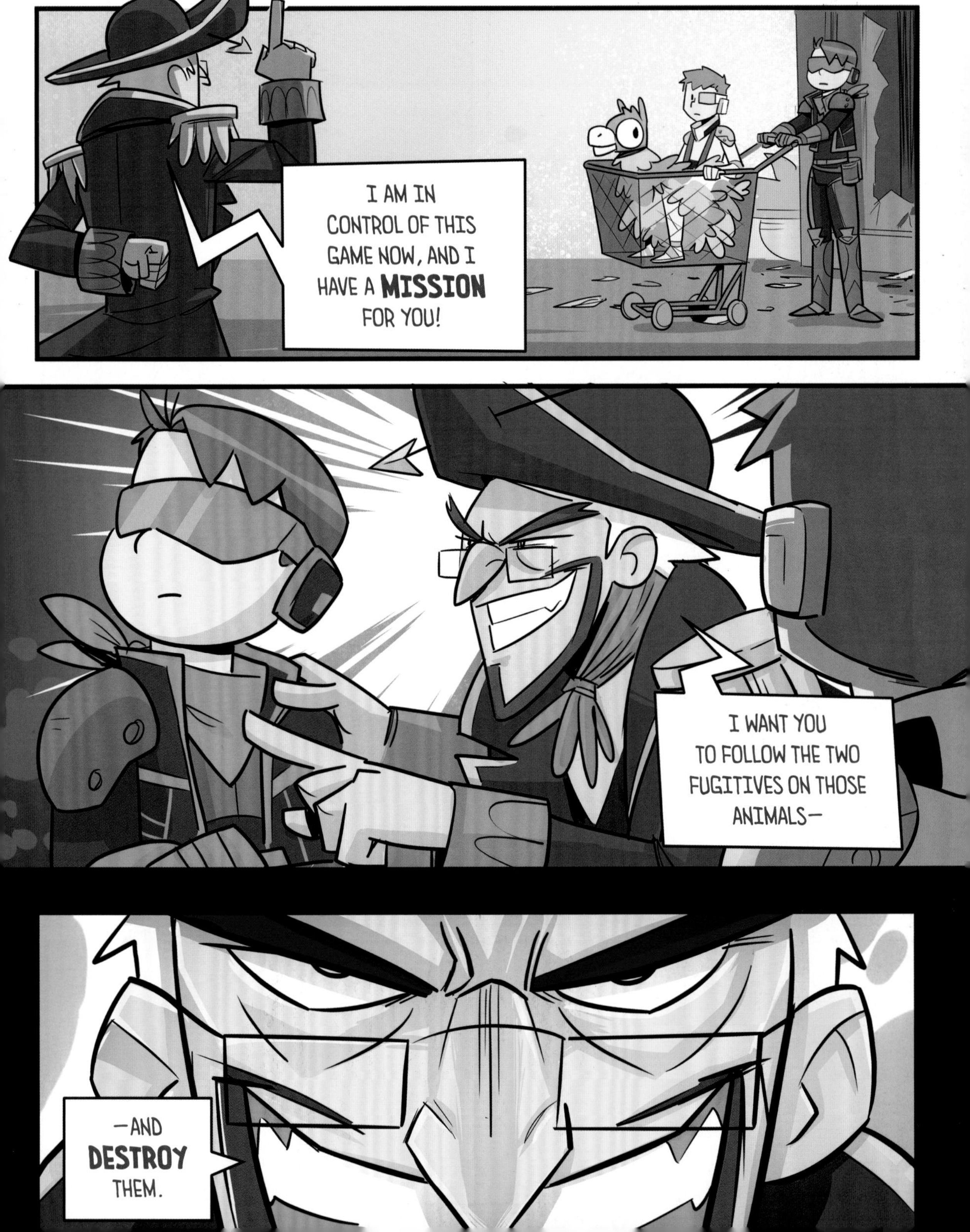
I AM IN CONTROL OF THIS GAME NOW, AND I HAVE A **MISSION** FOR YOU!
I WANT YOU TO FOLLOW THE TWO FUGITIVES ON THOSE ANIMALS—
—AND **DESTROY** THEM.

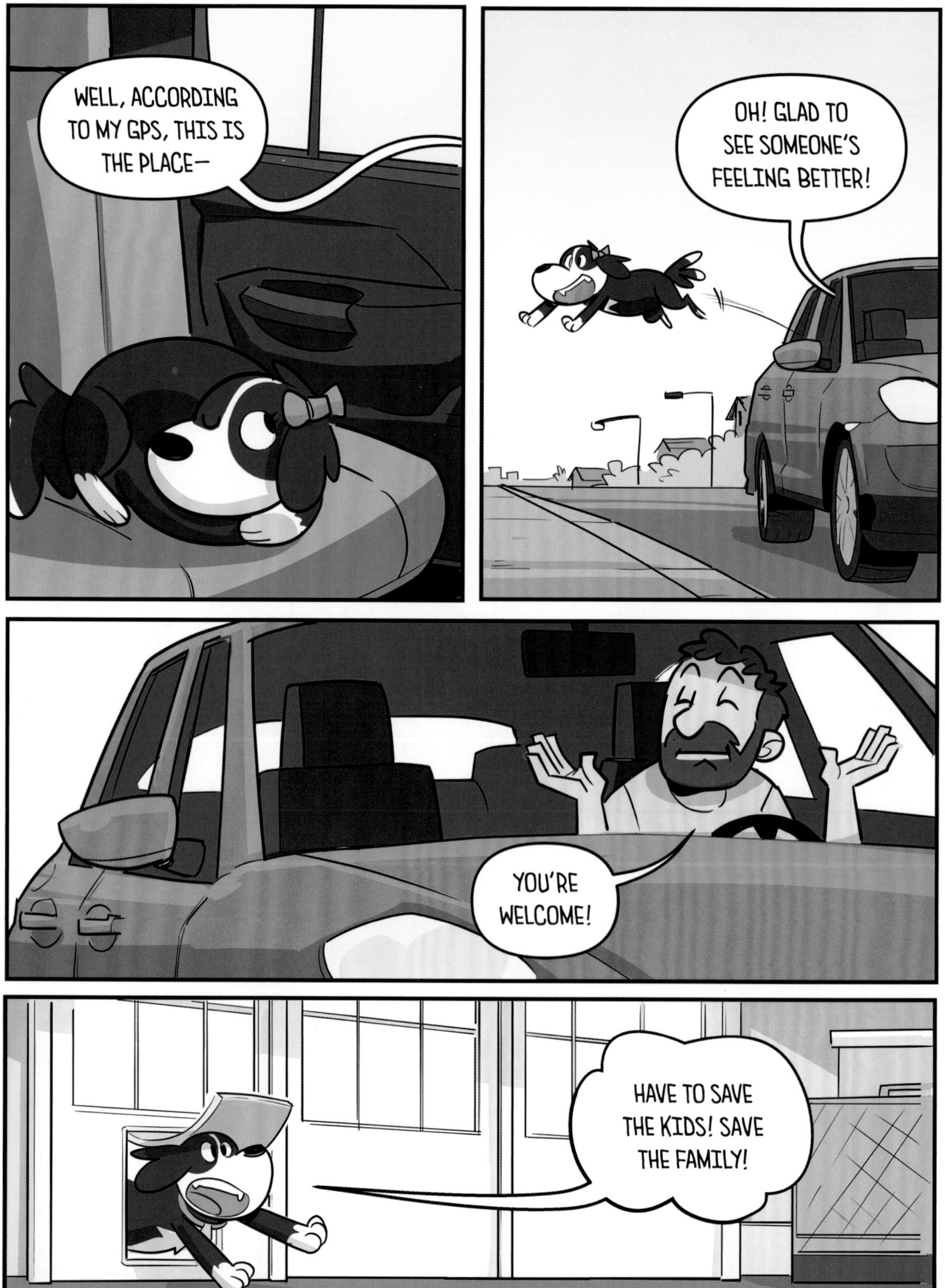
WELL, ACCORDING TO MY GPS, THIS IS THE PLACE—
OH! GLAD TO SEE SOMEONE'S FEELING BETTER!
YOU'RE WELCOME!
HAVE TO SAVE THE KIDS! SAVE THE FAMILY!

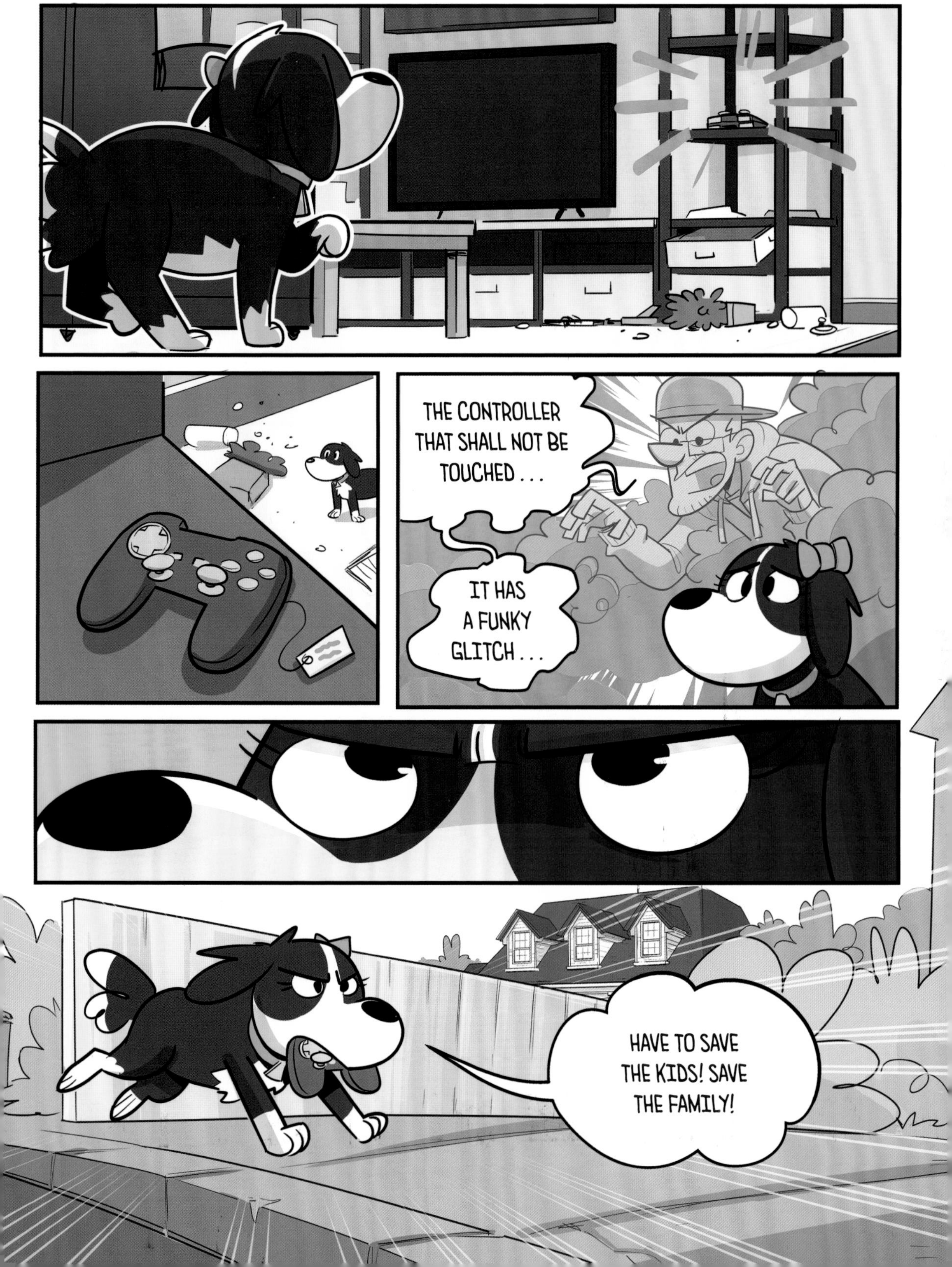
THE CONTROLLER THAT SHALL NOT BE TOUCHED . . .
IT HAS A FUNKY GLITCH . . .
HAVE TO SAVE THE KIDS! SAVE THE FAMILY!

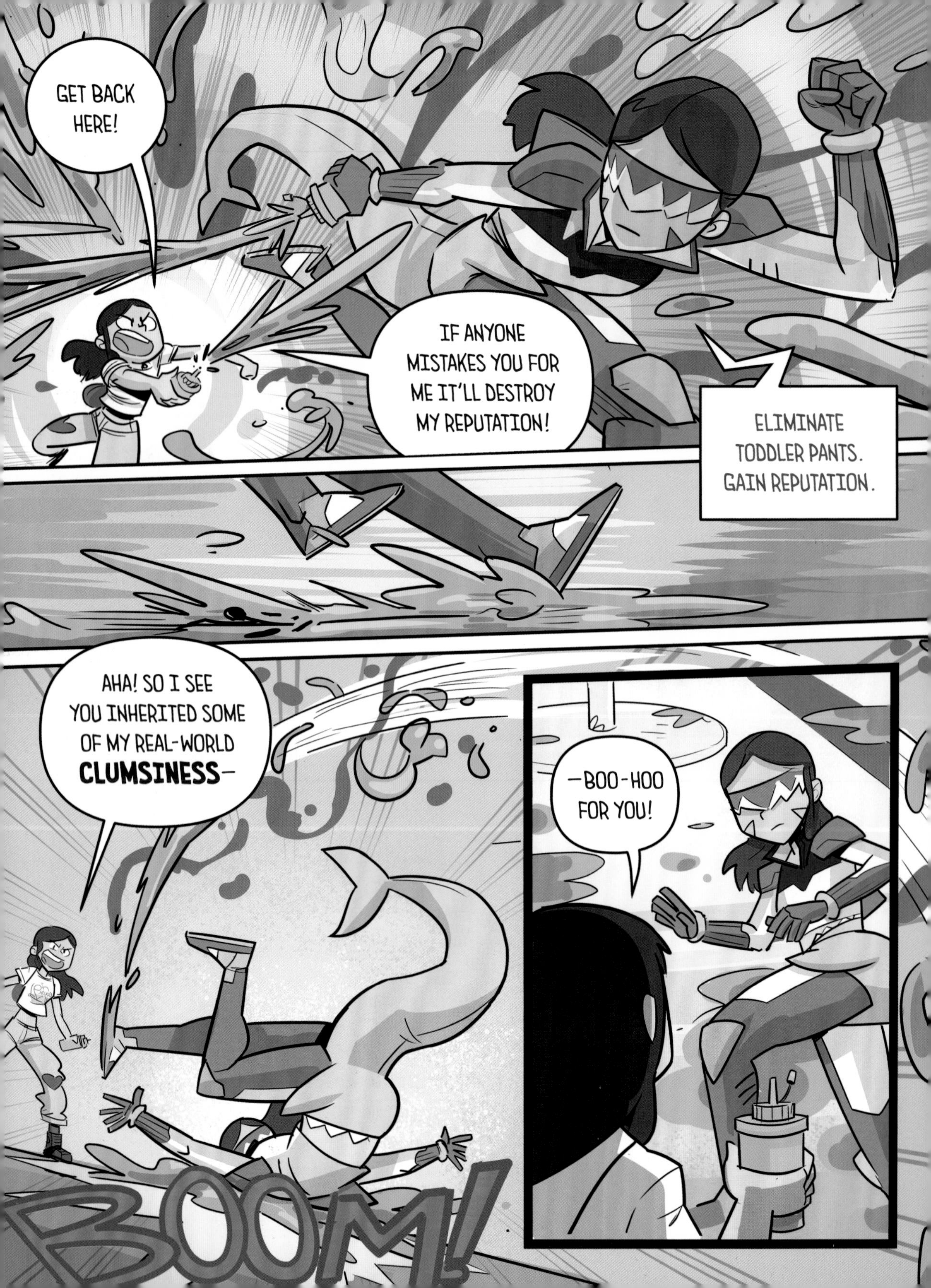
GET BACK HERE!
IF ANYONE MISTAKES YOU FOR ME IT'LL DESTROY MY REPUTATION!
ELIMINATE TODDLER PANTS. GAIN REPUTATION.
AHA! SO I SEE YOU INHERITED SOME OF MY REAL-WORLD **CLUMSINESS**—
—BOO-HOO FOR YOU!
BOOM!

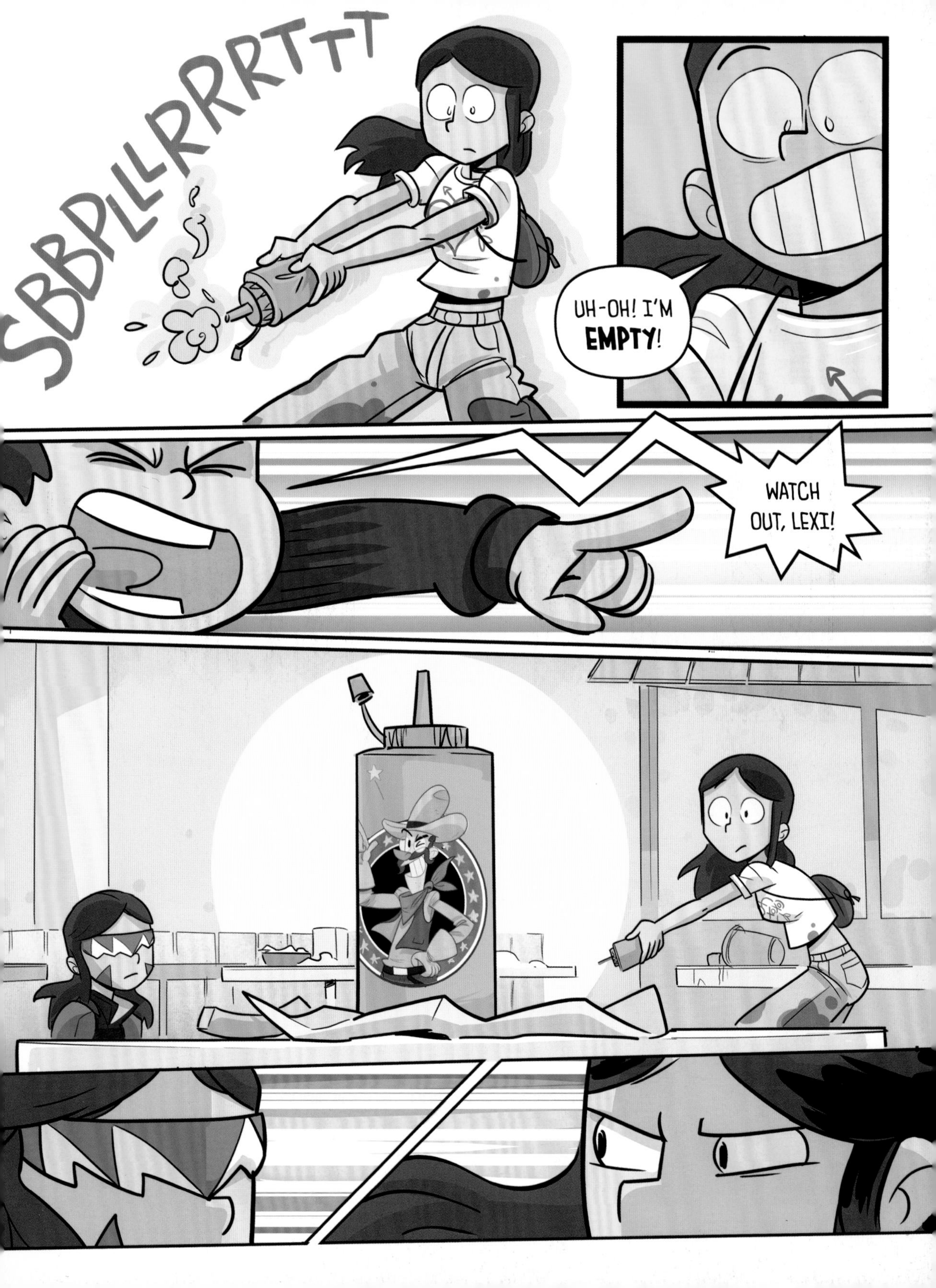
SBBPLLLRRRTTTT
UH-OH! I'M EMPTY!
WATCH OUT, LEXI!

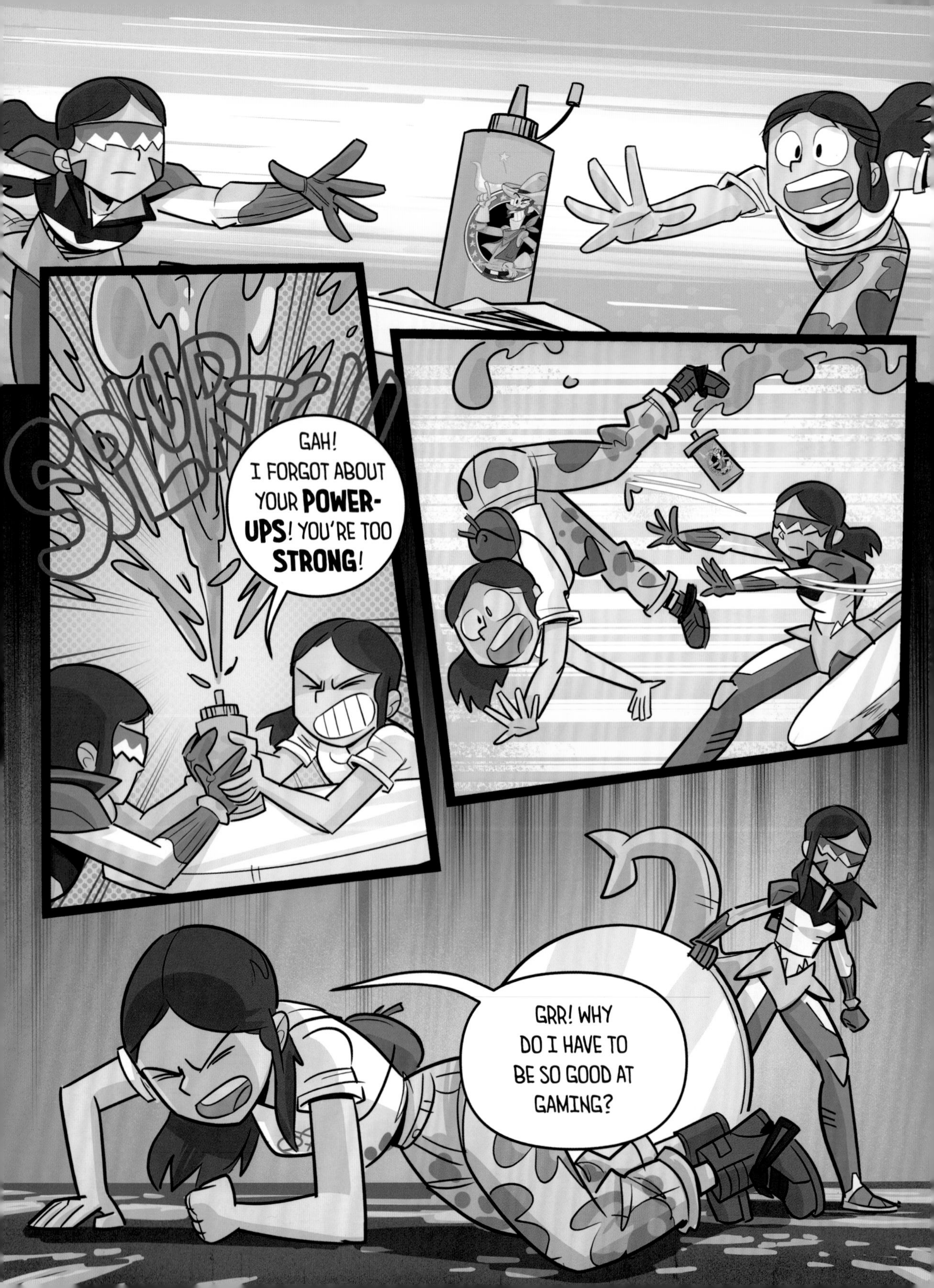
GAH! I FORGOT ABOUT YOUR **POWER-UPS**! YOU'RE TOO **STRONG**!
GRR! WHY DO I HAVE TO BE SO GOOD AT GAMING?

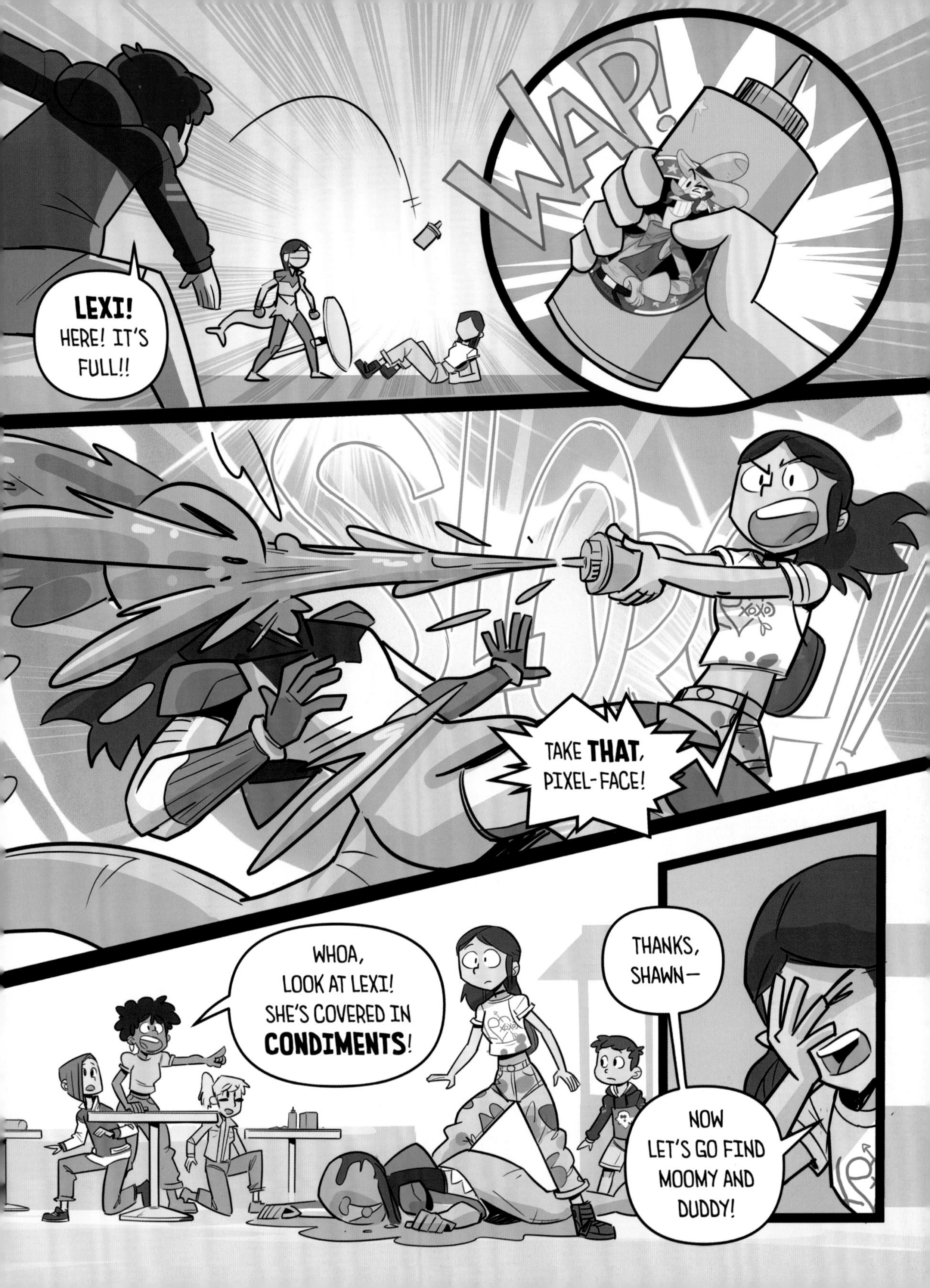
LEXI!
HERE! IT'S FULL!!
WAP!
TAKE THAT, PIXEL-FACE!
WHOA, LOOK AT LEXI! SHE'S COVERED IN CONDIMENTS!
THANKS, SHAWN—
NOW LET'S GO FIND MOOMY AND DUDDY!

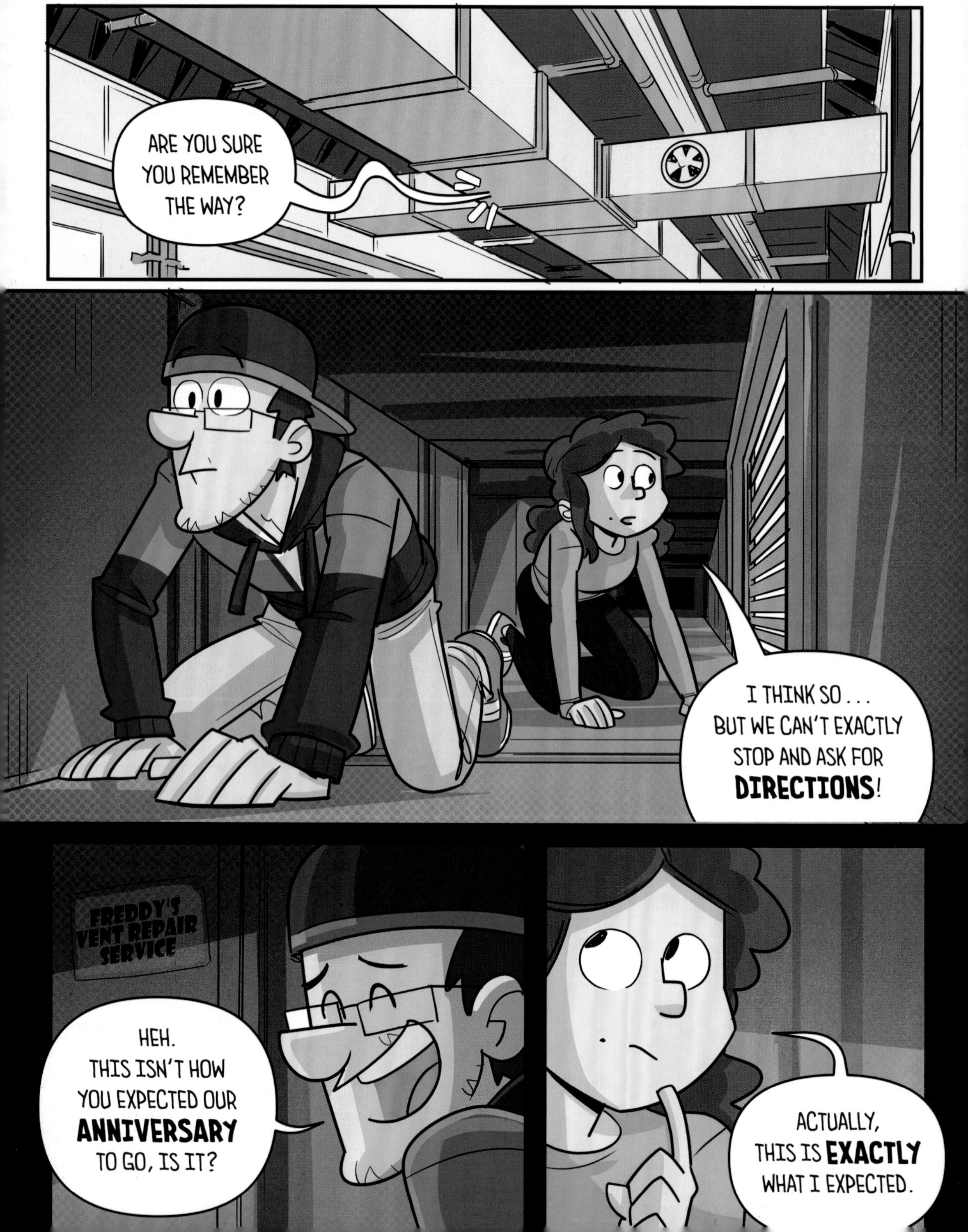

ARE YOU SURE YOU REMEMBER THE WAY?
I THINK SO . . . BUT WE CAN'T EXACTLY STOP AND ASK FOR **DIRECTIONS**!
FREDDY'S VENT REPAIR SERVICE
HEH. THIS ISN'T HOW YOU EXPECTED OUR **ANNIVERSARY** TO GO, IS IT?
ACTUALLY, THIS IS **EXACTLY** WHAT I EXPECTED.

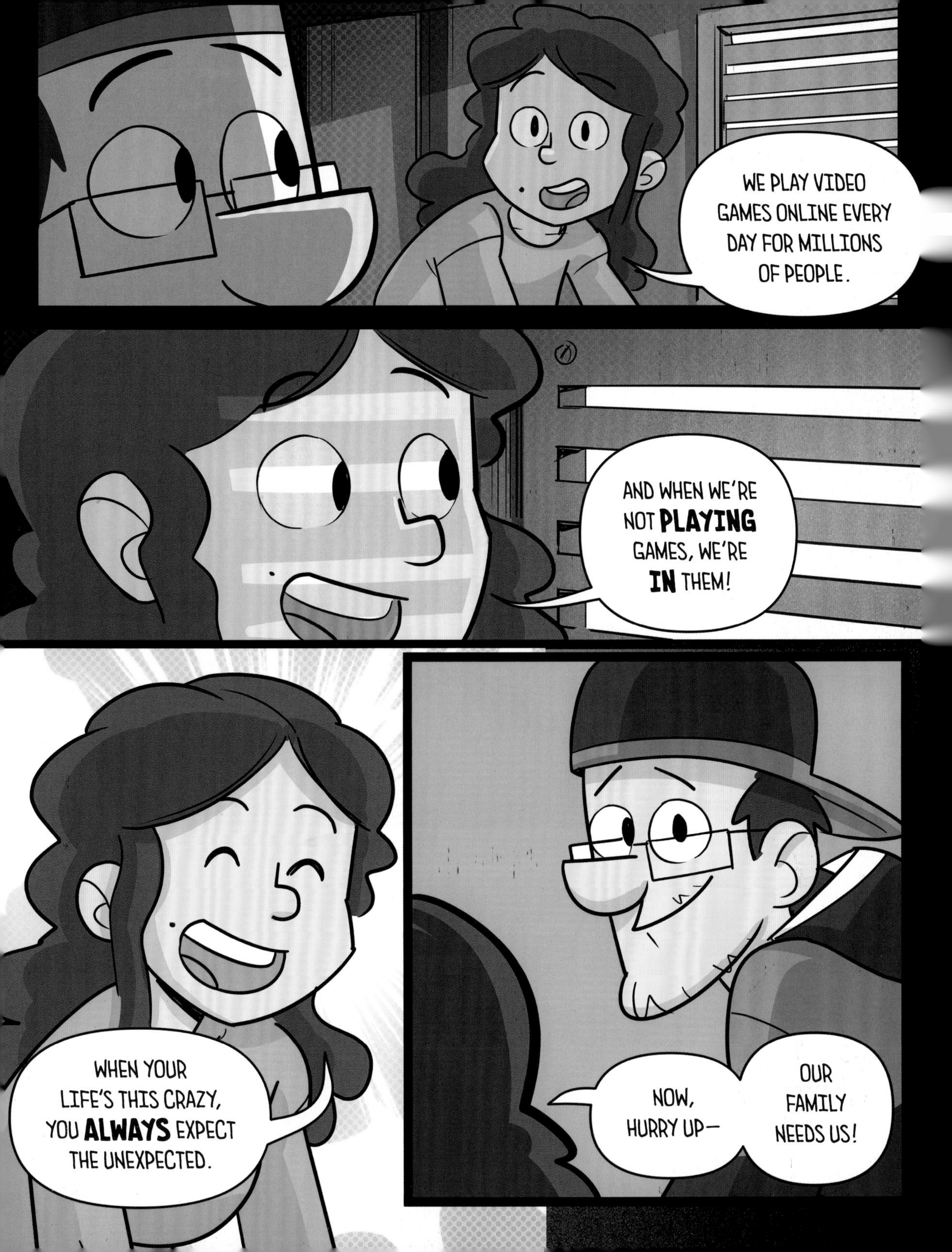
WE PLAY VIDEO GAMES ONLINE EVERY DAY FOR MILLIONS OF PEOPLE.
AND WHEN WE'RE NOT **PLAYING** GAMES, WE'RE **IN** THEM!
WHEN YOUR LIFE'S THIS CRAZY, YOU **ALWAYS** EXPECT THE UNEXPECTED.
NOW, HURRY UP—
OUR FAMILY NEEDS US!

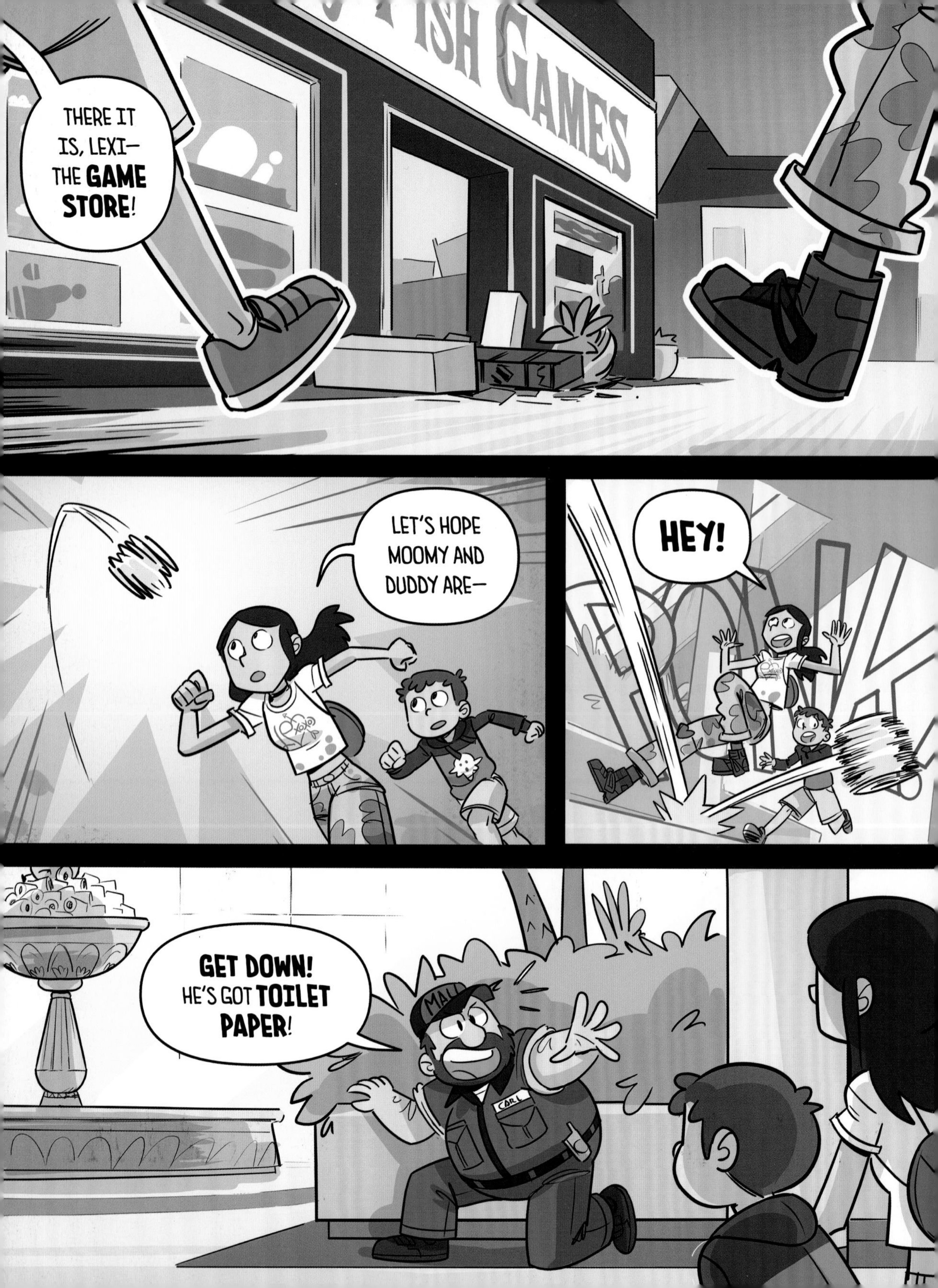
ISH GAMES
THERE IT IS, LEXI— THE GAME STORE!
LET'S HOPE MOOMY AND DUDDY ARE—
HEY!
GET DOWN! HE'S GOT TOILET PAPER!

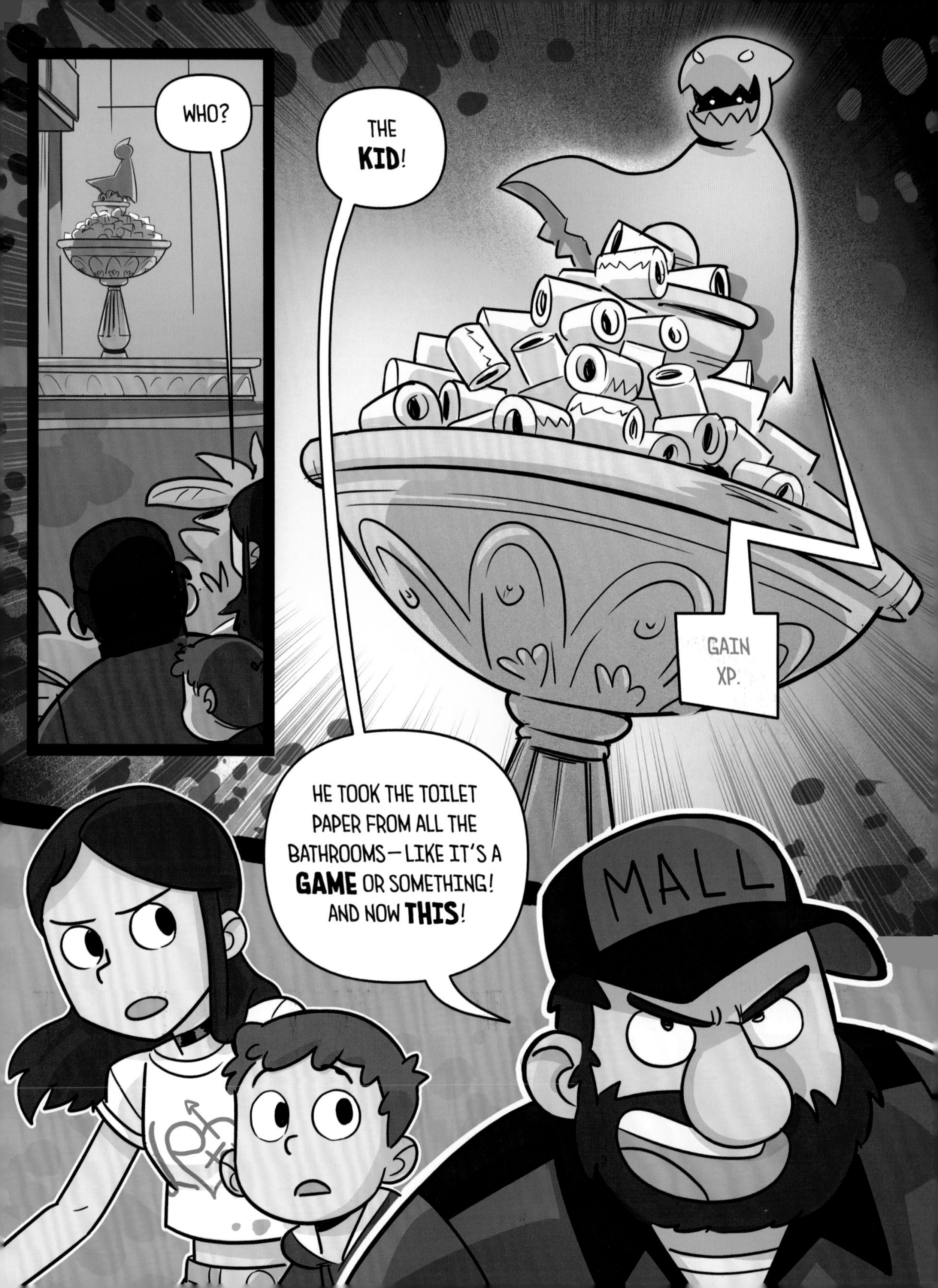
WHO?
THE KID!
GAIN XP.
HE TOOK THE TOILET PAPER FROM ALL THE BATHROOMS—LIKE IT'S A GAME OR SOMETHING! AND NOW THIS!
MALL

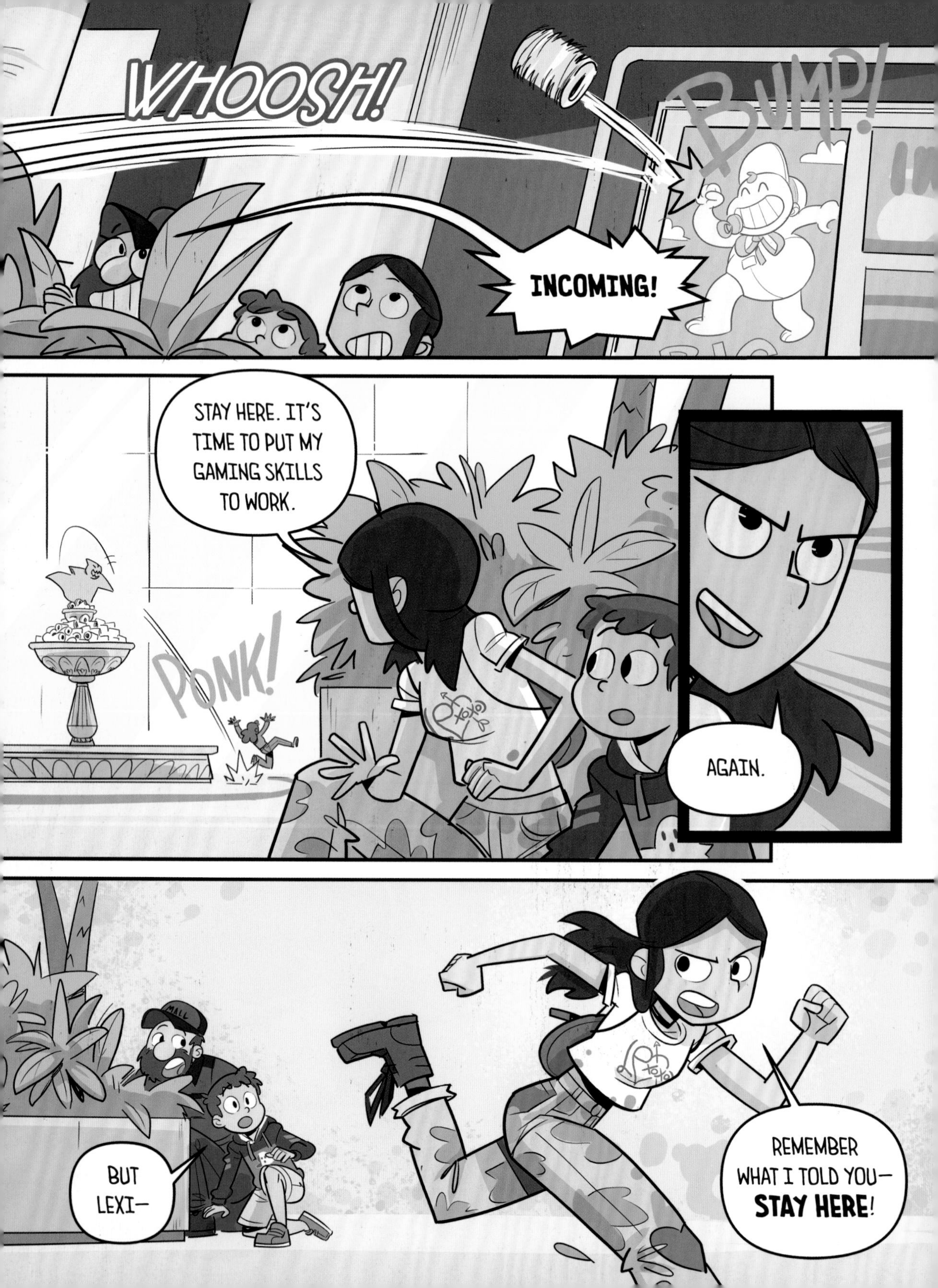
WHOOSH!
BUMP!
INCOMING!
STAY HERE. IT'S TIME TO PUT MY GAMING SKILLS TO WORK.
PONK!
AGAIN.
REMEMBER WHAT I TOLD YOU— **STAY HERE**!
BUT LEXI—

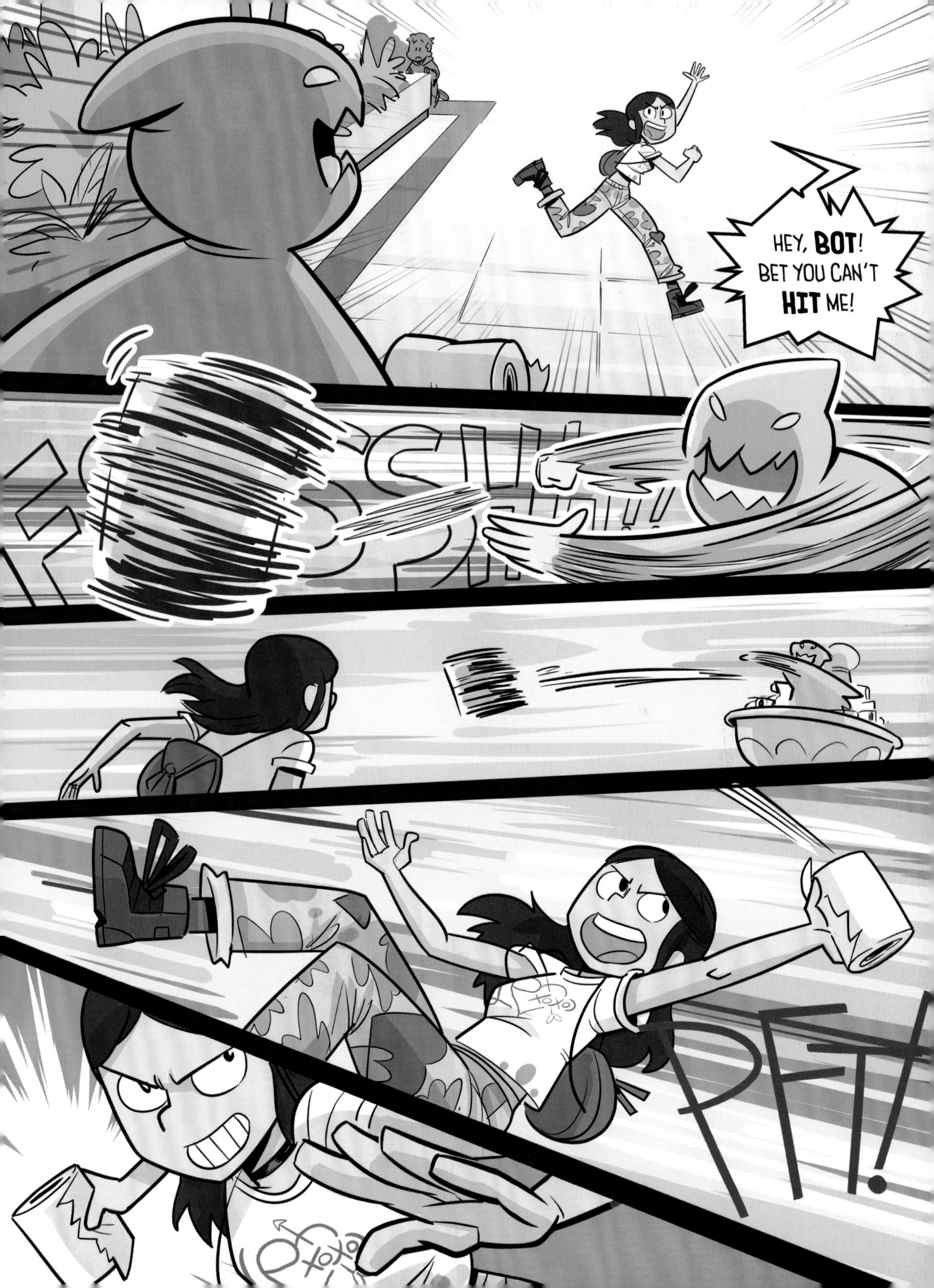
HEY, BOT! BET YOU CAN'T HIT ME!
PFT!

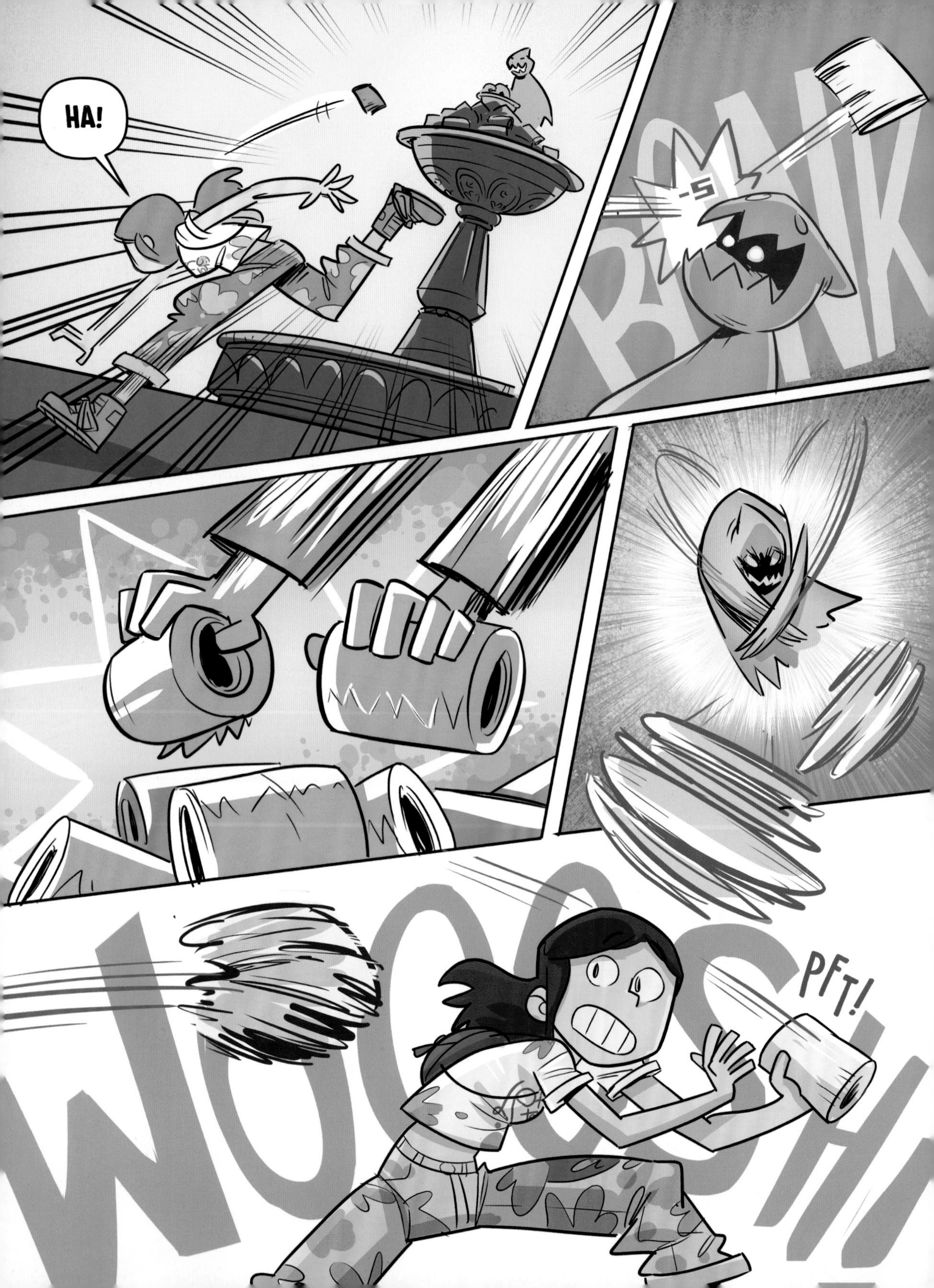
HA!
BONK
-5
WOOOSH
PFT!

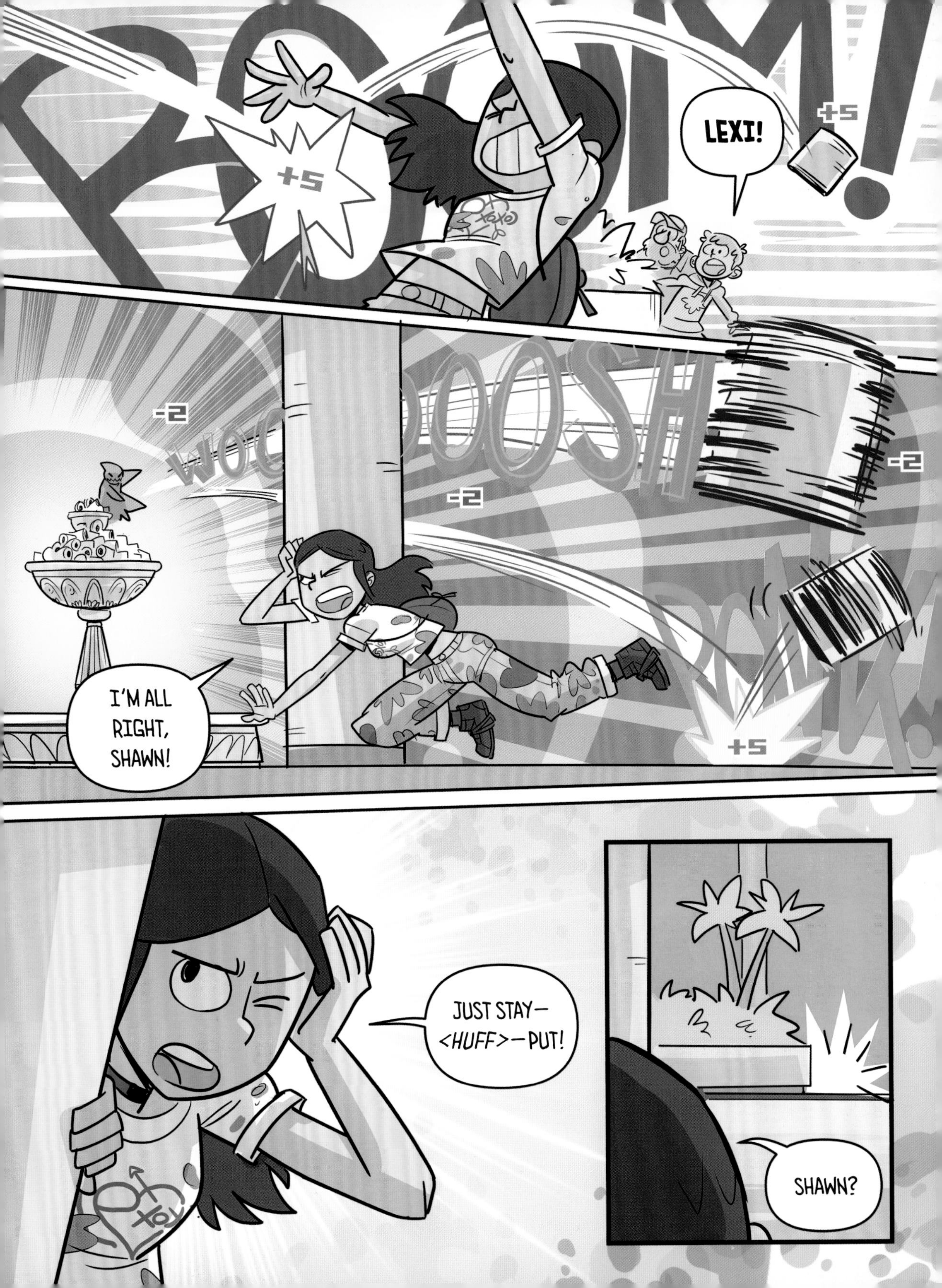
+5
LEXI!
+5
-2
-2
-2
I'M ALL RIGHT, SHAWN!
+5
JUST STAY— <HUFF>—PUT!
SHAWN?

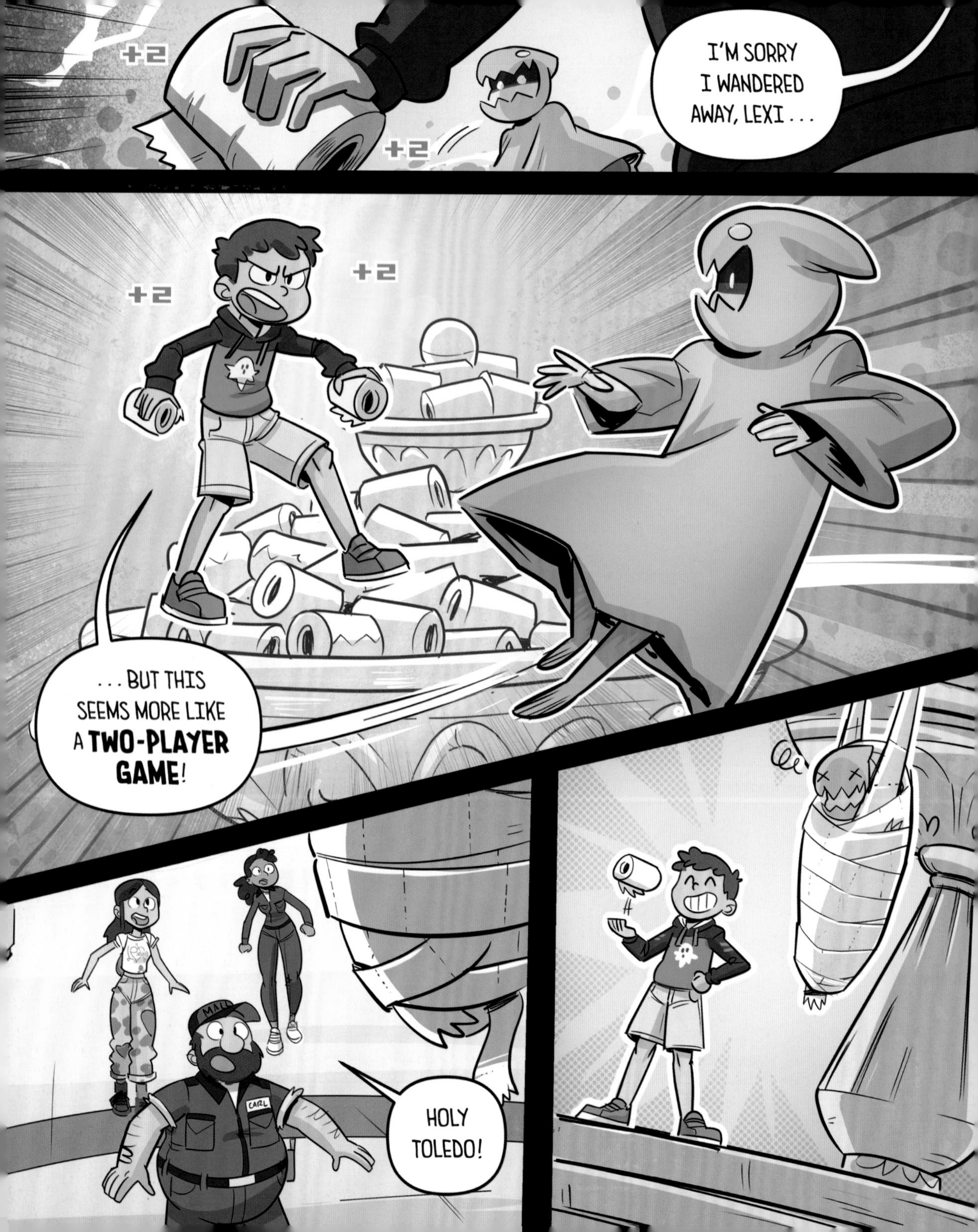
+2
+2
I'M SORRY I WANDERED AWAY, LEXI . . .
+2
+2
. . . BUT THIS SEEMS MORE LIKE A **TWO-PLAYER GAME**!
MALL
CARL
HOLY TOLEDO!

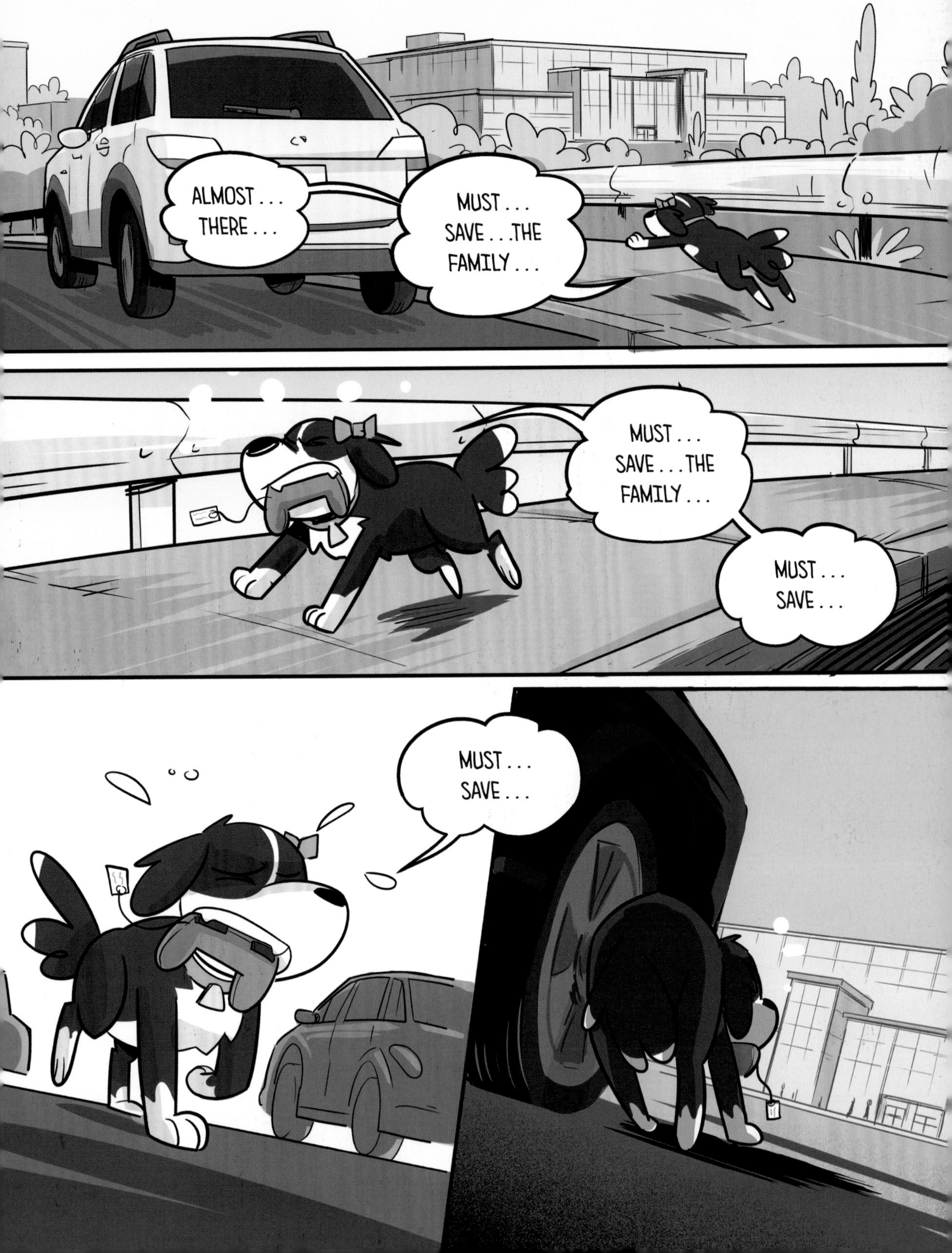
ALMOST . . . THERE . . .
MUST . . . SAVE . . . THE FAMILY . . .
MUST . . . SAVE . . . THE FAMILY . . .
MUST . . . SAVE . . .
MUST . . . SAVE . . .

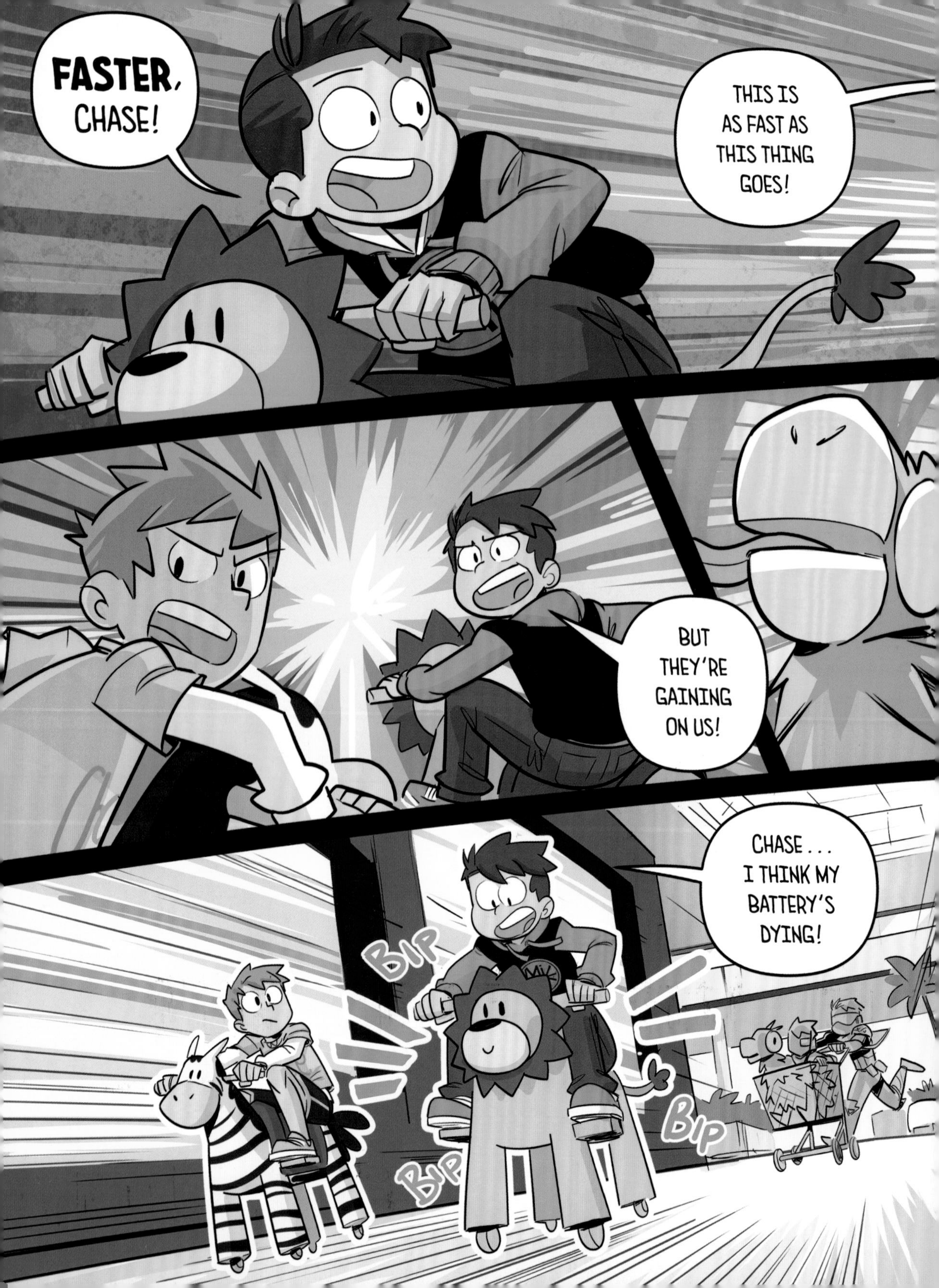
FASTER, CHASE!
THIS IS AS FAST AS THIS THING GOES!
BUT THEY'RE GAINING ON US!
CHASE . . . I THINK MY BATTERY'S DYING!
BIP
BIP
BIP

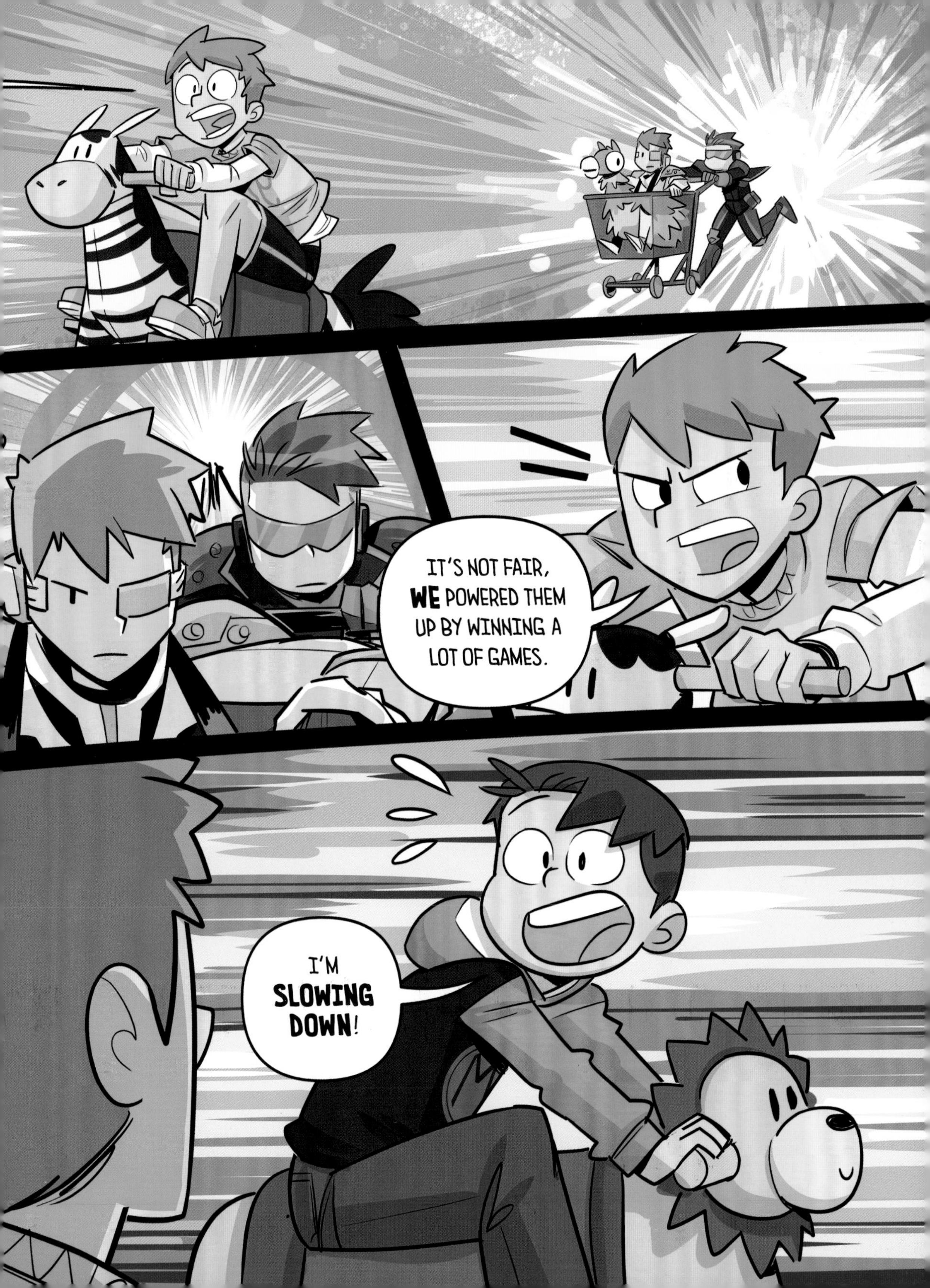
IT'S NOT FAIR, **WE** POWERED THEM UP BY WINNING A LOT OF GAMES.
I'M **SLOWING DOWN**!

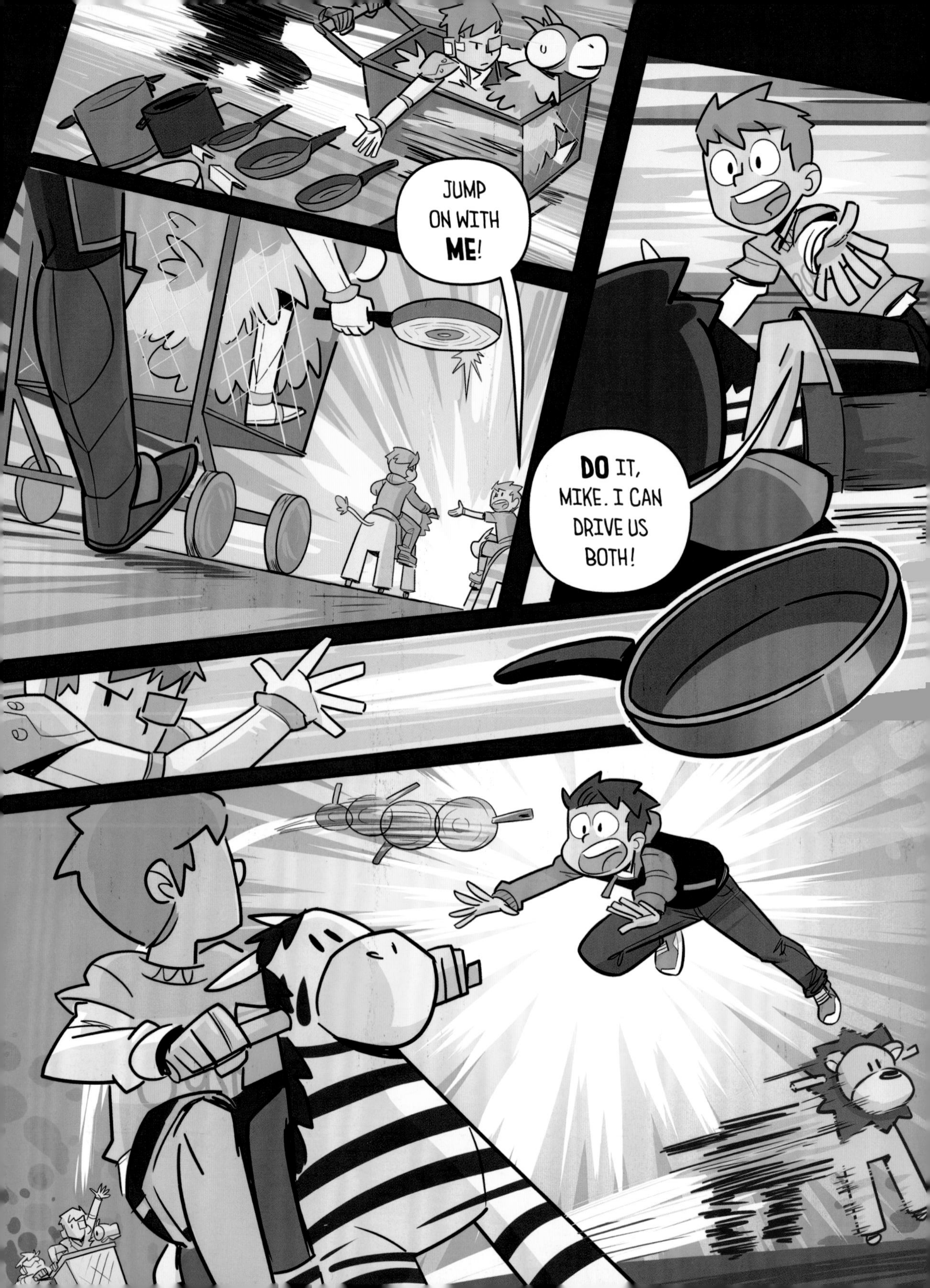
JUMP ON WITH **ME**!
DO IT, MIKE. I CAN DRIVE US BOTH!

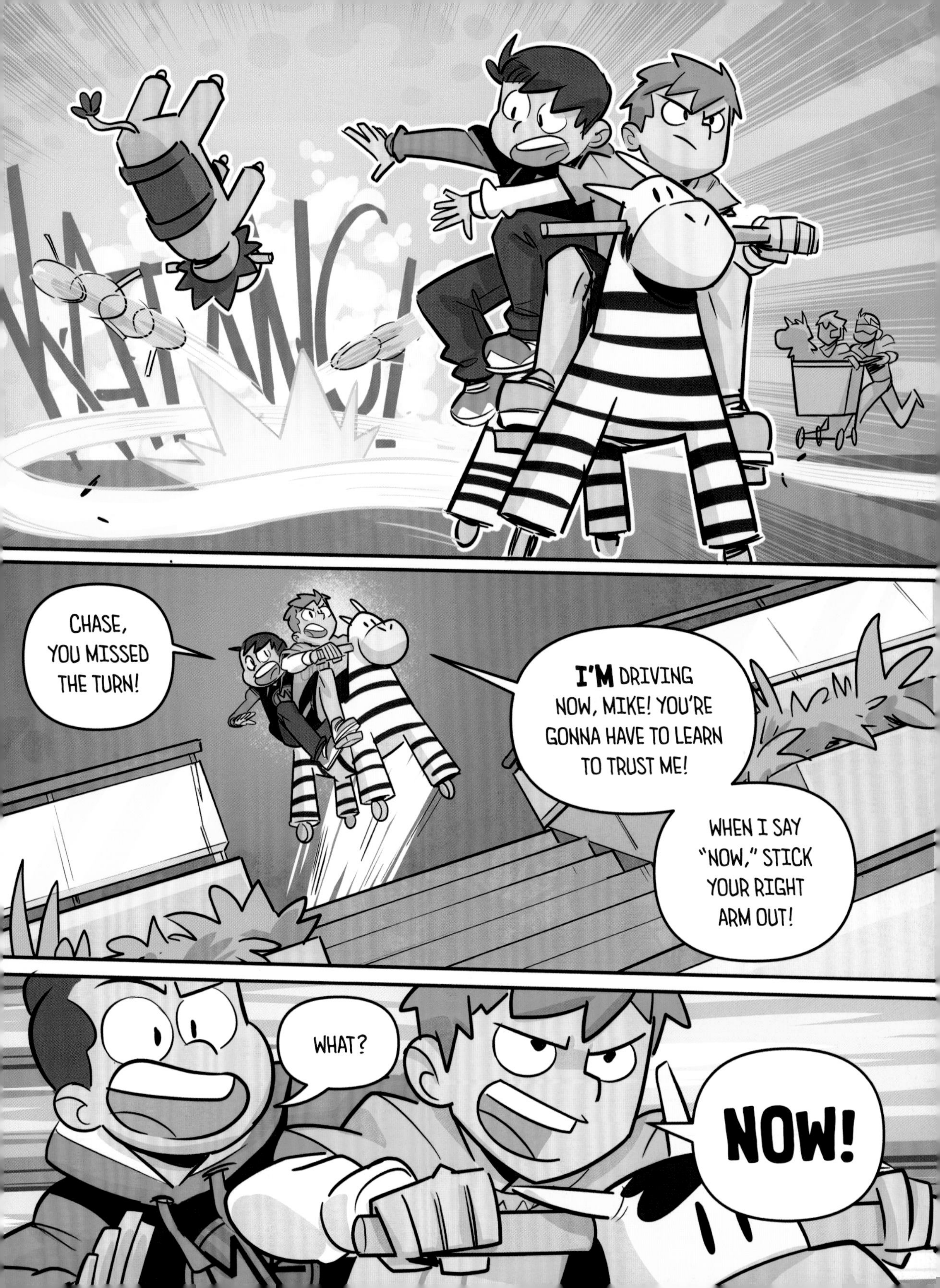
CHASE, YOU MISSED THE TURN!
I'M DRIVING NOW, MIKE! YOU'RE GONNA HAVE TO LEARN TO TRUST ME!
WHEN I SAY "NOW," STICK YOUR RIGHT ARM OUT!
WHAT?
NOW!

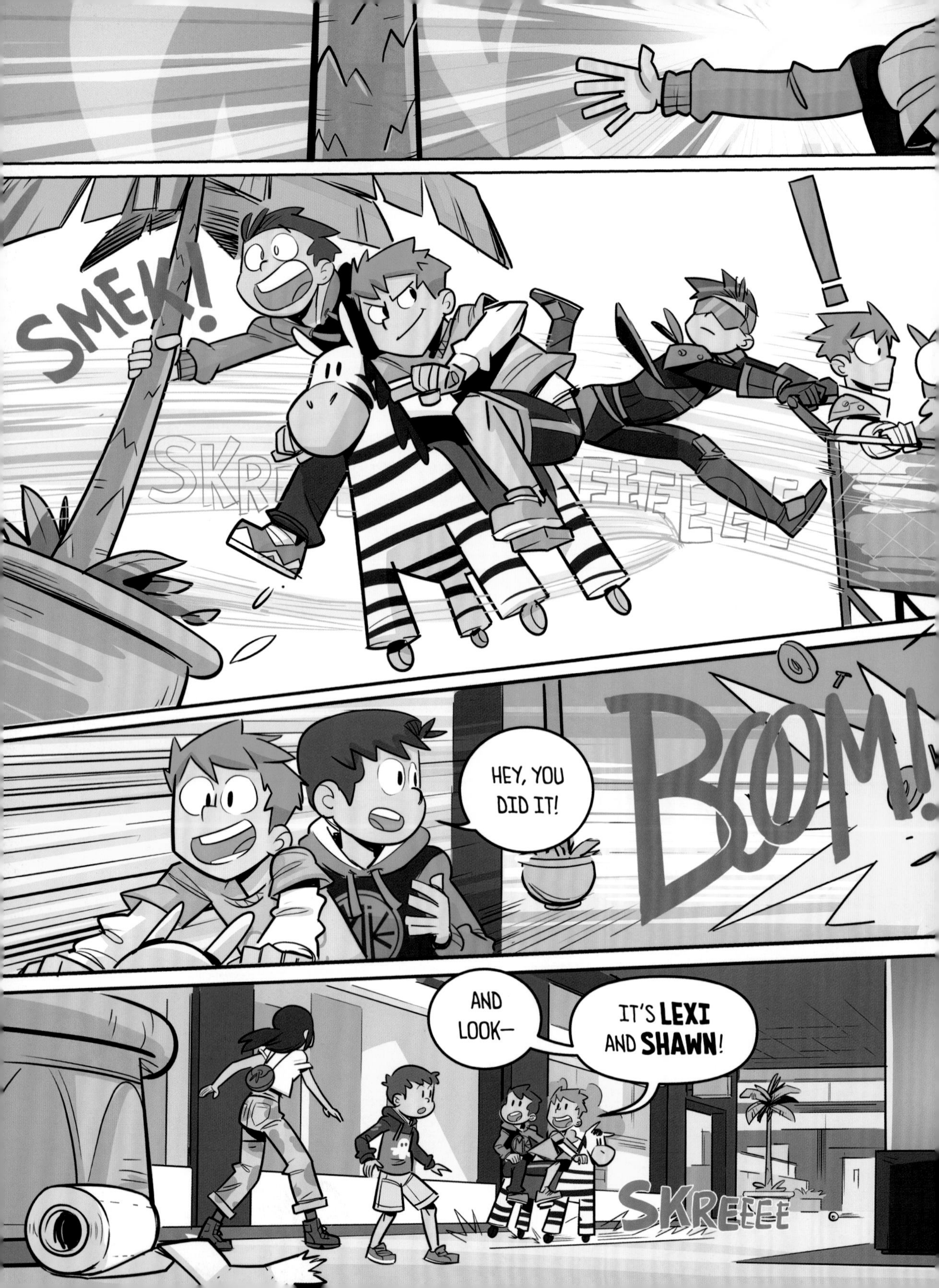
SMEK!
!
SKREEEEEEEGE
BOOM!
HEY, YOU DID IT!
AND LOOK—
IT'S LEXI AND SHAWN!
SKREEEE

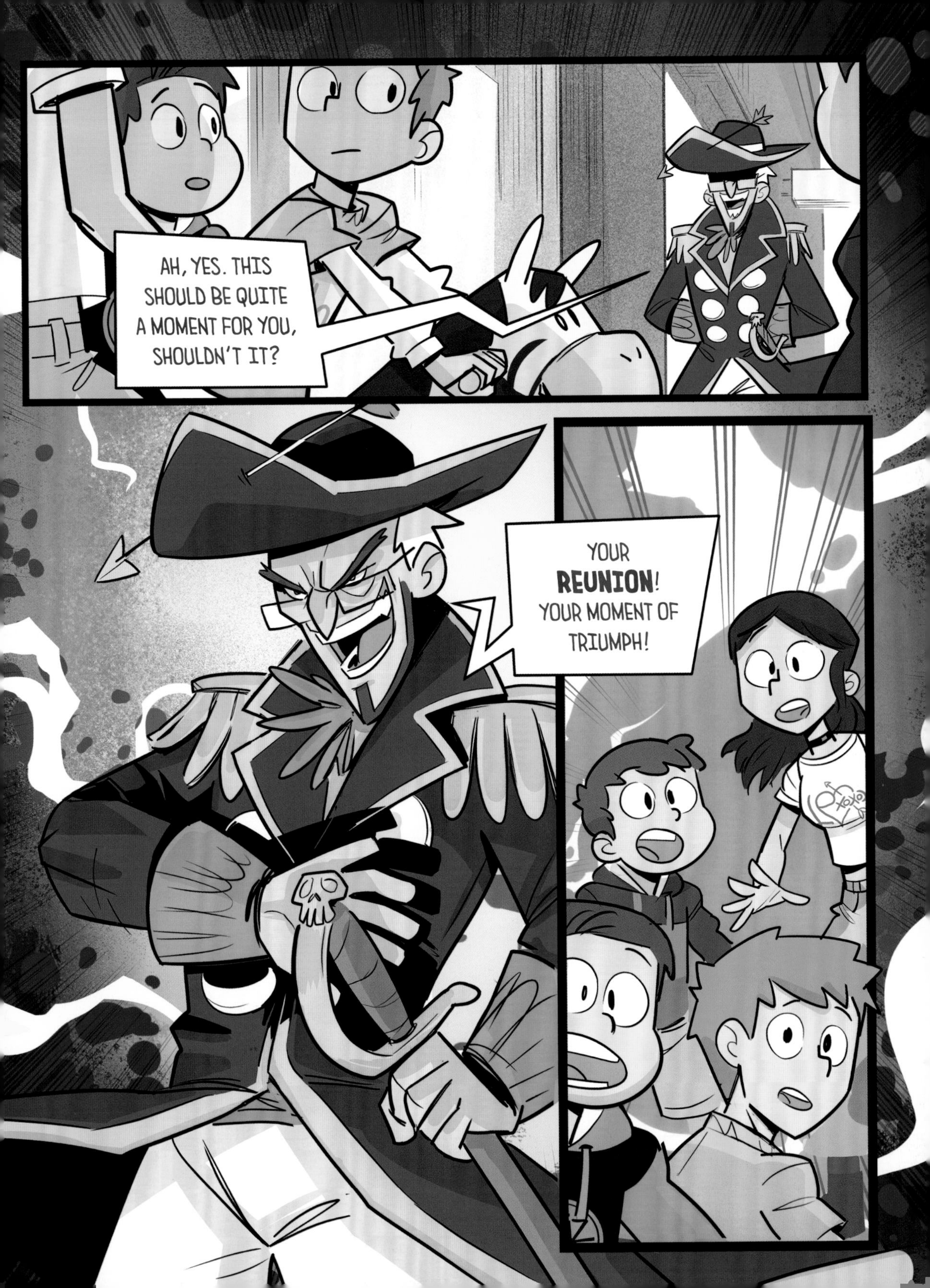
AH, YES. THIS SHOULD BE QUITE A MOMENT FOR YOU, SHOULDN'T IT?
YOUR **REUNION**! YOUR MOMENT OF TRIUMPH!

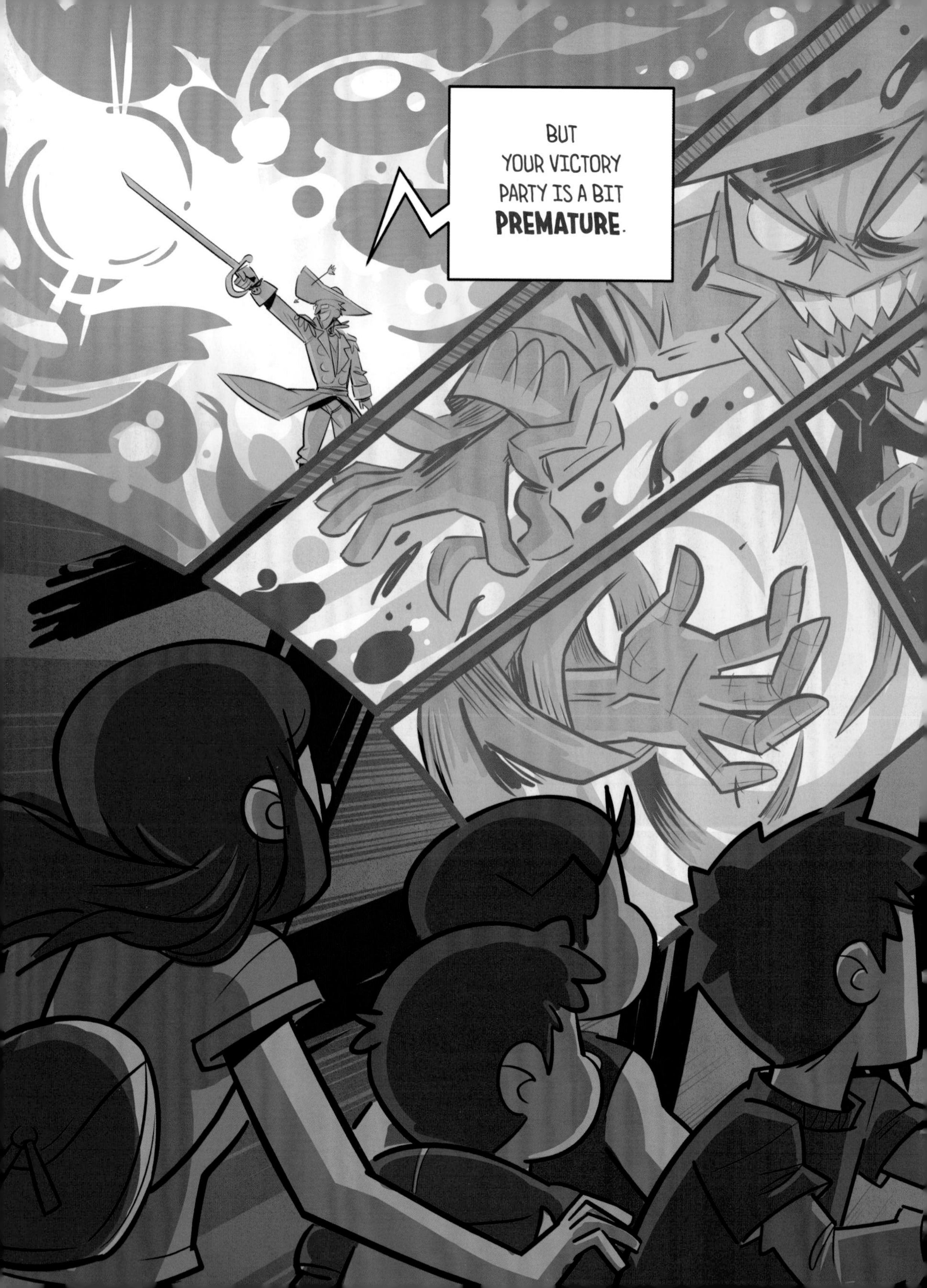
BUT YOUR VICTORY PARTY IS A BIT **PREMATURE**.

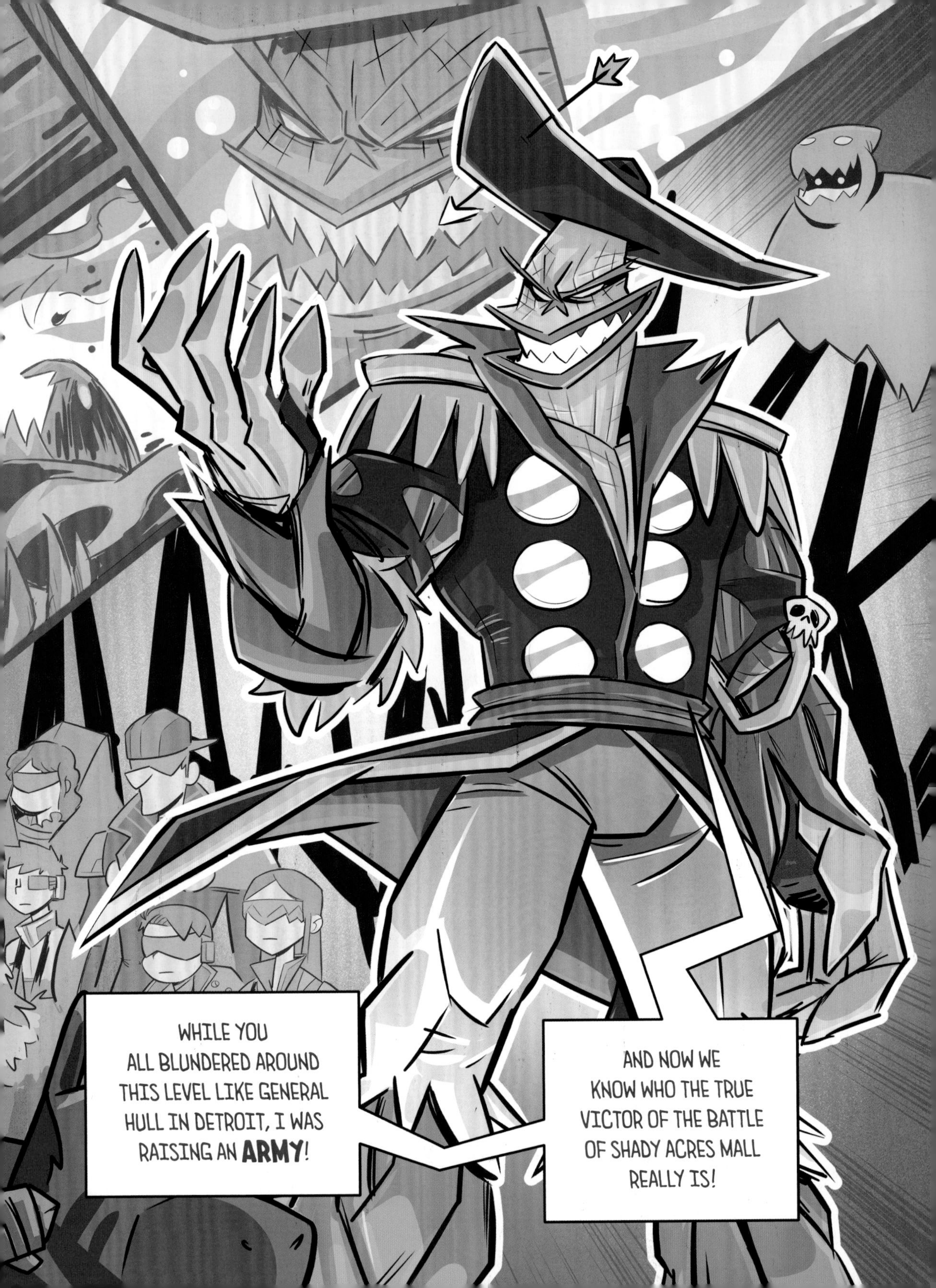
WHILE YOU ALL BLUNDERED AROUND THIS LEVEL LIKE GENERAL HULL IN DETROIT, I WAS RAISING AN ARMY!
AND NOW WE KNOW WHO THE TRUE VICTOR OF THE BATTLE OF SHADY ACRES MALL REALLY IS!

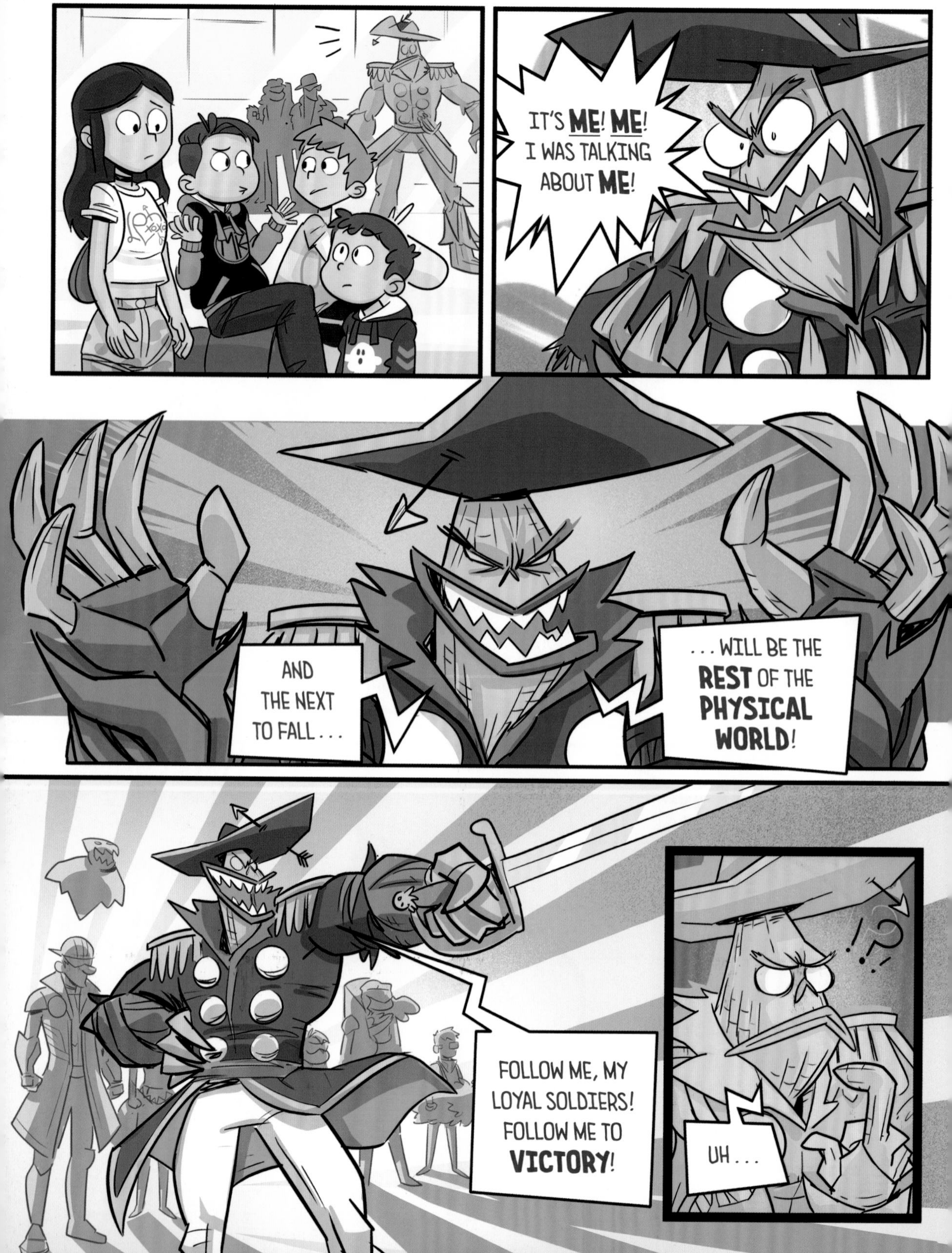
IT'S **ME**! **ME**! I WAS TALKING ABOUT **ME**!
AND THE NEXT TO FALL . . .
. . . WILL BE THE **REST** OF THE **PHYSICAL WORLD**!
FOLLOW ME, MY LOYAL SOLDIERS! FOLLOW ME TO **VICTORY**!
UH . . .

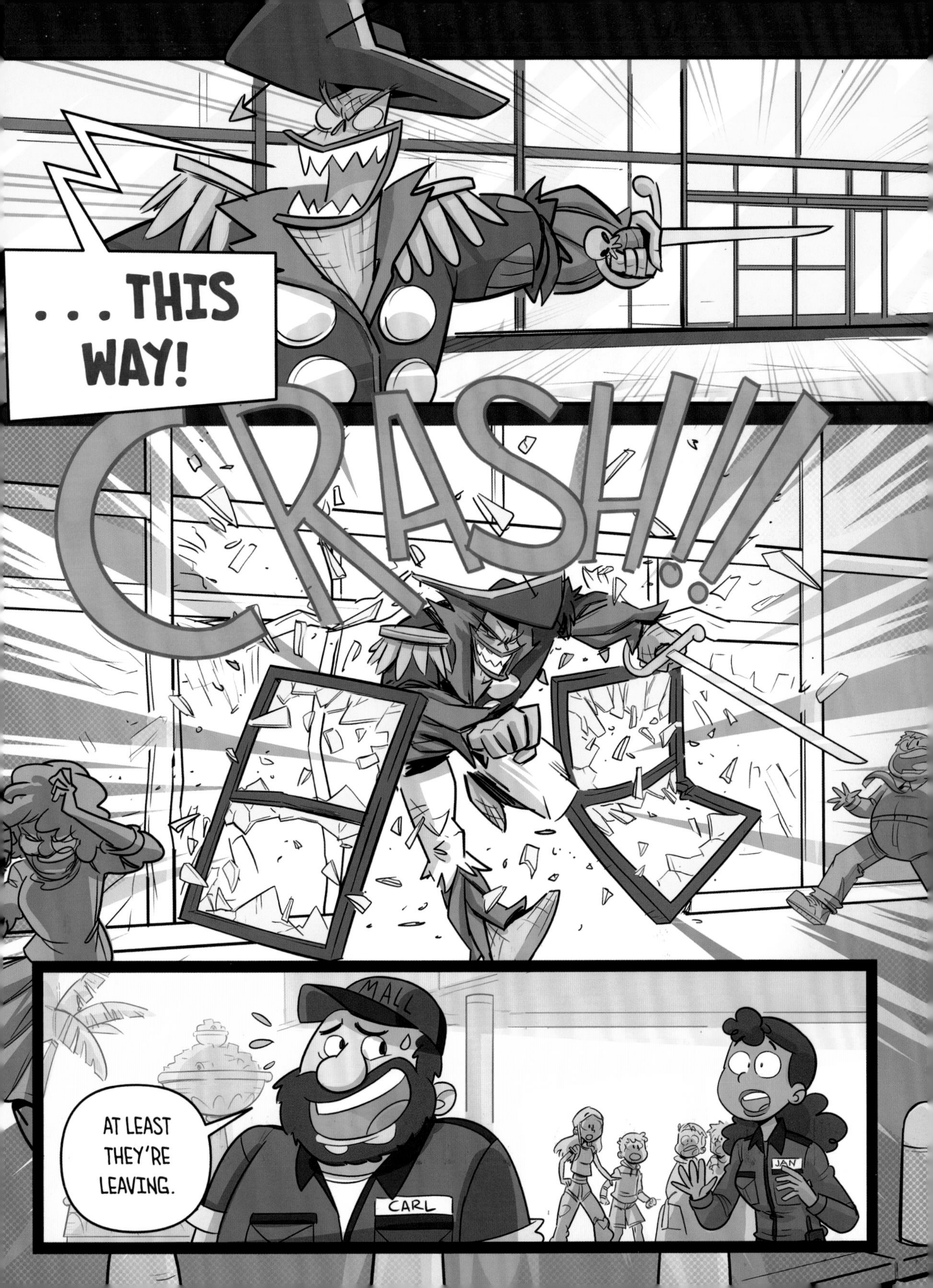
...THIS WAY!
CRASH!!!
MALL
CARL
JAN
AT LEAST THEY'RE LEAVING.

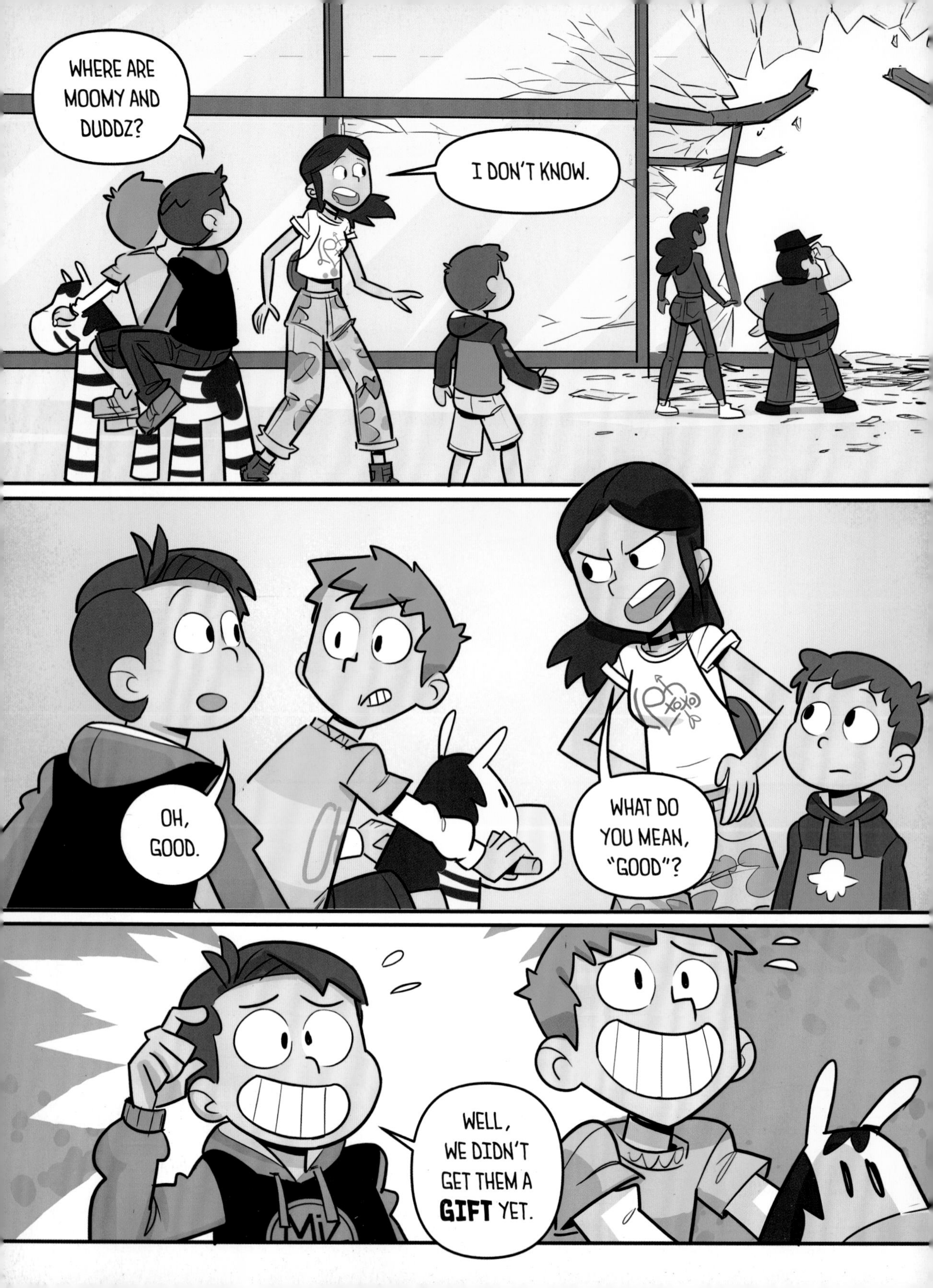
WHERE ARE MOOMY AND DUDDZ?
I DON'T KNOW.
OH, GOOD.
WHAT DO YOU MEAN, "GOOD"?
WELL, WE DIDN'T GET THEM A GIFT YET.

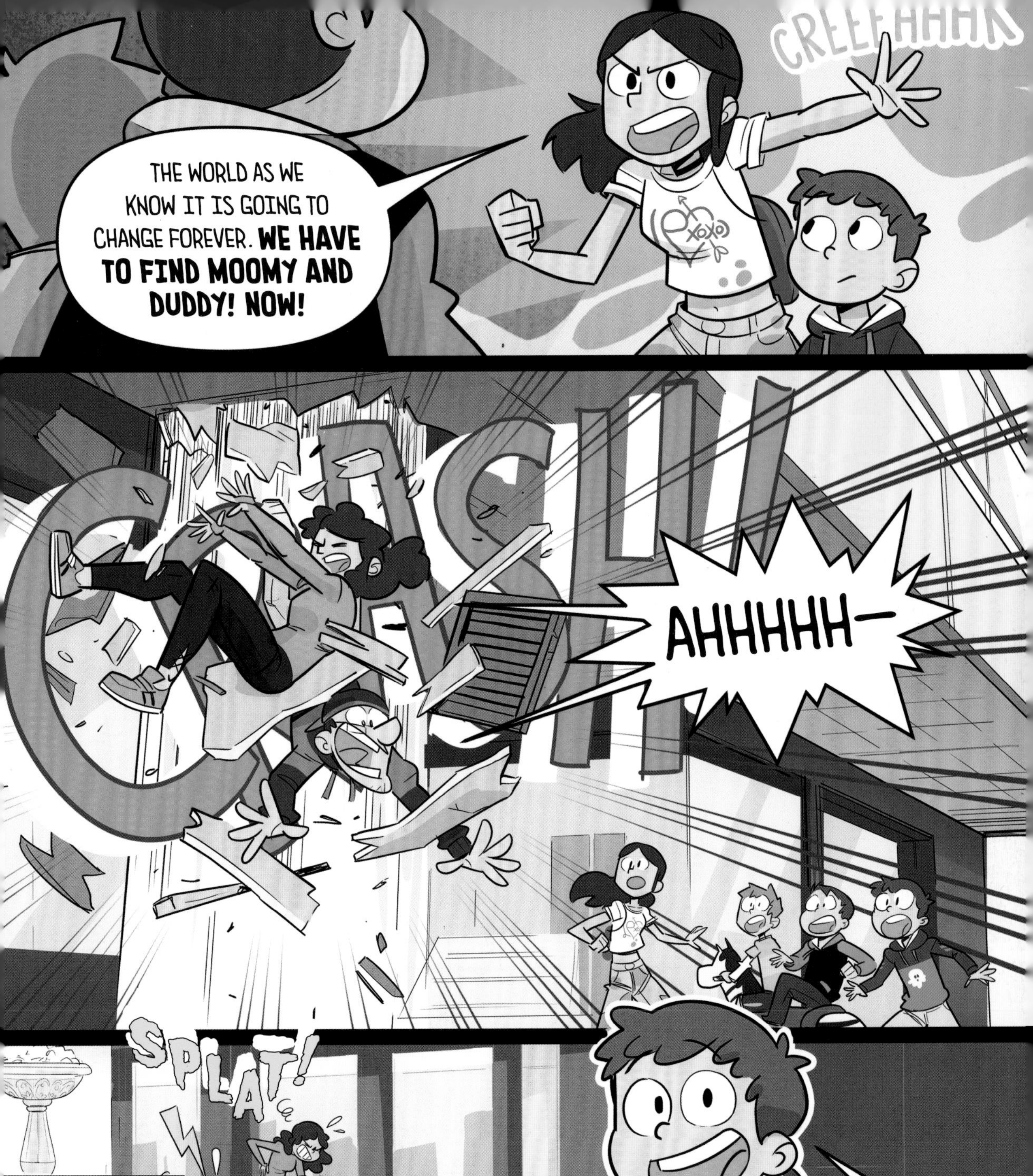
THE WORLD AS WE KNOW IT IS GOING TO CHANGE FOREVER. **WE HAVE TO FIND MOOMY AND DUDDY! NOW!**
CRASH
AHHHHH—
SPLAT!
I **FOUND** THEM!

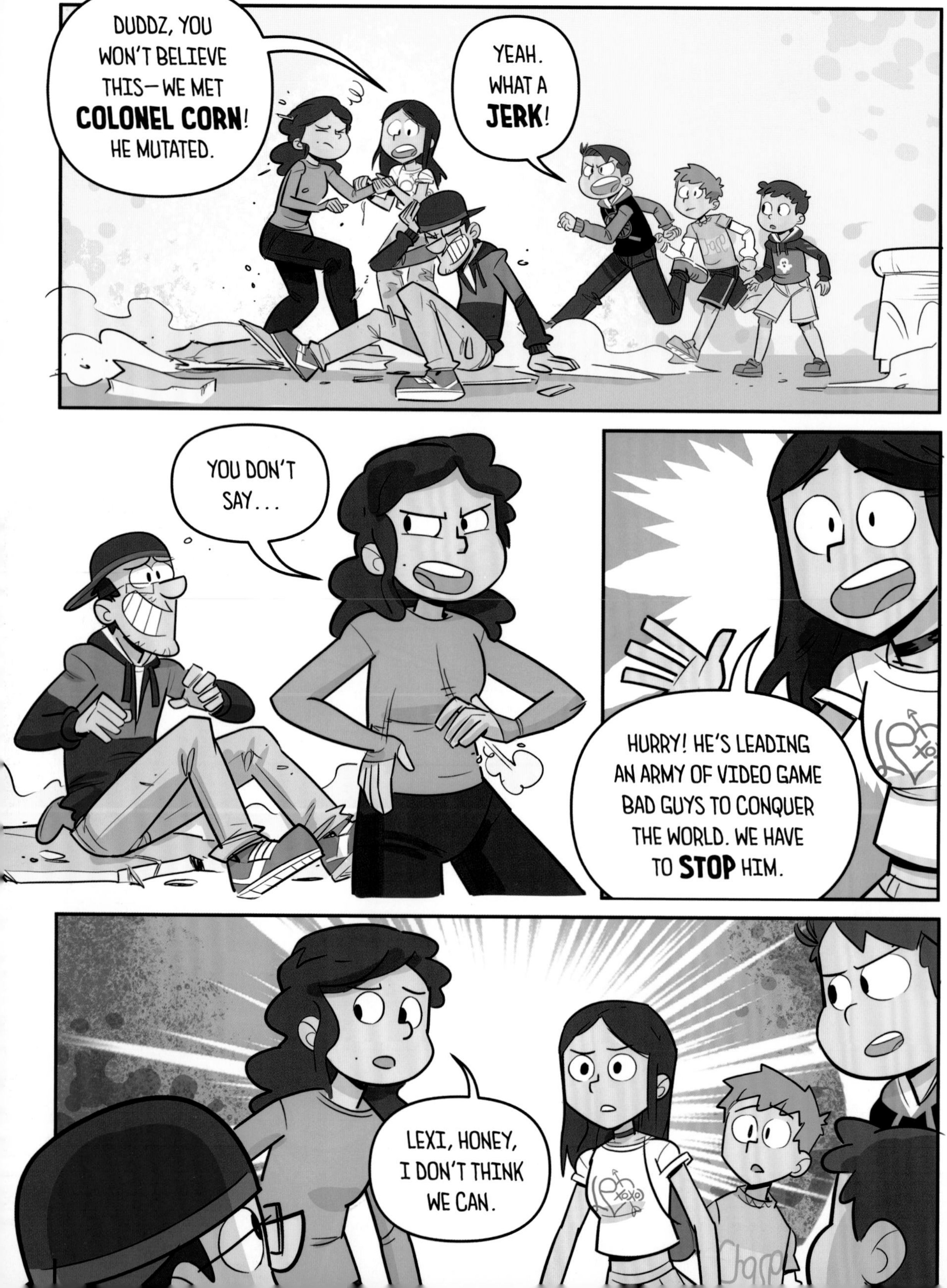
DUDDZ, YOU WON'T BELIEVE THIS— WE MET **COLONEL CORN**! HE MUTATED.
YEAH. WHAT A **JERK**!
YOU DON'T SAY...
HURRY! HE'S LEADING AN ARMY OF VIDEO GAME BAD GUYS TO CONQUER THE WORLD. WE HAVE TO **STOP** HIM.
LEXI, HONEY, I DON'T THINK WE CAN.

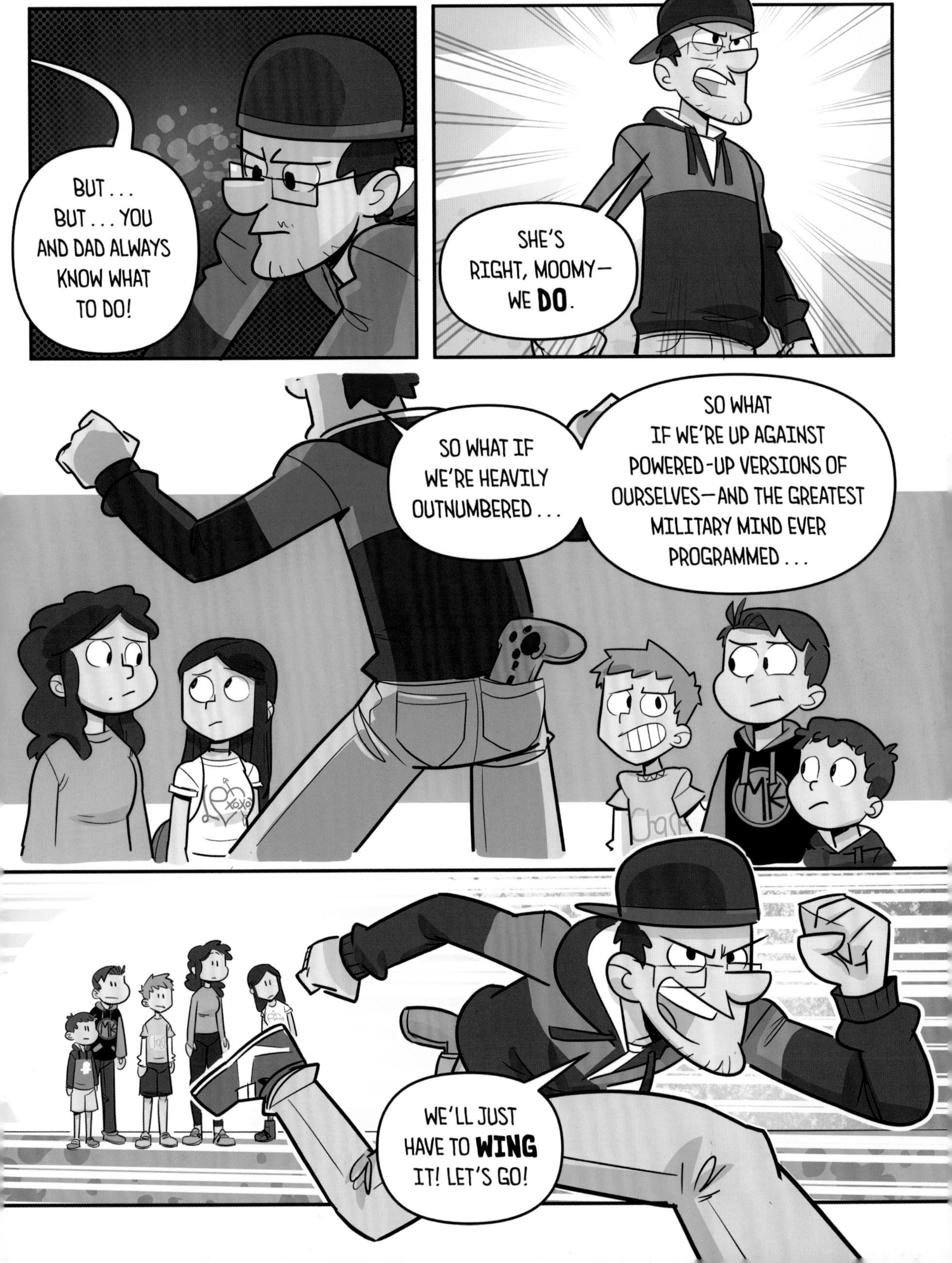
BUT . . . BUT . . . YOU AND DAD ALWAYS KNOW WHAT TO DO!
SHE'S RIGHT, MOOMY—WE **DO**.
SO WHAT IF WE'RE HEAVILY OUTNUMBERED . . .
SO WHAT IF WE'RE UP AGAINST POWERED-UP VERSIONS OF OURSELVES—AND THE GREATEST MILITARY MIND EVER PROGRAMMED . . .
WE'LL JUST HAVE TO **WING** IT! LET'S GO!

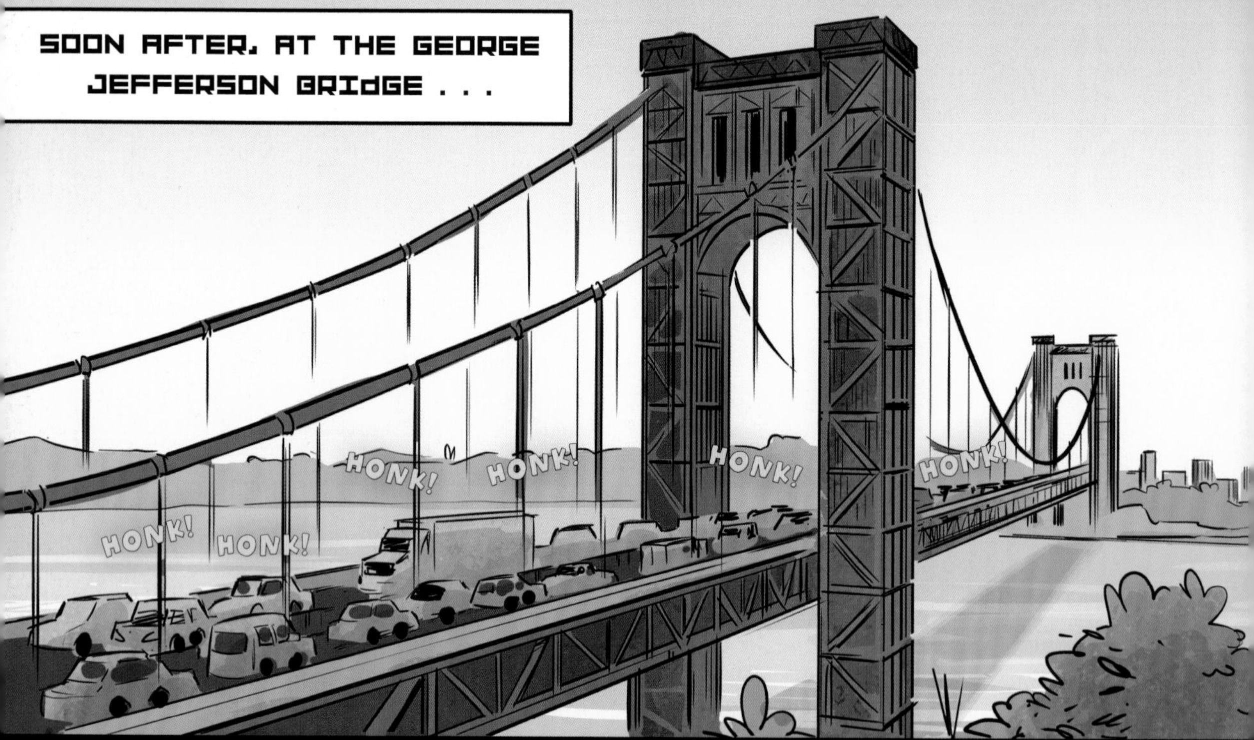
SOON AFTER, AT THE GEORGE JEFFERSON BRIDGE . . .
HONK!
HONK!
HONK!
HONK!
HONK!
HONK!

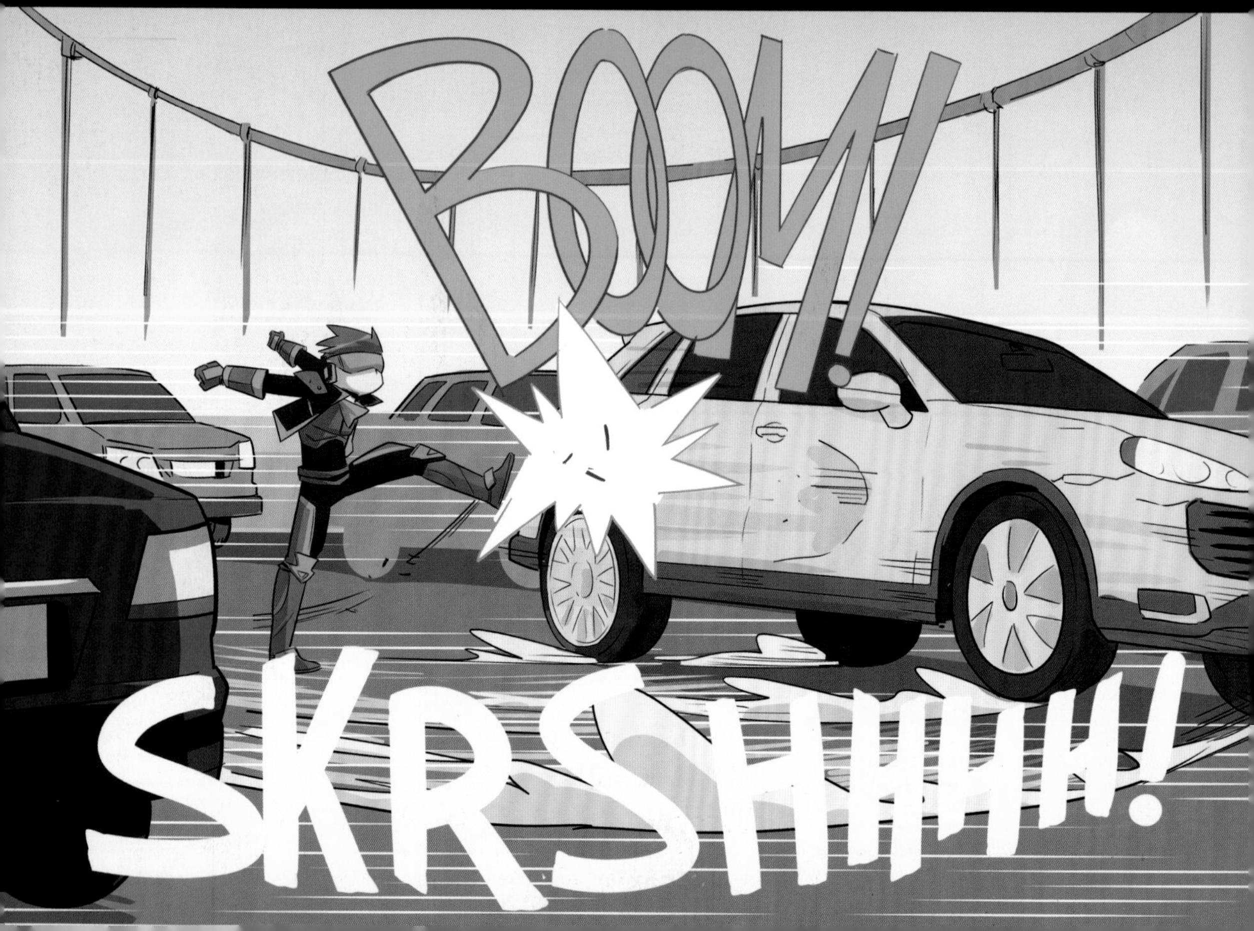
BOOM!
SKRSHHHH!

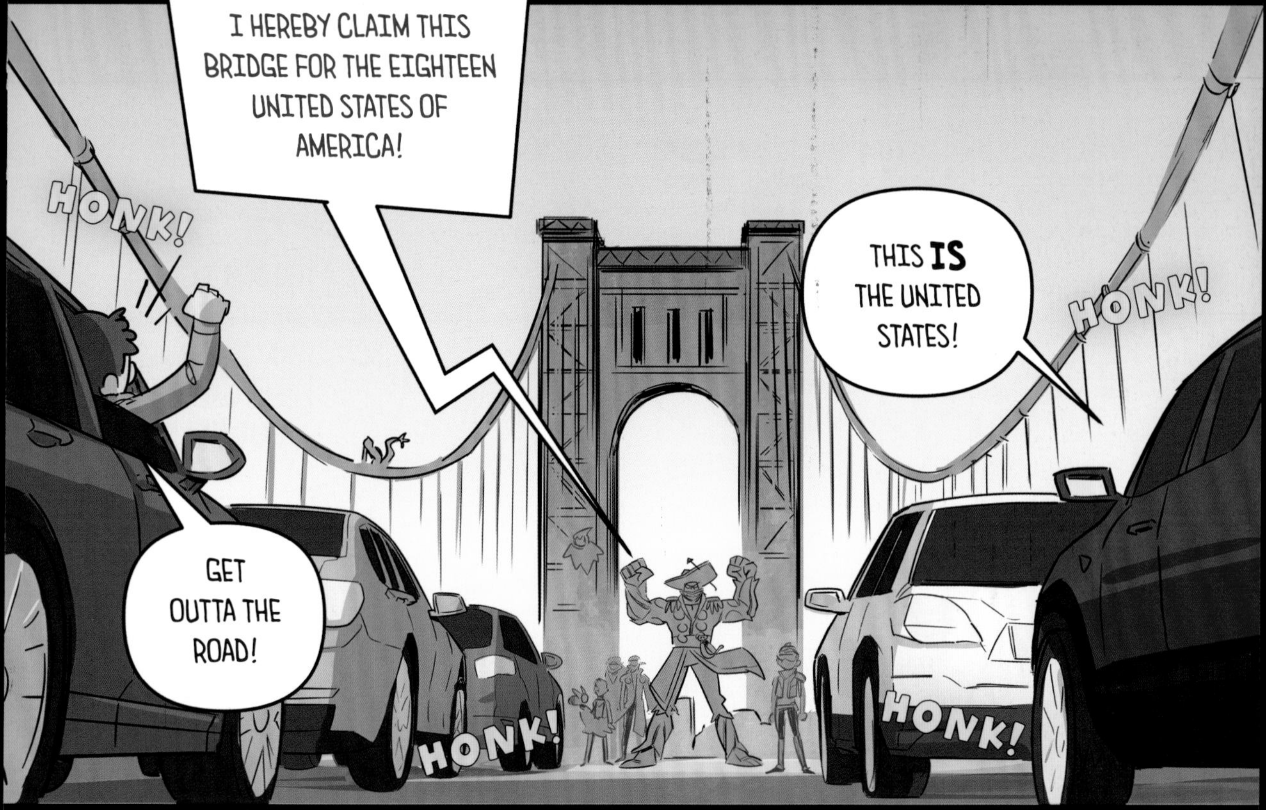
I HEREBY CLAIM THIS BRIDGE FOR THE EIGHTEEN UNITED STATES OF AMERICA!
HONK!
THIS IS THE UNITED STATES!
HONK!
GET OUTTA THE ROAD!
HONK!
HONK!

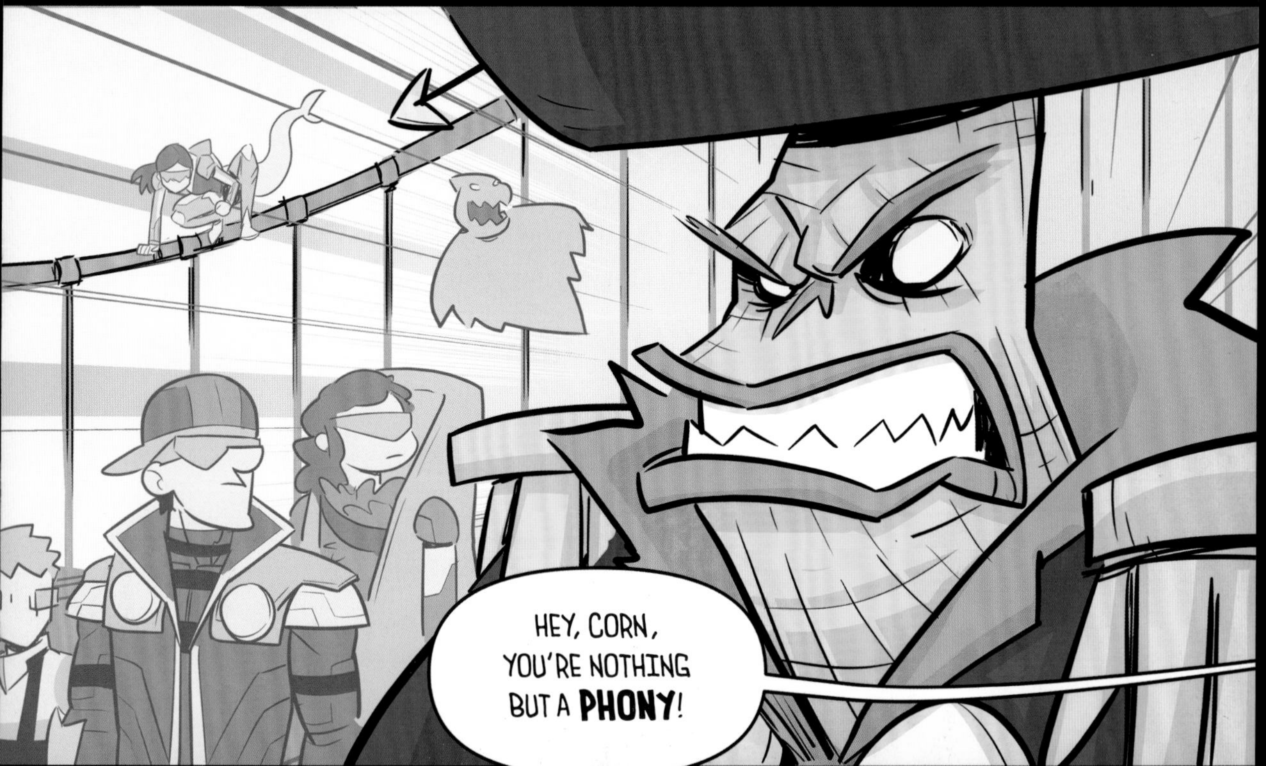
HEY, CORN, YOU'RE NOTHING BUT A **PHONY**!

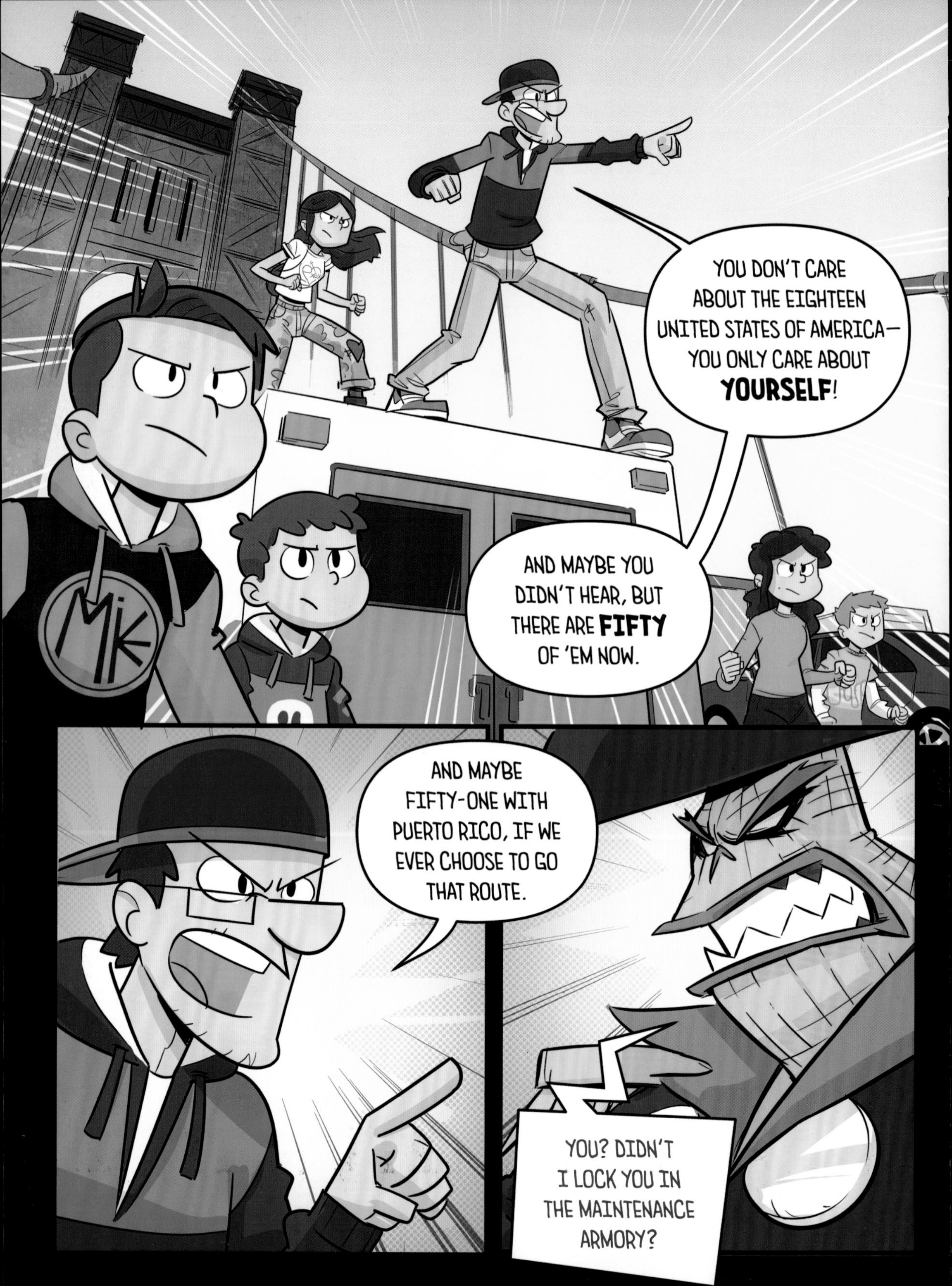
YOU DON'T CARE ABOUT THE EIGHTEEN UNITED STATES OF AMERICA—YOU ONLY CARE ABOUT **YOURSELF**!
AND MAYBE YOU DIDN'T HEAR, BUT THERE ARE **FIFTY** OF 'EM NOW.
AND MAYBE FIFTY-ONE WITH PUERTO RICO, IF WE EVER CHOOSE TO GO THAT ROUTE.
YOU? DIDN'T I LOCK YOU IN THE MAINTENANCE ARMORY?

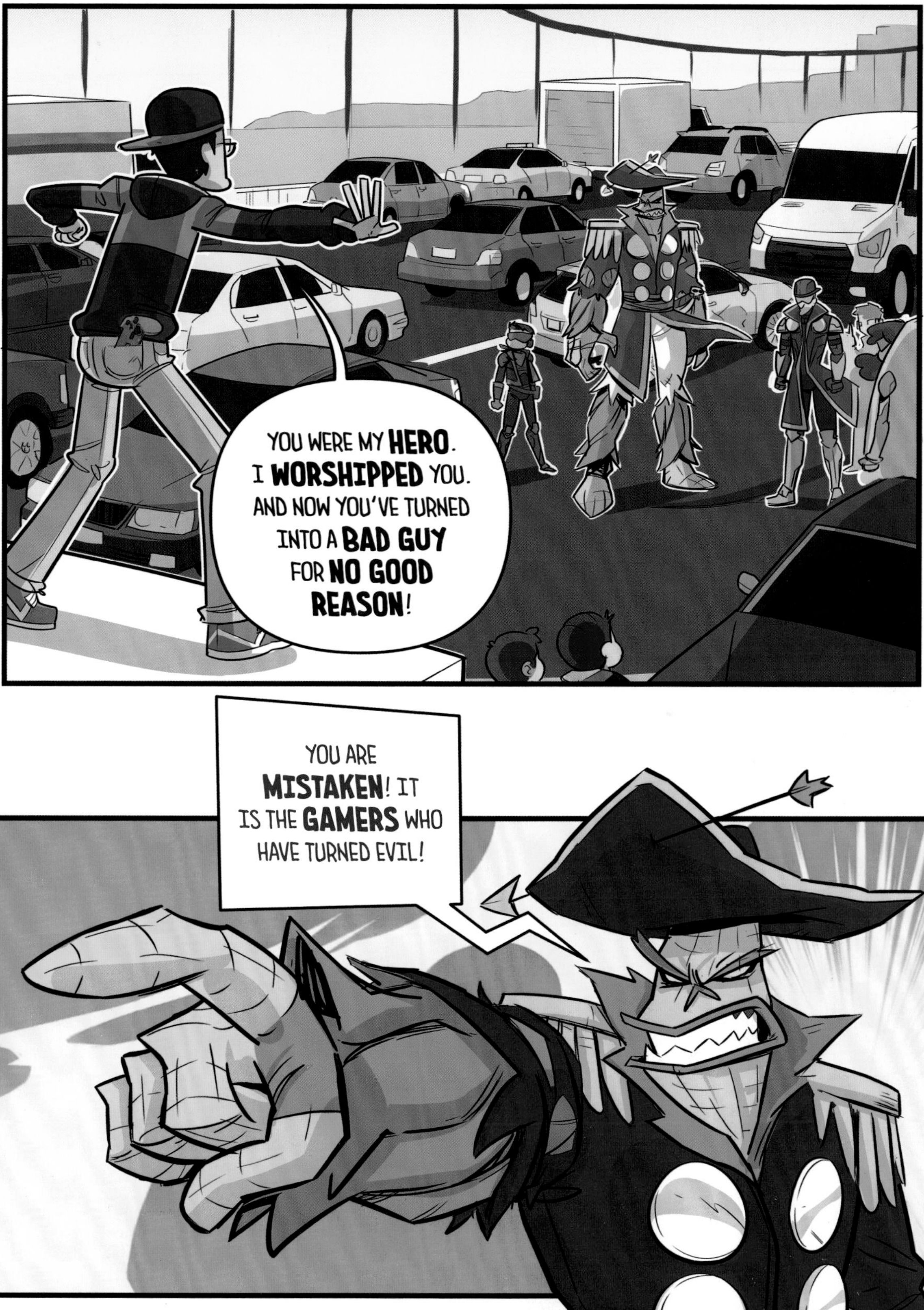
YOU WERE MY HERO. I WORSHIPPED YOU. AND NOW YOU'VE TURNED INTO A BAD GUY FOR NO GOOD REASON!
YOU ARE MISTAKEN! IT IS THE GAMERS WHO HAVE TURNED EVIL!

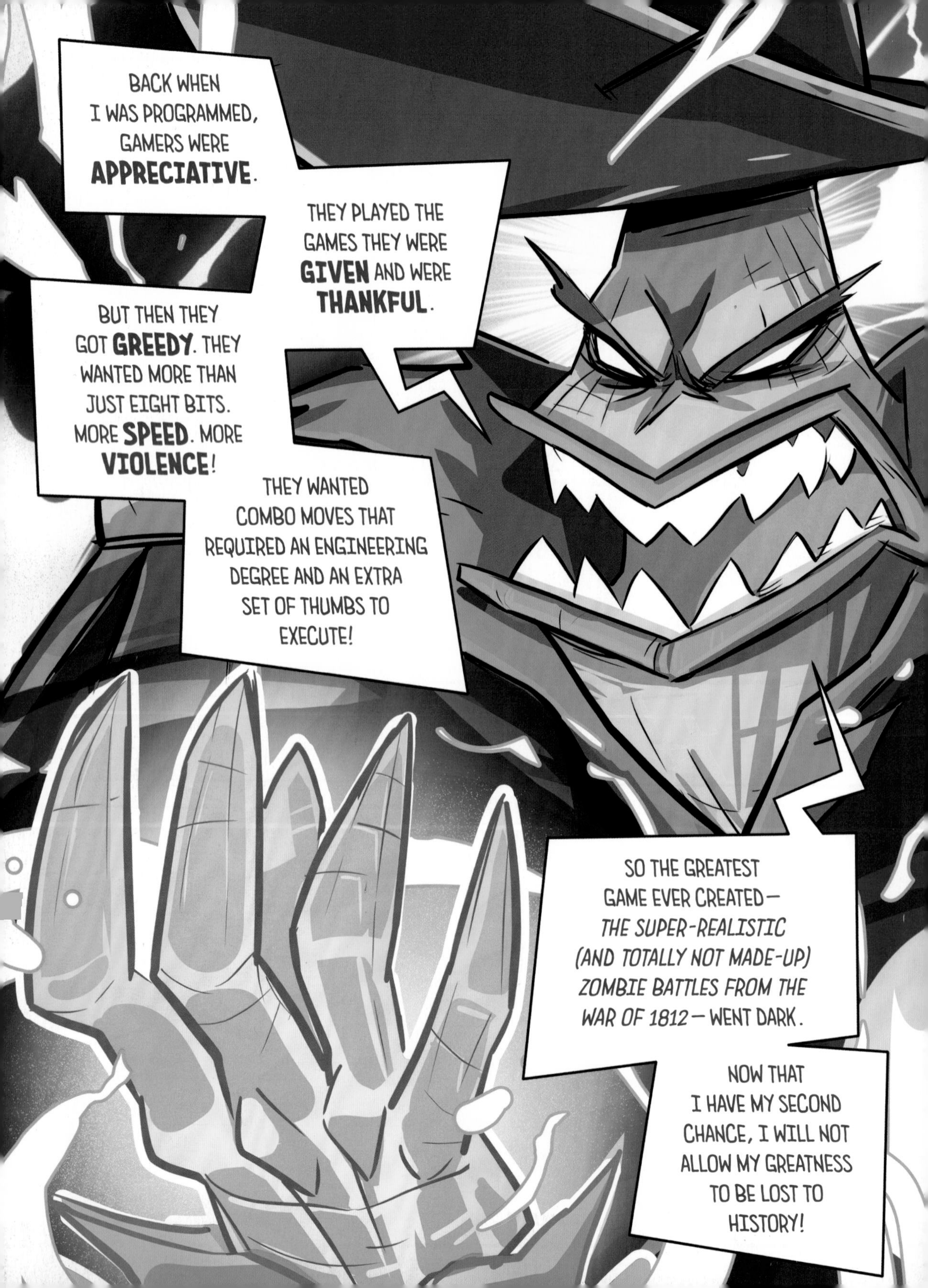

BACK WHEN I WAS PROGRAMMED, GAMERS WERE **APPRECIATIVE**.
THEY PLAYED THE GAMES THEY WERE **GIVEN** AND WERE **THANKFUL**.
BUT THEN THEY GOT **GREEDY**. THEY WANTED MORE THAN JUST EIGHT BITS. MORE **SPEED**. MORE **VIOLENCE**!
THEY WANTED COMBO MOVES THAT REQUIRED AN ENGINEERING DEGREE AND AN EXTRA SET OF THUMBS TO EXECUTE!
SO THE GREATEST GAME EVER CREATED—*THE SUPER-REALISTIC (AND TOTALLY NOT MADE-UP) ZOMBIE BATTLES FROM THE WAR OF 1812*—WENT DARK.
NOW THAT I HAVE MY SECOND CHANCE, I WILL NOT ALLOW MY GREATNESS TO BE LOST TO HISTORY!

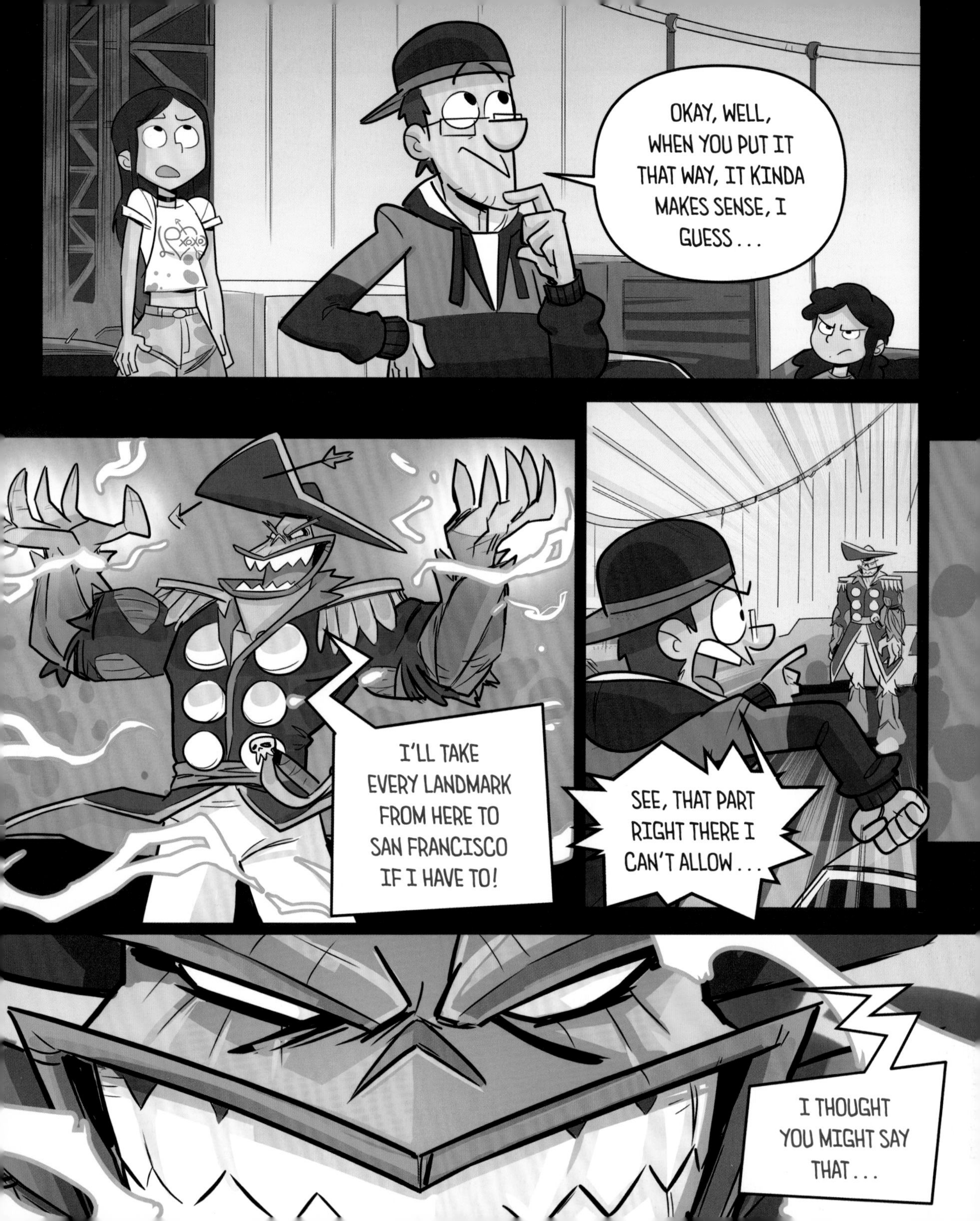
OKAY, WELL, WHEN YOU PUT IT THAT WAY, IT KINDA MAKES SENSE, I GUESS . . .
I'LL TAKE EVERY LANDMARK FROM HERE TO SAN FRANCISCO IF I HAVE TO!
SEE, THAT PART RIGHT THERE I CAN'T ALLOW . . .
I THOUGHT YOU MIGHT SAY THAT . . .

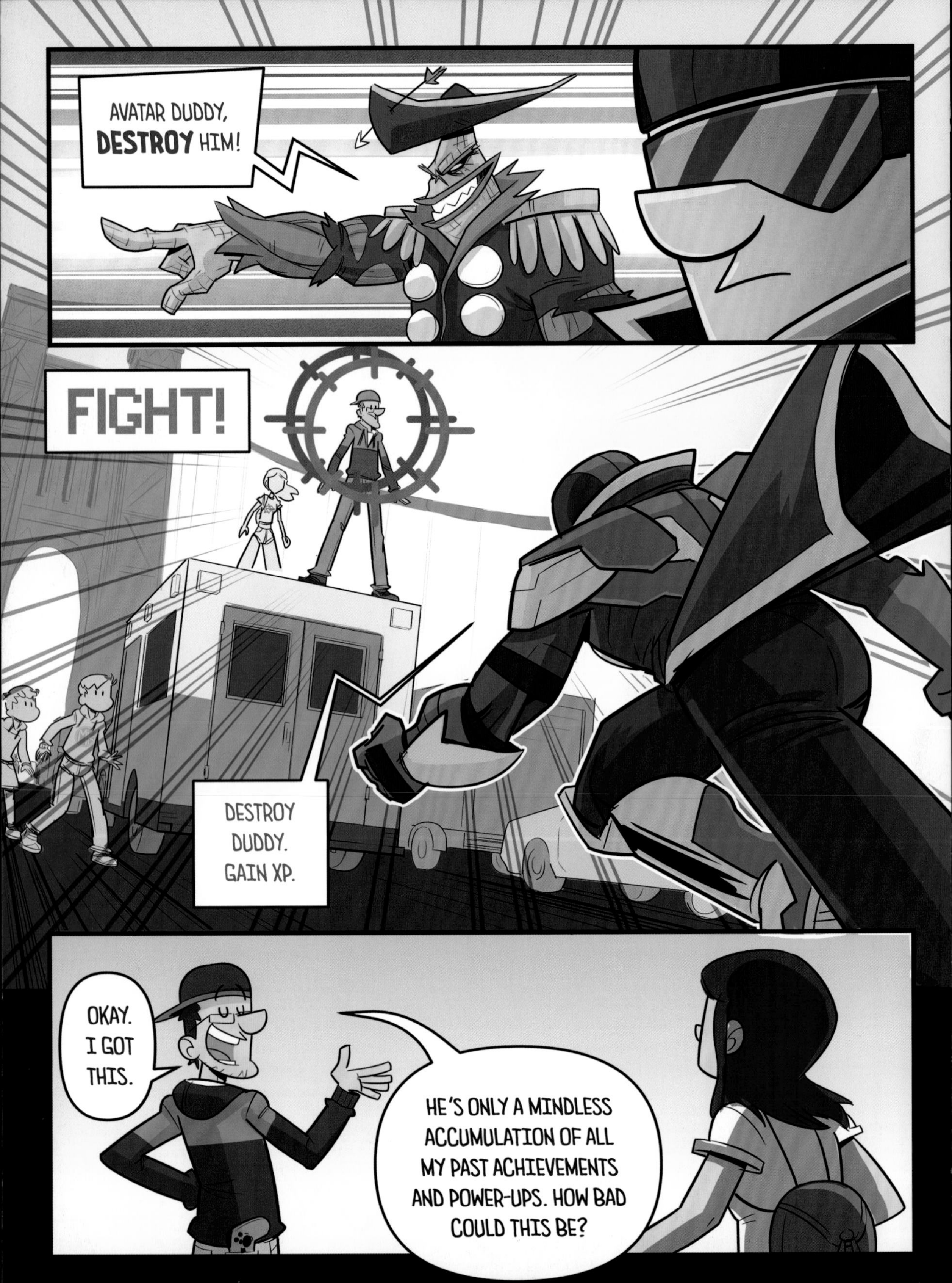
AVATAR DUDDY, **DESTROY** HIM!
FIGHT!
DESTROY DUDDY. GAIN XP.
OKAY. I GOT THIS.
HE'S ONLY A MINDLESS ACCUMULATION OF ALL MY PAST ACHIEVEMENTS AND POWER-UPS. HOW BAD COULD THIS BE?

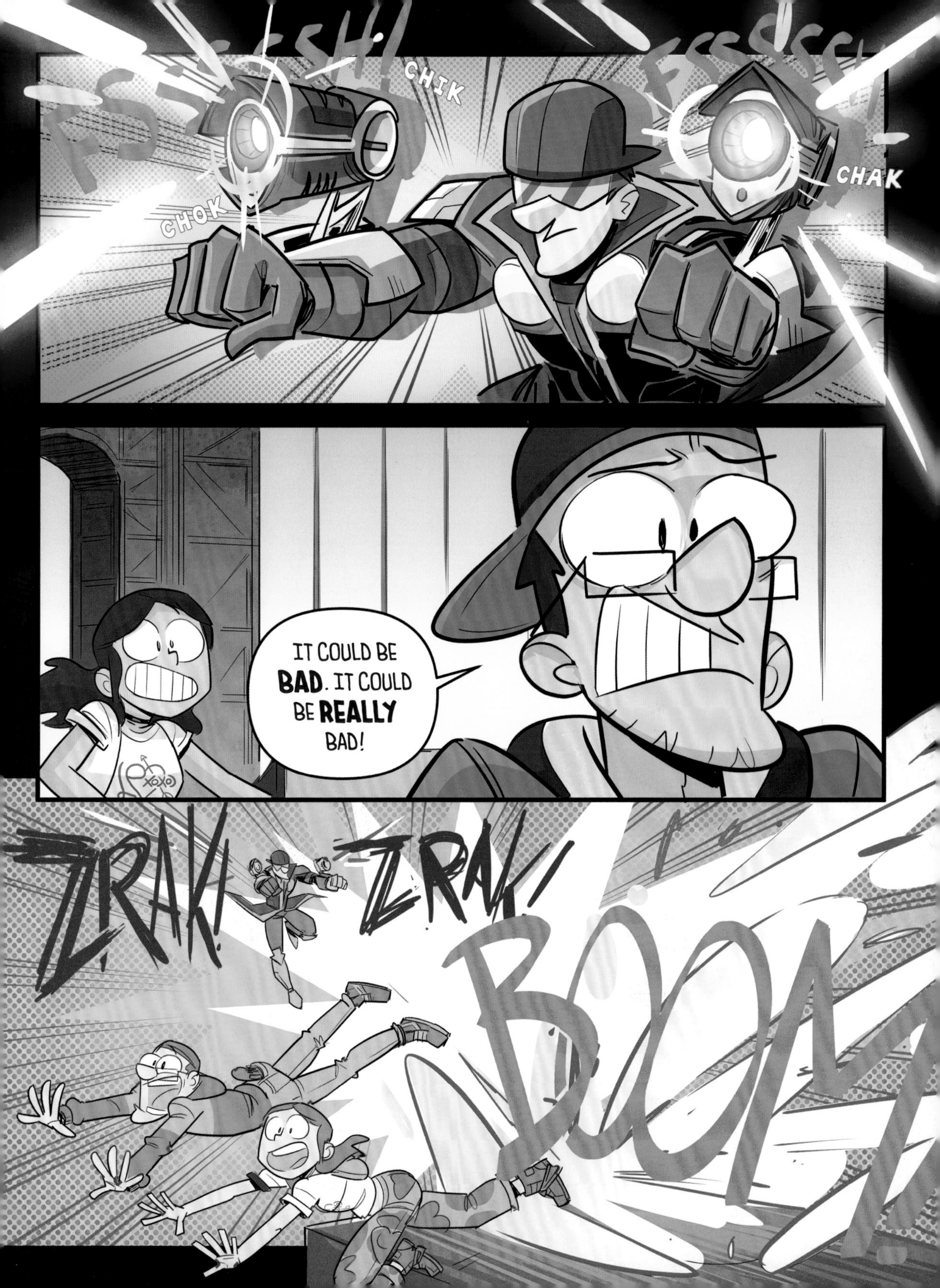
CHIK
CHOK
CHAK
IT COULD BE **BAD**. IT COULD BE **REALLY** BAD!
ZRAK!
ZRAK!
BOOM

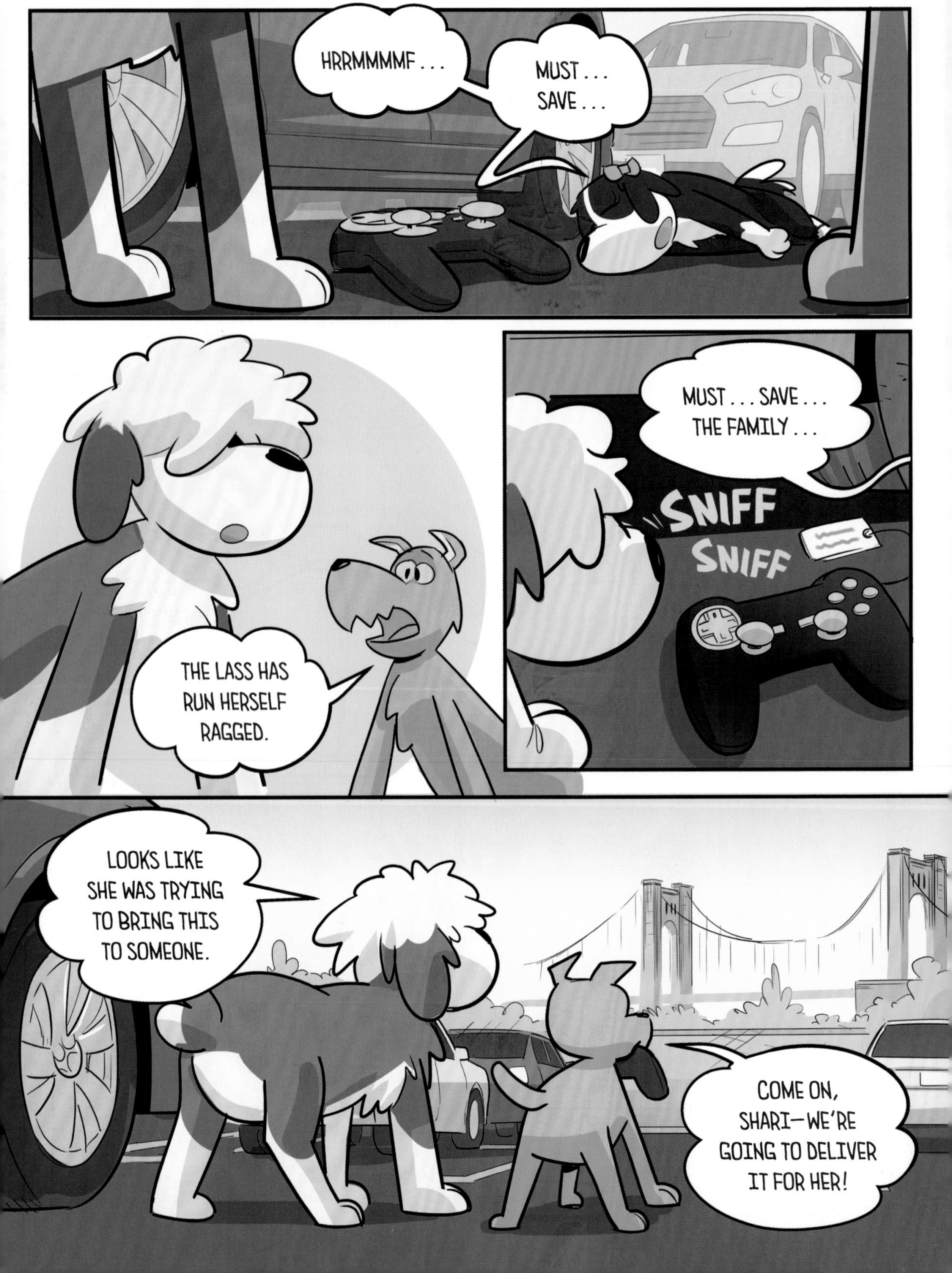
HRRMMMMF . . .
MUST . . .
SAVE . . .
MUST . . . SAVE . . .
THE FAMILY . . .
SNIFF
SNIFF
THE LASS HAS
RUN HERSELF
RAGGED.
LOOKS LIKE
SHE WAS TRYING
TO BRING THIS
TO SOMEONE.
COME ON,
SHARI—WE'RE
GOING TO DELIVER
IT FOR HER!

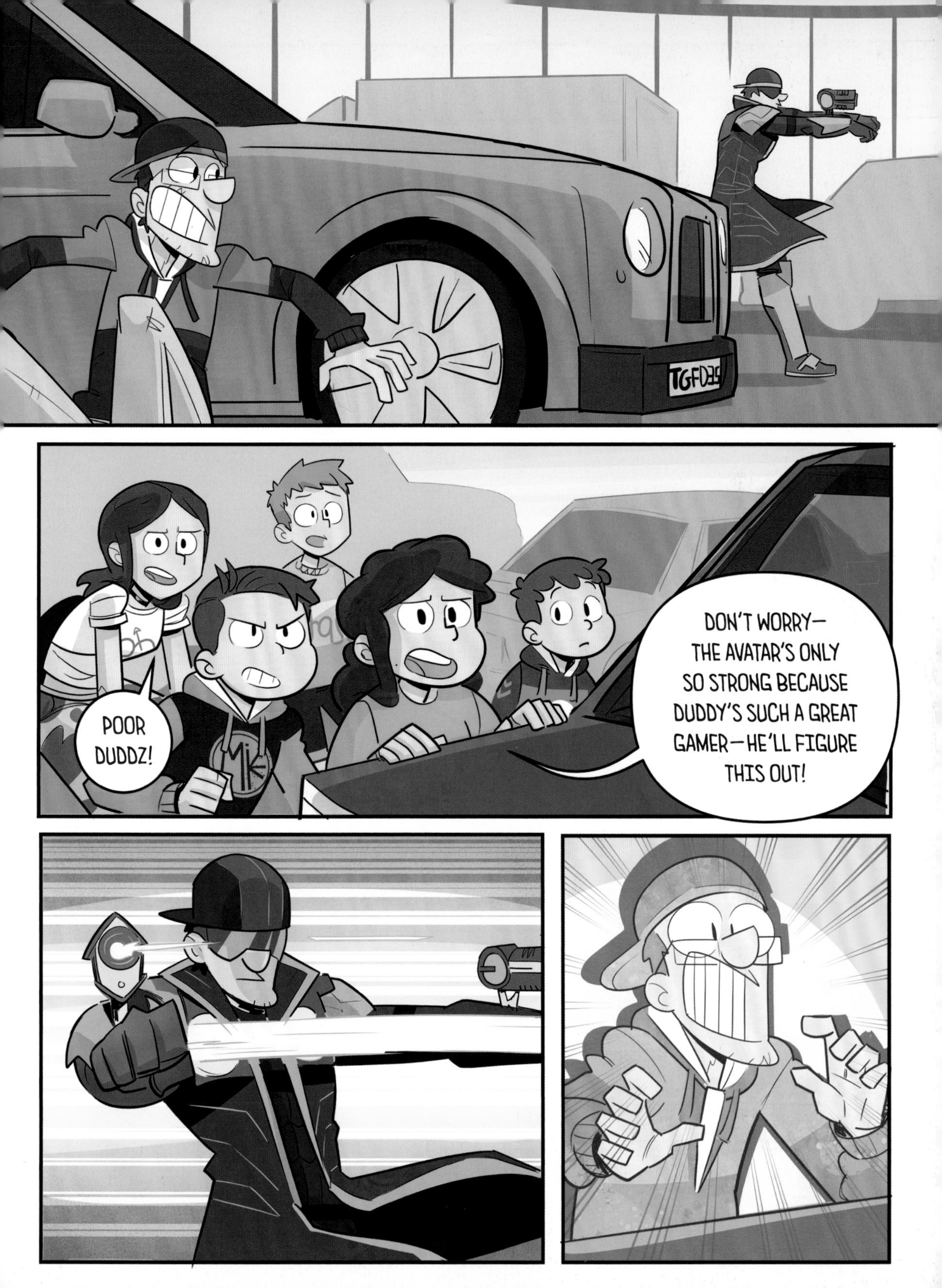
TGFD35
POOR DUDDZ!
DON'T WORRY—THE AVATAR'S ONLY SO STRONG BECAUSE DUDDY'S SUCH A GREAT GAMER—HE'LL FIGURE THIS OUT!

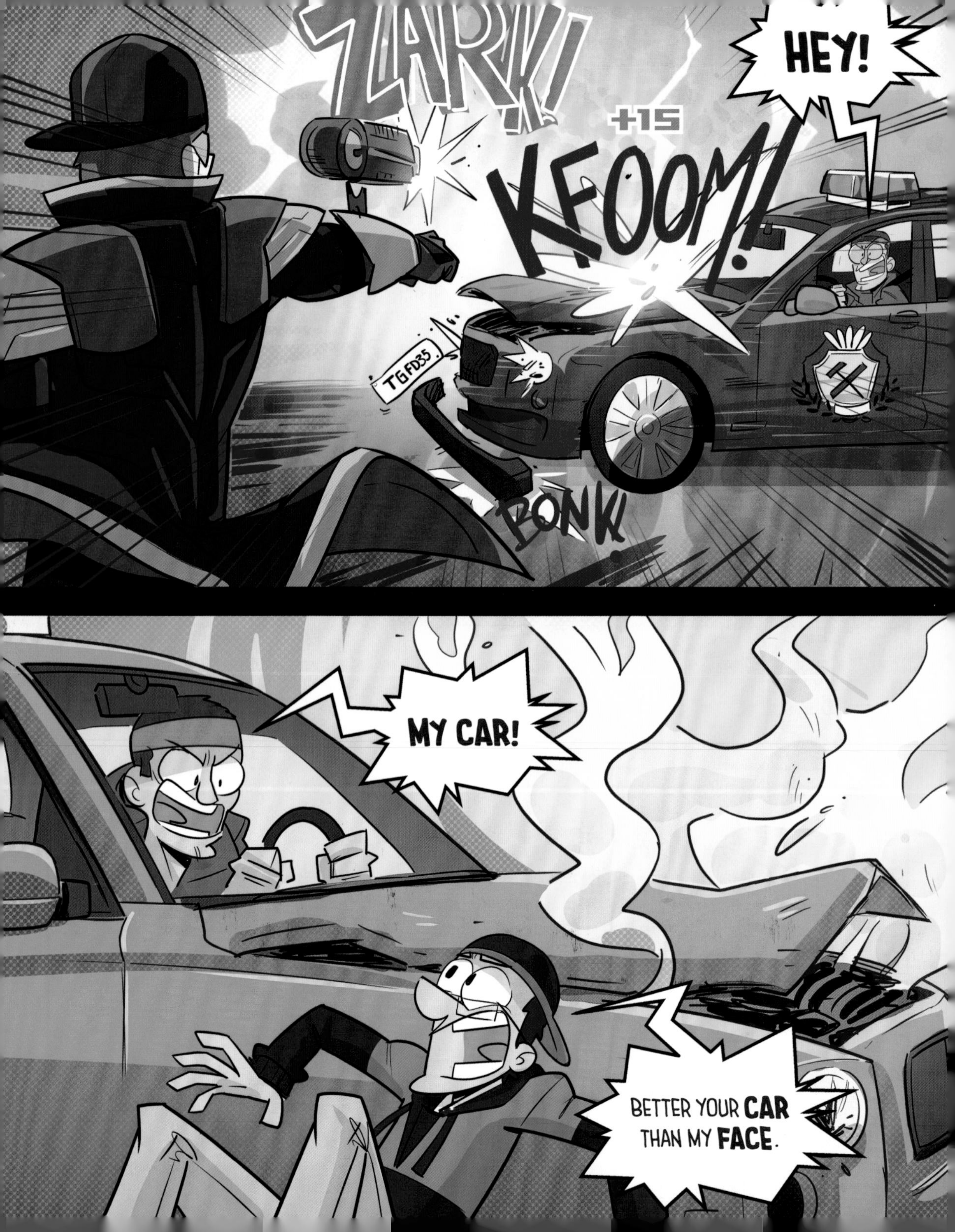
ZARK!
+15
KFOOM!
HEY!
TGFD35
BONK!
MY CAR!
BETTER YOUR CAR THAN MY FACE.

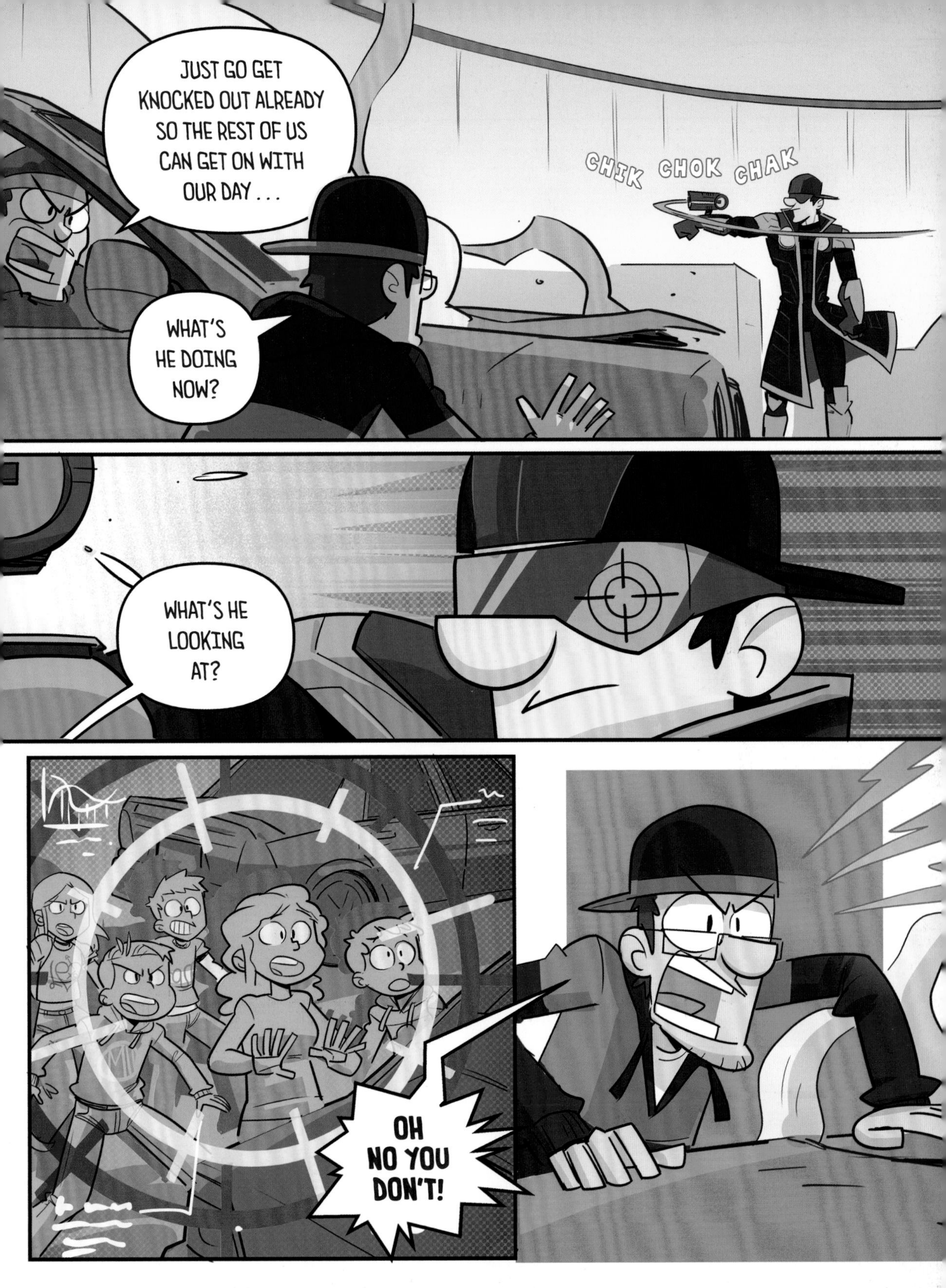
JUST GO GET KNOCKED OUT ALREADY SO THE REST OF US CAN GET ON WITH OUR DAY . . .
CHIK CHOK CHAK
WHAT'S HE DOING NOW?
WHAT'S HE LOOKING AT?
OH NO YOU DON'T!

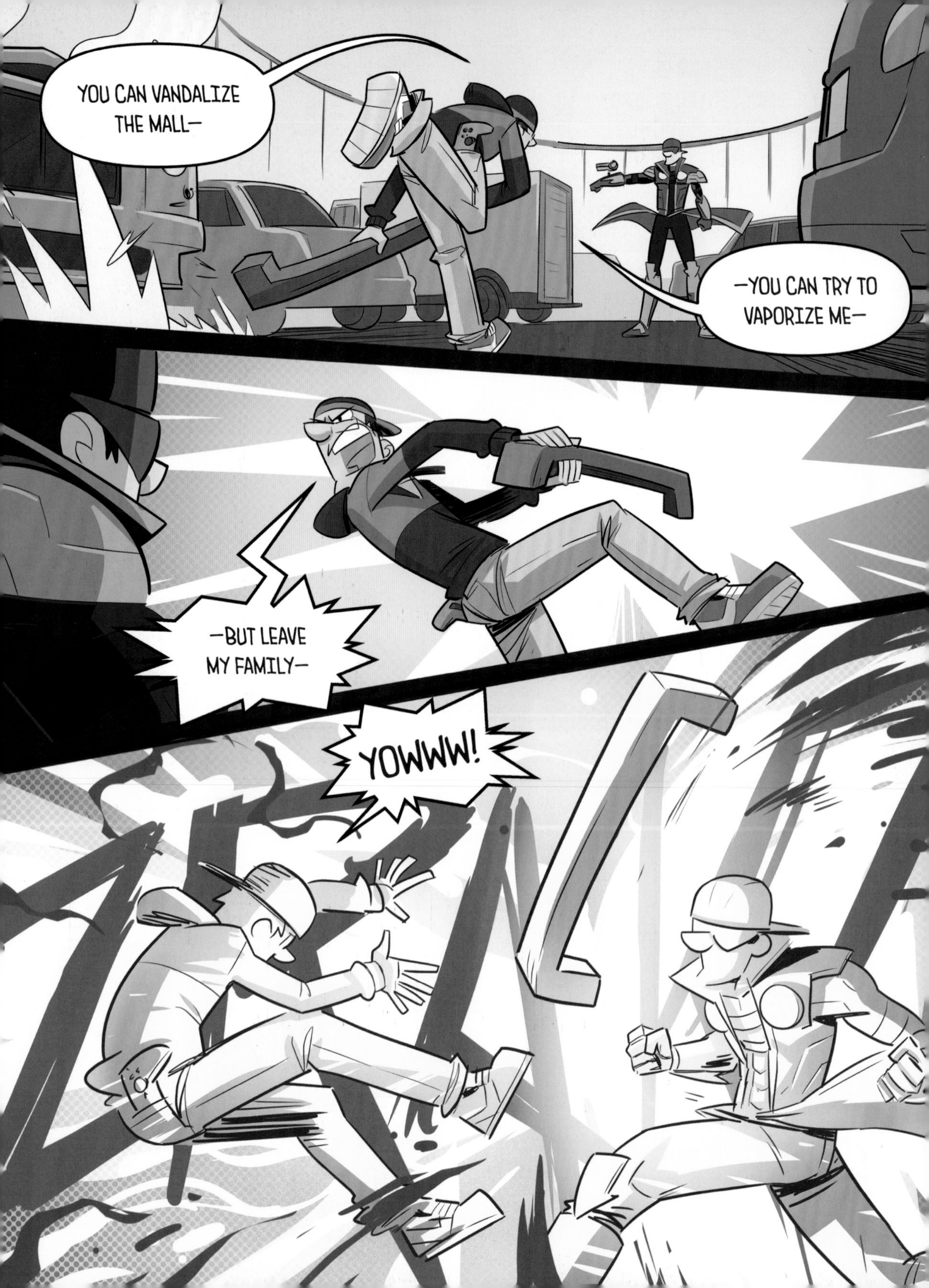
YOU CAN VANDALIZE THE MALL—
—YOU CAN TRY TO VAPORIZE ME—
—BUT LEAVE MY FAMILY—
YOWWW!

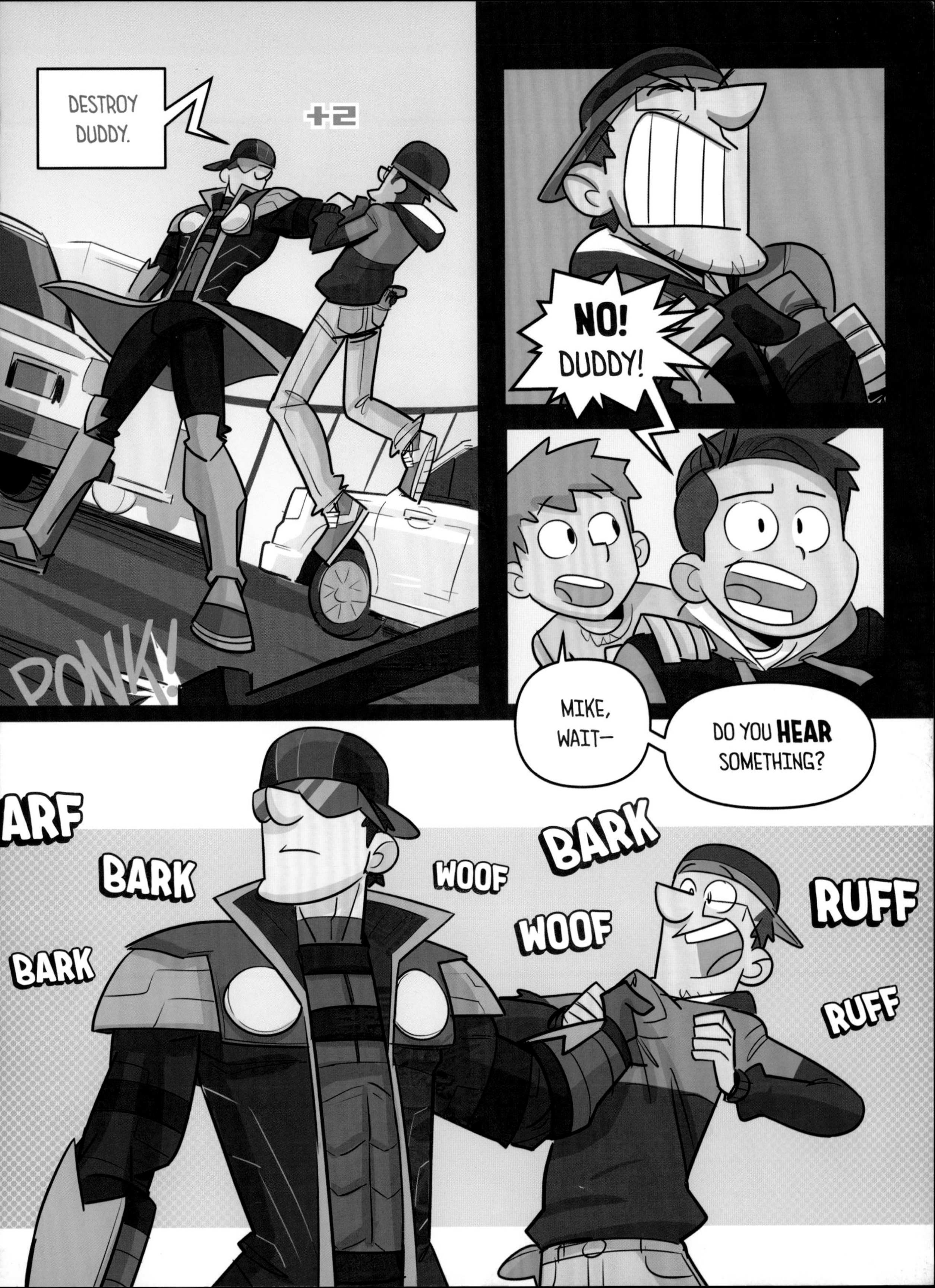
DESTROY DUDDY.
+2
PONK!
NO! DUDDY!
MIKE, WAIT—
DO YOU **HEAR** SOMETHING?
ARF
BARK
BARK
WOOF
BARK
WOOF
RUFF
RUFF

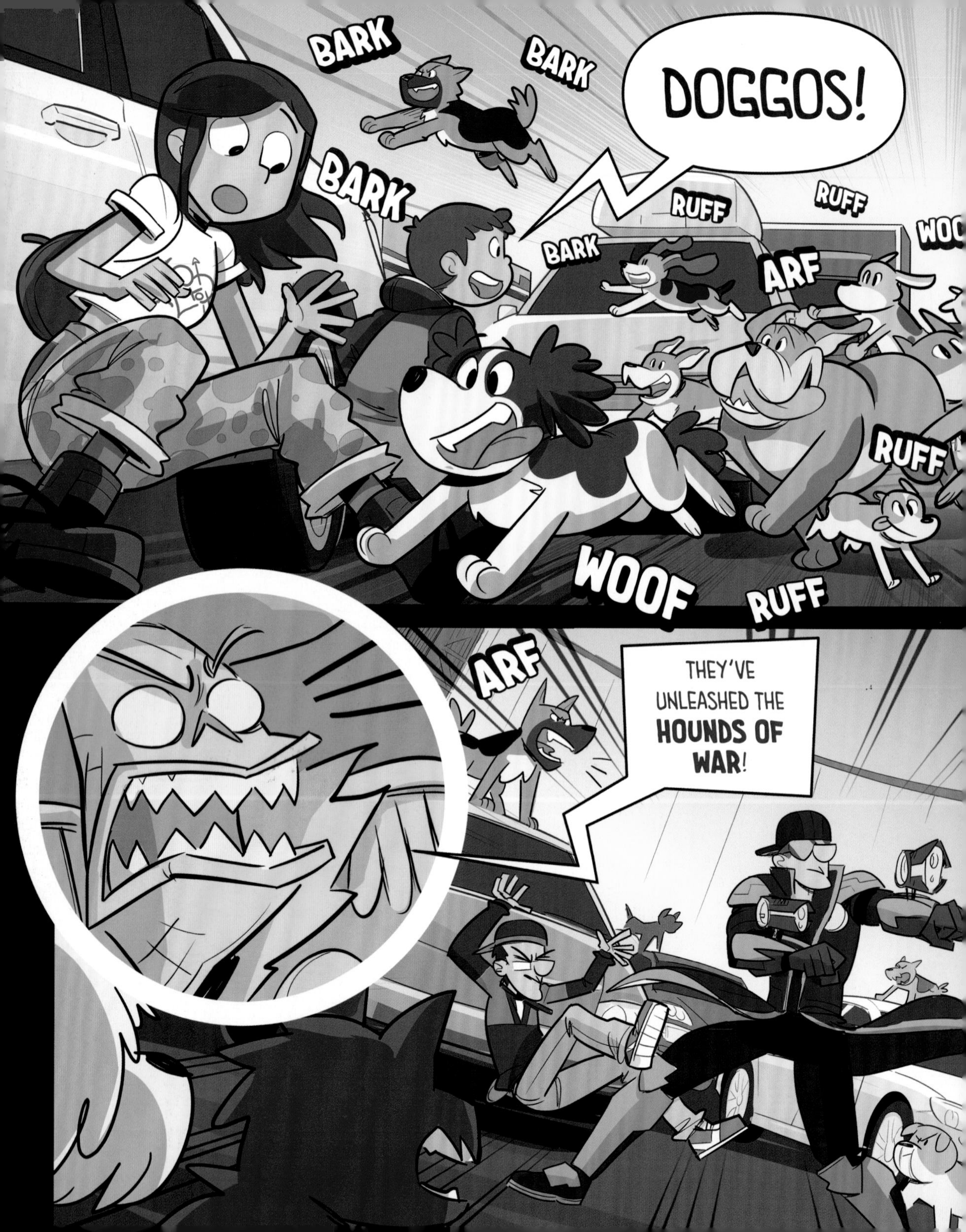
BARK
BARK
DOGGOS!
BARK
RUFF
RUFF
WOO
BARK
ARF
RUFF
WOOF
RUFF
ARF
THEY'VE UNLEASHED THE **HOUNDS OF WAR**!

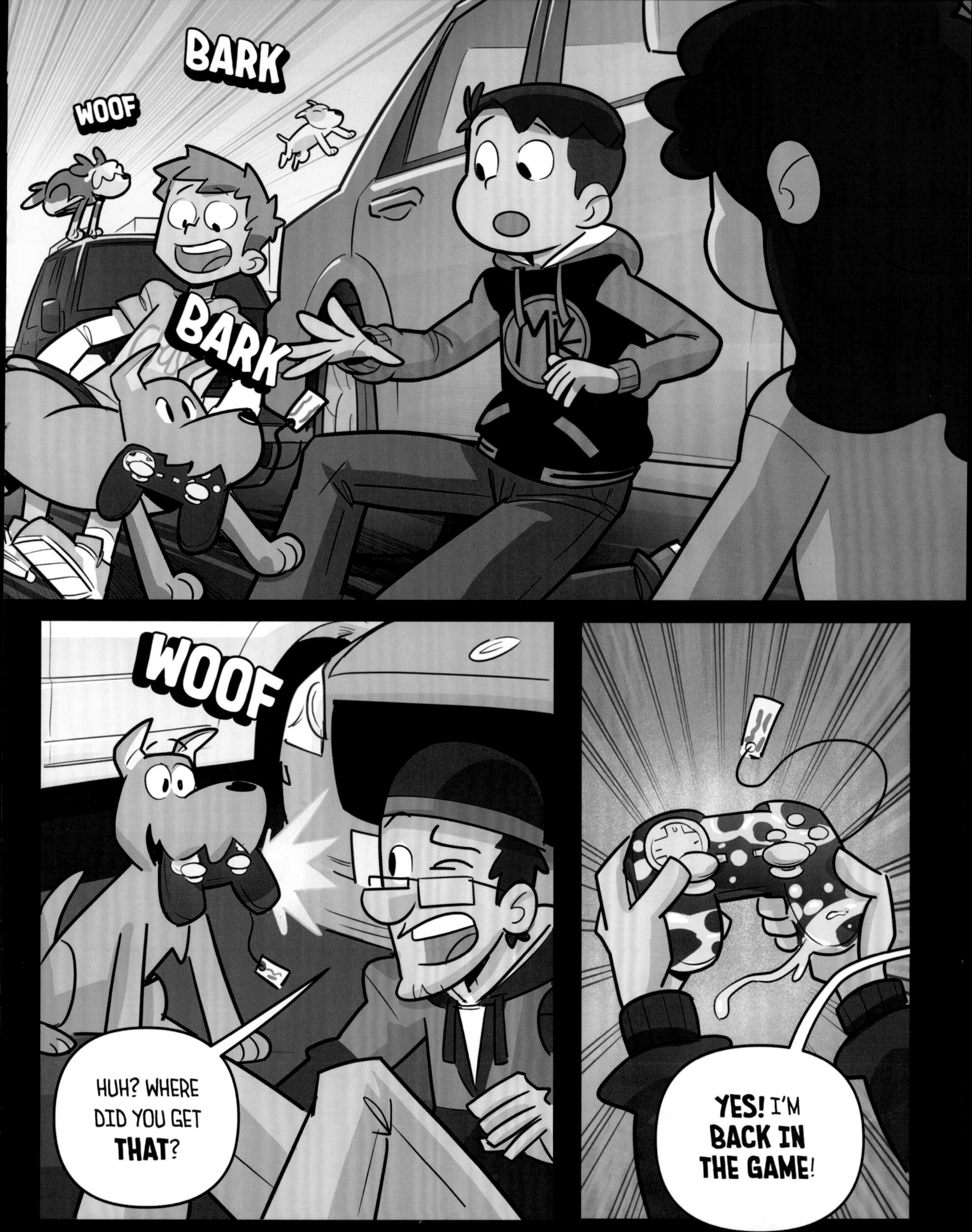
BARK
WOOF
BARK
WOOF
HUH? WHERE DID YOU GET THAT?
YES! I'M BACK IN THE GAME!

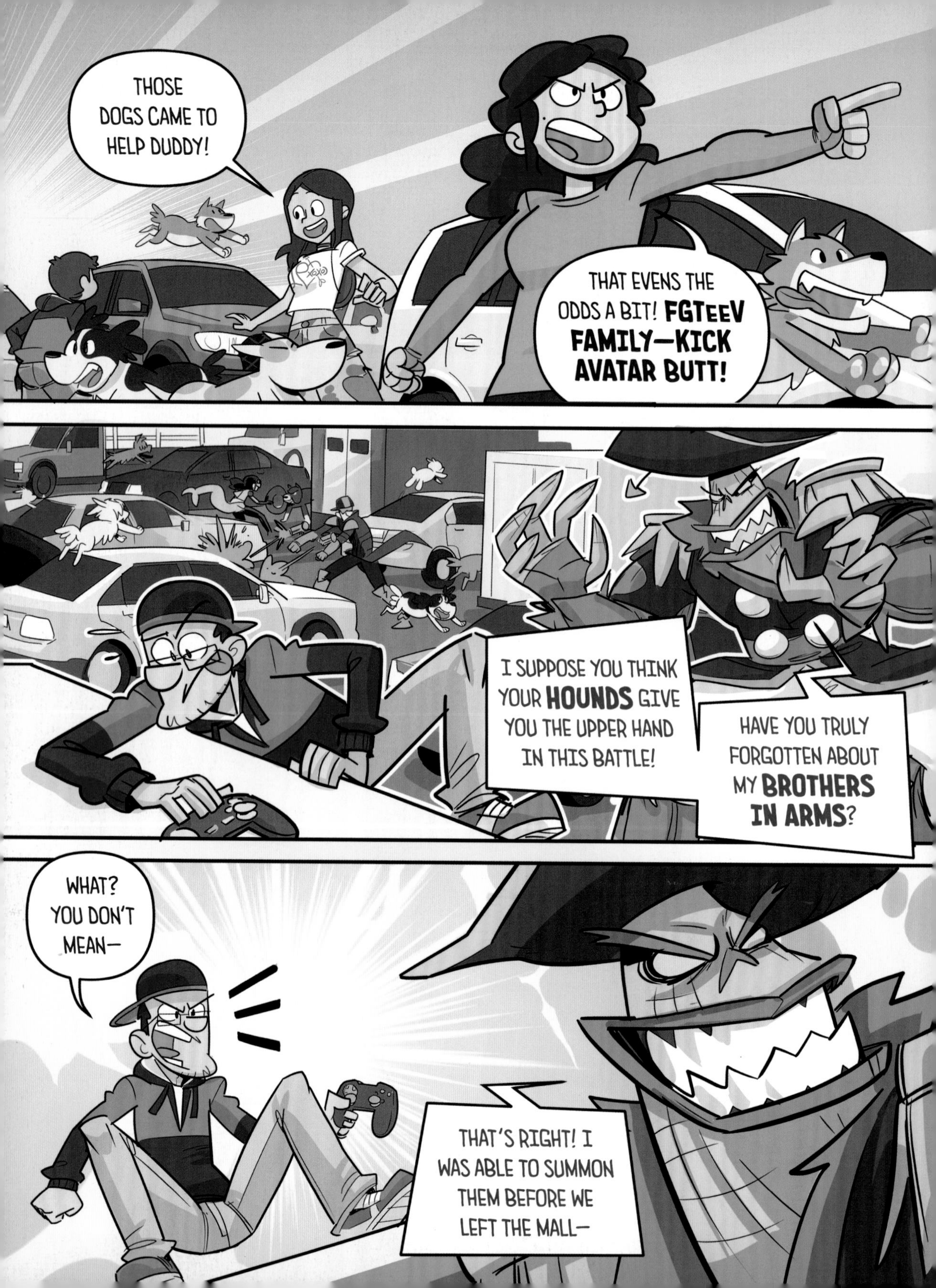
THOSE DOGS CAME TO HELP DUDDY!
THAT EVENS THE ODDS A BIT! FGTEEV FAMILY—KICK AVATAR BUTT!
I SUPPOSE YOU THINK YOUR HOUNDS GIVE YOU THE UPPER HAND IN THIS BATTLE!
HAVE YOU TRULY FORGOTTEN ABOUT MY BROTHERS IN ARMS?
WHAT? YOU DON'T MEAN—
THAT'S RIGHT! I WAS ABLE TO SUMMON THEM BEFORE WE LEFT THE MALL—

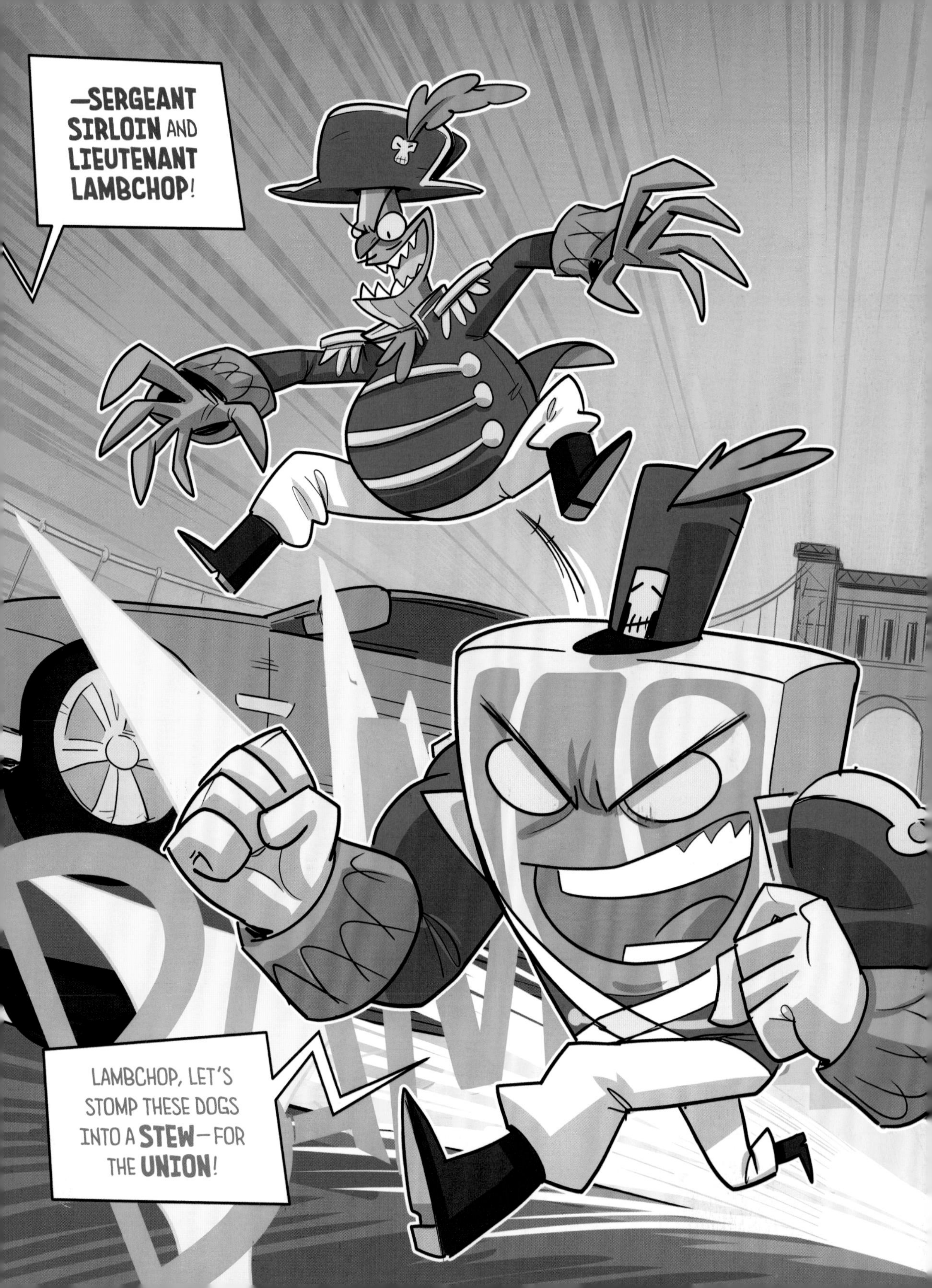
—SERGEANT SIRLOIN AND LIEUTENANT LAMBCHOP!
LAMBCHOP, LET'S STOMP THESE DOGS INTO A STEW—FOR THE UNION!

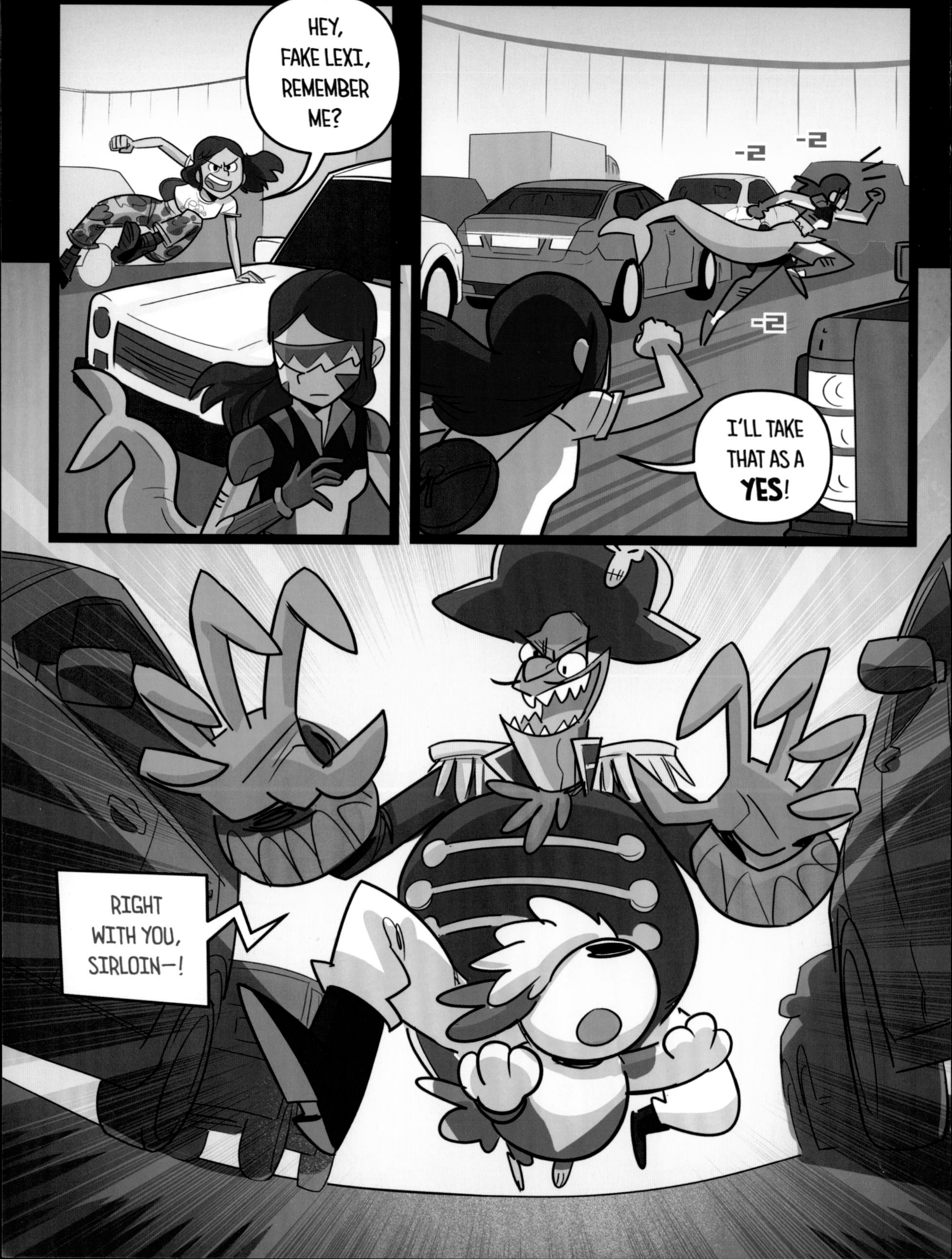
HEY, FAKE LEXI, REMEMBER ME?
-2
-2
-2
I'LL TAKE THAT AS A YES!
RIGHT WITH YOU, SIRLOIN—!

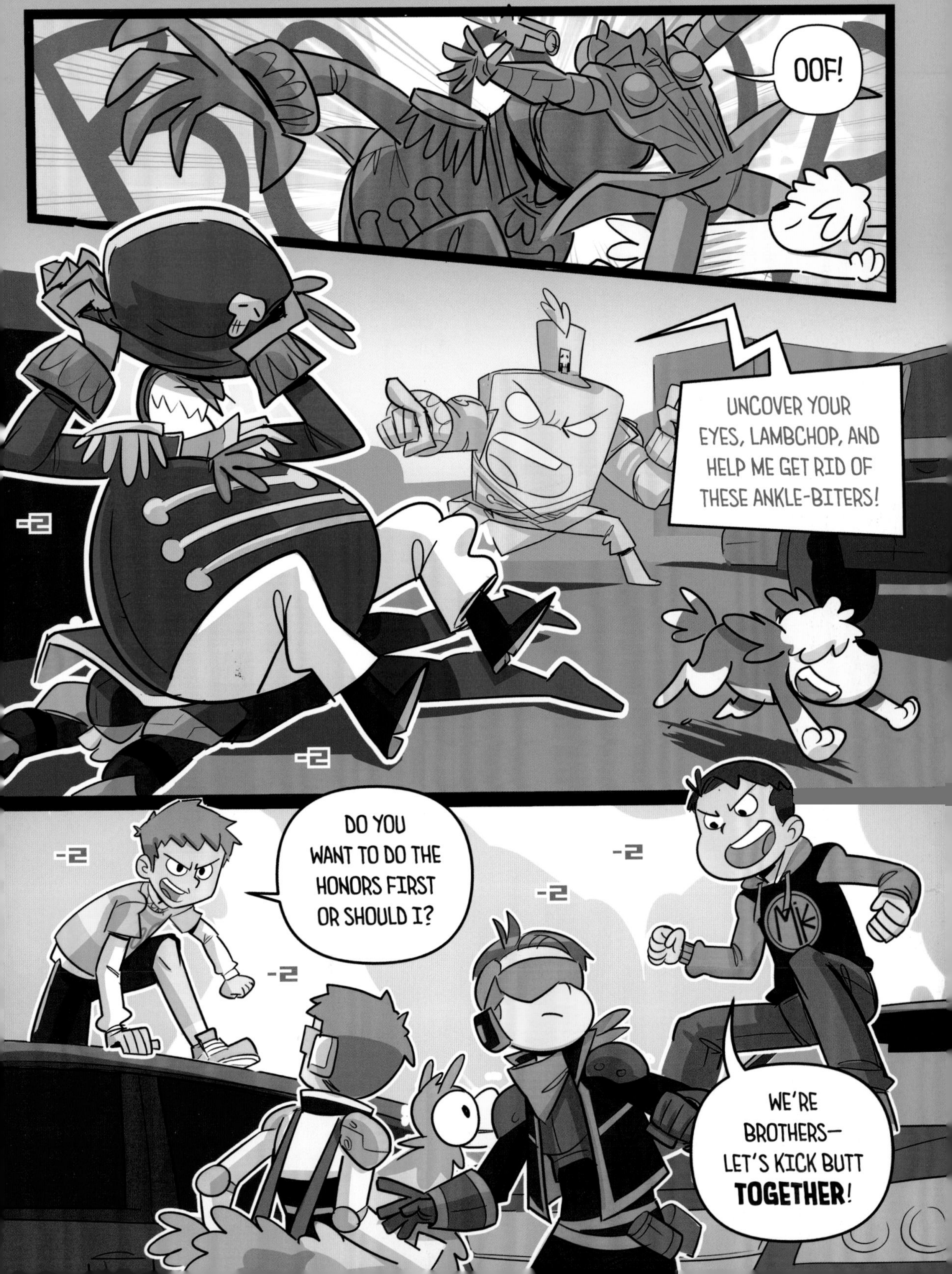
OOF!
UNCOVER YOUR EYES, LAMBCHOP, AND HELP ME GET RID OF THESE ANKLE-BITERS!
DO YOU WANT TO DO THE HONORS FIRST OR SHOULD I?
WE'RE BROTHERS—LET'S KICK BUTT TOGETHER!

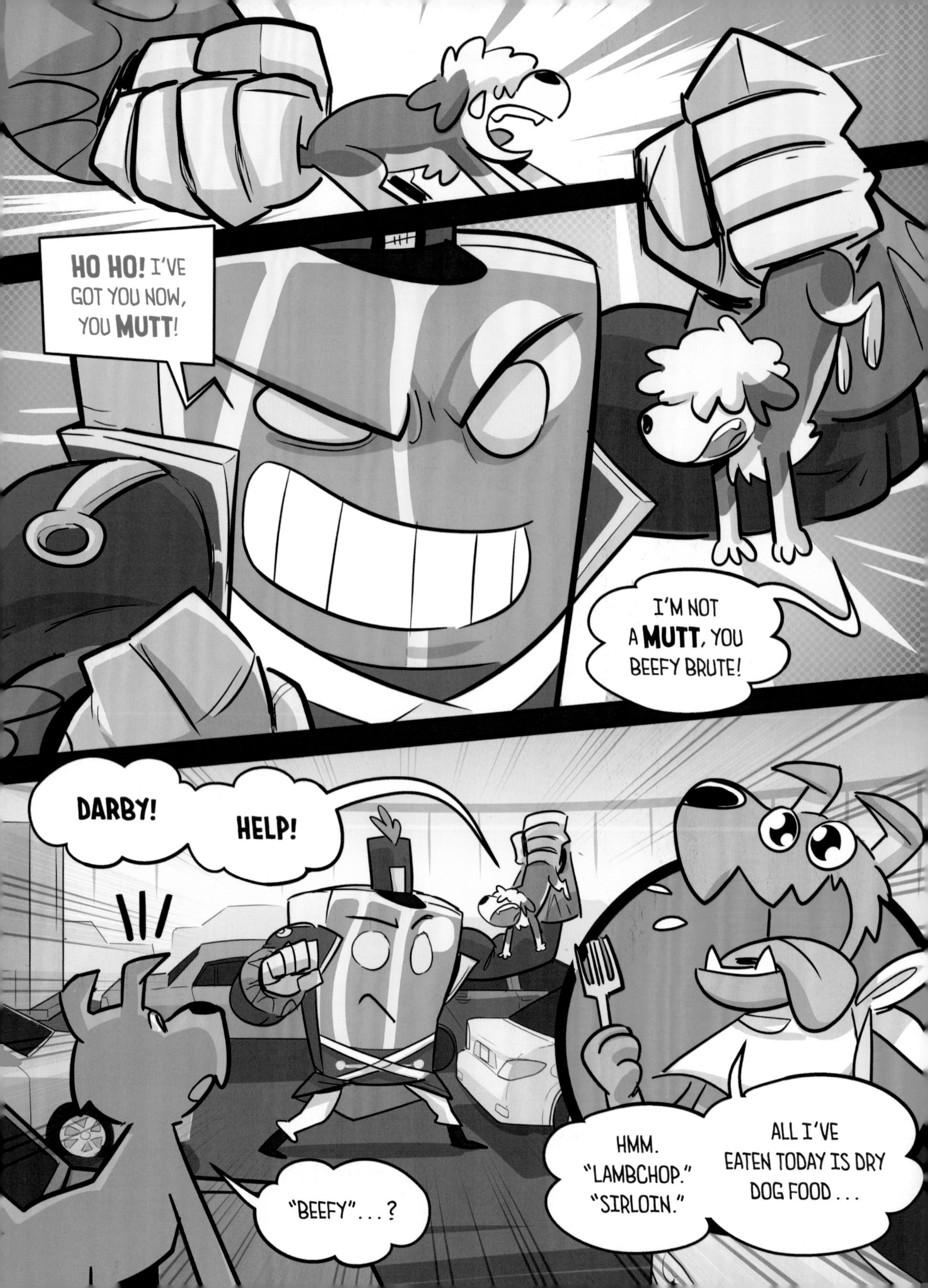
HO HO! I'VE GOT YOU NOW, YOU MUTT!
I'M NOT A MUTT, YOU BEEFY BRUTE!
DARBY!
HELP!
"BEEFY" . . . ?
HMM. "LAMBCHOP." "SIRLOIN."
ALL I'VE EATEN TODAY IS DRY DOG FOOD . . .

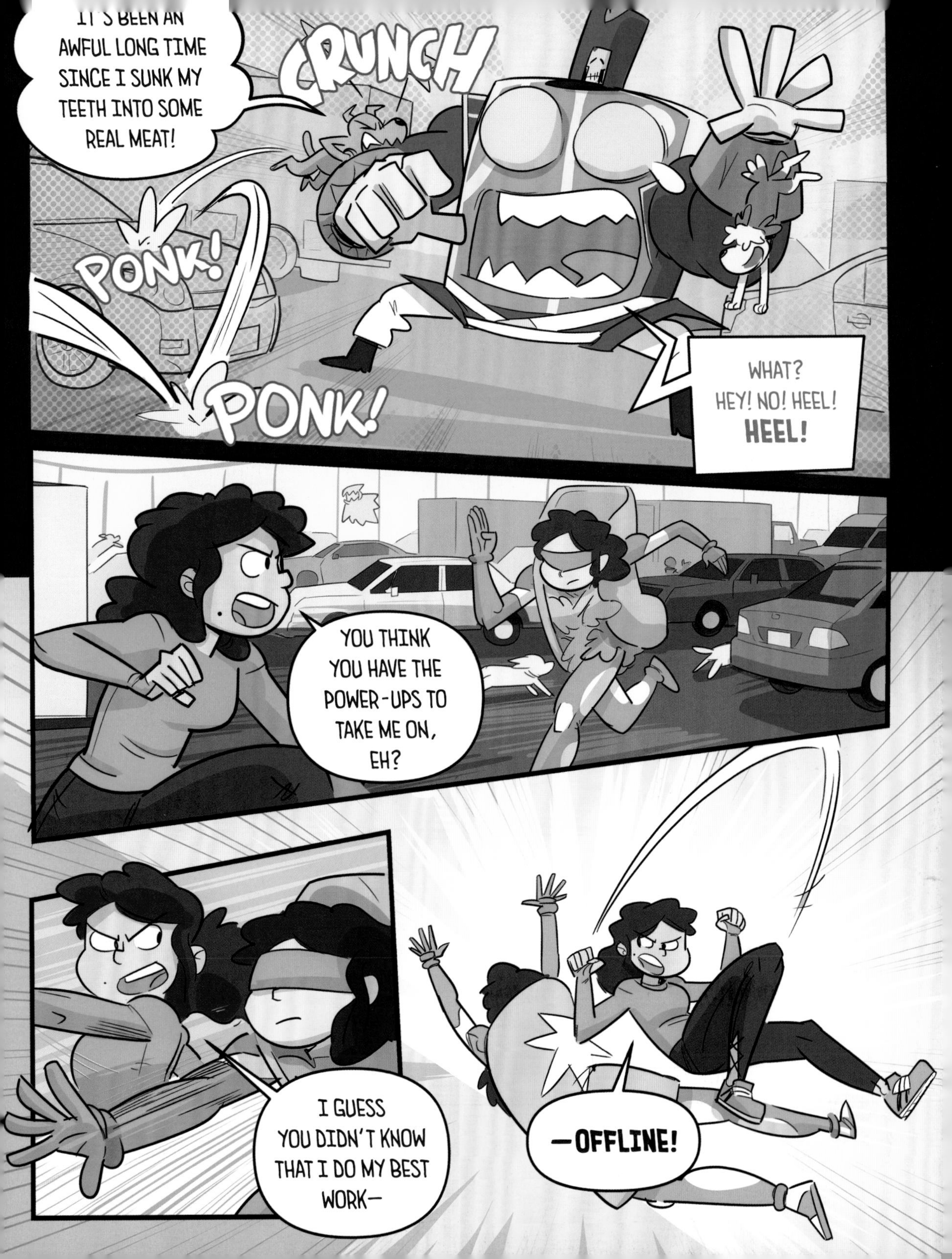
IT'S BEEN AN AWFUL LONG TIME SINCE I SUNK MY TEETH INTO SOME REAL MEAT!
CRUNCH
PONK!
PONK!
WHAT? HEY! NO! HEEL! **HEEL!**
YOU THINK YOU HAVE THE POWER-UPS TO TAKE ME ON, EH?
I GUESS YOU DIDN'T KNOW THAT I DO MY BEST WORK—
—**OFFLINE!**

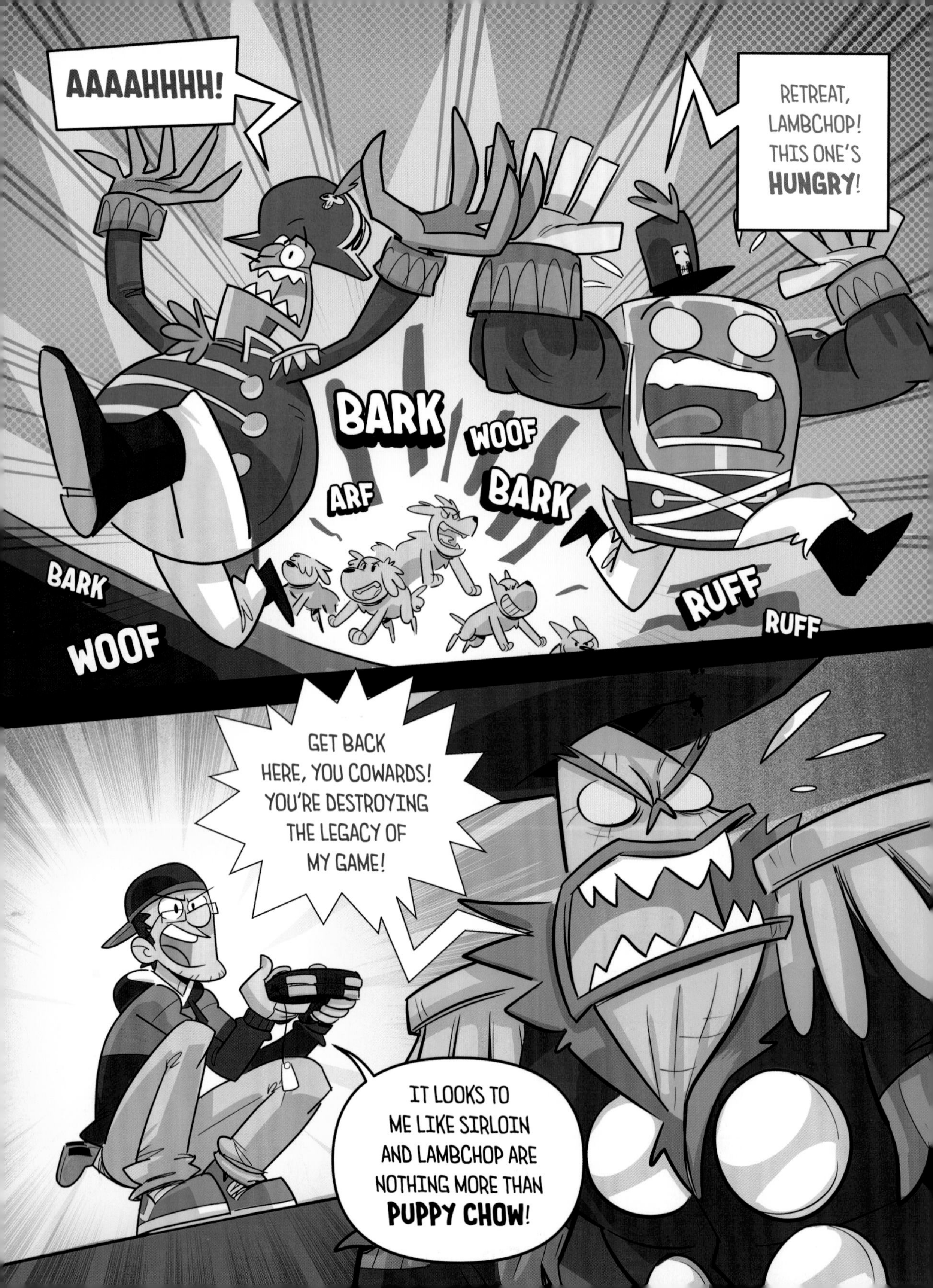
AAAAHHHH!
RETREAT, LAMBCHOP! THIS ONE'S **HUNGRY**!
BARK
WOOF
ARF
BARK
BARK
WOOF
RUFF
RUFF
GET BACK HERE, YOU COWARDS! YOU'RE DESTROYING THE LEGACY OF MY GAME!
IT LOOKS TO ME LIKE SIRLOIN AND LAMBCHOP ARE NOTHING MORE THAN **PUPPY CHOW**!

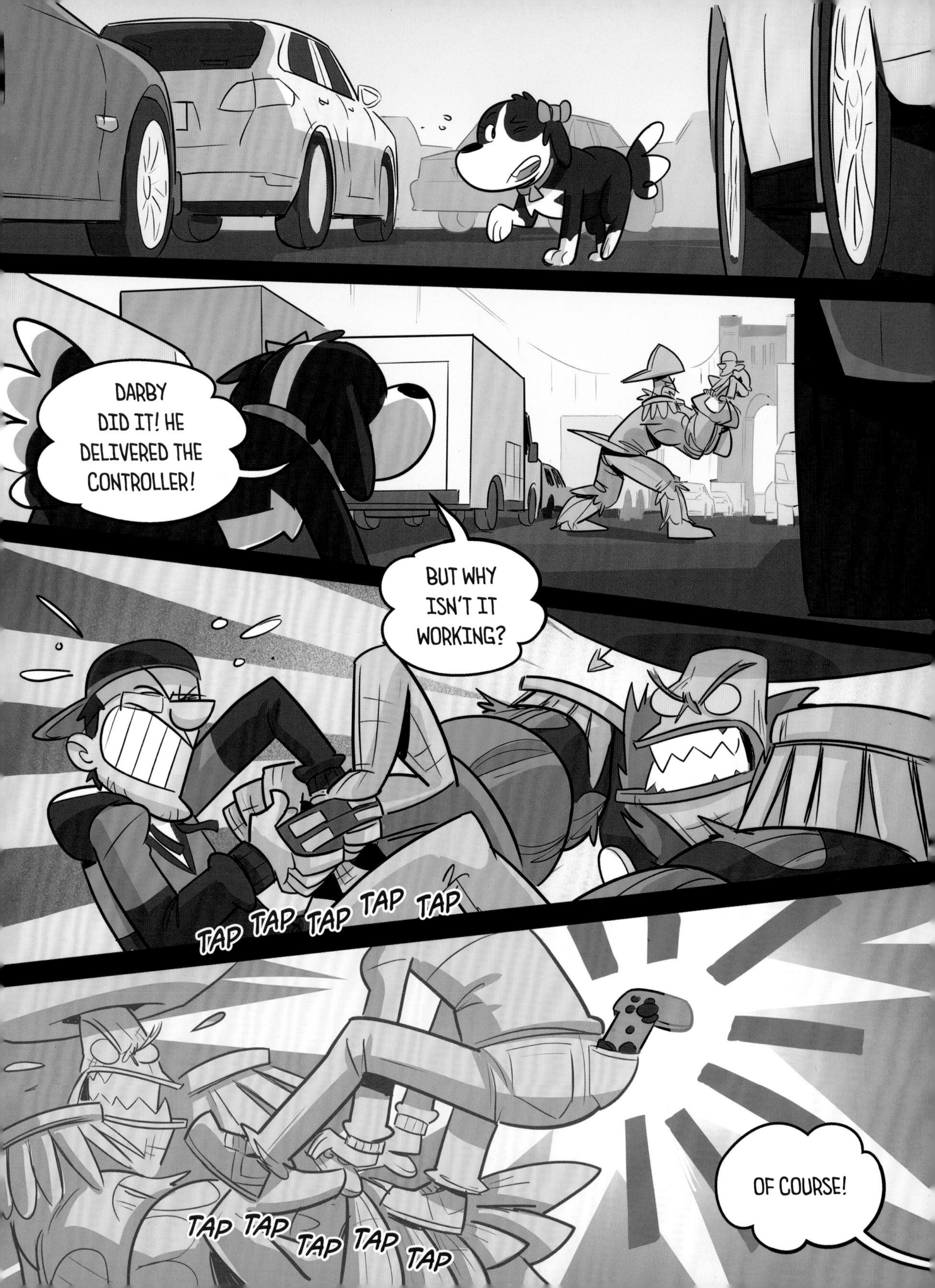
DARBY DID IT! HE DELIVERED THE CONTROLLER!
BUT WHY ISN'T IT WORKING?
TAP TAP TAP TAP TAP
TAP TAP TAP TAP TAP
OF COURSE!

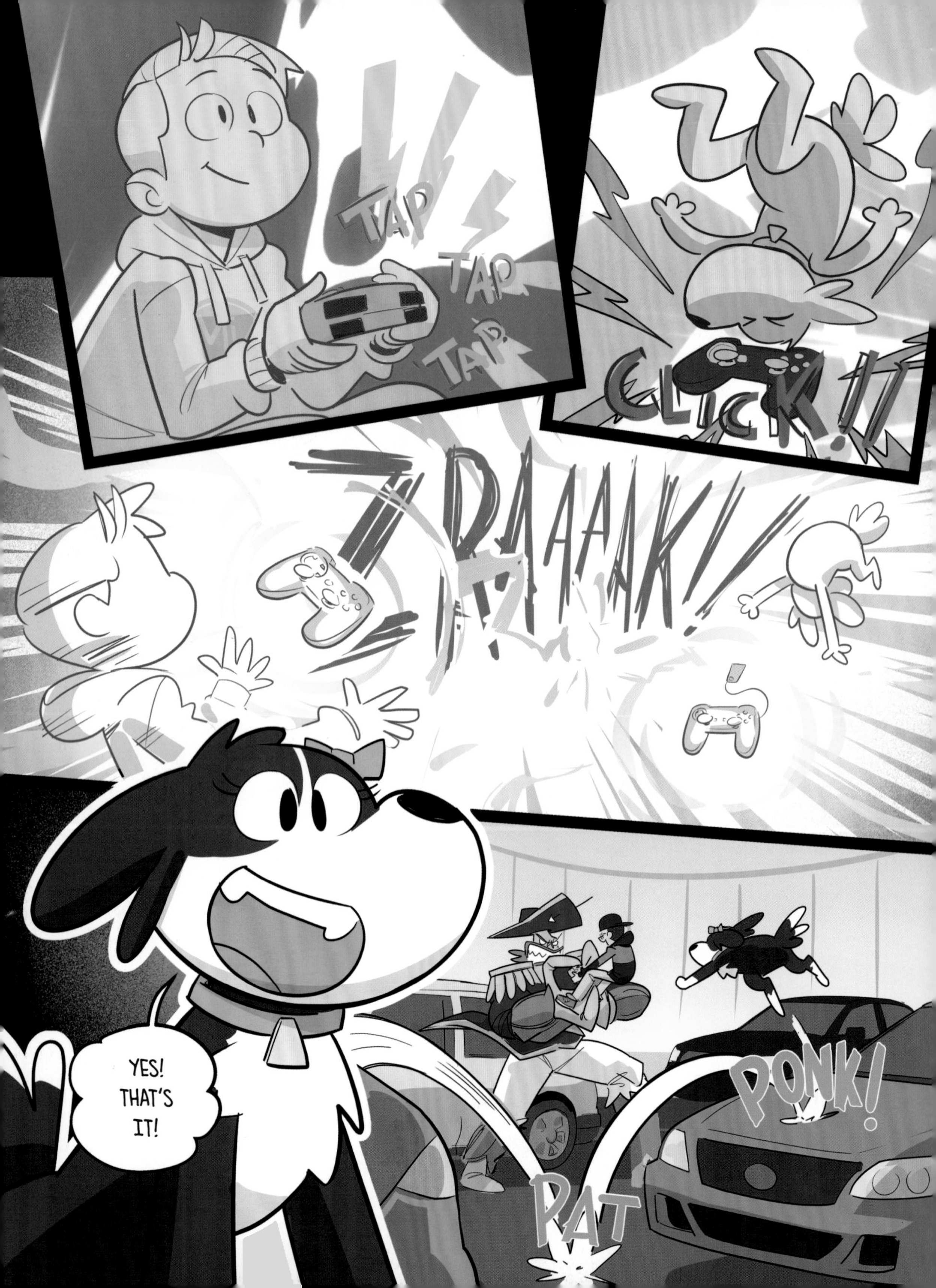
TAP
TAP
TAP
CLICK!!
ZRAAAAK!!
YES! THAT'S IT!
PONK!
PAT

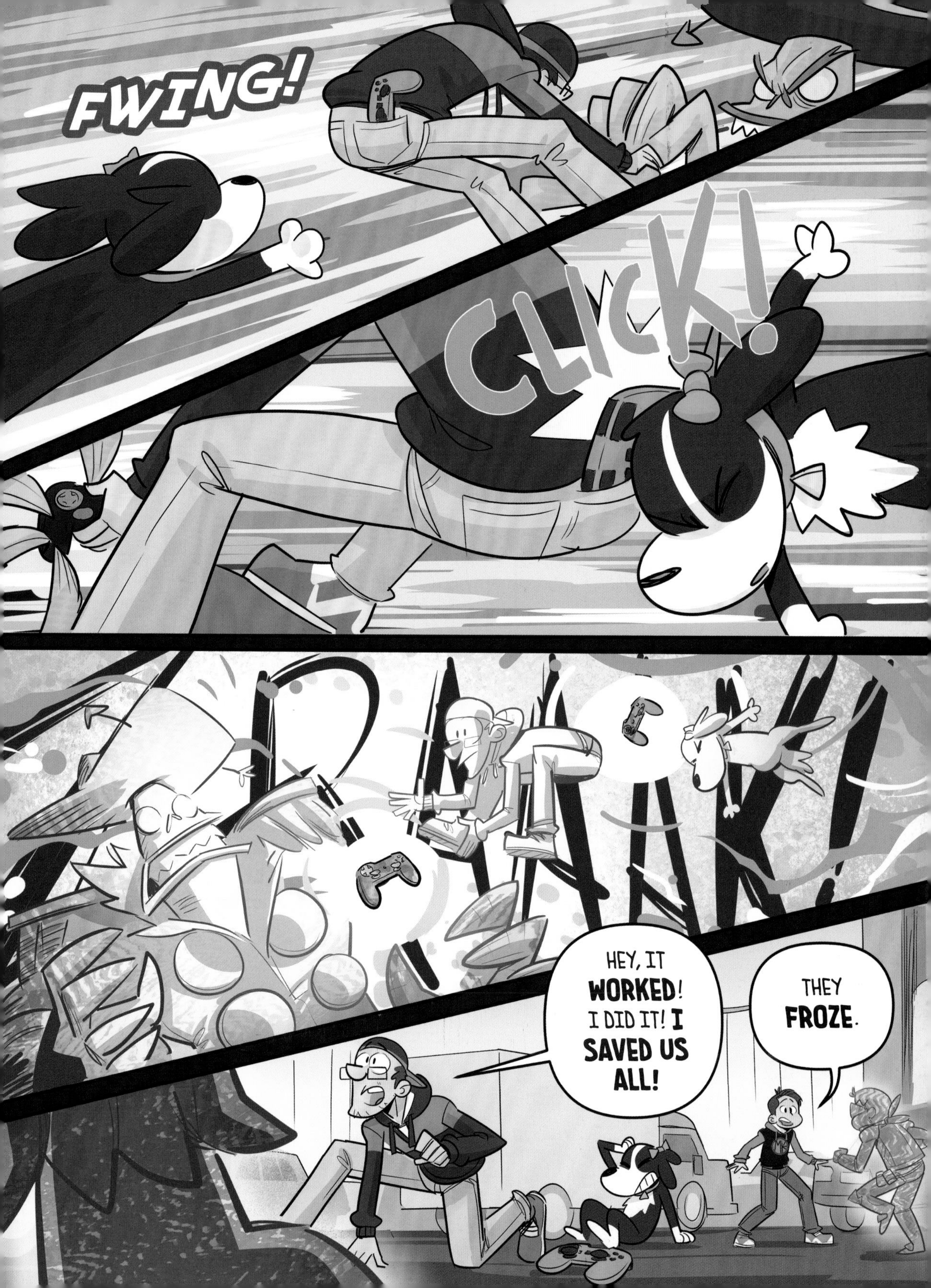
FWING!
CLICK!
HEY, IT WORKED! I DID IT! I SAVED US ALL!
THEY FROZE.

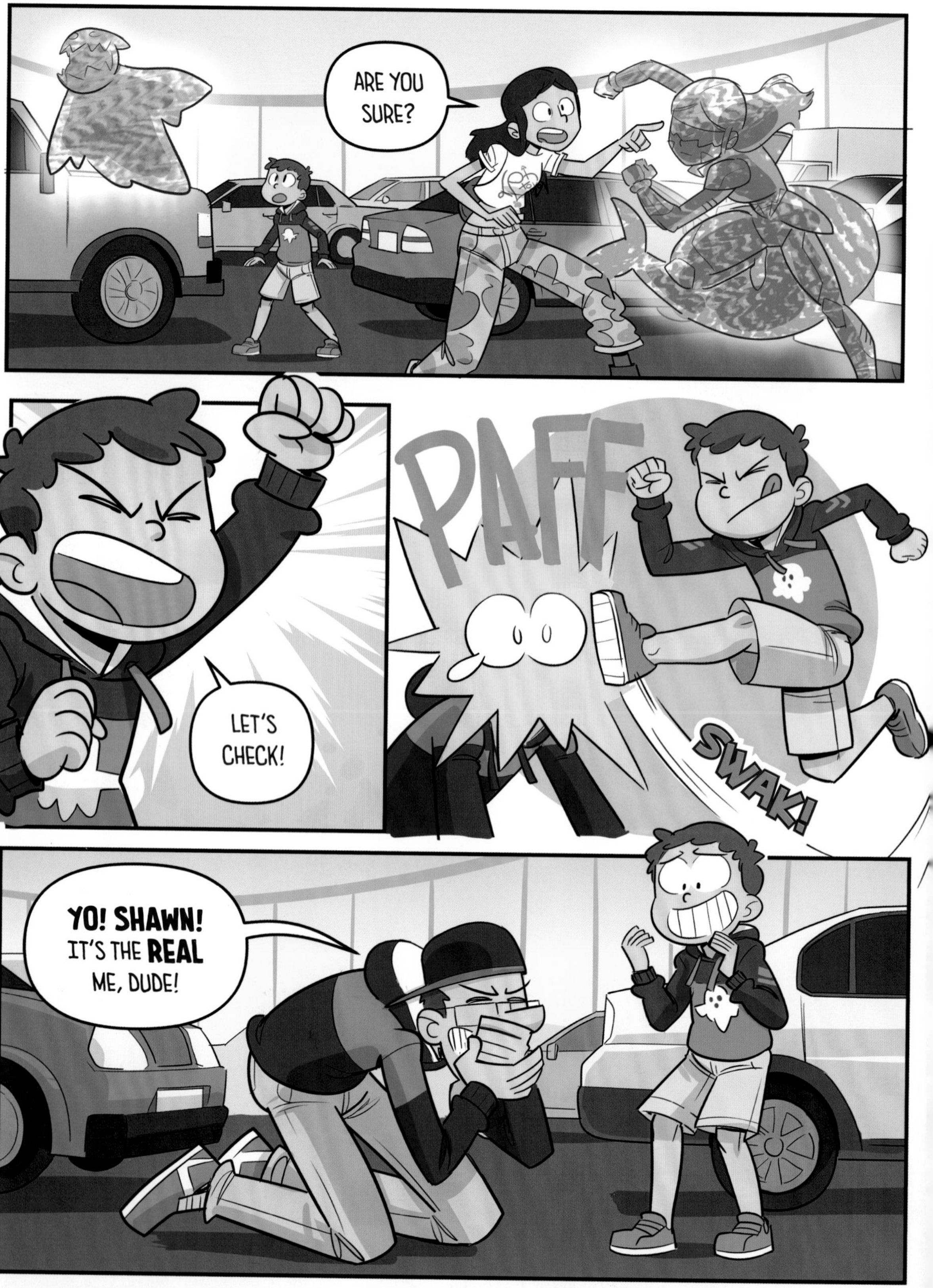
ARE YOU SURE?
LET'S CHECK!
PAFF
SWAK!
YO! SHAWN! IT'S THE REAL ME, DUDE!

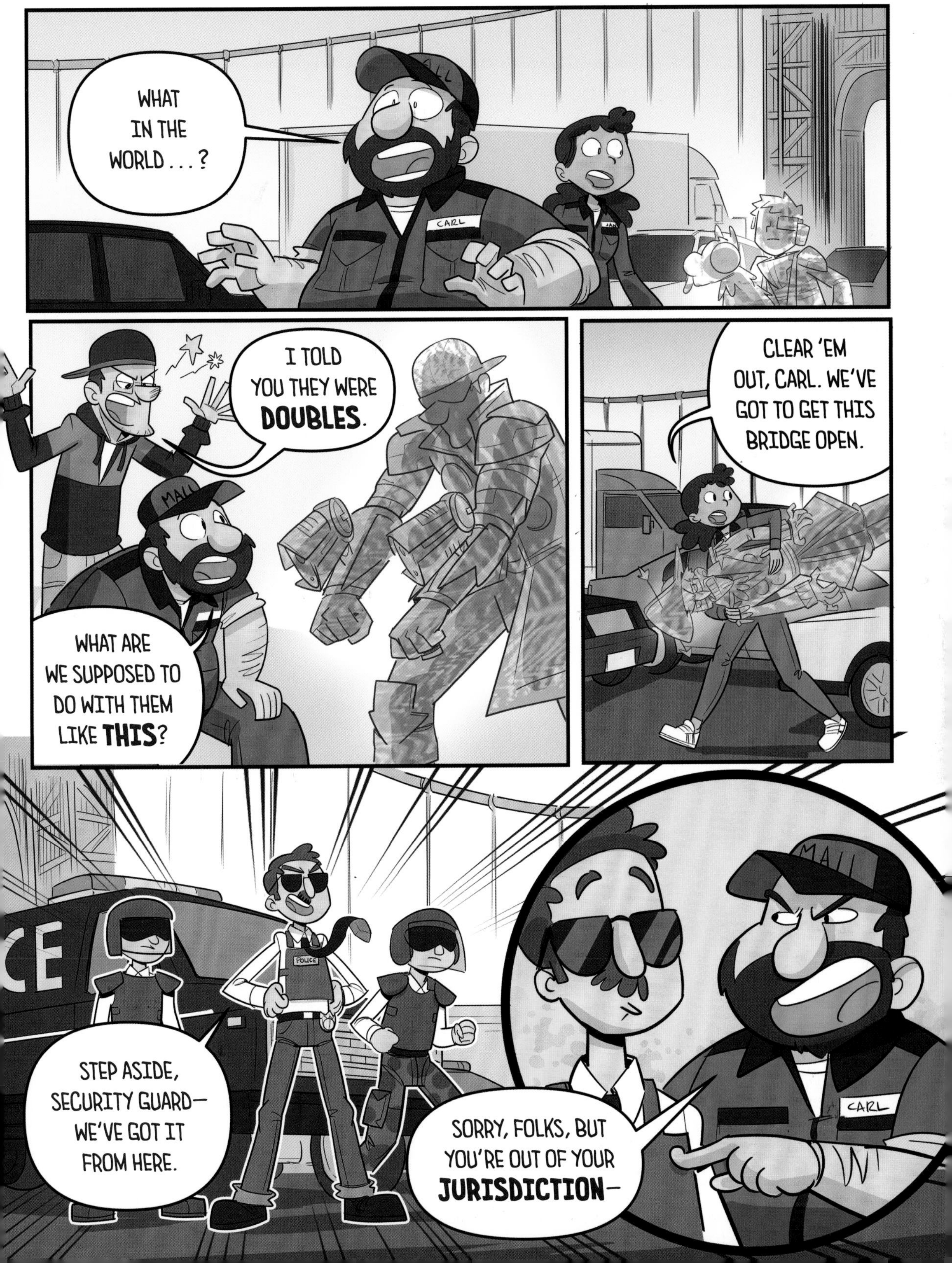
WHAT IN THE WORLD . . . ?
I TOLD YOU THEY WERE **DOUBLES**.
WHAT ARE WE SUPPOSED TO DO WITH THEM LIKE **THIS**?
CLEAR 'EM OUT, CARL. WE'VE GOT TO GET THIS BRIDGE OPEN.
STEP ASIDE, SECURITY GUARD—WE'VE GOT IT FROM HERE.
SORRY, FOLKS, BUT YOU'RE OUT OF YOUR **JURISDICTION**—

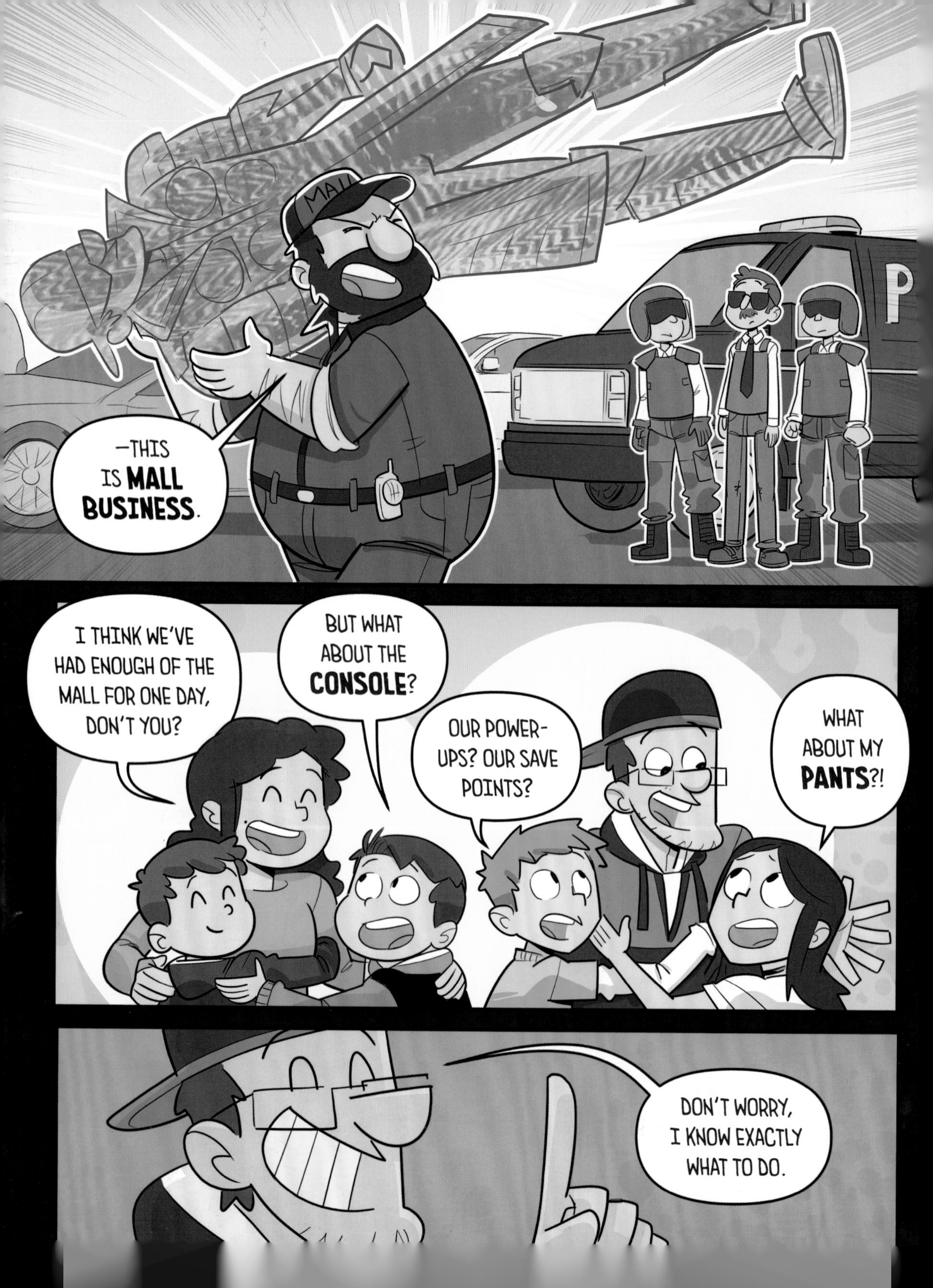
—THIS IS MALL BUSINESS.
I THINK WE'VE HAD ENOUGH OF THE MALL FOR ONE DAY, DON'T YOU?
BUT WHAT ABOUT THE CONSOLE?
OUR POWER-UPS? OUR SAVE POINTS?
WHAT ABOUT MY PANTS?!
DON'T WORRY, I KNOW EXACTLY WHAT TO DO.

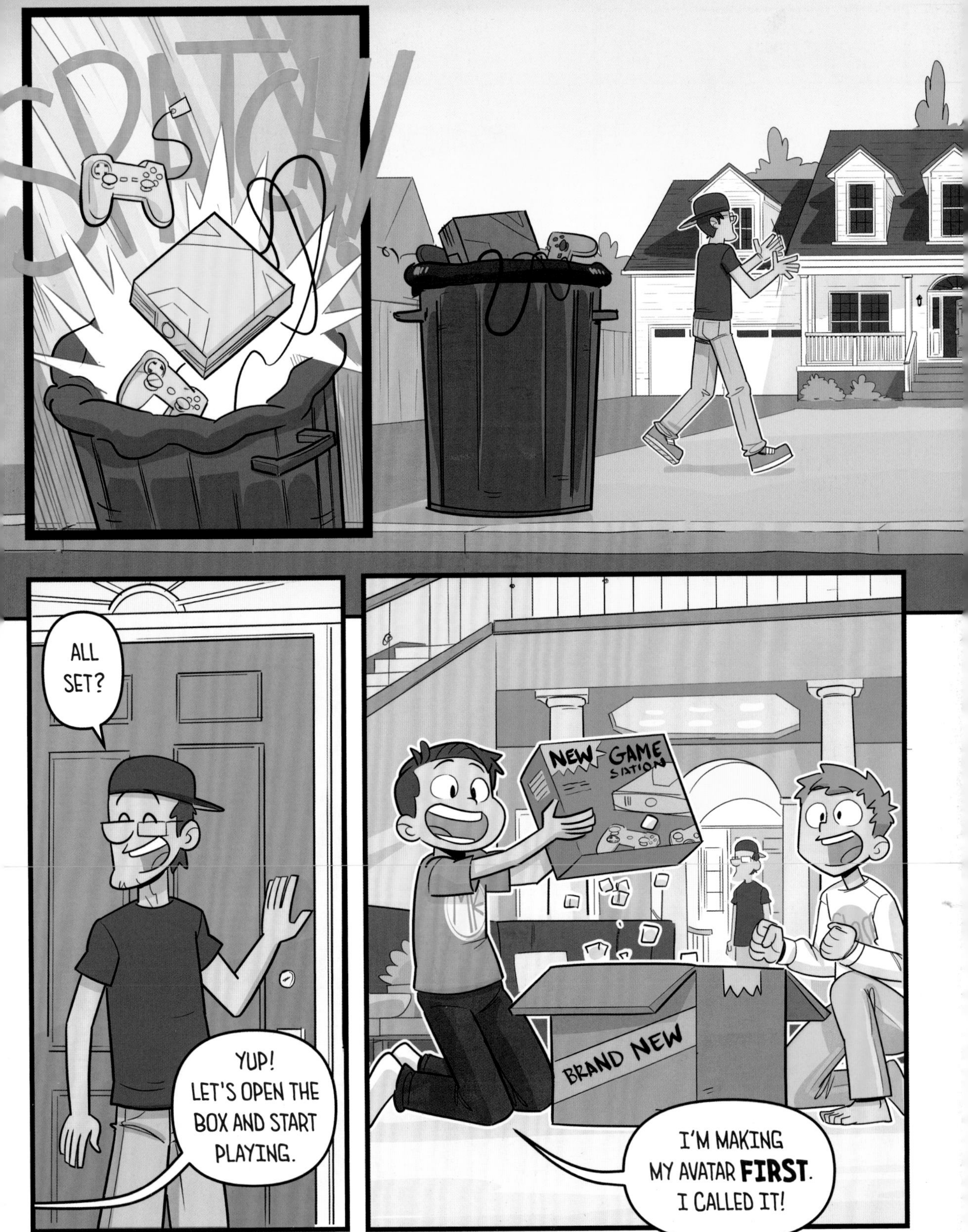
SPATCH!
NEW GAME STATION
ALL SET?
YUP! LET'S OPEN THE BOX AND START PLAYING.
BRAND NEW
I'M MAKING MY AVATAR FIRST. I CALLED IT!

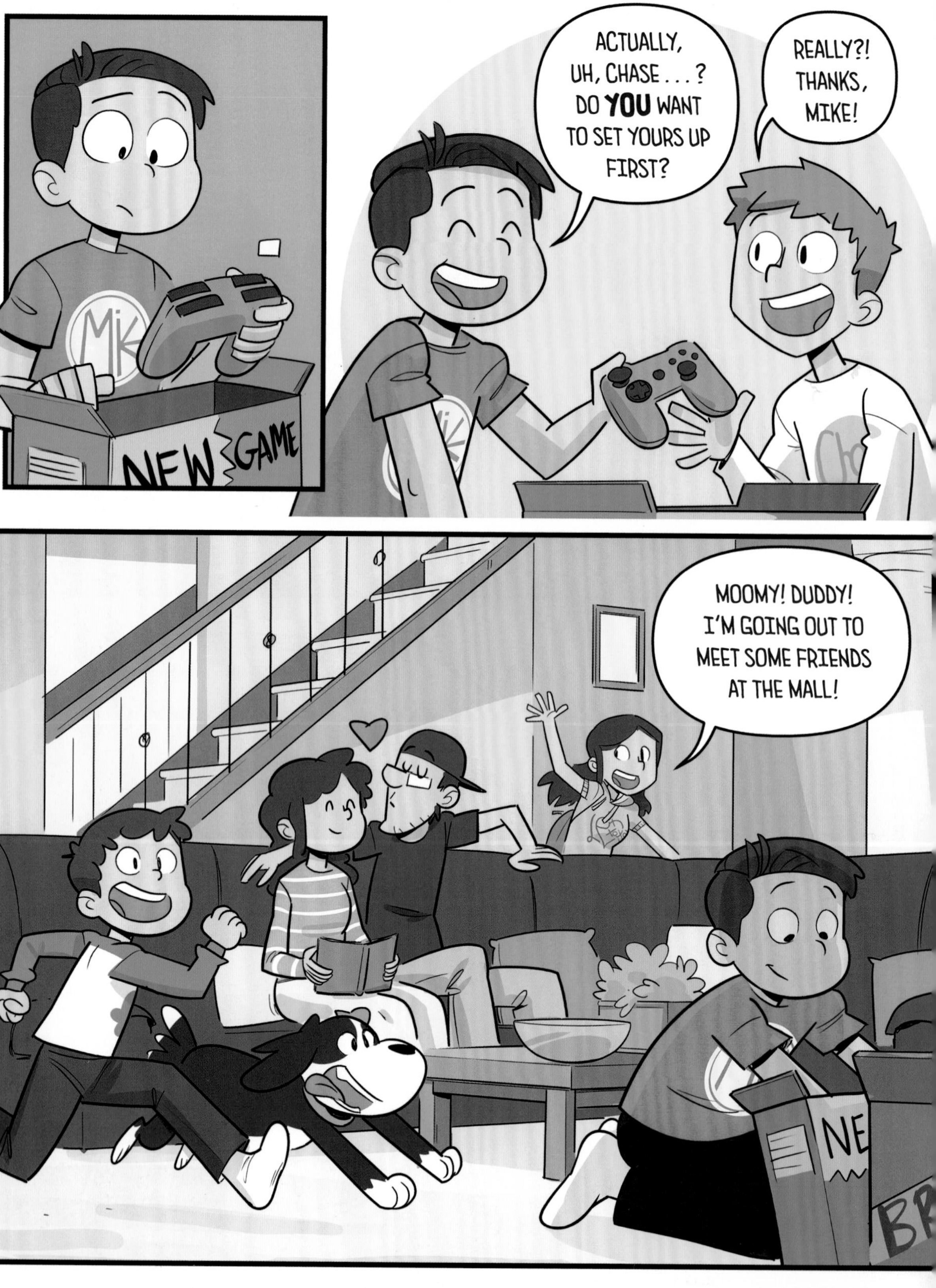
NEW GAME
ACTUALLY, UH, CHASE . . . ? DO **YOU** WANT TO SET YOURS UP FIRST?
REALLY?! THANKS, MIKE!
MOOMY! DUDDY! I'M GOING OUT TO MEET SOME FRIENDS AT THE MALL!

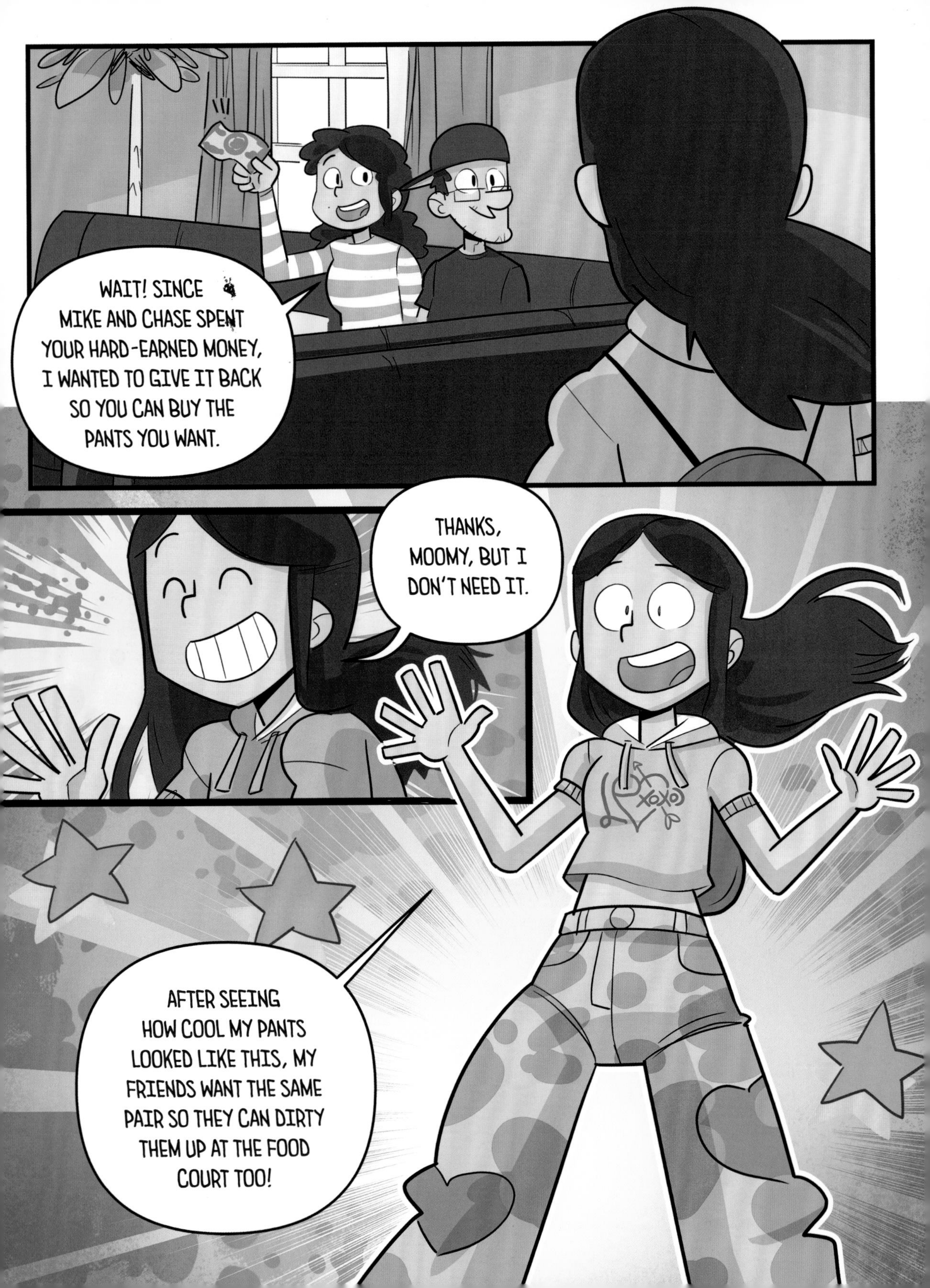
WAIT! SINCE MIKE AND CHASE SPENT YOUR HARD-EARNED MONEY, I WANTED TO GIVE IT BACK SO YOU CAN BUY THE PANTS YOU WANT.
THANKS, MOOMY, BUT I DON'T NEED IT.
AFTER SEEING HOW COOL MY PANTS LOOKED LIKE THIS, MY FRIENDS WANT THE SAME PAIR SO THEY CAN DIRTY THEM UP AT THE FOOD COURT TOO!
XOXO

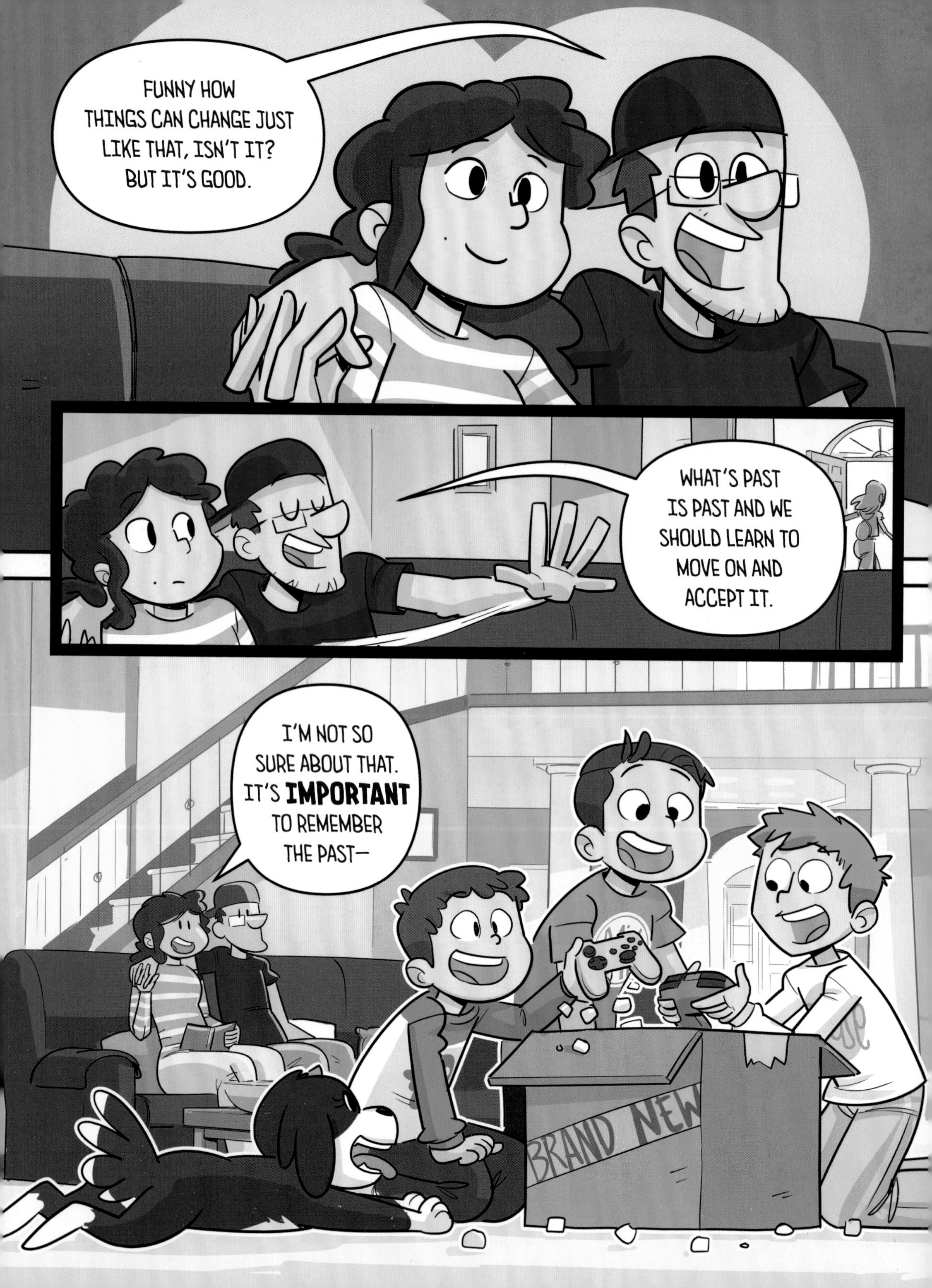
FUNNY HOW THINGS CAN CHANGE JUST LIKE THAT, ISN'T IT? BUT IT'S GOOD.
WHAT'S PAST IS PAST AND WE SHOULD LEARN TO MOVE ON AND ACCEPT IT.
I'M NOT SO SURE ABOUT THAT. IT'S **IMPORTANT** TO REMEMBER THE PAST—
BRAND NEW